Reade Met . . .

Emily Houghton is the author of *Before I Saw You*. She is an Essex girl at heart, but now spends most of her time between London and Suffolk. Emily worked in digital product management at Tesco and Barclays for seven years, and it was during a sabbatical from work, travelling around India, that her first book was born; the first draft is still written on her phone!

After a whirlwind few months, Emily quit her corporate job to live her dream of writing full-time. A true Gemini at heart, she's got many interests and is a trained spin and yoga teacher. She has a curiosity for life and a passion for all things well-being, one day hoping to create her own retreat space with a lot of dogs! Her writing, while centering around love stories, often touches on deeper emotional themes such as self-love, healing and the power of finding yourself.

Also by Emily Houghton

BEFORE I SAW YOU

and published by Penguin

LAST TIME WE MET

Emily Houghton

PENGUIN BOOKS

TRANSWORLD PUBLISHERS
Penguin Random House, One Embassy Gardens,
8 Viaduct Gardens, London SW11 7BW
www.penguin.co.uk

Penguin
Random House
UK

Transworld is part of the Penguin Random House group of companies
whose addresses can be found at global.penguinrandomhouse.com

Penguin paperback edition first published in 2022

A CIP catalogue record for this book
is available from the British Library.

ISBN 9781529176704

Typeset in 10.75/14.4pt Sabon by Jouve (UK), Milton Keynes.
Printed and bound in Great Britain by Clays Ltd, Elcograf S.p.A.

The authorized representative in the EEA is Penguin Random House Ireland,
Morrison Chambers, 32 Nassau Street, Dublin D02 YH68.

Penguin Random House is committed to a sustainable
future for our business, our readers and our planet. This book
is made from Forest Stewardship Council® certified paper.

1

For my Grandma, who so desperately wanted to read this but left us before she had a chance. I miss you every day.

And to anyone who has ever lost themselves in love, may we remember that we are deserving and worthy exactly as we are x

Then: Aged 13

Eleanor

'This is ridiculous.' Eleanor sighed, rolling over on to her back.

'Is it, Elles? How do I know that in twenty-two years' time you're not going to turn around and deny this entire conversation ever happened?' Fin's freckled face looked down at her from over the bed.

'Well, you don't but I won't,' she replied matter-of-factly.

'You say that now.' He poked her gently in the stomach. 'But what happens if we lose touch? What if I disappear off to India and become a yoga teacher or a spiritual leader and I leave my cult in search of *you*, ring in hand, down on one knee on your thirty-fifth birthday, and you claim that you don't even know me,' he cried incredulously.

'You're being ridiculous.' She turned back on to her stomach. Conversations with Fin often had a way of making her restless. 'Honestly, what goes on in that brain of yours? It exhausts me just thinking about it.'

'Sign the paper, Eleanor,' Fin declared.

'No. And it's weird when you call me Eleanor.'

'Eleanor Ruth Levy. Sign this pact immediately or risk

losing our friendship for ever.' He leapt off the bed and thrust the piece of paper under her nose.

Eleanor finally conceded and put down her book. She'd been desperately trying to focus on something other than Fin's ramblings for the last twenty minutes, but she knew it was pointless. When Fin wanted something, there was no way in hell he would stop until he got it.

'First of all' – she propped herself up on her elbows – 'you can't touch your toes or sit still for more than ten seconds at a time, so the chance of you becoming some sort of yoga guru is highly unlikely.' She sat up and continued quickly before he could interrupt with another stream of thoughts. 'Secondly, you know that even if I tried every second of every day for twenty-two years, I could never forget you. Look . . .' She jabbed her finger at the top of the piece of paper. 'Isn't this enough? We've already made our life plan together.'

Fin glanced down at the list of promises they had made. What had started off as silly rules to govern their friendship – don't lie to each other, don't go to sleep mad at each other, don't steal each other's stuff – had, over time, manifested into a combined to-do list for their lives. Finish high school together. Attend the same university (different courses allowed, but ideally the same number of years). Move to London after graduation and rent a flat together. And when, inevitably, marriage and babies occurred, they'd have to always live within at least twenty minutes of each other.

'And finally, I'm praying with all I have that we won't even need to use this pact, because quite frankly I don't fancy being alone at thirty-five. *But* because you're my best friend, and because I want to go back to reading my book, I'll sign it.'

Fin's eyes lit up with delight. He handed her his pen and winked.

'Ms Levy, if we could please have you sign once at the top and once at the bottom, I think we will be good to go.'

She grabbed the piece of paper and began to read.

I, Eleanor Ruth Levy, and I, Finley James Taylor, hereby declare that if such a time occurs at the ripe old age of thirty-five that both members of this agreement find themselves single then it shall be mandatory for the individual parties to wed each other. The marriage shall take place in accordance with this binding contract, willingly entered into by both.

Signed.

-------------   --------------

'Sorry, but when did you become some sort of legal expert? I didn't think you even knew half these words existed,' she exclaimed, half joking, half impressed.

'Well, that teaches you not to underestimate me, doesn't it?' He flashed her a proud smirk. 'Plus, my mum watches loads of crappy legal dramas on TV when my dad is away on business, so you pick up a few things.'

'I knew it wasn't just your natural intelligence,' Eleanor replied, turning her gaze back to the piece of paper and signing her name at the bottom. 'Done. Now, here's hoping we're not both single and lonely by the time we're thirty-five.' She sank herself back into the soft pink carpet and picked up her discarded book.

'Ew, thirty-five, that's old.'

'*So old.*'

'I don't know if I even want to live until I'm that old. Being an adult looks hard.'

'Fin!'

'What?' he exclaimed innocently.

'You know I hate it when you say things like that.' She kicked him gently and he came to lie by her side. 'You can't go anywhere. I need you too much.'

'Fine. For you, Elles, I'll stick around.' He nudged her softly and grinned. 'But only because you need me.'

'You really are ridiculous.' She rolled her eyes.

Fin rested his head gently on her shoulder. 'But you love me anyway.'

A ripple of warmth bloomed inside her stomach. 'The only person I love in this world is Leonardo DiCaprio.'

'Eurgh,' Fin grunted. 'So typical.'

'Don't get jealous,' she teased.

'Jealous? You wish!' He ran his hands through his wild flaming hair. 'Leo wishes he was as good-looking as me.' Fin proclaimed arrogantly.

'You're deluded,' she snorted.

Fin sighed and rolled over on to his back. 'You're my best, Elles.'

'You mean I'm *the* best, Fin,' she corrected.

'No. You're *my* best.' His voice had dropped to a whisper. His eyes lifted and locked with hers.

Eleanor's throat tightened as she felt his words hit her heavy in the chest. She prayed with every piece of her that she could press pause on this moment.

'You're my bestest, Fin.' She smiled.

'Of course I am, that's why you just agreed to marry me.' He winked and then suddenly stood up. 'I'm hungry. You want to get some pizza?'

And just like that, someone had pressed play again.

Now: Aged 34

Eleanor

Eleanor woke slowly, a heavy fog pressing in on her from all sides. She stretched out and felt the satisfactory click of her joints welcoming in the morning. She tried to sit up but a surge of nausea floored her.

Oh God.

The sweet taste of wine tickled the back of her throat, making her want to retch. Slowly she became aware of the heaviness in her body. The dull ache behind her eyes and the sandpaper that coated the inside of her mouth. She groaned pathetically and willed herself back to sleep. Suddenly a sound pierced her consciousness.

No!

Leave me alone.

But the loud beeping refused to go away. Eleanor reached for the source, her hands scrambling around until she found her phone discarded between the sheets. Without even thinking, she answered.

'Happy New Year, darling!' The unmistakable voice of her mother trilled down the phone. Eleanor cursed silently to herself, wishing she hadn't been so hasty in answering. 'Eleanor? Can you hear me?'

'Urgh.' Her mouth was devoid of any moisture and her voice was husky and cracked. 'Yes, I can hear you.' She rolled over and placed the phone on the pillow next to her.

'Ah, good. I'm out for a walk and it's a bit windy,' her mum continued to shout. 'What are you up to? No doubt lolling about like a wet blanket. You sound awful. Were you drunk last night? How much wine did you have?'

'*Please*, Mum. Not so many questions,' she groaned.

'Remember to eat something, won't you? Soak up any lingering alcohol that's left swishing around in that stomach of yours.'

'Uh-huh.' Eleanor felt her insides contract.

'So, is your plan to wallow all day, or do you have at least one productive thing scheduled for the start of this brand-new year? You know what I always say . . . opportunity awaits around every corner!' Her voice was reaching even greater heights of enthusiasm.

'Yeah, well it turns out there's not that much to do when you're an old spinster.'

'Stop that at once,' her mother snapped. 'I know last year was hard for you, but being single is not a life-threatening disease. You'll survive this, Eleanor. You've just got to let yourself move forward.'

Eleanor picked at the raw skin around her nail beds. The one good thing about being hungover was that she was too dehydrated to cry. It didn't stop her throat tightening and her heart hurting though.

Suddenly her body ran cold. 'Look, Mum, I think I might need to go.'

'Aha! That's more like it. Decided to seize the day, have

we? Well, good for you, sweetheart. Up and at 'em, that's what my mother always said!'

'Sure, Mum.' Eleanor could barely get the words out. Her stomach twisted angrily and sweat broke out all over her skin. 'I really have to go . . .'

'Fine, I'll leave you to it. Happy New Year, my darling,' her mother called, but before she could finish, Eleanor hung up and threw the phone across the room. There was no time for niceties.

After successfully expelling the remainder of last night's stomach contents into the toilet, Eleanor managed to drag herself downstairs and on to the sofa. It was strange. Every memory and thought of Oliver felt unbearable and yet living in the flat they had shared for nearly ten years didn't feel odd at all. It had surprised everyone that for the past few months he'd allowed her to stay there. Maybe even *he* knew that breaking her heart and kicking her out of her home was a little too cruel. Although picking up his share of the mortgage had been an eye-watering stretch on her budget, it had been worth it. This flat was her slice of tranquillity, nestled in amongst the madness of East London. Every detail, from the cushions to the wallpaper to the lighting to the cutlery, was all a piece of Eleanor. There was hardly any trace of Oliver to be found.

Maybe that's why he found it so easy to drop everything and leave.

The acidic thought shot through her mind, causing her already queasy stomach to lurch in protest. She stretched her crumpled legs out and closed her eyes. Could she stay hidden away for ever? Lying inanimately. Barely existing. It would surely be easier than facing real life.

Once again, her faithful phone buzzed her out of her stupor.

Incoming Call: Freya Sis.

Eleanor quickly answered. 'Hey, Frey.'

'You're alive then?' Her little sister's sarcasm was always cutting.

'I'm sorry I didn't message. I was in work and then at Sal's and then there was way too much wine and . . . you know how it is.'

'You're now lying on the sofa feeling sorry for yourself, barely able to move from the hangover?'

Eleanor laughed. 'Pretty much.'

'It's fine. I just worry about you.' She heard her sister feign despair. 'Christ, I'm becoming worse than Mum, aren't I?'

'No one is as bad as Mum. I've just been on the phone to her actually.'

'Ah.' Freya chuckled. 'Let me guess, more motivating and inspiring speeches about the wealth of opportunity that this life can offer if you'd only open your eyes to it?'

Eleanor snorted. Freya's impression of their mother was close to perfect. 'I stopped her before she could rile herself up too much. I've never been more grateful to vomit in my life.'

'How's that for perfect timing? Anyway, I just called to say Happy New Year!' The brightness and sparkle had returned to Freya's voice. Eleanor hated it when Freya was so serious, mainly because she knew that nowadays the only thing she was being serious about was Eleanor's fluctuating emotional state. No little sister should have to pick their big sister off the floor and put them back together. Guilt formed a tight knot in her stomach.

'Happy New Year, Frey. Thank you for everything . . . honestly, I don't know what I would have done without you.

I promise this year will be better. It's about time I got back to looking after you!'

'Oh, please,' Freya scoffed. 'You haven't looked after me since I was fourteen, and even then you were a hopeless babysitter.'

'Hey, I tried to be sensible. But it was like looking after two children, with Fin around.' A wave of nostalgia caught her by surprise.

'He really was the worst. Do you remember that time when he used all of his pocket money to order every item on the Domino's takeaway menu? The house stank of grease and cheese for weeks. Mum was livid.'

Eleanor's heart sank. Hangovers weren't the best time to be walking down memory lane.

'Anyway. How was your night?' she quickly deflected.

'All right. Sam took me to a pretty standard house party, but amazingly I'm not feeling too worse for wear today. In fact, I'm taking a leaf out of my big sister's book and am about to go for a run.'

'You're a better woman than I am. Do a couple of miles for me, please?'

'I'll try my best, although at this rate I reckon just getting to the end of the road will be a miracle.' Freya paused. 'Promise me you'll try not to spend all day moping, OK?' There was that motherly tone again. It seemed no one could have a conversation with Eleanor these days without a background note of anxiety. 'Why don't you make use of that beautiful journal thing I got you for Christmas? Everyone at work is raving about them. Good for the mind apparently.'

Eleanor sighed. Since the break-up, the once his-and-hers gifts were now replaced with every self-help and self-healing item available. Chocolate bars by the dozen. Journals and mindfulness books in piles. Spa vouchers (strictly applicable to solo treatments only). Scented candles. Face masks. All the ingredients required to transform yourself and your pain into something that at least smelt and looked heavenly on the outside.

'And don't knock it until you try it!' Freya scorned. 'I can practically hear your scepticism through the phone.'

Maybe Freya was right. Maybe it was time for Eleanor to start making her way through the contents of the 'sad singles bag', as Sal referred to it. In fairness, what else was she going to do with her day?

'Fiiiiine. You're right. New year, new me and all that.'

'Exactly! Now, if I don't go for a run now I never will. Shall we do dinner next week?'

'Of course. And I'll see you at Mum's tomorrow. *Please* say you're coming.'

Why had she suddenly become so needy?

'Come on, what do you take me for? I would never leave you alone in that situation!'

Eleanor breathed a sigh of relief. 'I'll pick you up at twelve, OK?'

'Perfect. Now, *go journal*!' Freya barked affectionately. 'I love you.'

'I love you too.' But before the words were even out of her mouth, her little sister had hung up on her. 'So much for respecting your elders,' Eleanor grumbled.

OK, come on, no more wallowing, Eleanor Levy. Sort your shit out.

Eleanor stretched out languidly one last time before forcing herself upright.

Well, at least some of your shit anyway.

*

Three cups of 'relax and restore' tea and half a packet of Lindt extra dark chocolate later, Eleanor was stuck. In truth, she'd been stuck on the first page of her Positive Mind journal since she opened it.

Question 1. How do you feel today?

Awful just didn't quite cut it. Dead inside? In total and complete despair?

Eleanor chewed the end of the pen anxiously, rereading the question in the vain hope that an inspired lie would force its way out and on to the page. She already felt bad enough; did she really need to see it written down in front of her?

'OK, this is pointless. What else have you got for me?' she mumbled, flicking through the rest of the crisp blank pages. 'Aha! Your monthly planner,' she read to no one. 'An opportunity to plan all the things you're looking forward to this month. This is more like it!' She smiled, embarrassingly delighted at finding a task that felt manageable.

Lunch at Mum's every other Sunday.

She marked the little squares reluctantly.

Kate's wedding! 15 January.

Panic coursed through her. The first event of the year where she'd be turning up solo. Her throat tightened. Could she cancel? She'd have to cancel. Maybe she could contract stomach flu the night before. Yes. There were plenty of ways she could get out of it, and surely Kate wouldn't even notice if she wasn't there? Being in love makes you too blind to care.

Eleanor reached for the chocolate again and shoved three squares into her mouth at once.

'That's right, Eleanor, go and eat your feelings. I'm sure that's going to help.' She sighed.

Jesus, you're full on talking to yourself now?

Come on, focus!

11

But this is miserable.

Eleanor shook her head violently, hoping at least some of the thoughts would dissipate in the process. Her brain hurt from all the thinking.

'Let's try something different.' She wasn't ready to give up on this just yet. The only other plan she had for the day was napping and she knew that, even with the best will in the world, she wouldn't be able to make that stretch longer than a few hours. A hazy memory crept into her mind from last night. 'Yes!' She slammed her fist down excitedly. 'New Year's resolutions.'

Sal had decided it was mandatory that they create at least three resolutions for the year ahead. Eleanor hadn't had a clue. In all honesty, the only thing she'd been working towards for the past month was staying alive. There had been no room in her head for any forward thinking, especially when faced with a future alone and heartbroken. Sal being Sal had easily reeled off a handful of goals and it got Eleanor to thinking, what *did* she want to do this year?

She flicked to a blank sheet of paper and dutifully wrote the title at the top.

New Year, New Me Resolutions
   1. <u>Go to the Maldives.</u>

'Start small, why don't you.' She chuckled to herself.

Ever since she was a little girl, Eleanor had dreamed of disappearing off to an island with white sands and crystal waters. The moment she started earning money, she decided that the Maldives was the spot. A two-week all-inclusive holiday had been on her bucket list for years, but somehow life always managed to get in the way. Then there was the fact that Oliver used to travel so much with work that when it came to holidays they always chose to go somewhere close. Normally France. Actually, always France. Did she even like France that much?

She tightened her grip on the pen and carried on writing.

2. <u>Drink less.</u>

That one felt particularly relevant as her head continued to pound.

3. <u>Call Mum more.</u>

These are pathetic, Eleanor. You're not twelve years old.
She paused slightly before writing the next one.

4. <u>Start painting again.</u>

Her mind instantly went to the little studio she'd made for herself upstairs. Eventually it was going to be repurposed for a nursery, when the time came, but until then Eleanor had fought hard to make it a temporary space for her and her art. Unfortunately, all that had filled the room were unopened paint pots and blank canvases. Oliver never really thought much of painting.

'Stop thinking about him,' she scorned loudly.

Everyone had said it would take time to let go and move on with her life, but the fact that he still occupied such a large portion of her mind made her insides ache.

You have to stop this.

What would Angela Levy do?

'Turn the pain into positives,' she announced, in her best impression of her mother.

If Oliver leaving had taught her anything, it was that nothing is guaranteed. So much of her existence had been spent in the safety of security. And where had that got her? Nowhere. Now it was time to go wild and enjoy life a little! She scribbled out her number four and instead wrote in bold capital letters:

4. <u>DO THINGS THAT SCARE YOU!</u>

Painting definitely came under that category.

'Voila!' Eleanor placed the pen down with self-satisfied finality. 'A list that even Sal would be proud of,' she announced to herself.

Just as she was about to close the book, she hastily grabbed the pen and wrote a tiny note at the bottom of the page.

5. <u>Find love?</u>

She felt the clouds of the hangover grow heavier in her mind as she closed the book and slid it to the side. She shoved the last remaining squares of chocolate into her mouth and made her way over to the lounge. 'Right, *Mrs Doubtfire* and a nap, I think.'

Eleanor curled up on the sofa and felt the tides of sadness lap at her feet.

Is there anyone in the world hating this day as much as me?

Fin

Fin had been pacing up and down his living room for the past half-hour. He knew this wasn't going to be a nice conversation, and although there were a million other ways he'd rather be spending his New Year's Eve, he knew he couldn't avoid it any longer. When would he learn? Situations left unattended could swiftly turn septic and deadly. In fact, wasn't that what had got him into this mess in the first place? You could ignore something all you want, but eventually it would turn around and bite you in the arse.

Fin heard the key turn in the lock.

'Cam?' he called out nervously.

'Hey, babe,' Camilla replied, her sing-song LA accent brimming with enthusiasm.

He sat on the edge of the sofa, unsure whether to stand or stay seated.

'Sorry I'm late, the traffic was insane today!' she continued brightly. The sound of her footsteps stopped abruptly. Fin felt his heart drop a little lower in his chest.

'Why is your suitcase in the hallway?' she asked, her

heeled boots beginning to stamp their way towards him. 'Hey, Fin, can you hear me?'

The moment she saw his face, her voice changed completely. Fin felt the entire atmosphere freeze as her arms folded across her chest. 'What's going on? Why is your suitcase packed?'

'I . . .' He took a deep breath and willed himself to just say it. 'I'm heading back to London tomorrow.'

Camilla's face contracted into a confused scowl. 'London? Don't tell me this is another one of Rob's last-minute urgent job requests.' The disdain in her voice was blatant.

'No, it's not for work.'

'OK, so what is it for?' she demanded. Fin could sense her very limited patience was already wearing thin.

'My mum's not well so I'm going to go and visit her.'

'Your mom?' Camilla's confusion was increasing rapidly. 'I thought you didn't talk to your mom?'

'I don't.'

'Well, why are you going back then?' she huffed.

'Because it sounds bad. Like . . . end-of-the-road kind of bad.'

Camilla's edges softened slightly. 'OK, that's obviously not ideal.' She flicked her long, golden hair over her shoulder in irritation. 'How long will you be gone for?'

'That's the thing.' Fin stood and shook his head. 'I don't know.'

'What do you *mean* you don't know?' She flared. 'Surely you've booked a flight home?'

'No,' he mumbled, his eyes fixed to the floor. 'Not yet.'

'Why not?' Her voice rose in a wave of outrage.

'Because funnily enough there isn't a neat schedule of when someone is going to die, Cam,' he snapped.

'You don't need to be like that.' She pouted. 'I'm just saying . . . It's New Year's Eve, for Christ's sake.' She stamped her foot in frustration.

'I wish I could have given you more notice, but I only found out a couple of days ago. It's not my fault that my mum has dementia and is now living in a care home, and on top of that has been diagnosed with terminal cancer.' He hadn't meant to lose his temper, but his head was filling up with so many thoughts that he was quickly reaching boiling point. 'It's not easy for me either, you know?'

Camilla stepped back, her dark brown eyes wide with shock. 'Why didn't you tell me sooner?'

Fin shrugged. 'I don't know. I needed to think about some things, I guess.' He knew it was a pathetic answer, but he had never been good at difficult conversations.

'Right, so *now* it's OK to tell me, when you're dropping everything to fly across the world to be by the bedside of a woman you haven't seen in nearly fifteen years.' She paused. 'You're not expecting me to come with, are you? Work is crazy at the moment.'

'No. I don't want to do that to you.'

'Fine.' Her face noticeably relaxed. 'Long distance it is. Surely if her condition is that bad, it won't be too long before you'll be back.'

Fin gritted his teeth at her lack of tact, but tried to keep his voice as calm and controlled as possible. 'I don't want to do that either.'

'Excuse me?' Camilla jerked her head.

'I . . .' He paused, gathering the dreaded words up and forcing them out of his mouth. 'I don't want to do long distance.'

'What does that mean?' She stepped a little closer, her neatly painted eyes boring into his. 'Are you breaking up with me?'

Fin forced himself to keep eye contact, the intensity of the moment threatening to crush him.

Just say it.

Be an adult and tell the truth.

'Yes.' The tiny word fell feebly out on to the floor between them. 'I think I am.'

'Are you *fucking* kidding me!' Camilla screamed, her entire being pulsing with rage. 'Is this some sort of sick joke?'

Fin tried to swallow but his throat was too dry.

'At least answer me, Fin!' she screeched.

'No.' He hung his head. 'It's not a joke.'

The next thing he knew, he was being pelted with every available item that Camilla could get her hands on.

'Come on, Cam,' he tried to reason. 'You know things haven't been great for a while. We barely see each other and when we do . . . the only time we really talk is when we argue.'

Her face cemented into a thunderous expression.

'Happy New Year to you too, you total arsehole,' she yelled, grabbing her handbag and storming into the bedroom.

The sound of doors slamming echoed around the apartment. An ocean of emotions flooded him. Guilt and rage, grief and relief all swirled amongst one another and crashed over him in waves.

It's for the best.

You know it's ultimately for the best.

*

18

It didn't take long for Camilla to clear out the stuff she'd kept at his apartment and leave. Strangely the place felt a lot lighter without her, as though it could breathe again. Things hadn't been right between them for weeks, and the weight of their constant bickering and fighting had become unbearable.

Happy bloody New Year's Eve.

Fin slumped down on to the sofa and allowed the dying rays of sunshine to bathe his face as they poured in through the window. Considering he was a redhead with too many freckles to count, his skin seemed to relish the hot weather. How the hell was he going to cope living under the dreary grey skies of London?

Suddenly he felt his phone buzz in his pocket. Reluctantly he pulled it out, desperate not to see Camilla's name flashing up on the screen. He couldn't take any more of her shouting right now. He smiled when he saw the name of his best friend pop up instead.

'Happy last night of the year, buddy,' Rob cheered down the phone.

'How are you doing?' Fin forced his voice to resemble some sort of upbeat excitement.

'Good, man, good. Just having a few beers before we head to Nick's tonight. Are you sure you and Cam don't want to join us?'

There was a sickening twist in Fin's stomach. 'Nah, thanks though. We have plans.' The lie tasted bitter on his tongue.

'Well, the offer's there if you change your mind.'

'Thanks, Rob.'

'Are you sure you're all right?' his friend pressed. 'You sound a little off.'

'I'm fine. It's just this stuff with my mum. Really thrown

19

a spanner in the works.' Fin felt a spasm of guilt ping against his chest. He hated keeping things from his friend, but right now the thought of deep-diving into his break-up with Camilla was too exhausting. There would be plenty of time to analyse why Fin couldn't seem to keep a girlfriend for more than two years, and why he was most likely an idiot for dating yet another high-maintenance and highly strung LA socialite.

'Of course. Must be pretty tough, I'm not surprised you're a bit blindsided by it. You know I'm here if you want to talk about it, don't you?'

'Thanks, mate.' He knew Rob wasn't the best at emotional conversations either, but Fin felt a swell of gratitude at his attempt. 'Also, are you sure I can stay at your place?'

'Course! *Mi casa, su casa* and all that. Besides, it's been sat empty for months so it would be good to have someone check everything's all working and stuff,' Rob confessed.

'Oh, to have a spare flat lying around in London,' Fin teased. As much as Rob liked to pretend he was from humble beginnings, Fin liked to remind him otherwise.

'Oi. Come off it.'

'I'm kidding, I'm really grateful for this. You know that, right?'

'I do.' Rob sighed despondently. 'Man, I'm going to miss you while you're gone. Who the hell am I going to hang around with?'

'I'm sure you'll cope.'

'You'd better hope I do.' Rob laughed. 'Anyway, buddy, I got to go and get stuff sorted before tonight. Safe flight and call me when you're in the flat.'

'Cheers. Will do.'

'Oh, and Fin?' Rob called, just as Fin was about to hang up.

'Yeah?'

'Happy New Year, mate.'

Fin smiled. 'Happy New Year to you too.'

*

3.05 a.m.

Fin cursed himself for looking. He knew that, realistically, no more than an hour could have passed since his last glance, but fifteen minutes! Time was toying with him.

Could he get up now? Most people were probably still out celebrating. Would it be totally insane to go and join them at an after party? A younger version of himself wouldn't have even thought twice about it; he'd be half a bottle of Jack Daniel's down and on his way in an Uber.

A drop of whiskey wouldn't go amiss right now.

He scrunched his eyes tightly and willed the urge to dissipate from his body. Funny how the temptation could spring up on him even after all this time.

'Come on, sleep. Come on, come on, come on!' He threw his head back on to the pillow with every word, frustration rising up inside him. He reached for his phone once again.

3.30 a.m.

He'd have to get up soon, this was becoming unbearable. When was his flight anyway?

Fin scrolled through his emails looking for the confirmation, a task made far more difficult than it needed to be by the constant stream of messages flooding his phone screen. He kept his eyes focused on the emails, trying to avoid looking at the New Year's well wishes and drunken tokens of affection that were ungraciously interrupting his task. Rob must have messaged him over twenty times already.

'British Airways . . . British Airways, where the hell are you?' he muttered, scrolling through his inbox. 'Aha! Dear Mr Taylor, please find this as confirmation of your flight . . .' He scanned the screen. 'Here we go! Flight departure 1 p.m.'

His heart sank. There was no way he could face turning up to the airport over five hours early, especially as his default setting was always at least ten minutes late. It was a habit that for his entire life he'd never been able to shake, much to the dismay of everyone who had ever known him.

'Speaking of late,' he whispered, catching her name in the long list of emails. 'Would it be ridiculous?' he asked himself.

Fin opened the 'save the date' email he'd received months ago and stared at it. He'd told his friend he couldn't make it to her wedding; he'd RSVP'd the very next day with a decline. He knew Kate wouldn't be surprised or especially upset. He hadn't been back home in so long that he was shocked to even have made the guest list. But Kate was one of his oldest friends and despite their long stretches of no contact, she always seemed to make the effort to check in with him at least once a year. Now he would be in the UK at the same time as her big day . . . surely it would be the perfect opportunity to go?

'Why not?' he mused. The worst that could happen was that she said no.

Email to Kate Crossley:

Hey Kate. How's it going? Happy New Year! I know this is super last-minute and your wedding is only two weeks away, but I'm actually now going to be in London for a few weeks, and so if there's room for a little one at the reception I'd love to come and celebrate with you! Totally understand if not, would be great to catch up regardless. X

He couldn't help but laugh at his own audacity. He imagined the look on Kate's face when she read his email. It was something that both she and Eleanor would have scorned him for.

Eleanor.

His stomach dropped. God, he hadn't thought of her in ages. Like nearly everything else in his past, she'd been banished into the far-flung corners of his mind. Maybe it was inevitable; he was after all going back to the place that was full of her. Suddenly a prickle of panic rippled over his skin. Was he really going to be able to do this?

'You don't have a choice,' he affirmed, heaving himself out of the bed and throwing himself under the shower.

Eleanor

In the beginning of their relationship, Sundays had been Eleanor's favourite day. It was the one time in the week that her and Oliver's schedules seemed to actually align. Lazy mornings, long runs, indulgent dinners, and a deep desire to soak up every precious moment before the obligatory Monday blues hit. Maybe she should have read the signs better, as over the years the Sundays they managed to spend together became few and far between. There were still lazy mornings, long runs and indulgent dinners, but Eleanor often found herself doing them solo. Now every other Sunday involved lunch with her mother. An occasion she'd previously managed to schedule for once a month at best.

'I told you we should have left earlier,' Freya chided.

Eleanor swore as yet another traffic light turned red.

'Seriously, Frey?' Eleanor gripped the steering wheel tighter.

'Mum's going to think we did it on purpose, you know.'

'I know! That's why I'm feeling even *more* stressed than normal. I hate driving in London at the best of times.' She shot her sister a fierce glare, but unsurprisingly she was on her phone and paying absolutely no attention.

'You're also probably still hungover, right?' her sister goaded.

'No.' Eleanor felt the haze of the wine still hovering at the edges of her mind. 'OK, maybe a little bit. Anyway, why do we even have to go to these lunches? Every two weeks is a bit excessive, no?' Eleanor noticed the whining had crept back into her voice. Could heartbreak steal your soul and revert you to a stroppy teenager all at once?

'Because Mum loves us. And . . .' Freya glanced awkwardly over at Eleanor.

'And everyone was scared how crazy I'd go when Oliver left me?'

Freya snorted. 'Exactly.'

'But that was months ago now. Look at me, I'm fine. What's the big deal?' Eleanor pushed her foot down hard on the accelerator and lurched the little Yaris forward.

'Jesus, Eleanor. I'd rather be late than turn up in an ambulance. Slow down!'

'Sorry. Sorry.' She took a deep breath in and held it for a moment. As she exhaled, she felt some of the frustration drain out of her body.

'We just care about you.' Freya reached out and laid her hand gently on top of Eleanor's.

'I know.' That sickly feeling of guilt crawled in the pit of her stomach.

'I've texted Mum and told her we're running late. She says it's fine, no rush.'

'Thank you.' Eleanor smiled and didn't even flinch when the light ahead turned red. 'Frey?' She swallowed the knot of fear that had tangled itself in her throat.

'Uh-huh?' Her sister was listening but had once again become absorbed in the vortex of her Instagram feed.

'When Oliver left . . .' Eleanor closed her eyes briefly, allowing the words to tumble out. 'How bad was I?'

Her sister put her phone down and laid her head back on the headrest. 'Pretty bad.' Eleanor desperately wanted to reach for her but knew she needed to focus now more than ever on driving. 'You disappeared for a while. It's like you were here but not. Some days you'd sleep all day. You wouldn't eat. I preferred it when you cried to be honest, at least I knew you were conscious.'

Jesus Christ.

Eleanor's heart began to race furiously in her chest. How had she managed to erase that completely from her mind? Every time she tried to think back, to recall any moment after Oliver walked away from her, all she was met with was a void.

'I'm sorry,' was all she could pathetically muster.

'You don't need to be.' Freya leant over and planted a kiss on her cheek. 'Now. Let's blast out some Tina Turner before we have to deal with lunch. It always helps me feel better prepared.' She flashed her a daring smile and reached for the volume button.

*

'*Darlings!* My gorgeous little offspring, there you are at last!' The bright pink front door opened to reveal the formidable Angela Levy. 'Look at you both. How can I even be one tiny bit mad at you for being late when you look so delicious?' She pulled them into a very tight hug.

Eleanor's nose filled with the sweet scent of her mother's perfume. Jasmine. The smell of her childhood. She could just about make out Freya's groans as she was pulled closer into their mother's firm embrace.

'Mum, let us breathe!' Freya wrangled herself free from the layers of turquoise chiffon that were starting to wrap themselves around them both.

'I'm sorry, sweetie. I can't help it if I miss you so *much* that I want to squeeze every ounce of juice from you both.' She held Eleanor out in front of her and sighed. 'Now, how is my eldest baby doing?'

'I'm good, thanks.' Eleanor forced her lips into a strange version of a smile. 'Honestly.'

'Hmmmm.' Her mum's heavily lined eyes narrowed suspiciously. 'You still look a little worse for wear. Your skin is drier than your grandmother's roast chicken, God rest her soul. And you're still a bit too thin for my liking. Us Levy girls look better with a bit of meat on our bones. You can't look like a sparrow when you're built to be a swan.' She hadn't even paused for breath. 'Let's eat!'

Eleanor was pulled through to the kitchen, Freya sniggering behind her. As expected, there was enough food to feed at least ten people. In this household, nothing said love better than a twelve-course meal.

'Sit sit sit, both of you.' Their mother flapped wildly at them. 'Tuck in, it's all vegan and gluten free. Eat well, live well – that's what they say, isn't it?' she sang.

'Sure,' Eleanor mumbled, obediently sitting and starting to spoon tiny portions of everything on to her plate. She knew this lunch was going to be a marathon, and to win the race one had to pace oneself carefully.

'Now, Freya dear. Tell me about Samuel. How is he doing? When can I meet him? I've told all the girls at the shop about him. Rita was practically frothing at the mouth with jealousy. Neither of her girls are even being sniffed at, let alone currently dating an ex-*rugby star*!' Their mother's eyes sparkled, her entire body humming with excitement.

Freya rolled her eyes. 'Mum, come on. I told you he played rugby for his university, that's all. He's not some professional athlete or anything.' She groaned, playing despondently with a piece of spinach on her plate. 'And he's fine. Getting a bit boring, if I'm being honest.'

'Oh.' Angela's face dropped immediately. 'Well, don't get rid of him just yet. I need to gloat a little more before I end up back in the same league as Rita.'

'What league is that, then?' Eleanor felt the anger spark inside her. 'The league of women with two embarrassingly single daughters?' She felt her teeth grind together.

'Eleanor, please!' her mother replied curtly. 'Don't be so ridiculous. That's not what I meant at all.' She smoothed down her silk scarf and took a large sip of her wine, expertly avoiding Eleanor's eye the entire time. 'Anger doesn't look good on you, it never did.'

There was a heavy silence.

'How's the shop going, Mum?' Freya tentatively asked, squeezing Eleanor's hand under the table.

'Fantastically, thank you for asking. As you know, they are putting me forward for Regional Manager. I still can't believe it, but it's true. We're thriving, according to the numbers. Thriving!'

Eleanor couldn't help but feel a little swell of pride for her mum. For all her misguided advice and eccentricities, she really was a force to be reckoned with.

'I am loath to ask, but have you been to visit your dad lately?' Her mum's stare was all-knowing but her voice remained bright and breezy.

Eleanor looked guiltily at her sister, praying she was just as negligent.

'Right, well could you try? You know he'll appreciate it.'

'But . . .' Freya went to speak.

'But nothing, Freya Isabelle. You're his daughters. It's the least you can do.'

The stony look on their mother's face was enough to tell them that this wasn't a fight worth picking.

'Sorry,' they both mumbled guiltily.

And then, just like that, Angela Levy broke into a dazzling smile once more.

'I was thinking . . .' Her thick-painted eyebrows arched in glee. 'How about we book a girls' weekend for my birthday this year? Can you imagine the fun we'd have!'

Eleanor had to shove another mouthful of vegan lasagne into her mouth to avoid screaming out in protest.

'Freya, you check your diary, make sure you get a weekend where Sam isn't planning to wine and dine you.' She winked exaggeratedly. 'Eleanor, I've already got you down as a yes.'

'What about my calendar! I might have plans,' she said indignantly.

Her mum reached over and patted her hand. 'Sweetheart, you're a newly single thirty-four-year-old. Let's not kid ourselves, shall we? Plus, you deserve a little sprucing up before we get you back riding that dating horse. Your attendance is a must.'

Eleanor wanted to scream and cry all at once, but she was so shocked the only thing she could manage was dumbfounded silence.

'Are we all done here?' Her mother swooped in and gathered the plates from under their noses. 'I'll get the dessert.

You need fattening up, my little bird.' She pinched Eleanor's cheek and skipped over to the sink. 'Your father always used to tell me that men don't like bones.'

Freya shuffled over closer to Eleanor. 'How about I ask Mum if we can make these visits less regular.' She squeezed her arm supportively.

'Don't ask her,' Eleanor growled. '*Tell* her.'

'Speaking of calendars,' her mother called. 'I won't see you for a while now, will I, Eleanor sweetheart?' She appeared all at once with a gigantic apple pie that was placed proudly in the centre of the table.

'What do you mean?' Eleanor replied, her stomach already weeping at the thought of consuming any more food.

'Well, you've got Kate's wedding the weekend of our next Sunday lunch, haven't you?'

Eleanor froze. How the hell did her mum know about that?

'It's the fifteenth, isn't it?' her mother continued, serving a pile of steaming pudding into a bowl.

'Yeah, it is . . .' Eleanor's eyes shifted to Freya, who was already shovelling a spoonful of pie into her mouth.

'Pass on my best, will you? Oooh, what are you going to wear? Surely nothing of yours fits any more.' Her mother handed over a bowl that unsurprisingly seemed to be the fullest.

'I'm . . . I'm not sure I'm going to go, actually.'

Her mother snatched the bowl back and scowled. 'What on earth do you mean, you're not sure you're going to go?'

Eleanor felt her face flush. She hadn't told anyone of her plans to skip Kate's wedding yet and she wasn't adequately prepared for her mother's interrogation.

'It might be strange going by myself. I'm not sure I'm ready for it.'

Her mother slammed her spoon down, sending stewed apples flying across the table. 'Not ready? Not ready to see your friend of over twenty years get married to the love of her life? Eleanor Ruth, shame on you.'

'But it will be *embarrassing*. Turning up alone whilst everyone is there with their partners. It's too hard.' Eleanor knew how pathetic she sounded, but she didn't care. She was sick of everyone assuming that just because she wasn't curled up in a ball crying every hour of every day miraculously her heartache had vanished.

'And you think I find it easy turning up to things by myself, do you? You think I *enjoy* being the only one at reunions or dinner parties without a partner? You think Freya relished being the only single one at every family meal before Sam came along?' Her mother's voice was getting louder and louder.

Eleanor could feel the shame radiating off her. Every word her mother spoke pricked her with guilt, but at the same time there was a latent anger that refused to subside. 'You can't compare me to Freya. She chose to be single.'

'And what about me? I chose to be by myself, did I?' Angela stood up abruptly, flinging her shawl over her shoulders. 'I'm sorry that Oliver hurt you. I'm especially sorry that he managed to fool us into thinking he was actually a nice guy for all those years. But some things in life suck, Eleanor. In fact, most things in life suck, but we have to get on with it or risk not living a life at all. Now, eat your dessert before it gets cold.'

Fin

'Bloody hell, it's cold.' Fin pulled his jacket closer around his body as he stepped out of the taxi and on to the bustling streets of North London. It wasn't even lunchtime and the sky had already turned a miserable shade of grey. His skin wept at the absence of sun, his mood immediately darker just from looking at the thick blanket of clouds. The flight had been long and fairly uncomfortable. All his body wanted was a warm shower and bed, but he knew he had to fight the jetlag for as long as he could.

'Welcome back,' he mumbled to himself, placing the key in the lock and opening the front door.

Rob hadn't been wrong when he'd warned Fin that his flat might be a little unlived in. Cobwebs hung like candy floss from the corners of the hallway and a fine layer of dust coated every available surface. Still, it was better than haemorrhaging his savings on overpriced accommodation or a soulless Premier Inn. Life as a freelance photographer paid well enough that he had a comfortable amount stashed away for emergencies such as this, but who knew how long he'd be here for? He couldn't afford to be careless with his money.

'Heating . . . heating . . . where the hell is the heating?' He dropped his suitcase on the floor and made his way further into the flat, eyes hungrily searching for the thermostat. 'Come on, where are you!' he cried, rubbing his hands together. After twenty minutes of fruitless searching, Fin felt his phone vibrate in his pocket.

'Have you trashed the place yet or what?' Rob's familiar drawl greeted him.

'Not yet, but if I don't find the damn heating switch soon I will. It's *freezing* here.'

'It's in the cupboard in the hallway, behind the washing machine.' Rob stifled a yawn. 'Glad to know you got there safely though. How was the flight?'

'Yeah, fine,' Fin replied distractedly, peering into the tiny cupboard and feeling around for the switch. 'Aha, gotcha!' he cried jubilantly. 'Wait, isn't it like 2 a.m. over there? What are you doing up?'

'Working,' Rob grumbled. 'Essentially trying to make up for being completely trashed last night and doing nothing all day. It was a great party though. We missed you.'

Fin laid himself out on the sofa and sighed. He knew where this conversation was heading and he didn't know if he had the energy to steer it off course.

'You wouldn't have even known I was there. I bet you were completely wasted and can't remember anything before midnight.'

'Not true!' Rob exclaimed. 'I remember everything, right up until just *after* midnight. To be honest, the rest is a bit of a blank. Although I do distinctly recall seeing Camilla there . . . by herself.'

'Did you.' It wasn't a question.

'You know I did.' Rob paused. 'Do you want to talk about it?'

Fin laughed. 'When do I ever want to talk about it?'

'This is true, and normally I would be more than happy to avoid any form of emotional conversation, but what with your mum and all . . .' There was an awkward hesitation. 'Is everything OK? Are *you* OK?'

'Apart from the fact I'm holed up in this dirty as hell, freezing flat of yours by myself, jetlagged up to my eyeballs and missing out on a shedload of freelance work, I'm fine.' Fin stood up and forced himself to walk around; he knew the longer he stayed on that sofa, the more likely it was he would never be able to get back up.

'How ungrateful!' Rob protested. 'I told you it hadn't been lived in for a while and that you were welcome to reject my kind offer of staying indefinitely in my house for free, and go and pay for a nice little hotel room, but nope. You made your bed, you lie in it!'

Fin felt a weight lift from his chest; they were off the emotional talk and back on safer ground now. 'Speaking of beds . . . when was the last time you changed the sheets, do you reckon?'

'Ten years ago. If you're lucky.'

'You bastard!' Fin snorted. 'I'd better go and do some domestication of this little hole then, hadn't I? Try and get some sleep, OK, buddy?'

'I'll try my hardest. Let me know how it goes with everything, yeah? I hope your mum is . . . well . . . you know . . . I hope it goes all right.'

'Thanks, Rob.'

Fin felt the lump in his throat grow tighter. Since he had

received the fateful phone call it had become a permanent feature of his anatomy, growing and shrinking in size, loosening and tightening its grip but always present. He tried to shake the memory of the conversation from his tired mind but it was never far from the forefront of his thoughts. He had been working from home that morning when his phone had rung. He didn't recognize the number, but the calling code was one he would never forget.

'Hello, is this Mr Finley Taylor?'

The English accent had made his stomach flip immediately.

'Yes, speaking.'

'My name is Nurse Clara and I'm calling from St Catherine's Care Home here in Watford. Your mother is Eileen Taylor – is that correct?'

Fin's heart began to beat furiously in his chest. Even after twenty years of being divorced, she still refused to drop his father's name. A spark of anger flared up inside him.

'Uh-huh, that's right.'

A small pause. A sharp intake of breath. The preparation for bad news.

'I'm afraid your mother is sick. Really quite sick, in fact.' The nurse's voice was clear and to the point, but there was a warmth lingering at the edges that instantly made Fin trust her. 'She's been a patient of ours for some time now but things are, unfortunately, deteriorating, and I wanted to let you know with enough time.'

Fin's mind stalled. A thousand questions flooded his consciousness, making everything blur into a chaotic racket.

'Enough time?' he repeated dumbly.

'Yes. Things are progressing fast and I wanted to call sooner rather than later.' She paused; her silence felt heavy and loaded. 'I'm sorry to have to deliver such bad news.'

Fin felt his grip tighten around his phone. This couldn't be real. Surely this couldn't be real? Suddenly a thought struck him. 'Does she know you're calling me?' he asked.

'At St Catherine's, we are empowered to make decisions about when is the right time to inform family members,' she stated firmly. 'You're down as the only next of kin.'

'But she doesn't know, does she?' A cascade of emotions assaulted him. 'She hasn't told you to call me?'

'No,' the nurse confirmed. 'No, she hasn't.'

'Shouldn't you tell her?' He ran his hands anxiously through his hair. How could this be happening?

'As I said . . . we are empowered to make the decision when a patient is not fully able to do so themselves.'

'What do you mean, not fully able to do so themselves?'

'Unfortunately, your mother has dementia.'

'Right . . .' Fin had to use every morsel of strength to keep focused on this stranger and her words. The room was spinning from the number of thoughts whirring around in his head. 'Is that what's killing her?'

'No. She was diagnosed with terminal cancer a few months ago.'

'Shit,' he breathed, completely thrown by this entire conversation.

'Quite.' The nurse paused. 'I'm very sorry that you had to find out this way, Mr Taylor, and I don't know what happened between you two – quite frankly it's none of my business – but what I will say is, whether it's a good or bad day, you're all she talks about.'

Fin felt his breath catch in his chest. 'Really?'

'Really.'

Neither spoke for a moment and Fin desperately tried to sort his chaotic thoughts into some form of order.

'How long has she got?' he asked, clutching the phone tightly to his ear.

'It's hard to say. But in these situations, we'd always advise you to get here as quickly as you can.'

*

He'd managed to stay up until just past 8 p.m. before the waves of exhaustion took hold and swept him away. Despite Rob's musty sheets, which he hadn't bothered to change in the end, Fin had slept surprisingly well. In fact, he probably would have slept right through until the afternoon if he hadn't been rudely awoken by the incessant buzzing of his phone.

Bleary-eyed, he reached over and answered.

'Erm hello,' he mumbled groggily.

'*Fin*?' a voice whispered down the phone. 'Is that you?'

'Uh-huh.' He tried to stifle a yawn whilst silently unfurling his limbs from their curled-up sleeping position.

'Oh my God, it's me . . . Kate!' his overexcited friend announced loudly.

Fin sat up and rubbed his eyes. 'Oh, hey Kate. You all right?' He was suddenly conscious of the American twang that had crept into his voice over the years. No wonder she didn't recognize the sound of him.

'I'm great. I'm sorry, did I wake you?'

'No, I'm just a bit jetlagged. I flew in yesterday.'

'I am *so* excited you're here! I couldn't believe it when I saw your email. I mean, classic you to message me less than two weeks before the wedding!'

'Yeah, about that . . .' He tried to backtrack, feeling increasingly foolish for even thinking about asking to come, let alone sending the message. 'It was stupid of me – ignore it.'

'Absolutely not! Turns out one of George's cousins is pretty much about to give birth, and so she and her wife have decided to stay home and avoid risking the journey.' There was a hint of bitterness in her voice. 'Which *means . . .* there's a space for you! For the whole day, if you want it? You'll be stuck with her menu choice, but from what I can remember you eat pretty much anything, right?'

Fin hesitated for a moment. Doubt began to inch its way to the surface of his mind. Was he really going to do this?

You sent the email in the first place.

'Only if you're sure?' he replied cautiously.

'Yes, I'm sure! This is such brilliant news. How long has it been since I last saw you? It has to be like twenty years or something crazy.'

'Not quite, but yeah, definitely a long time.' He smiled to himself. After all these years, she was still the same one-thousand-miles-an-hour Kate he'd grown up with. 'How are you feeling about the big day? Nervous?'

'There's still a couple of bits left to do but we are pretty much ready to go.'

'I can't believe little Kate Crossley is getting married.' He yawned as he indulged in another long stretch. 'When did we get so old, hey?' He forced himself up and out of bed.

'Don't! I'm getting about ten new wrinkles a night these days.' She groaned. 'Anyway, I won't keep you, I'm sure you've got loads to be doing and people to be catching up with. I only wanted to check in and make sure you were all sorted for transport and accommodation and everything?'

'All good, Kate, no need to worry about me.'

'Wonderful. I'll see you next Saturday, then?'

He couldn't help but laugh at the ever-present element of doubt that he would show up.

'You bet. See you then.'

Fin stared around at the apartment, Kate's words echoing in his head.

I'm sure you've got loads to be doing and people to be catching up with.

There was a reason that Fin had left home and never come back. London held nothing for him any more. There was nobody here for him to catch up with. No friends to reach out to and surprise with his unplanned visit. There was only one person he needed to catch up with, only one person he'd flown all this way to see, and despite time being of the essence he knew deep down that he wasn't going to be able to face his mum today. There was never a good time, in Fin's mind, for emotional confrontations, but to do it when jet-lagged and tired? No. He needed more time to prepare, to ready himself to face the situation.

'Tomorrow,' he bargained with himself. 'I'll go and see her tomorrow.'

Eleanor

Find dress for Kate's. Call Freya. Buy more wine. Send Catherine new proposal deck. Find dress for Kate's. Call Freya. Buy more wine. Send Catherine new proposal deck.

The thoughts were going round and round as she pounded the pavement. Wasn't running supposed to switch off her thinking brain? Ten miles later and she still hadn't managed to turn the volume down on her thoughts. Her legs felt good today though. Strong and surprisingly full of life after another sleepless night. If only she'd had the luxury of time, she would have gone for another five more, but life wasn't going to afford her that.

Stretch. Shower. Coffee. Breakfast.

Her stomach instantly contracted. She was trying; she really was. But food had lost all meaning and enjoyment since the break-up. No matter what she put in her mouth, the moment it touched her lips it seemed to transform into a heavy ball of cardboard. Cloying. Claggy. Inedible. The days she did manage to force something down, it would sit like a rock in the pit of her stomach. Besides, she had enough weight to carry in her heart without adding more to the pile.

Eleanor hadn't noticed the weight loss at first; in fact she hadn't noticed much at all in the days after the break-up. The inky mist of grief had filled every corner of her consciousness, blanking out everything but her own pain. But now, as she pulled off her sweaty running kit, she couldn't ignore the sharp angles of her body. The bones rising to the surface, stretching the skin back to reveal their pointed peaks. Eleanor closed her eyes; it was easier not to look some days.

Her mother's voice rang out shrilly in her mind: 'men don't like bones'.

Fuck what men like.

One quick shower, a change of clothes and a shot of espresso later, and Eleanor was on her way to work. As she settled herself on the Overground, she reached for her phone. Although her commute was a deliciously short thirty minutes, she still had to find a way to fill every second. The busier she was, the less time she had to drown herself in memories. Her fingers found their way almost unconsciously to Kate's number.

Could she honestly face turning up to the wedding by herself?

Just as she was about to message, she remembered the New Year promises she'd made to herself. What was the last one?

Find love.

No. The other last one.

Do things that scare you.

'Fine,' she groaned, stuffing her phone back into her bag and pushing all thoughts of Kate's wedding out of her mind.

*

'Good morning, love of my working life. How are we?' Sal planted herself and two large coffees down next to Eleanor.

'Miserable and already loathing every second spent in this office,' Eleanor fired back grimly. Every week she tried to convince herself that she could pretend to love her job. And if not love, then at least not despise, but the moment she set foot in the office come Monday, the lack of fulfilment and the despair would strike.

'Ah, the joys of another week,' Sal replied sarcastically. 'But remember, things could always be worse,' she bleated cheerfully.

Eleanor narrowed her eyes suspiciously. 'Wow, someone is feeling bright and breezy today.' Sal was not a morning person and she was especially not a Monday morning person.

'Is it a crime to want to bring a little positivity into my best girl's life?' Sal grinned widely.

Eleanor stopped typing and turned in her chair to take in her friend fully. 'I know you're up to something. Tell me!'

Sal clasped her chest in mock offence. '*Me*? Up to something? How dare you accuse me of such things.'

'Because the only time you're in this mood is when you're drunk, you've had sex, or you're plotting something wicked.'

Sal laughed so loudly that Doreen, her boss's assistant, nearly fell out of her seat. There was nothing small or subtle about Sal. She was bold and brash and filled up every inch of space that she could. Eleanor admired her for it. In fact, it was one of the main reasons why she loved her so much.

'I wish I'd had sex, and part of me kind of wishes I was drunk. Mondays suck.' She frowned. 'But you're right, as always. Although I wouldn't call it *plotting*. I simply have a proposal for you. Please think about it and don't just say no straight away . . .'

Realization struck Eleanor, and before Sal could even utter another word, she turned her head back to her computer and began typing furiously.

'No. No. Absolutely not.'

'Come *on*, you don't even know what I'm going to say yet.' Sal pulled her back round to face her.

'Let me guess. You know this guy who just happens to be single and available and oh . . . guess who else is single? Me! Could it be that you want to set us up on a date?'

'Now, why on earth would you think I'd do something like that?' Sal frowned.

'Because you're Sally Moreno, my bullish, stubborn and determined-for-me-to-be-happy best friend?' Eleanor smiled affectionately. 'And I can read you like a book.'

'You forgot the bit about me knowing what's best for you too.' She leant closer, her eyes large and pleading. 'Come *on*, Eleanor. What else have you got going on apart from drowning your sorrows with me in the pub once a week and going for hideously long runs?'

Eleanor felt a little stab of annoyance at this. She had stuff to do. In fact, she had plenty of things to be doing.

'Can I remind you of the last time we attempted this?'

Sal's face instantly dropped. 'Hold on, that's not f—'

'What part wasn't fair *exactly*?' Eleanor cut across. 'The bit where you set me up with your friend Curtis who, it transpired, was still completely in love with his ex-girlfriend? Or the part where he ran away during our date. Or maybe . . .' – Eleanor's voice was growing louder and louder – 'it was when I had to chase him down the road for about a mile and then counsel him for the rest of the afternoon about how to win his ex-girlfriend back.'

Sal seemed to have shrunk considerably by the time

43

Eleanor had finished talking. 'Well . . . I appreciate that might not have been the *most* successful date, *but* you can't tar everyone with the same brush.' She puffed up her chest indignantly. 'Curtis practically begged me to set you two up – how was I to know he was still pining after his ex?'

Eleanor laughed. The memory of that fateful afternoon hit her with full force. She reached out and took Sal's hand in hers.

'I know you want me to meet someone. It seems like the whole bloody world wants me to meet someone, but I promise . . . I'm OK by myself at the moment.'

They both stared at her tiny frame, with her clothes hanging loosely off her.

Sal squeezed Eleanor's hand and took a gigantic swig from her coffee. 'I wouldn't go that far. But fine. Let me know if you change your mind, though; this one is a real gem, I promise you. Definitely not a flight risk.' She winked.

'Sure.' Eleanor laughed. 'Anyway, I have bigger problems right now.'

'Go on . . .'

'I've got my friend Kate's wedding this Saturday.'

'Who on earth is Kate?' Sal asked bluntly. 'And why do you have other friends apart from me?' she joked.

'She's a girl I went to school with. We used to do a lot of "couples dates" when Oliver and I were together.' Eleanor felt the bitterness sting her throat. 'Anyway, I didn't really want to go, but my mum has successfully guilt-tripped me into saying yes and I have absolutely nothing to wear.' She paused and pulled at her baggy jumper. 'Well, nothing that fits.'

'Good job you have me as a best friend then.' Sal clapped her hands together decisively. 'It's this Saturday, right?'

Eleanor nodded in response.

'Fine. I'll order some options this afternoon and they will be with you to try on tomorrow. Sorted.'

'Thank you!' Eleanor beamed. If she thought she was organized, it was nothing compared to Sal. 'Nothing too fancy though, and not too much skin, please.'

'OK, Grandma,' Sal shot back. 'Let the professional handle this, I know what I'm doing.' A wicked smile had crept on to her face.

'Sal, I'm serious,' Eleanor warned.

'Trust me. I'll get you something absolutely gorgeous. And besides, you never know, there may be some cute single guys there you need to make a good impression on.'

'Christ, you're nearly as bad as my mum,' she groaned.

'I'll take that as a compliment, thank you very much.' Sal grinned smugly as she walked away.

Fin

'Kate is going to kill me ... she's going to absolutely kill me,' Fin moaned to himself, as he checked the map on his phone once again. 'Two minutes, my arse.' He grumbled at the directions, willing his legs to move as quickly as possible over the cobbled streets. Had driving everywhere in LA ruined his ability to walk places? He wiped the sweat from his brow and hurriedly turned yet another corner.

Some people were born with musical talents. Others, an innate art for learning languages. For Fin, it was an infuriating talent for being late. Even when he tried especially hard to be on time, minutes would accumulate and somehow he'd be even later than usual. It was something that many people had attempted to stamp out of him over the course of his lifetime, but to no avail. Fin's lateness was as much a part of his DNA as his bright red hair and his freckles.

'Aha! There you are.' He beamed. At the end of the road up ahead stood the little church where, right about now, his friend Kate was probably already saying 'I do.'

He nervously checked his watch; he was now officially half an hour late.

Weddings never start on time.

You're fine.

Just run!

He reached the front doors of the church and placed his ear against the cool wood. He could hear the rousing congregation, their voices singing out the words of a familiar hymn. Part of him wanted to stay outside, hidden from view; the thought of disturbing this moment filled him with dread. Would opening the doors somehow break the magic that was brewing inside?

'Glad I'm not the only one that's turning up with their tail between their legs,' a voice from behind whispered close to his ear.

'Jesus!' Fin shouted, his insides momentarily jumping out of his body. He spun round to find a sheepish, rather harried-looking man standing to his side. 'They nearly had a funeral on their hands as well as a wedding there for a second.' Fin felt his heart straining against his chest.

'Sorry, didn't mean to give you a fright.' The man held out his weathered-looking hand and Fin shook it firmly. 'I'm Jack.'

'Hey, Jack. I'm Fin.' He turned back and listened again at the door. 'They're still singing; do you reckon we go in now?'

'Don't think there's going to be a better time, mate.' Jack shrugged his shoulders.

Fin took a deep breath and pushed against the heavy door. Slowly the inside of the church came into view through the crack: the backs of hundreds of heads, coiffed, gelled and adorned with hats. Luckily there was more than enough room at the back for the pair of latecomers to linger. Fin felt his chest swell with affection as his eyes found the glowing couple standing at the front of the altar, the stained-glass window throwing its rainbow colours across them both, their faces reflecting the light back tenfold.

'Good work, my friend.' Jack leant over. 'I think we might have got away with that one.' He punched Fin rather hard on the arm. Fin nodded in agreement, eyes fixed forward on the scene unfolding before him. Vows being exchanged, rings in hand.

'Are you with the bride or the groom?' Jack hissed, pulling at his suit uncomfortably. Fin didn't reply but Jack didn't seem to notice. 'I'm with the groom. In fact it's probably best I'm hidden at the back—'

'Shhhh!' A fierce-looking lady turned her head and scowled at them both. Fin smiled weakly as Jack held his hands up apologetically.

'Sorry,' he half shouted, half whispered at the woman, who replied with an even more deadly stare.

Thankfully Jack managed to restrain himself for the rest of the ceremony, only using his voice to sing as loudly as humanly possible during the hymns. It was a beautiful ceremony, and there wasn't a dry eye in the church as Kate and her new husband George walked out of the doors as man and wife. Fin watched eagerly as they passed, followed up by a trail of red-eyed family members. Soon it was their turn to leave and Jack seemed in a particular rush to go, almost pushing Fin out of the door.

'Come on, if we get caught behind this lot we'll be stuck for hours and I, for one, certainly want to make use of the free bar as soon as I can.' He chuckled, anxiously looking behind him at the stream of people moving through the aisles.

For a January day the weather had been surprisingly kind, the bleary sun trying its hardest to shed its rays on the happy gathering below. Fin stood a little to the side as the photographer swarmed around the family, herding everyone into position. Jack hovered by Fin's side, fumbling in his pocket for a crumpled pack of cigarettes.

'You want one?' he offered. Fin shook his head, eyes eagerly watching the congregation for any signs of familiar faces. 'How are you getting to the reception, by the way?'

Fin grimaced. 'Erm, no idea. Taxi?' Even as the words came out of his mouth, he realized it was foolish. They were in a tiny rural village in the middle of nowhere.

Jack scoffed. 'Oh yeah, all those Ubers just queuing up. I'm guessing you didn't book a place on the coach then?' His eyebrow arched gleefully.

'Nope.'

'No worries. I'll drive you if you want? My car's just over there.' He waved his hand vaguely to the left. 'The two renegades have to stick together – am I right?' He smirked.

Fin returned the smile. 'Thanks, mate.'

It seemed that their lateness was going to bond them for the entire wedding, not that he minded; Jack was now the third person aside from the couple that he knew. There was always safety in numbers.

'No sweat.' Suddenly Jack's face dropped. He threw the half-smoked cigarette on the floor and stamped it out viciously. 'But we have to go . . . right now.' He grabbed Fin's arm and started to pull him away from the church.

'All right, calm down! What's the rush?' But before Jack could answer, Fin saw a small woman push her way through the throng of people and head directly towards them. She looked like a gift-wrapped pit bull clad in coral. Even the delicate curls on her head seemed to suddenly stiffen in anger.

'Jack Clements. Where the *hell* have you been!' she barked.

'Oooh, someone really is in trouble,' Fin teased.

'Wouldn't you be if you turned up late to your step-brother's wedding?' Jack was still trying to drag Fin away from the approaching woman, whose eyes seemed to grow narrower with every step she took.

Fin couldn't hold back the laughter any longer. 'Jack, I thought you were a renegade! Surely a daredevil like you isn't afraid of your own mum?'

'I don't know what kind of woman gave birth to you, buddy, but mine is not one you want to cross,' he hissed, stumbling over a clump of raised earth. 'Now, go!' he ordered, practically hurling Fin towards the car park.

*

After they'd arrived at the old barn, Jack had unceremoniously been whisked away and Fin hadn't seen him since. Over the years, as he'd watched almost all of his friends pair off and get married, Fin had learnt that the best place to be at weddings was as close to the kitchen as humanly possible. It was loud and busy, which didn't lend itself well to small talk. It also meant you were afforded first dibs on the canapes, which was always a bonus.

'Ladies and gentlemen, if you would like to take your seats it's time to eat!' the master of ceremonies called out across the room. Fin joined the mass of guests wending their way into the dining hall, his eyes searching for his table amongst the crowd. He caught a sheepish-looking Jack being forced into a chair at the front, his mother staring at him with a less ferocious gaze but still with an intense air of dislike. He suddenly felt a solid body knock into his shoulder.

'God, I'm so sorry.' He turned around, feeling the sensation of warm liquid soaking into his jacket. 'I wasn't looking where I was going, totally my fa—' But the rest of his words seemed to dissolve instantly at the sight of her.

'Eleanor.' Saying her name out loud felt strange after all this time.

'Fin?' she gasped, her eyes growing exponentially in size.

'Hi.' He lifted his hand in a lame attempt at a wave, as thousands of memories hit him at once. He blinked them away and forced himself to focus on the woman standing in front of him now. 'Nothing spilt on you, did it? I'm so sorry, I didn't even see you there. I can get you another glass if you want?' He anxiously checked to see how much of her drink she had left.

'No, no. It's fine,' she replied, her face still frozen in shock. 'What are you doing here? I mean . . .' She shook her head. 'I didn't know you were even in the country.'

'I wasn't. Until a couple of weeks ago.'

'I see.'

Fin felt his face redden; he'd known if they ever saw each other again it might be awkward, but the sheer terror that seemed to be written across her face was quite the unexpected reaction. 'I thought I'd show my face at the wedding while I was here, you know.' He tried to sound casual and prayed that Eleanor didn't decide to probe. She'd always had a way of getting him to confess the truth about things.

'Right. Makes sense.' She nodded curtly.

'What table are you?' he asked.

'Seventeen.'

'Ah, me too.'

Fin couldn't help but notice Eleanor's face twitch in response. Was it out of anger? Frustration? It seemed his ability to read her little quirks had been lost over the years.

'No, you're not. I checked the seating plan. Your name wasn't on it.'

Fin put his hands in his trouser pockets and smiled awkwardly. 'I was actually a bit of a last-minute addition so I'm not sure there was time to officially change the names. Technically I'm down as George's pregnant cousin.' He tried to joke, willing even a hint of a smile to appear on her face.

'I see.' She nodded. 'Well, we'd better go – everyone is seated.'

'Of course.' He gestured ahead. 'After you.'

The pair made their way silently across the room. Fin could feel the tension grabbing hold of every cell in his body, squeezing and twisting until it felt like screaming.

'I have to be honest.' Eleanor's voice was only just audible over the rolling waves of surrounding chatter. 'I'm quite surprised to see you here. I didn't think you came back that much any more.'

Fin faltered, the honest answer forcing its way to the surface. He swallowed it down hard and smiled.

'Every decade or so.' He laughed uncomfortably at his poor joke. Eleanor returned an equally half-hearted smile.

'Talking of surprises . . .' Fin tried to divert the conversation away from his unexpected visit. 'Where's Oliver? Or have I missed him?'

Eleanor stopped dead in her tracks, her champagne spilling out of the glass once again. She gave her head a little shake and then continued walking.

'He's not coming,' she replied flatly.

'Oh, still working hard as ever?' Table seventeen was fast approaching and Fin could already see his name place standing tall and proud, beckoning him over. He looked either side and saw names he didn't recognize. If he hadn't been so distracted trying to find where exactly Eleanor was seated, he might have noticed the tears that had gathered in the corners of her eyes. Only when he heard her strained voice did he stop and pay attention.

'We . . . we aren't together any more.'

He felt the bottom drop out of his stomach.

Oh, well done, you bloody idiot.

Time seemed to slow to an excruciating crawl.

Say something.

Anything.

But no words came. How had he managed to lose all form of social etiquette in the space of five minutes?

'I'm so sorry.' He reached his hand out to comfort her, but she'd already taken a step forward and so it hung limply in mid-air. 'Honestly, you know how useless I am when it comes to this.'

She turned to face him and wiped the tear that was rolling down her face. 'What, talking to people?' A hint of a smile flickered across her face.

'Yeah, pretty much.' He shrugged.

She carried on walking. 'It's OK. We broke up last year; I'm going to blame the tears on this.' She held up her half-spilt champagne.

'Honestly, I'm an idiot, I didn't mean to upset you, Elles.' He ran his hand anxiously through his hair.

'It's fine.' She gave a tiny whisper of a laugh. 'Besides . . . this wouldn't be the first wedding you've ruined, would it?'

Then: Aged 15

Eleanor

'Remind me why we have to go to this again?'

'You have to go because it's your dad's wedding. And I have to come to supervise you.'

Fin ran his hands through his already wildly out of control hair and sighed. 'And I'll ask the question again . . . why? It's not like it's the romance story of the year, is it? He's marrying the woman he cheated on my mum with.'

Eleanor stopped and pulled her friend in for a hug. She breathed in the smell of his brand-new suit mixed with the familiar scent of his warm skin. 'No one is denying that this is beyond weird, and if I could make this less awkward and terrible for you, I would. But it's important for your dad. You know we have to go. Plus, we get a free three-course meal. Not even you can say no to that.'

He squeezed her tightly and whispered in her ear, 'Ever my voice of reason, hey, Elles?'

She smiled and held him out in front of her. 'And you never know, Ancka's friends might have some attractive daughters for you to hang out with.'

'I would rather date *you* than risk being even more closely tied to that witch.'

'Wow. Jesus Christ, Fin, talk about insulting.' Eleanor slapped him gently on the arm and carried on walking towards the church. She heard him running up behind her.

'Oh, come on, Elles.' He draped his arm across her shoulder. 'You know what I mean. You're like my sister.' He nudged her gently.

'Yes, I know.' She shrugged his arm off her and rearranged her hair. 'Now, just because you're not remotely interested in me doesn't mean that no one else will be. So quit ruining my hair and let's get this over with.'

'Right you are, captain.' He grabbed her hand and squeezed it tight. Eleanor looked at him and instantly saw the little boy she'd grown up with hidden, not so discreetly, under the layers of adolescent confidence.

'Let's do it! Let's go watch your dad get hitched.' She took his hand and led him into the church.

*

'Congratulations, Brian. And thank you so much for inviting me.' Eleanor held out her hand but Fin's dad had already pulled her in for a hug. Brian Taylor was a huge bear of a man, loud and gruff, with a voice that could be heard from a mile off. Looking at Fin and his dad side by side, the only vague hint that the two men were related was the red hair they wore proudly on their heads. Brian squeezed Eleanor hard and she felt her lungs crumple in on themselves.

'Don't be silly, Eleanor! You're practically family, you know that. Wouldn't be the same without you.' He lowered his voice to almost a whisper. 'Now, where the hell is that son of mine?'

Eleanor's heart sank. She'd been praying that Fin's absence hadn't been noticed, but clearly she'd been kidding herself.

'I'll go find him. I'm sure he's just flirting with one of the waitresses somewhere.' She tried to force a laugh but it came out like a stilted squawk.

'Why on earth would he be doing that when he only has eyes for one girl?' he teased, releasing her from his embrace.

'Brian!' The new Mrs Taylor was waving frantically at her husband with a look of impatience etched into her delicately made up face. 'Brian, come and say hello to Francine, please.'

'I'd better go. But I want to see that boy on the dance floor within the hour, OK? He promised me he'd behave today. I *need* him to behave today.' He flashed her a pleading smile, then joined Aneka and her gaggle of friends on the dance floor.

Where the hell are you, Fin?

Eleanor had been trying to subtly look for him ever since dessert. He'd been sitting opposite her at the meal – thankfully she was sandwiched between Fin's two cousins who she'd met countless times before and so there were no awkward silences or forced conversations. What that did mean, however, was that she hadn't been paying too much attention to Fin, who, according to his aunt, had said he was getting some fresh air but never returned.

'You know what he's like, darling. Probably made some new friends and lost track of the time. That boy will speak to anyone!' his aunt had chortled, as Eleanor accosted her for the third time for more information.

Eleanor had tried to smile, but the fear had sunk its claws into her stomach and unease crept over her like a chilling frost.

'You're probably right, but I'll just go and have another look. You know how much he loves dessert. He'll kill me if he misses it.'

Nearly an hour later and Eleanor had searched everywhere, but there was simply no sign of Fin. She'd taken to hanging around outside the male toilets for a good ten minutes before having to embarrassedly ask one of Fin's uncles whether he could check the stalls to see if he was locked in there. She'd even asked the hotel reception to keep an eye out. Until he was found, all she had to do was keep calm and act like everything was under control. Except now people were noticing and Eleanor's anxiety was threatening to bubble over.

She'd decided to do one last loop of the venue when she saw him, half walking, half swaying across the dance floor. His suit jacket was hanging off his shoulder and he was holding a bottle of champagne in his hand.

This wasn't good. This was not good at all. She tried to run and divert his path, but by the time she'd made it through the crowd of dancing guests he'd already reached his target.

'Finley! There you are, son! We were about to send out the search party.' His dad clapped his son firmly on the back.

Fin stumbled backwards. He could barely keep his head up, let alone stand still; his body was rocking back and forth. Each time he steadied himself, the bottle of champagne slipped a little further out of his grasp.

'Fin, why don't we go and sit down for a second.' Eleanor was by his side, trying to sound soothing. Her grip was vice-like around his arms in a subtle attempt to keep him upright.

'No,' he mumbled.

'Fin, please.' She lowered her voice so only he could hear her plea. 'Come on. Let's go.'

'*No*.' His voice rang out loudly over the music. The bottle of champagne dropped on to the floor as he toppled into Eleanor. 'I want to speak to my dad on this happy *happy* occasion.'

Eleanor couldn't bear to look at the faces of the guests. Hushed whispers rippled around them as the scene unfolded.

'Son.' His dad stepped towards them, his voice flat and solid. 'I think you need to go and lie down. Just for a bit, and I'll be up in a moment to check on you, OK?'

Eleanor felt Fin lurch forward. 'How about . . . no!' He pushed his dad square in the chest, but the motion took him so far forward he tripped over his shoes and landed on the floor.

'Brian! Get. Him. Out. Of. Here.' Aneka marched over, the venom in her voice making Eleanor wince. '*Now*.'

'Oh, hello, *Mum*.' Fin was on his back now, pointing up at Aneka. '*Mum*.' He burst out laughing. 'Can you believe I get to call a stuck-up bitch like you my mum now? Only . . . what is it . . . only a year after my real mum was left heart-broken and alone?'

The look on Aneka's face as she took in the sight of Fin rolling around on the floor was terrifying. It was as though her skin had folded in on itself and melted into pure fury. Eleanor wanted the ground to swallow them both up. Her heart was breaking for Fin as the tears rolled thick and fast down his face. She dropped to her knees and threw herself over him.

'Fin, please. Please come with me. You need to get up and you need to go.' She grabbed his hand and squeezed it tightly.

'I hate her. I fucking hate her.' He hadn't adjusted the volume of his voice, so the words came out loud and clear.

'*Enough*. Eleanor, move, please.' She barely had a second to react before Fin's dad had reached down and hauled his son up to standing. 'Get out of here right now. I don't want to see you for the rest of the evening.' The look on his face was mutinous. Both men, father and son, glared at each other with such anger that Eleanor could feel it thundering through the floor.

Then Fin broke. The tears erupted from deep inside him.

'Fine, pick her. See if I care.'

Eleanor grabbed his hand and led him gently away. The moment they were outside he collapsed on to her, his body shaking with the force of grief.

'I'm sorry. I'm so sorry.'

'It's OK,' she cooed, lowering them both on to the ground. 'You're OK. I'm just going to call Dad to come and get us.'

'Elles. Please never leave me.'

'Uh-huh Fin, hold on, keep your head up for me if you can.'

'Promise me?' he whispered, as he laid his head on her shoulder.

'Promise you what?'

'Promise me that you'll never leave me.'

She took a deep breath and kissed the top of his head.

'I promise you, Fin. I'll always be here. No matter what.'

Now

Eleanor

It had been three days since the wedding and Eleanor still hadn't got over the unexpected presence of Finley Taylor. Ideally, she would have behaved like she'd had at least some level of social skills and not stared at him, mouth open, fumbling over her words, but what was there to say? It had been years since they had spoken. Probably decades! The last thing she needed at her first solo event post-break-up was that sort of surprise being thrust upon her. Luckily, Eleanor had been sitting next to Kate's extremely chatty uncle and so barely had time to breathe, let alone engage in conversation with anyone else at the table. After dinner she had purposefully disappeared off to the toilets, latched on to one of Kate's work colleagues, and spent the rest of the evening downing tequila shots at the bar. Fin, she hoped, would stay clear of that particular area, and thankfully their paths didn't cross again.

'Oi. Are you even listening to me?' Sal snapped. 'You look like you're off on another planet!'

'Sorry,' Eleanor apologized. 'What did you say?'

'I *said*,' Sal huffed, opening the door of the pub and reeling from the swell of noise and smell of beer that hit them, 'will you go on a date with my friend?'

'Oh. Absolutely not.'

'But it's been nearly three months!' Sal cried incredulously, as they forced their way through the heaving mass of bodies.

'And?' Eleanor shouted over her shoulder. The little pub across the road from their office was always packed after work; if you managed to get a space at the bar you were lucky, let alone a seat at a table. Thankfully Sal knew the manager, and without fail there would always be a corner seat reserved for her and Eleanor whenever they needed it.

'And?' Sal shot the group of rowdy men next to her a deadly glare as one very nearly spilt his entire pint on to her shoulder. 'I think you should at least give it a go. Look how far you've come. You went to a bloody wedding by yourself and it won't be long until you're back to your carbohydrate inhaling, sleeping eight hours a night self! Next step is surely a date?'

Eleanor laughed as she eventually reached the little reserved booth nestled in the back of the bar. 'There's not some sort of heartbreak recovery checklist, you know? Just because I'm not crying every five minutes and consuming 90 per cent liquid, doesn't mean I'm ready to date.'

Sal frowned, sliding into the seat opposite her. Eleanor knew that eventually she would have to succumb – there were only so many times her friend could take no for an answer – but right now she was willing to try and keep her at bay for just a little longer.

'You deserve some happiness, that's all.' Sal grabbed the bottle of wine and poured them both a large glass. 'Oh shit, I forgot to get one for Freya.'

Eleanor's eyes narrowed instantly. 'Can you two stop being friends behind my back, please. It's weird.' She grabbed her glass and angrily sipped her wine.

'You've only got yourself to blame. If you hadn't disappeared off the face of the earth when Oliver left then I wouldn't have had to contact your sister to check if you were alive,' Sal shot back. Eleanor felt her face redden with a potent mix of embarrassment and frustration. 'We only talk because we care about *you*.' Her friend reached across and clinked her glass against Eleanor's.

'Fine.' She felt her body soften slightly. 'Anyway, why is everyone so obsessed with me meeting someone?' she whined, clumsily changing the subject. Eleanor had always counted herself lucky. She had never technically had to date anyone before. High school boyfriends were acquired in the very emotionally mature way of passing notes or slow dancing at the annual disco. Then came university, and it just so happened that on the first night of Freshers' Week she met Oliver Fitzpatrick, and after ten Jägerbombs and some neon paint, the pair had become inseparable. Now she cursed her lack of experience. How could she be on the cusp of turning thirty-five, having never had a proper first date? She thought it only fair to discount the one where Curtis had legged it halfway through.

'Because the longer you leave it, the harder it will be. I'm not saying it's going to be easy. Trust me, I've had my fair share of dates and it can be unbelievably depressing at times.'

'Remind me again how you're VP of Sales and Marketing with this kind of pitch?' Eleanor cut in.

'*But.*' Sal grabbed her hand and squeezed it. 'You deserve to find someone. And trust me, you're not going to find them holed up in that flat of yours or having Sunday lunch with your mum. We have to get you out of your comfort zone!'

The words triggered something in her brain. Eleanor's mind flashed back to the New Year's resolutions she'd written.

Number 4: Do things that scare you.

Eleanor exhaled deeply and remembered the tiny note she'd added to the bottom of the page.

Find love?

'Fine. If I agree to go on *one* more date' – she pointed her finger sternly at Sal, whose face had already lit up – 'will you promise to get off my back about the whole thing?'

'One million per cent.'

'And if he runs away from me, I swear I will kill you.' She took another large mouthful of wine. 'Do you have a picture of him?'

Sal's eyes glittered mischievously. 'Of course.' She scrolled through her phone and then slid it across the table triumphantly. Eleanor had barely had time to focus on the screen when her sister's voice rang out.

'Sorry I'm late, this place is a *nightmare*. It took me about twenty minutes to fight my way across the room!' Freya planted herself down and looked at the two glasses of wine on the table. 'You're kidding me? I have to battle my way through that all over again.' She groaned.

Eleanor handed over her glass. 'Just share mine for now.' She tried to sneakily glance down at the face of the man staring up at her from Sal's phone.

'So, what do you think?' Sal purred.

'About what?' Freya quipped. 'What are we looking at?' She craned her neck over the screen.

'Nothing,' Eleanor replied, a little too defensively. Freya's face crumpled into a scowl.

'Come on, you can't invite me for drinks then exclude me from the conversation. Didn't Mum teach you any manners?'

'*I* didn't invite you,' Eleanor murmured petulantly.

'Excuse me!' Freya exclaimed, snatching Sal's phone from her grasp. 'Well hello, he's gorgeous. Is this your new date, Sal?'

Eleanor shot Sal a look that she prayed screamed, 'Please lie and say he's yours.'

'Nope, not mine,' Sal replied innocently, avoiding Eleanor's gaze.

'Aha! Now I understand why you were being all snappy,' Freya teased. 'He's fit, Eleanor. When are you meeting him?'

'I don't know.' She could feel her entire body bristling with embarrassment. 'I don't even know his name.'

'Ben. His name's Ben and he is super excited to meet you on Saturday . . .' Sal grinned.

'What?!' Eleanor slammed the glass down on the table. 'You already said yes?'

Sal shrugged her shoulders. 'I had a hunch you'd like him, that's all. Besides, these days there really isn't much time to waste.'

'I'm not *that* old.'

'I didn't mean that. I *meant*, if you wait around dithering, a man like Ben will be snapped up before you know it. Trust me. He's a good one and they don't hang around for long.'

'Fine,' Eleanor conceded. 'But the same rules apply as before. No dinner, no drinks, afternoon dates only and absolutely no or—'

'Organized activity.' Sal finished the sentence, rolling her eyes in exasperation. 'Yes, I know. I've already told him to take you for coffee.'

'Good.' Eleanor nodded, satisfied. 'Although I don't know why everyone just assumes I'm free all the time – I may have had plans for Saturday.'

Sal scoffed into her wine.

'Hey!' Eleanor shouted indignantly.

'Stop grumbling and tell us how the wedding was,' Freya interrupted.

'Ooh yes, how was it?' Sal chimed, eager to move the subject on now the date had been confirmed.

'It was actually all right. It felt a bit odd being there by myself, but as soon as everything kicked off it was fine. Kate looked stunning, the venue was beautiful, and the food was amazing. She did very well.'

'And how drunk did you get? Any secret smooches with a wayward cousin in the corner of the bar?' Sal's eyes twinkled.

'Surprisingly . . . no.' She chuckled.

'Boring,' Freya groaned.

'Sorry to disappoint.' Eleanor shrugged.

'You're telling me that there was nobody, not even one single interesting person at the wedding for you to report back on.' Sal folded her arms crossly.

'I mean . . .' Eleanor fiddled with the stem of her wine glass.

Don't mention it.

It's not worth it.

'Eleanor?' Freya pressed, sensing the hesitation.

'It's nothing like that.' Eleanor glanced over at Freya.

'What! Who was there?'

'Fin.'

'Excuse me?' Freya spluttered.

'You heard me,' she replied curtly.

'Fin, as in . . .?' Her sister's expression was one of total incomprehension.

'Yes, *Fin*.'

'Well? How did he look? Was it weird?' Freya babbled excitedly. 'How long is he in town for? I didn't think he came back here any more.'

'I don't know,' Eleanor snapped.

'Well, didn't you speak to him?'

'Only for a bit.' She shrugged. 'He seems fine.'

'Excuse me? Back up a second,' Sal interrupted. 'Who on earth is Fin?'

Freya opened her mouth to answer but Eleanor cut across. 'Just an old friend,' she replied casually, hoping it was enough to satisfy Sal's curiosity.

'I see.' Sal eyed the sisters suspiciously.

'Old friend is a bit of an understatement,' Freya contested. 'Those two were practically joined at the hip for the entirety of their childhood. He was like a brother to us.'

Eleanor winced at Freya's words.

'What happened?' Sal leant forward across the table. 'How come I've never heard of him if he was such a good friend?'

'Because I haven't spoken to the guy in decades.' Eleanor stood up suddenly, keeping her eyes firmly away from Sal's piercing gaze. This was a conversation she did not want to be getting into right now.

'And before you start,' she warned, 'nothing happened. We just drifted apart, that's all.'

'I see,' Sal replied unconvincingly.

'Now, Frey, you need your own glass.' She changed the subject quickly. 'And while I'm up I'll get us another bottle.'

Eleanor didn't even wait to hear their reply as she shifted out of her seat and into the pulsing, intoxicated crowd of suits. In her opinion, there was nothing more to say about Finley Taylor.

For all she knew, he could be halfway back to LA by now, never to be seen again.

Fin

It had now been just over two weeks since his arrival in London, and the only things Fin had managed to accomplish successfully were eating his way through the neighbourhood's selection of takeout restaurants, watching nearly everything that Netflix had to offer, and sleeping. He wasn't quite sure he could count Kate's wedding a success. Not only had he been late, but that awkward interaction with Eleanor was still playing heavily on his mind. The look of dread that flashed across her face when she saw him was not something that was easily forgotten.

'Stupid idiot,' Fin muttered to himself as he replayed the moment once again, this time in ultra-slow motion. Before he had any further opportunity to chastise himself, he felt his phone vibrate from somewhere deep inside the cushions of the sofa. He reached down, trying not to think about what his fingers might be touching, and grabbed it.

'Hello?' Fin answered, without even checking who was on the other end.

'Jesus, have you forgotten who I am already?' Rob quipped sarcastically. 'You've only been gone two weeks.'

'Sorry, mate, what can I say? You're just not that memorable.' Fin grinned, feeling lighter at once at the sound of his friend's voice.

'Bastard,' Rob sniped. 'Anyway, what's happening over there? How is the flat, everything all good? Not trashed it completely and broken everything in sight?'

Fin looked around at the piles of empty takeaway cartons and the dirty laundry gathering in small groups across the room. 'Trashed isn't quite the word I'd use.' He laughed. 'But no, everything is fine, I promise.'

'Cool. How's your mum doing?'

A sickening feeling of guilt churned in his stomach. Every day he'd planned to go and visit his mother and yet every day he'd found an excuse not to. He knew he was being a coward, but seeing Eleanor had been enough of a visit down memory lane; could he really handle any more?

'She's all right, not great but . . . you know, doing OK,' Fin lied, praying his friend wouldn't be able to sense the dishonesty.

'I'm sorry, man. It must be tough.'

Yeah, really tough sitting around doing sweet nothing all day.

Fin's guilt raged even stronger. 'Thanks, mate, I appreciate it. Anyway, how are you doing?'

'Me? I'm all good. Missing you. Working every hour the good Lord sends, but fine.'

'What poor soul have you roped in to replace me while I'm gone, then?'

Rob burst out laughing. 'I knew it wouldn't be long until you asked me about work.' He sighed in mock exasperation. 'Some newbie from the agency. Not a patch on you, don't worry. He's a sweet kid but he's got some stuff to learn.'

'Don't we all, mate,' Fin replied whimsically.

'You're not wrong there, buddy. Anyway, speaking of work, I'd better go. I'm already running late to my shoot and I only wanted to check in and say hi. Send your mum my love. I'm assuming you've told her all about me.' He chuckled childishly.

Fin felt the guilt practically clawing its way up his throat. 'Sure thing. Bye, mate.'

As the phone went dead, all Fin could hear were the conflicting thoughts that were whirling around his head. Yes, it would be hard seeing his dying mother after all this time. Yes, it would mean facing all the things he ran away from so long ago. But was he really going to come all this way to wallow in empty chow-mein packets in his friend's freezing cold apartment?

Just one visit. That's all it is.

*

St Catherine's Care Home was not, as he had imagined, a sterile block of a hospital building. In fact, if there hadn't been the big white sign outside the driveway, he probably would have mistaken it for just another large Victorian house on the street. Seeing it, he felt a swell of relief; in spite of everything that had happened between them, he still wouldn't want his mum to be holed up in some lifeless, dank place.

'Hello! Can I help you?' a small woman called out as he stepped into the reception. Her close-cropped wispy hair and large, round glasses made her look like a little owl, perched dutifully behind the desk. He smiled sheepishly, noting the name tag placed proudly on her chest.

'Hi, Nurse Clara? My name's Finley Taylor. We spoke on the phone a couple of weeks ago.'

Her face broke into a smile. 'Ah, Mr Taylor, I'm so glad you came.'

'Please, call me Fin.' The nerves in his stomach were reaching peak intensity.

'As you wish.' Nurse Clara gathered up some papers and placed them to one side. 'Shall I show you through to see your mother?'

'Sure,' Fin replied, shuffling nervously from one foot to the other, willing them not to turn around and run back out from where they had come.

'Eileen won't know what's hit her. Two visitors in one day.' Nurse Clara beamed; her harsh features softening instantly with her smile. 'She's just down here.' The nurse opened the door to the side of the desk and walked briskly ahead, her tiny legs moving with efficiency. 'Her friend should be finishing up soon; she only stays for half an hour or so. Luckily for you both, your mum is fairly lucid today. Fingers crossed it stays that way.'

'About that.' Fin paused, halfway through the door. 'How bad is she? Like . . . what happens?'

Nurse Clara ushered him through and continued to stride down the long, red-carpeted hallway. 'On good days it's mainly just moments of confusion. Maybe some disorientation and forgetfulness. Bad days can sometimes mean she doesn't remember where she is. How old she is. Who she is. There can be a lot of distress and anger on a bad day.' She stopped and looked at him kindly. 'Understandably, of course. It's a terrible disease.'

'Of course.' Fin nodded, trying as hard as he could to digest all the information being given to him.

'But like I said on the phone, your name never fails to crop up in conversation.' The nurse patted his arm softly and stood outside the door at the very end of the corridor. 'Here we go.' She knocked loudly on the door. 'Eileen, it's your lucky day . . . we have another visitor for you.' She smiled and winked at Fin, whose stomach surged with nausea.

'Perfect timing, I'm just leaving,' a voice called out from within. 'Eileen darling, I'll see you next week, OK? Stay strong and keep eating. Low blood sugars don't help anyone.'

Fin felt his entire body freeze.

No.

It can't be.

Before he had another moment to think, the door flew open to reveal none other than Angela Levy.

'Good God!' she cried, her eyes so wide they were filling half of her face. 'Fin?' She breathed his name, stepping forward to inspect him.

'Angela, hi.' He waved pathetically.

'Look at you.' She gesticulated wildly up and down the length of his body. 'I can't believe you're here! Your mother is going to be *so* happy to see you.' All at once he was pulled into a fierce embrace.

'Now' – Angela held him out at arm's length – 'be prepared. She's going to look a little different. But . . .' She squeezed him firmly, interrupting his thoughts. 'She's still Eileen. She's still your mum. Don't forget that, OK?'

Fin nodded dutifully and stepped to the side to let her pass.

'How long are you planning on staying for?' she asked.

'Not sure yet. I guess it depends on . . .' He dropped his gaze slightly. 'On how my mum does.'

'Of course.' Angela patted his arm sympathetically. 'Well, while you're here, you *must* come over for Sunday lunch. We're still in the same place as we've always been.'

Fin was about to open his mouth and fire off any excuse he could think of, when Angela planted a firm kiss on his cheek and began to stroll off down the corridor. 'And you know I won't take no for an answer,' she called back, her layers of purple chiffon flapping wildly out behind her. 'I'll be in touch, darling.'

Both Nurse Clara and Fin stood silently for a moment.

'She's a force to be reckoned with, that one is.' Nurse Clara chuckled. 'And that's coming from me!' She adjusted her glasses and placed her small hand firmly on his back. 'Are you ready, Fin?' she asked softly.

'Uh-huh.' He nodded meekly, still a little dazed from the whirlwind of Angela.

'I'll be down the corridor if you need me, all right?' She gently pushed him into the room, closing the door quietly behind him.

It took a moment for Fin's eyes to adjust without the stark strip lighting of the corridor. The room itself was fairly small and strangely dark.

'Hello?' a faint voice murmured feebly.

Fin forced his eyes to focus. There in front of him was a large hospital-type bed, and tucked up under the covers seemed to be a mass of skin and bone. If he hadn't known it was his mother lying there, he could have been persuaded it was nothing more than crepe paper and matchsticks. An artistic interpretation of a human being. A sketch of life.

Slowly her head turned in his direction and recognition flickered in her large glassy eyes.

'Oh my,' she gasped.

Fin stood there frozen. The only thing his body seemed able to do was blink and breathe.

'Fin?' The wispy figure reached out a tentative hand, as though his mother were grasping for a mere memory of him. 'Is that really you?' Her eyes narrowed.

He shuffled forward so that she could see him a little better. All at once her withered face lit up. 'My word. You look . . . you look so grown-up.'

Fin could feel his entire body prickle with emotion. The regret. The anger. The shame. They all piled in, one on top of the other, scrabbling for top spot, whilst he stood there silently.

'Sit, please.' His mother pointed at the empty chair by the side of her bed. Fin approached cautiously and sat down.

'How did you even know where I was?' A bewildered look fell across her sunken face.

'One of the nurses called me,' he mumbled, still unable to believe that this was what his mother had become.

'I see.' Her lips pursed and her face darkened. 'I didn't know. If I did, I would have told them not to bother you. They like to make a fuss here.'

'Well, dementia and cancer kind of feels like something to make a fuss over.' With every word spoken, Fin could feel the weight of tension growing heavier on his shoulders. 'But maybe that's just me.' He shrugged, noting how petulant his sarcasm sounded.

'I didn't want to inconvenience you, that's all. I'm sorry you've had to come all this way.'

'It's fine.' He tried to sound like he meant it, but it was proving trickier than he thought. 'How are you feeling?'

She forced her face into a reassuring smile. 'Most of the time I'm OK.'

Silence fell over them both. There were so many things to say, so many questions to ask, but none of them seemed appropriate given the circumstances. Fin looked around the room, trying to find anything to distract from the stilted, uncomfortable atmosphere. The layout, he assumed, was standard for every resident at the home. Dark wooden furniture, pale green wallpaper, and hospital equipment hidden in the corners, ready to be called upon at a moment's notice.

Suddenly his eyes clocked the photograph by her bedside. His mum and dad on their wedding day. Fury tore through him. How? How, after everything that had happened, could she still bear to look at him?

'You look well.' His mother's weak voice cut across his thoughts. 'America clearly suits you.'

'Thanks.'

Another deafening silence. He could practically see the effort of his mum's brain as it tried to search for any topic of conversation that might lighten the mood.

'Did you see Angela as you came in?' A twinkle of joy danced in her pale eyes.

'Yeah, we passed each other in the corridor.'

'She's still the same as ever. Mad as a bloody hatter, but God love her, she comes and sees me every week without fail. After everything that's happened to her, she still manages to find time.'

Fin clenched his fists. Was that a dig at him?

'That's good of her,' he replied flatly.

'Can you believe we've been friends for over thirty years?'

his mum continued. 'I always thought you and Eleanor would follow suit.' She shook her head sadly.

'Yeah, well . . . things don't always go the way you planned, do they?'

His mother turned and fixed her eyes on his.

'No, Fin. No, they don't.'

Eleanor

Despite her best efforts to be exactly on time for her date, Eleanor had arrived early. It had all felt quite innocent when she'd agreed to it in the pub. But now Eleanor actually had to go and meet this stranger, and pretend not to be counting down the minutes until she could respectfully leave, it didn't seem so fun.

It will be fine.

Just one coffee, that's all it is.

Her phone buzzed in her pocket and she was grateful for the distraction. Her stomach was flip-flopping wildly, making the double espresso and granola she'd inhaled for breakfast dangerously at risk of coming back up to greet her.

Eleanor stared down at the screen and saw her mother's name flashing up at her. She took a deep breath in and answered. 'Hey, Mum. Everything OK?'

'Darling . . . you will *never* guess who I just saw?'

Angela's voice was even louder than usual, the excitement physically assaulting Eleanor's ears.

'I don't know . . . Brad Pitt?'

'*Please*, if I had seen Brad Pitt, you wouldn't hear a peep from me for weeks. We'd be too busy wrapped up in each other for me to call.'

Eleanor shuddered. 'Ew, enough, Mum. I don't need that image in my head.'

'Don't be such a prude, Eleanor dear.' She chuckled wickedly.

'I'm not a prude,' Eleanor huffed childishly. 'Anyway, tell me who you saw.' She closed her eyes, readying herself for a very disappointing story about an old neighbour's brother's cat-sitter.

'Finley Taylor!'

Eleanor's body jolted violently.

'He's still here?'

'Yes!' her mother exclaimed joyfully. 'Wait . . . what do you mean he's *still* here? Did you already know he was back in the country?' Angela bristled with irritation.

Dammit.

'Erm . . .' Eleanor searched her scattered brain for any way out of this.

'Eleanor?' her mother pressed.

'I *may* have seen him at Kate's wedding,' she admitted.

'And you didn't tell me?' Her mum was aghast. 'How could you!'

'Sorry, it totally slipped my mind.'

'Oh, sure,' Angela quipped sarcastically.

'It did.'

'You weren't rude to him, were you, Eleanor dear? I know what you can be like.' Angela tutted.

'Jesus, Mum, give me a break, will you? I'm not quite the monster you make me out to be, you know?'

'All I'm saying is that heartbreak does terrible things to even the best of us.'

Eleanor's heart twinged in acknowledgement. 'Where did you see him?'

'When I went to see Eileen. Things aren't looking great so I assume the home must have called him.'

'Oh, right.' How could she have been so stupid? Obviously he hadn't come back solely for Kate's wedding. She hadn't even asked about his mum. The shock of seeing him so unexpectedly at the wedding had thrown Eleanor completely.

'Yes, it's all very sad. I've invited him round for lunch tomorrow. Poor soul must need something to do other than visiting his sick mother in that care home. Is that OK with you, darling?'

Eleanor paused, biting back the urge to scream 'no' down the phone.

'Erm . . .' But guilt and surprise and cold terror about her imminent date were blurring her thoughts and making forming a response incredibly difficult.

'Wonderful! I knew you wouldn't mind. It will be lovely having you all back together again. I still don't know why you let him disappear off around the world and out of your life. He was always such a lovely boy.' She sighed nostalgically.

I didn't let him disappear; he chose to go.

'It wasn't quite like th—' Eleanor tried to explain.

'Anyway, darling, I need to go, the shop practically crumbles without me there! I'll see you tomorrow, sweetheart. Have a lovely rest of the day.'

'Thanks, Mum, I'll try,' Eleanor replied, but her mother had hung up almost instantly. And although Eleanor's brain was buzzing, she didn't have time to properly digest the conversation that had just occurred. There was something far more pressing she had to deal with. Her date.

I can't do this. I cannot do this.

'Yes, you can,' she affirmed, looking up at the entrance to the coffee shop, as nerves flickered their tiny butterfly wings inside her stomach.

They'd agreed to meet somewhere central, halfway between them both. It was a cute little independent place that he, her date, had suggested. Why she found it so difficult to refer to him by his name escaped her – maybe it was a way to dehumanize him. Meeting 'the date' felt less real than meeting Ben Ryans, forty, from New Cross.

Eleanor spotted him the moment she walked into the cafe, nestled in the corner with two steaming mugs and two slices of cake. She breathed a small sigh of relief; Sal hadn't been wrong and the photographs hadn't lied. He was handsome. He looked clean.

Why would he not be clean?

She pulled self-consciously at the hem of her jumper and slowly made her way over to him.

'Hi, you must be Eleanor?' He stood and reached out to hug her.

Eleanor smiled and awkwardly allowed herself to be held, her arms planted rigidly by her sides. Why did this not get any easier?

'Hi,' she managed.

He smelt of oranges and soap, and his body was wonderfully warm.

'Sit, please.' He proffered the empty seat in front of him. 'I took the liberty of ordering; Sal gave me strict instructions to go for carrot cake and a flat white. Please tell me she wasn't tricking me?' The look of fear that dawned on his face made Eleanor snort with laughter.

'Well, I have to say I'm glad Sal's tough love treatment isn't reserved solely for me.' Eleanor sat and took a sip of her drink. 'But don't worry, you got it spot on.'

'Phew!' He smiled, rubbing his hands through his short-cropped hair. It instantly reminded her of Fin and her heart contracted painfully. 'I have to confess I'm really not very good at these things. I think this is my first date in nearly a year, so I'm sorry if I'm a bit rusty.'

Eleanor's stomach dropped. Sal promised that this wouldn't be like the last time.

I may as well get up and go now.

'Oh, but no, wait.' He blushed. 'To be clear, I am completely over my ex and I am very much ready to meet someone.'

Eleanor couldn't help but burst out laughing. 'I'm guessing Sal told you about the *very* successful first date she tried to set me up on, then?'

'Maybe.' He rubbed his golden stubble anxiously with his hands. 'I was meant to be subtle about this. I've not done a great job so far, have I?'

'Trust me, you're doing better than the last. And bearing in mind this is only my second-ever date in thirty-five years, you don't have much to be worried about.' She picked the corner off the cake.

'Thirty-five years. As if!' His dark blue eyes were now wide with shock. 'How is that even possible?'

She shrugged. 'I met my first serious boyfriend in Freshers' Week at university and we were together ever since.' She shuffled uncomfortably in the squashy armchair. 'Well, until recently.'

'Wow. Firstly, I'm really glad that Sal wore you down

enough to give dating another chance.' Eleanor felt the heat in her cheeks. 'And secondly, I can only apologize it's nothing grander than a coffee shop, but Sal gave me limited options!'

There was something incredibly comforting about Ben. His entire face seemed to radiate kindness and his smile was big and bright.

Eleanor grinned shyly. 'Yeah, that one might have been my doing, actually. Sorry.'

He laughed. 'In case I turned out to be a psycho?'

'Pretty much.' She sank back in the chair, enjoying the easy back-and-forth they'd settled into.

'Let me assure you, I'm not a psychopath.'

Eleanor smirked. 'Surely a psychopath wouldn't actually admit they were a psychopath.'

'Wow, not even half an hour in and we're talking about psychopaths.' Ben shook his head. 'Anyway, how do you know Sal?'

'We work together. I loved her the moment I saw her. It's hard to find someone with much personality in the corporate world and in she walked, practically dripping in it.' Eleanor's heart lifted at the memory of it. 'How about you?'

'I used to work with her too, so I know exactly what you mean. She isn't one to be messed with, is she? It took a while for her to accept me as a friend and not a colleague, but I ground her down and here we are!' He took a nervous sip of his drink. 'I like your hair, by the way.'

Eleanor's hand instinctively flew to her head. 'Really?'

'Yeah.' He chuckled. 'I'm sensing you don't?' His eyebrows knitted in curiosity.

'Erm, I don't mind it.' Eleanor felt the familiar sense of sadness uncoil itself from its hiding place.

'But?'

'But my ex never liked it curly.'

'What!' Ben exclaimed. 'Why?'

Eleanor shrugged. 'I don't know, he said it was too much. Made me look unsophisticated or something. I always used to straighten it.' She couldn't look Ben in the eye so she fixed her gaze determinedly on the half-eaten cake in front of her.

'Really? What an idiot,' Ben joked, taking a bite of his blueberry muffin. 'What else did he make you do – change your clothes?'

Eleanor's face dropped as a memory flashed across her mind, her old brightly coloured wardrobe now full of grey, black and white. Unease sat heavy on her chest but she willed herself back to the present moment.

'Eleanor, are you OK?' Ben reached his hand across the table. 'Sorry, I shouldn't have said that; I was only joking. I didn't mean anything by it.' All the calm and lightness seemed to have been sucked from the room.

'It's fine, honestly.' She painfully forced her mouth into a smile. 'Maybe we should move off exes for a bit, though?'

'Deal.' Ben raised his cup in agreement.

He's a nice guy, Eleanor.

So was Oliver at first . . .

Stop!

'So . . .' he continued. 'Sal tells me you're a UX designer?'

'I used to be.' Eleanor settled back into the squashy armchair. 'Now my job consists mainly of meetings and PowerPoint presentations.'

'Ah.' He grinned. 'Let me guess – you got promoted to management?'

'You bet.' She took a long, slow sip of her drink. 'It's crazy, isn't it? You get promoted because you're good at your job, and then you end up doing everything *but* the job you were so good at!'

'I take it you're not overly enamoured with work right now?' He laughed.

'Is it that obvious?'

'A little,' he replied kindly. 'But I totally get it. It's all stupid corporate bullshit at the end of the day. We're just the idiots who put up with it, right?' He winked cheekily at her and Eleanor felt a strange surge of warmth spread through her body.

'Exactly.' She felt her cheeks blush as she finished the dregs of her coffee.

'Can I buy you another?' He nodded at her empty cup.

Eleanor didn't even hesitate. 'That would be lovely, thank you.'

Fin

After a rather jarring series of encounters with his past, the last place Fin expected to find himself was seated at Angela Levy's kitchen table that very Sunday lunchtime. He had barely been home for an hour after visiting his mother when his phone had rung; foolishly he'd answered, only to be told in no uncertain terms that he would be joining Angela and the girls for lunch the next day. How had she got his number? Which poor soul at the home had she interrogated for his information? It seemed that despite many things changing over the years, Angela Levy's determination was not one of them.

'Are you sure I can't offer you something a little stronger, darling?' Angela held out two bottles of wine.

Fin tightened his grip around his cup of tea and shook his head. 'No, I'm all good, thank you.'

'If you say so.' She shrugged, opening the bottle of white and pouring herself a generous glass. 'You don't mind if I treat myself to one, do you?' she asked, already placing the glass to her brightly painted lips. Even though Fin had never particularly cared for the taste of wine, its alcoholic smell sent waves of longing through him.

'Absolutely not. You deserve a whole bottle after the feast you've made,' Fin commented, staring at the table, already piled high with nibbles and cold starters.

Angela blushed and waved him away affectionately. 'Don't be silly, darling, it's really nothing. In fact, it's a pleasure to have people to cook for. Makes a change when it's usually just little old me to feed.'

'Yeah, cooking for one isn't exactly inspiring, is it?'

'No, it's not.' Angela took a large swig of wine and came to join him at the table. 'That's why I worry about Eleanor so much. She assures me she's eating and cooking for herself, but ever since Oliver left she's practically disappeared before my very eyes.'

Fin shifted uncomfortably in his chair. 'I was surprised not to see him at the wedding. She said they had split up.'

Angela let out a short, sharp laugh. 'Split up? That makes it sound amicable, my dear. He left her. Upped and left without so much as a backwards glance. Poor girl was devastated, as you'd expect. It was completely out of the blue.'

Fin felt waves of anger rise up from deep inside him.

'We all thought he was a nice guy. Perhaps a little boring, but still, nice,' Angela continued, oblivious to the shift in Fin's mood. 'Did you ever meet him? It would be interesting to get your thoughts on him. You know, the male perspective and all that.'

'Erm.' He hurriedly grabbed a handful of crisps and shoved them into his mouth. 'I don't think I did. I don't really remember, to be honest.'

'True, I suppose it was an awfully long time ago now,' she lamented. 'Although, sometimes I think if Eleanor had kept friends like you around, maybe this whole sorry mess could have been avoided.'

Before Fin had time to try and formulate a response, the doorbell rang.

'Aha! Here they are.' Angela leapt up from her seat. 'Go make yourself another tea, sweetheart, and I'll let the girls in,' she instructed, before disappearing out of the room in a whirl of beaded silk, leaving Fin to stare into the dregs of his tea.

You could have done something.

You knew he was wrong for her.

Fin stood abruptly, hoping the haunting words would fall from his head and out on to the floor beneath him. He couldn't go back there, not now. He had to keep it together, at least in front of Eleanor. Suddenly, the kitchen door burst open and before he knew it Fin was being thrown backwards by the force of Freya, who had run directly at him.

'*Fin!*' she shouted. 'As if you're here!'

'Hey, Frey,' he mumbled into the top of her head. 'That's the best hello I've had in years.'

She pulled away and stared at him. 'You literally look exactly the same.' Her eyes scanned the full length of his body.

'I'm not sure if that's a good thing.' He felt very self-conscious all of a sudden, running his hands through his hair without thinking.

'Aha!' She pointed at him excitedly. 'You're still doing that old hair-ruffling thing. This is so *weird*. How's it being back? How long are you staying for?'

Fin couldn't help but laugh. It was as though the little Freya he'd known growing up had burst out from within the adult woman standing in front of him. The constant questioning and endless enthusiasm; underneath it all, she hadn't changed a bit either.

'Leave the poor man alone, Freya. Let him breathe!' Angela swooped in, practically dragging Eleanor into the kitchen behind her.

'Hey, Eleanor.' He performed another one of his lame waves, shuffling awkwardly into the middle of the room.

'Hey,' she replied, distinctly less horrified than the last time they met.

'I was just about to make a cup of tea.' He hurried over to the kettle, very aware of Freya's and Angela's eyes flicking back and forth between him and Eleanor. He was also very aware that his voice seemed to have risen by at least an octave and had become extremely formal in its tone. 'Would anyone else like one?'

'I'll take a coffee, if that's all right,' Eleanor replied, equally as polite and restrained.

'Same for me, please,' Freya chimed loudly.

'I'm good with my drop of poison, Finley darling.' Angela chortled. 'Now, Frey . . . can I borrow you for a second? I need some help upstairs.'

'Argh, can't it wait? I'm starving,' she groaned, eyeing the table full of treats in front of her.

'No, it absolutely cannot wait. Come . . .'

Fin tried to hide his amusement as he watched Freya being reluctantly hauled from the room, her complaints echoing loudly down the hallway.

'Some things never change, hey?' Eleanor smiled, passing Fin a bottle of milk from the fridge.

'Thanks.' He took it from her hands, unable to ignore her tiny birdlike wrists. Angela was right: she was so much smaller than he remembered.

'I'm sorry to hear about your mum, by the way,' she continued quietly, her words stilted, rubbing up against one another awkwardly. 'I knew she wasn't well but I didn't know it had got quite so bad.'

Fin focused his attention on the rapidly bubbling water. 'Yeah. It's not ideal.'

'I can imagine,' she whispered. 'I suppose I should have put two and two together – here was me thinking you were only back for Kate's wedding!' Her laugh was forced and Fin could feel her willing the situation to lighten.

'It would take more than a free bar and a white dress to drag me back to this place.' He grinned, taking the kettle and filling the empty mugs. 'Weddings aren't really my thing.'

'I remember,' she replied softly.

A comfortable silence fell over them both, as Fin emptied the teabags into the bin.

'Did you have fun at Kate's? I hardly saw you after the dinner,' he remarked.

'Yeah, it was great, although I left quite early in the end.'

'Ah. I see.' Fin added a heaped spoonful of sugar to his tea.

'Can't party like I used to.' She rested her back against the cabinets.

'You're telling me,' Fin chuckled. 'I could barely get out of bed the next day and I wasn't even hungover.'

A darkness clouded Eleanor's expression and Fin felt the years of painful memories start to rear their ugly heads once more.

'Somebody give me strength!' Freya's voice interrupted, as she entered the room carrying a huge cardboard box. 'Mum's just made me go up into the bloody attic. You know how much I hate heights and spiders and dark places. I'm completely covered in dust. It's *gross*,' she moaned.

'Do you want me to put some whiskey in your coffee?' Fin offered.

'More like coffee in my whiskey, please. Mum is on one today, Eleanor, I swear.'

'Excuse me?' Angela trilled, entering the room with a devilish grin on her face. 'Did you say something about me, darling? You have dust in your hair, by the way.'

'Eurgh.' Freya began to frantically pat down her hair. 'There'd better be some kind of family riches in that box you're about to hand out to us.'

'Riches come in many forms, dear girl. I thought while we have the pleasure of Fin's company we could have a look through some of the old memory boxes your father and I kept in the loft. It needs to be cleared out at some point and who doesn't love a little trip down memory lane, hey?'

Fin felt his entire body tense.

'Do we really need to do this right now?' Eleanor frowned. 'Can't we eat first? I'm starving.'

'Lunch won't be ready for an hour. Judging by the timing of your last few visits I expected you to be anything but on time, and there was no way I was going to risk serving our special guest here dry chicken.' Fin felt Angela grip his shoulders tightly, giving him a little encouraging shake. 'So, stop being a spoilsport and let's get stuck in!' She flung open the box, sending specks of dust everywhere.

'Well, would you look at *this*,' Angela gasped, lifting a large photograph up for closer inspection. 'Your school photograph. I can't believe you were ever this small. Look at you, Eleanor. Lord knows why we decided to give you that awful bowl haircut.'

Eleanor scowled. 'Because you claimed you didn't have time to do my hair every morning.'

'It really was much simpler when it was short,' Angela clucked.

'Yeah, but really, *really* ugly,' Freya snorted, grabbing another photograph of Eleanor as a child and holding it proudly in the air.

'Now, now, let's all play nice, shall we?' Angela cooed. 'Ah. This is a good one.' She took another picture from the box. 'The three of you all dressed up for Halloween.' She handed the photograph to Fin, who couldn't help but smile. There they were, standing side by side outside the front door of this very house.

'Freya is looking pretty pissed off dressed as a . . . wait . . . what is that? A beach ball?' He laughed.

She snatched the picture from him and shot him a scathing look. 'No! If I remember rightly, I was *meant* to be a pumpkin on holiday. You and Eleanor were going as a corpse bride and groom on honeymoon, and you told me the only way you'd let me come trick or treating with you was if I dressed up as a beach pumpkin.' She sighed, still sore from the memory. 'I look awful.'

Eleanor glanced at him from the corner of her eye and smiled wryly, taking the photo from her sister's hands and eyeing it carefully. 'That doesn't sound like something we'd do. Besides, it looks like we're dressed as Teenage Mutant Ninja Turtles.'

'*I know!*' Freya cried. 'You decided to change outfits at the last minute without telling me. It was the worst Halloween ever.'

Fin nearly choked on his cup of tea. 'Sorry, Frey. I didn't realize we were that mean.'

91

'You were the worst,' she sniped, reaching for a handful of crisps and shoving them angrily into her mouth.

'Yes, you really were quite the pair.' Angela sighed affectionately, yanking the photograph from Eleanor's hands and placing it to the side. 'We had to move heaven and earth to keep you apart back in those days.'

Fin felt his face flush but Angela continued oblivious. 'Oooh, what do we have here?' She unfolded a crumpled piece of paper and laid it flat on the table. Fin's stomach jolted at the sight of the handwriting. How could he ever forget his childish scrawl? He didn't dare look at Eleanor; it was enough that the entire room seemed to extinguish itself of sound.

'Eleanor and Fin's Friendship Rules,' Freya read out loud, and Fin prayed the ground would swallow him up.

'Number one,' Angela continued gleefully. 'Best friends don't lie to each other. Ever. Not even little white lies. Oh, how funny, Eleanor, you've added "this applies mainly to you, Finley Taylor" and underlined it three times.' She chuckled to herself. 'You always were a bossy child. Headstrong, your father liked to say. More like bullish, in my opinion!'

'OK, we get the gist,' Eleanor cut in, her face starting to shine red.

'Number two,' Freya carried on, ignoring the deadly stare her sister was shooting her. Fin remained silent. 'Best friends don't go to sleep mad at each other. Fights must be forgiven before bedtime (see exceptions to this rule overleaf).'

'I think we may have missed a trick here; we should have been lawyers, judging by this!' Fin joked, helplessly trying to find a thread of lightness amongst the web of tension.

'Are we done?' Eleanor grimaced.

'Hell no, look at this thing at the bottom!' Freya pointed out. 'It's some sort of contract.'

'What does it say here . . .' Angela scowled, reading the messy attempt at writing, sprawled haphazardly across the page. 'I, Eleanor Ruth Levy, and I, Finley James Taylor, hereby declare that if such a time occurs at the ripe old age of thirty-five that both members of this agreement find themselves single then it shall be mandatory for the individual parties to wed each other.' Angela laughed, reaching for Fin's cheeks and squeezing them hard. 'Oh my! Shall I get my hat?'

'Unfortunately for you I'm still thirty-four,' Eleanor said sarcastically, snatching the piece of paper and throwing it back in the box.

'That may be, my darling, but thirty-five is not far off. And I don't see much of an effort being made to change your single status, so maybe a back-up isn't a bad idea.'

Fin could feel Eleanor's anger from across the table; it was radiating off her in thick undulating waves. He grabbed inside the box to try and find anything to divert the conversation.

'Not this again, *please*,' Eleanor growled.

'Ohh, someone is a bit tetchy, aren't they?' Freya teased. 'You wouldn't want to marry her anyway, Fin, she's so grumpy these days.'

Fin's body temperature began to rise rapidly. Why was he so hopeless in these situations?

'Well, for all we know, Fin could be in a happy relationship with the woman of his dreams.' Angela winked.

'Of course!' Eleanor cried, not giving Fin even a second to speak. 'It's probably just poor old spinster Eleanor who's the only one single and alone.' She began vigorously repacking the box. 'Now, can we *please* eat?'

'I'm alone too,' he shouted, the words bursting out of him uncontrollably.

Nobody spoke, and with every passing second of silence Fin could feel his cheeks burning brighter.

'I just meant that I'm not with anyone either.' He hung his head and began to fiddle nervously with the edge of the tablecloth. 'You're not the only single person here.'

'Well, I'm sure you will be snapped up in a heartbeat. With a face like yours? The ladies of London better watch out!' Angela cried.

'Mum, stop embarrassing everyone,' Eleanor pleaded. 'Can we eat already?'

The joy in Angela's eyes receded a little. 'I really don't know where you get your impatience from, darling. It definitely isn't from me or your father.' She tutted, turning towards the oven with a wave of silk. 'Clear the table for me then, will you, and I'll serve up.'

Eleanor

If Eleanor had thought the weekend was hard, she knew that Monday morning was only going to be tougher. She'd ignored all of Sal's texts and calls demanding updates about how her date with Ben went. She'd also left the message from Ben himself unanswered. The message that she'd received last night. The message asking for a second date . . .

'Aha, so she *lives*, does she?' Sal barked across the office floor. Eleanor dropped her head even lower behind her monitor.

'I know you're there, Eleanor,' Sal continued to shout, as she made her way towards her. Eleanor groaned and laid her head on the desk, catching the very disapproving eye of Doreen across the way.

Suddenly a loud thump landed next to Eleanor's ear. She looked up tentatively and saw a large coffee cup with her name written on it.

'You're mad but you still buy me coffee?' She smiled sheepishly.

'It's my way of making you feel even more guilty about

being a terrible unresponsive friend.' Sal pulled up an empty chair and planted herself firmly in it.

'I'm sorry,' Eleanor replied meekly.

'I need more than an apology.' Sal folded her arms and frowned.

'I'll buy lunch?' Eleanor offered sweetly.

'I'm on a diet. Try again . . .'

'Then a chocolate brownie won't work either.' Eleanor lifted her head off the desk and took a sip of her coffee.

'Don't,' Sal moaned, forgetting her role of hard-done-by friend instantly. 'I'm so hungry.'

'Eat something then!' Eleanor cried, happily keeping the subject away from Sal's anger at her. 'I don't know why you even bother with these diets. You are the most gorgeous thing I've ever laid eyes on.'

Sal's face melted momentarily, before realizing the direction the conversation had gone in. 'Wait, no! I mean, thank you.' She placed her hand over Eleanor's briefly and squeezed. 'But no! We can come back to me after we finish with *you*.' Her large amber eyes flashed wickedly.

'*Fine*.' Eleanor threw herself back in her chair.

'I want you to agree to go on a second date with Ben,' Sal stated flatly.

Eleanor sat up so quickly she felt her neck jar. 'How do you even know he wants to go on a second date?'

'Because, my darling Eleanor, you ignored my texts and calls all weekend and I simply *had* to know how the date went,' she purred, her voice overflowing with smug delight. 'So, I went directly to the source and asked Ben. He told me he was going to ask you out again and he's not the kind of guy to lie, so I assume he's messaged you already asking?' Her perfectly pencilled eyebrow arched gleefully.

'You are unbelievable!' Eleanor hissed. Sal sat there silently awaiting her answer. 'Yes, OK, he has messaged me. But he only sent it yesterday so it's not like I've ignored him for days,' she added defensively.

'And how do you feel about a second date?' Sal asked gently.

Eleanor closed her eyes for a moment and brought the image of Ben to her mind. She couldn't deny that they'd had fun. What more could she have asked for? He was kind. He was gorgeous. He had made her laugh. And he had stayed by her side the entire date. The only person at risk of running away right now was her.

'I'll message him tonight when I get home.' She saw Sal about to protest. 'I promise.' Eleanor knew her word would be powerful enough for Sal to concede and she was right. Her friend took a large sip of her drink and smiled.

'Wonderful. Now, how was the rest of your weekend? Angela stuff another seven courses down your throat yesterday whilst calling you too thin?'

Eleanor snorted. 'Not quite. Thankfully the attention wasn't on me for once. She'd invited Fin along as a surprise.'

'Who the hell is this Fin again?' Sal seemed to be scouring her memory for any trace of recollection.

'That old friend I saw at Kate's wedding.'

'He must have been a pretty close friend if your mum is inviting him round for lunch. Not even I have managed to swindle one of those invites,' Sal said, a little put out.

'We *were* close, until about fifteen years ago. His mum and my mum were – well, are still – friends. Turns out his mum has cancer, which is why he's over here visiting. I think he's staying until she . . . well, you know.' Eleanor couldn't bear to say the words out loud.

'Shit. That's sad.'

'Yeah. It sucks.' Eleanor could feel the legacy of her own loss starting to rear its ugly head again. 'But what sucks even more is my mother's campaign to make me his babysitter while he's here.'

'What do you mean?' Sal frowned.

'Look!' Eleanor pointed at her screen. This morning alone she'd received five emails from her mother, all with the subject title 'FUN THINGS TO DO WITH FIN'.

'Ahhh.' Sal sniggered. 'I see.'

'It's like she's got shares in London tourist attractions or something. Honestly, when this woman gets an idea in her head, she cannot let it go.'

'Can't you tell her you're busy?'

Eleanor threw her friend a deadly look. 'First of all, the woman assumes because I'm single at thirty-four that my diary is a blank bloody canvas.'

'Which isn't exactly *incorrect*,' Sal quipped smugly. 'Whereas if you went on a date with Benny boy . . . I'm sure that diary could be filled up nice and quickly.'

'You really are just as bad as her.'

'Calm down, will you. I have an idea.'

'Go on . . .' Eleanor huffed.

'I'm throwing a dinner party in a couple of weeks; you should invite Fin along.'

Eleanor's eyes narrowed. 'Why? The point is to *avoid* hanging out with him.'

'Yes, but this way you get your mum off your back and you don't actually have to spend any time with him. We can put him at the other end of the table. Voila . . . you've done your daughter duties and Fin can make some new friends to hang out with.' Sal clapped her hands together. 'I really am brilliant sometimes.'

Eleanor leant back in her chair. 'I mean, it's not the worst idea in the world.'

'Exactly! And you never know . . . if he's cute . . . maybe he could become more than my friend for a bit.'

'For Christ's sake, Sal, he's here to say goodbye to his dying mum, not to have a holiday romance.' Eleanor could feel her cheeks flushing red.

'All the more reason for him to do something that doesn't involve hospitals and death. Unless . . .' Sal cocked her head to the side, a slow realization dawning on her face. 'Did something happen between you two? Is that why this whole thing is so weird and awkward?'

Eleanor snorted. 'No!'

'Why are you literally turning the colour of Doreen's bad hair dye then?' Sal laughed, making Eleanor's face turn an even deeper shade of red.

'I'm not.' She forced her voice to be calm and composed.

'So, you're telling me nothing ever happened with you and Fin? Not even one tiny little drunken kiss after the school disco?'

'First of all, I don't know how old you were when you started drinking, but the only things we had at our school disco were lemonade and Panda Pops. And secondly, Fin was like family. There has never been anything remotely romantic between us at all.' She dropped her gaze briefly. 'Trust me.'

'OK, if you say so . . .'

'I do say so.' She forced her face into a willing smile. 'Besides, I don't think he's your type.'

'And that is for me to decide, isn't it?' Sal stood up and planted a kiss on Eleanor's cheek. 'I'll send the details over later. Email Angela now and tell her to back off – you've got important creative management work to do!' she said gleefully, striding away through the office.

'Oh, don't I just . . .' Eleanor grumbled.

Then: Aged 11

Eleanor

'Eleanor! Fin's here,' her mother shouted from downstairs.

'OK. I'll be down in a minute,' she called back.

'Eleanor. Did you hear me? Finley is here.' Her mum's voice boomed even louder.

Eleanor opened the bathroom door and stuck her head out. *'I know. I said I'll be down in a minute.'*

'All right, darling, there's no need to scream like a banshee.' Her mother was halfway up the stairs. 'Well, don't you look a pretty picture. Do my eyes deceive me or are you wearing make-up?'

'No.' Eleanor quickly tried to close the door.

'I think you are.' She waggled her finger. 'Come on, let me have a look.'

Eleanor cautiously stepped out on to the landing. She knew even if she locked the door her mum would find a way in.

'Sweetheart, you look lovely.' Her mum stepped towards her and smoothed down her straightened hair. 'I was expecting the usual dungarees and Converse but this . . . this is

101

very nice. Is there someone special you're trying to impress tonight?' She winked exaggeratedly.

'No,' Eleanor snapped defensively, jerking her head back. 'Kate and I said we'd match, that's all. I let her pick the outfit.'

Her mum's eyes widened and she nodded slowly. 'I see. Either way, you look a treat.'

'Thanks,' Eleanor grumbled. 'Can I finish getting ready now?'

'As you were, my darling. But don't be too long, you know what your father's like . . . he'll be asking Fin to help in the shed if he's left to his own devices, and goodness knows that's no fun for anyone.'

Eleanor retreated into the bathroom and stared at herself in the mirror. Under the layers of foundation and concealer, she could just about recognize herself. Her eyes felt heavy with mascara, and her lips were so thick with lip gloss that every time she breathed all she could taste was a sweet cloying vanilla.

This is ridiculous.

No, it's not. All the magazines say pink eyeshadow is on trend.

So?

You look like a Barbie doll.

And what's wrong with that?

Suddenly she heard an almighty squeal as Fin and Freya ran up the stairs like a pair of wild animals.

Eleanor ran to the bathroom door and locked it. She couldn't risk anyone else seeing her before she was ready.

'Fin, stop, please stop!' Freya squeaked, her breathing heavy and her voice exploding with joy. 'Eleanor, help me. Fin's trying to catch me and tickle me,' she cried loudly.

'Elles, come out, come out, wherever you are,' he called. 'Your little sister needs rescuing.'

'*Eleanor!*' her sister screamed. 'Help!'

Eleanor could hear the two bodies slumping down on to the carpet just outside the bathroom. The temptation to join in their games was outweighing her desire to fuss with her face any more. Slowly Eleanor unbolted the door. She was going to give them the fright of their life.

'Where is she anyway?' Fin asked breathlessly.

'I don't know. She's been getting ready for *hours*,' her sister whined. 'She hasn't played with me once all afternoon.'

'I don't know why girls bother,' he huffed. 'I didn't think Elles cared about that stuff.'

Eleanor's hand paused just over the door handle.

'Maybe she cares what *you* think,' Freya teased.

Eleanor's heart leapt to her throat. She pressed her ear against the door and closed her eyes.

'Of course she cares what I think. I'm her best friend,' he stated matter-of-factly.

Freya let out a giggle. 'Yes . . . but maybe she doesn't want you to be her best friend. Maybe she wants you to be her *boyfriend*.'

Eleanor's entire body froze; the only audible sound was her heart beating in her chest.

'Ew!' Fin cried. 'That's *gross*. She's like my sister.'

Freya started making kissing noises.

'Stop that right now, Freya, or I'll be sick on you.'

The overexaggerated smooching noises continued.

'I would *never* kiss my sister. Ew. Ew. Ew.' All at once Freya's kissing sounds were joined by a loud retching from Fin. 'I'm going to be sick on you, Freya. You can run but you can't hide!'

Eleanor heard the thuds of their footsteps descend down the stairs once more. She ran over to the mirror and gasped. Her carefully painted face was now smeared and smudged. Black streaks of mascara ran down her face, and her tears had made tracks through her layers of orange foundation.

'You are stupid. Stupid, stupid, stupid,' she cursed, wiping the remnants of the make-up off her face. 'This was all so stupid.' She threw herself on to the floor and cried.

She heard a tentative knock on the door.

'Eleanor darling, we really need to be going. Is everything all right in there?'

'Yes, Dad. Give me five minutes and I'll be down.' Her voice was thick with tears.

'You don't sound OK, sweetheart. Are you sure you don't want me to come in?'

Eleanor took a deep breath and tried to compose herself.

'I'm fine, honestly. I . . . I think I just inhaled too much perfume.' She was an awful liar and they both knew it.

Slowly she heard the door creak open. The soft familiar footsteps of her dad padded across the tiles.

'What are you doing all the way down there?' he mumbled, lowering himself slowly down to join her.

Eleanor shrugged her shoulders.

'Come, now. You've got a disco to get to, haven't you?'

'I don't want to go,' she whispered.

'Ah, yes you do. You've just made the silly mistake of putting on someone else's clothes, that's all. No one wants to go to a party pretending to be someone they're not.' He placed his finger under her chin and lifted it. 'Why don't you change into those gorgeous dungarees of yours, put your trainers on and show everyone how stunningly beautiful Eleanor Levy is . . . just as she is.'

Eleanor smiled, her heart swelling with affection for her dad, his kind blue eyes and crepe-paper face. She nodded slowly.

'That's my girl.' He kissed her lightly on her powder-caked forehead.

Now

Fin

Over the next couple of weeks, Fin found himself settling into a comfortable and much more productive routine. He visited his mum every Monday, Wednesday and Friday afternoon, timing his visits, with the help and intel of Nurse Clara, so as to avoid any future crossovers with Angela. He felt bad – she'd tried to call him a few times since their reunion lunch – but he hadn't had the heart or the energy to return her messages.

It's not like you've got anything better to do.

Excuse me . . . wallowing in self-pity and eating chocolate digestives is very time-consuming.

Fin reached down and fished out the last biscuit from the packet. 'Another day, another packet eaten.' He sighed proudly. There was a very good chance that Fin would return to America paler, fatter and much poorer than he'd been before he left. Maybe Camilla would be grateful he'd dumped her after all. A pang of regret struck his heart. Since the moment she'd walked out of his apartment, he'd heard nothing from her. Not even one angry, heartbroken, raging WhatsApp message. Funny really; his life in LA seemed so solid and permanent, but ever since he'd left, the only person he'd spoken to was Rob.

That's not funny. It's downright sad.

Fin grabbed his phone and fired off a message to his friend. Less than a second passed before it began to ring in his hand.

'Hello, my man, how's everything going over there in rainy England?' Rob's sunshine voice beamed in Fin's ear.

'Why the hell are you up so early? And why do you sound so happy?'

'Can't a man be happy to speak to his best mate at five in the morning?' Fin could hear his friend's smile all the way from LA.

'Partying on a Monday? You are a braver man than me.'

'I had a date, actually,' Rob corrected. 'I've just come from dropping her home, like the true gent I am, and I thought . . . who can I call to celebrate this wonderful evening with but my best friend in the whole world?'

'I don't think a 5 a.m. drop-off is very gentlemanly, but hey, what do I know.' Fin shrugged. 'Go on then . . . tell me everything . . .'

'Her name is Rachel. She's one of Doug's friends – you know the girl he's been on at me to go out with for months?'

'Uh-huh.' Fin tried to search his memory for this long-forgotten piece of information.

'It's her! I honestly don't know why it took me so long to say yes to a date. She's amazing. *So* fit, but it's more than that. We got on so well. She's a high school teacher. Lives by herself. Super into running. She's a vegetarian, but to be honest I barely eat meat these days.'

Fin stifled a laugh. 'Rob, you're the man who won the title of most chicken wings eaten in a minute in your entire hometown just last year.'

'All right, but she doesn't have to know that, does she!' he bit back defensively. 'Besides, people can change.'

'True.' Fin hadn't meant to dampen his friend's spirits, but seeing someone consume that much meat in sixty seconds isn't something you forget easily. 'So, what made you change your mind about going on the date?'

'Well, after three years of being single I just thought, why the hell not? And with you not around I found I didn't really have that much to do. I think we need to reassess how much time we spend together when you get home. No wonder all your girlfriends hated me.' Rob chuckled.

'Yeah, mate. I've been trying to shake you for years but you're just too needy!'

'Oh, *please*. I bet you're lost without me over there.'

Fin sighed, crumpling the empty biscuit packet in his hand. 'I won't say I'm having the most fun.'

'How are things with your mum?'

'Not great.' Fin closed his eyes and brought the image of his fading mother to mind. 'It's awkward and sad and uncomfortable and not the nicest way to spend the day.'

'I'm sorry, buddy.'

'I know, thanks, man.' Fin felt bad for deflating his friend's mood. 'Anyway, what else is new over in sunny California?'

'Absolutely nothing, dude. The wheels keep turning and everyone is just doing the same old shit every day. Any idea when you'll be back?'

'Nope.'

'Heard from Cam?'

'Nope. Have you?'

Rob paused and Fin instantly knew what was about to follow. Strangely, he was OK with it.

'Yeah. I ran into her and her new man out at the beach. He looks like a moron, if that's any consolation.'

'It's fine, I kind of guessed it wouldn't take her long to find someone else.'

'That's what you get when you date chicks like Cam. I told you . . . the only way you're going to break this two-year curse is by dating someone who cares about more than Instagram filters and juice diets.'

'Don't start, Rob.' Fin sighed. 'Fixing my inability to have a relationship longer than two years is not my top priority right now. Besides, have you ever considered it's me and not them?'

'You?' Rob asked.

'Yeah.'

'Nah. You're bloody perfect to me, buddy.'

Fin burst out laughing. 'If only you knew. Anyway, I'd better go, I'm visiting my mum today and I'm not even showered yet. Catch you soon?'

'You bet. I hope it all goes all right, mate.'

'Yeah, me too, Rob.'

Fin was just about to haul his unwashed self up from the sofa when he felt his phone vibrate.

From: Unknown Number.

Intrigued, Fin clicked on the text and very nearly had to sit back down again.

Hi Fin, it's Eleanor. I hope you don't mind me messaging. I got your number from my mum. My friend is hosting a dinner party on Thursday night and I was wondering if you fancied coming along? No pressure at all, I'm sure you have other plans. Let me know either way.

Fin stared at the message unblinking. He had to read it at least three times to make sure the words truly registered. Eleanor was asking him to hang out?

Well, technically you and a dinner party full of other people, but still . . .

He began searching his mental calendar and then stopped suddenly. Of course he was free, what else would he be doing? A tiny bubble of excitement formed in his stomach as he quickly fired off his reply, rereading the text one last time.

'I'm sure you have other plans.' He snorted, laughing to himself. 'If only you knew, Elles . . .'

*

'Ah, I was worried you weren't going to show today, Fin. You're usually here much earlier.' Nurse Clara looked relieved as he stepped through the door later that day.

Since his arrival in the UK, the small owlish Nurse Clara had become the closest thing to a friend Fin had. Some days, the dread of seeing his mother fading away before his very eyes felt too overwhelming, and it was only her presence at the front desk welcoming him in and waving him off that helped him to keep showing up. In fact, he'd become such a regular that if things were especially quiet in the home, Nurse Clara would insist that Fin stayed for a cup of tea. Normally this involved him sitting silently listening to her stories whilst deftly avoiding any questions she threw his way, but he didn't mind. As long as there were biscuits, Fin didn't mind at all.

'Sorry, I should have warned you, I am terrible with time-keeping.' He shook the rain from his hair and felt his feet squelch in his sodden trainers.

'You're just like my Neil.' She tutted affectionately. 'He's

110

a boy that time constantly seems to escape. Come on, I'll walk you down to your mum's. I need to head that way anyway.'

'How's she doing today?' Fin asked, as he followed the short, determined strides of the nurse down the hallway. It was the same question every time he visited, and usually an identical answer. Today, however, Nurse Clara gave the briefest of hesitations, which sent Fin's stomach free-falling.

'Today is not a good one, I'm afraid. She's very disorientated.'

'Oh,' Fin replied. 'Do you think it's still a good idea for me to pop in?'

His visits with his mum were awkward enough when she was lucid; he didn't dare think about how difficult this encounter would be.

'Definitely. It helps having people around who she knows. It will be fine,' Nurse Clara reassured him. 'And remember, I'm just here if you need me.' She nodded to a door on her left. 'I'll be waiting for you in the normal spot when you're done. It was one of the residents' birthdays at the weekend so we still have some of the good biscuits left over,' Nurse Clara noted. 'And remind me . . . I need to ask you something!'

'Oh, really?' Fin's interest was piqued.

'Later.' She waved him away. 'Now go, or you'll be even later for your mother,' she warned before disappearing behind the door to his left.

Fin steeled himself and continued down the corridor, counting the doors until he reached his mum's room. He'd barely opened the door a crack before he heard her faint voice calling out.

'Hello?'

He took a deep breath and forced himself to smile. 'Hi. Sorry I'm late.'

'Hello? Who's there?' she repeated, her distress growing rapidly.

'Mum . . . it's me.' He stepped further into the room but she remained confused, her eyes searching his face for answers. 'It's Fin, Mum. Do you remember me?'

Suddenly her eyes widened and her face broke into a beaming smile.

'Goodness me, look at your hair.' She beckoned him over, her withered fingers clawing at the air between them. 'It's such a beautiful colour. My son has hair just like that, you know.'

Fin's heart tripped over itself, but he forced a smile on to his face and came to sit next to his mum. 'Does he? He must be a lucky man then.'

Jesus, this is weird.

'He always hated it.' She chuckled. 'Said it made him stick out like a sore thumb.'

It still does.

A brief shadow passed across her face. 'It also reminded him of his dad and he really hated that.'

'Ah. I see.' Fin wrung his hands, wondering how much of a terrible human he would be if he left now.

'Are you close with your parents?' she asked brightly.

Change the subject. Say anything to change the subject!

'Erm, not really.'

His mother shook her head. 'We stopped talking, my son and I. A long time ago now.'

'That's a shame.' Fin had no idea what to do next. Part of him wanted to get up and leave without saying another word. Another part of him was intrigued at hearing his mother talk about him in this way.

'It is. He was such a good little boy.' She sighed.

'I'm sure he was. Anyway, how are you feeling today?' he asked, trying to divert the conversation.

'He doesn't understand,' his mother cut across him forcefully. 'He never understood why I loved his father so much.' She pointed to the wedding photograph standing proudly on her bedside table.

Fin could feel the cold tendrils of anxiety snake up through his chest and into his throat, closing down his airway so all he could do was nod meekly. Images of his father flashed through his mind, each memory as toxic and painful as the last.

'But love doesn't make sense, does it? I thought things would change. I thought we could get through anything together.'

Fin's fists were balled so tightly he started to feel the prickles of pins and needles in the ends of his fingers. He needed to leave; he couldn't stand hearing any more. But his mother continued, blissfully unaware.

'They say love is the most powerful drug in the world. Have you ever been in love . . . ?' She paused.

'Erm . . .' Was he really going to get into this conversation? His brain was so full of thoughts he couldn't think straight.

'Sorry,' his mum apologised. 'Look at me asking such personal questions, and I don't even know your name! Are you a new nurse here?'

'Yes, that's right.' Fin stood, quickly latching on to the ready-made excuse she'd just handed him.

Her face fell. 'Are you going already?'

'I have to,' he stated firmly. 'I only came in to do a quick check-up.'

'Are you sure you can't stay a little longer? You remind me so much of my son and I haven't seen him in such a long time. It's nice to look at you and pretend he's here!' she pleaded.

'No.' He brushed himself down and turned to leave. 'I'm sorry, I have to go. Someone will be in to see you later.'

'Oh. OK then.' Her sallow face sagged with disappointment. 'Goodbye then.'

*

Fin helped himself to another biscuit and clasped his hands tightly around his steaming mug of tea. Normally Nurse Clara would bring the drinks out into reception – that way she could still keep a watchful eye over proceedings – but today was different. Today she'd invited him into the private little nurses' room, tucked away at the back of the building.

'Are you sure you're OK, Fin?' she pressed, eyeing him warily over the rim of her cup. 'It's always difficult the first time.'

'I'm fine.'

'Did she recognize you?'

'In a way.' He closed his eyes. 'She said I looked like her son.'

'Ah, I see.' Nurse Clara smiled. 'No matter how bad her day is, she always remembers she has a son.'

'And a prick of an ex-husband, I bet,' Fin spat viciously.

'Mmm,' the nurse replied softly.

'Sorry, I'm not exactly being the best company, am I?'

'It's fine. Families are complex things and the past

can hold more pain than we realize.' She sipped her tea wisely.

'True.' He nodded. 'Wait . . . didn't you want to ask me something?'

Nurse Clara stood and dusted the crumbs off her uniform. 'Yes, but maybe now is not a good time.'

'Please,' he said. 'I need to think about something else.'

'OK then, as you wish. I have a favour to ask you.' She began to pace up and down the small room. 'It's not so much for me. It's more for the patients.' She paused before correcting herself. 'One patient in particular.'

'You want *me* to help a patient?' he asked.

'Well, technically I want your photography skills to help a patient.' She stopped pacing. 'There's a lady who lives here called Rudi. She's been with us for longer than I care to remember, but it's unlikely she'll be around much longer. She's been asking repeatedly for the past few weeks for someone to come and take her picture. It's been on my list of things to do, but I hadn't managed to get round to sorting anything and now . . .' Her voice faltered, revealing a tiny crack in her steely facade. 'Now she's worsening rapidly. And then it hit me, the other day when you told me about your work back in LA. Here's the answer! You're the answer. Our own fully fledged professional photographer. I was wondering if you would do the honours?'

'But I take pictures for advertising campaigns. With professional models. And abstract backgrounds . . .'

'And? Surely a person is a person whether they are a model or not?' the nurse retorted brusquely.

'True,' Fin conceded. 'I just don't know if I'll be able to give her what she's looking for, that's all.'

'How will you know if you don't try?'

'Are you going to let me say anything but yes?' He sighed.

'No.'

'Well then fine, I'll do it.'

She clapped her hands together in delight. 'Thank you, Fin!' The joy that lit up her face was quickly replaced with a serious frown. 'Now, what's the plan? What do you need me to do to help you get this started?'

'Erm.' Fin ran his hands through his hair and willed his brain to kick back into work mode. 'Luckily I brought my camera with me, but there might be other equipment I need to rent depending on what Rudi wants exactly. I'll need to speak to her beforehand, if that's possible.'

'Certainly. I'll let her know this afternoon and maybe we can get you back here tomorrow?'

'Really? So soon?'

'Time is of the essence with this one.'

'Of course. Tomorrow should be fine.'

'I thought so.' She grinned. 'No offence, but a man who willingly spends three afternoons a week having tea with an old nurse he just met doesn't seem too snowed under with plans.'

'Wow.' He sat back in the chair and folded his arms across his chest. 'That one hurt!'

'The truth often does.' She smirked.

Eleanor

Eleanor wrapped her coat tighter around her body and rocked back and forth on her heels. Brixton station was heaving with commuters and she had to keep craning her neck for any glimpse of Fin's bright ginger hair.

'Hurry up, Fin, it's freezing out here,' she moaned quietly.

Why had she let Sal convince her this was a good idea? And more importantly, why couldn't she say no to her mother? It was Angela's insistence that she and Fin hang out that had forced her into inviting him for dinner in the first place. Just because *she* had no problem living in the past did not mean Eleanor felt the same way. Some things should be left well alone, and she had a sneaking suspicion that Fin was one of them. A part of her had prayed that he would be busy or at least have the foresight to decline the pity invite. Unfortunately, he had accepted without hesitation.

It wasn't that bad at lunch the other day.

So? That doesn't make us friends again.

Eleanor dodged out of the way as two screaming children hurtled down the pavement, chasing after one another. Their faces were wild with excitement and their laughter so loud it could be heard over the madness of Brixton High Street. Eleanor's mind drifted back to the Halloween photograph her mother had found. How different things had been back then. How much *easier* everything had been when they were kids. A part of her had wished for so long that it could have stayed that way for ever, but she knew that life didn't work that way. Things changed. People changed.

We're not the same as we were.

We'll never be the same.

'I'm sorry. I am so, *so* sorry.' A mass of auburn hair hurled itself at her through the crowd, practically knocking her backwards. Fin's freckled face was flushed and his green eyes sparkled under the streetlights. There he was. Under all the layers of time, the boy she'd grown up with. 'Would you believe me if I said I even left twenty minutes early?'

Eleanor cocked her head and smiled. 'Strangely, I would.'

It seemed, even after all these years, her ability to stay angry at Fin was lacking.

'I hope your friend won't be mad or anything? I will apologize profusely when we arrive.' He grinned shyly. 'If I'm still invited, that is.'

'Another five minutes and you may not have been.' She laughed, feeling her frustration melt a little more. 'Come on, it's just down here.'

Eleanor led the way, guiding the pair of them through the queues of people waiting at the bus stops.

'God, London is *so busy*,' Fin marvelled, lagging slightly behind.

'Isn't it like this in LA? I thought it was huge,' Eleanor called back over her shoulder.

'It's big but . . . I don't know. It's not like this.'

They fought their way through the mayhem and turned down a quieter street. Despite this being their third encounter, conversation still felt a little stilted and forced. How the hell was she going to survive a whole dinner party with him?

You won't. He's here to make other friends, remember?

'How's your mum doing?' she asked tentatively.

Fin shrugged. 'She's OK. Saw her on a bad day for the first time . . . it wasn't great. She didn't even know who I was.'

'That sucks.'

'Just a bit.'

Eleanor offered a weak conciliatory smile.

'Is there anything they can do?' she asked hopefully.

'No, not really.' He shook his head glumly.

Eleanor continued walking. There were so many things she knew she should say, condolences to pass on and questions to ask, but for some reason she couldn't bring herself to speak.

'Anyway, enough of the sick and infirm,' Fin joked, breaking the silence. 'Who is this friend whose dinner I'm crashing tonight? I don't even know her name!'

Eleanor turned another corner, grateful for the change in conversation. 'Her name's Sally, but everyone calls her Sal.'

'How do you know her?'

'I met her at work. She's brilliant, absolutely terrifying but brilliant.' She hesitated slightly. 'She's my best friend.' The words felt like a cheap dig and Eleanor could see a flicker of emotion pass over Fin's face.

'Ah, so I'd better be on good behaviour then?' He chuckled nervously.

'Do you even know the meaning of the word?'

'I'm a changed man these days, I'll have you know.'

'A changed man that's still always late?' she goaded.

'Some things are just part of our DNA. Being late is in my blood. Always has been and always will be.'

Eleanor rolled her eyes.

'Like being efficiently organized is in yours,' he added casually.

'Excuse me.' She stiffened. 'I could have become a completely free-spirited, spontaneous wild woman over the years.'

'You were always a wild woman at heart, Elles.' He looked at her affectionately.

'Elles,' she murmured, the familiarity a little too close for comfort.

'Wait, sorry, force of habit. Does anyone still call you that?' he blustered.

'No. Although . . .' She tucked her hands deeper into her pockets. 'No one ever did apart from you.'

A heavy silence fell over the pair as they continued to make their way along the street. After a while Eleanor didn't even bother to try and think of things to ask; she simply followed her feet in the direction of Sal's house. Thankfully it wasn't far from the station.

'It's just this door here,' she announced loudly, turning to face Fin. 'Are you ready? I have to warn you, she's a bit of a whirlwind.'

'Ready as I'll ever be.' Fin reached out and knocked loudly.

Before Eleanor had time to offer some last-minute words of encouragement, the door was flung open to reveal an incredibly well-dressed and made-up Sal.

'At last! I was about to call for a search party. It's completely unheard of for you to be the last through the door, Eleanor.'

'Sorry, that's my fault,' Fin admitted guiltily.

'Aha, so you must be the famous Fin?' Sal pulled him into a ferocious hug and then quickly held him out in front of her. Her eyes ran up and down the length of him. 'So lovely to meet you. In you come.'

Fin was unceremoniously pulled into the hallway whilst Sal gave Eleanor a slightly more delicate embrace. 'You were right, definitely not my type,' she whispered in her ear.

Eleanor squeezed her tightly. 'I hate to say I told you so.'

'Come in, come in. I think you might recognize a few faces . . .'

Before Eleanor had a chance to ask who Sal meant, she saw him. Standing at the end of the hallway was none other than Ben Ryans.

'Come on then, go and say hi!' Sal grabbed her hand and pulled her inside. Eleanor's mind went blank. Every inch of her body began to sweat. 'I know you haven't texted him back yet so I thought I'd handle the situation myself.'

Could she leave?

No. What would everybody think!

'Ben, darling,' Sal cried. 'You remember Eleanor, don't you?' Her words were dripping in delight.

'Ah. Yes, I believe we met once?' Ben smiled and held out his hand.

Eleanor took it silently and shook it. Why were her palms so clammy?

'Hi,' she mumbled.

He pulled her into a hug. The smell of oranges and soap filled her nostrils and her stomach cartwheeled in recognition.

'I'm sorry about this. I didn't know you'd be here. The she-devil Sal strikes again, am I right?' His deep voice rumbled against her cheek.

Eleanor laughed and felt her body relax. 'I'm sorry for not

replying to your message, it's just the—' But before she could finish her excuses, Ben's voice cut across.

'It's fine. Honestly, don't worry about it.' Eleanor could hear the sincerity in his voice. 'Can I get you a drink?'

'Erm, yes please, that would be great.' She tried to check her reflection in the window behind him, praying her face wasn't as bright red and flushed as it felt.

'White or red?' Ben held aloft two bottles from the counter-top, blocking her view.

'White, please.'

I am going to kill you, Sally Moreno. I am going to bloody kill you.

Ben handed her a large glass of wine. 'Here you go.'

'Thank you very much.' Eleanor smiled sweetly, forcing all aggressive thoughts of Sal out of her mind.

'Sal told me you were coming here with an old friend. I'm assuming he's the redhead I just saw?' Ben asked.

'Erm.' She took a large gulp. 'Yeah, that's him.'

'That's cool. How do you two know each other?'

'We grew up together.' Eleanor took another large mouth-ful of wine.

'Aha! So, he's the person I need to befriend if I want to know all your secrets? Where's he got to? Maybe I need to introduce myself again,' he joked, exaggeratedly looking around the room.

'That's a good point. I actually have no idea. Sal has prob-ably got him cornered somewhere.'

'You'd better go and save him then.'

'No, he'll be fine.' Eleanor waved the air flippantly.

'Go!' Ben urged. 'I don't mind sharing you for tonight.' He flashed her a mischievous grin, which did nothing to help Eleanor's already flushed face.

'OK.' She nodded, aware that she probably should try to avoid appearing like a cold-hearted friend in front of the guy she wanted to impress.

You want to impress him?

Oh, shut up . . .

'I'll see you in a bit?'

'I'll be here all night.' Ben smiled.

God, he's so handsome when he smiles.

Eleanor turned away and began to scan the room for Fin's trademark hair. There were about twenty people crammed into Sal's moderately sized kitchen diner, which made it very noisy and very busy. It didn't take long to spot him though, talking to a couple of friends that Eleanor recognized from Sal's previous parties. She made her way over to the other side of the room, nodding polite hellos to familiar faces as she went.

'Eleanor!' The man talking to Fin waved her over enthusiastically.

'Hi Marcus, how are you?' She kissed him once on each cheek and turned to greet his wife. 'Hi Amy. You look amazing, congratulations!' She pointed to the swollen tummy that was peeking out beneath the folds of her dress.

'Thanks, five months gone already, how mad is that?' Amy gushed. 'Fin here tells us you were friends at school.'

'That's right.' Eleanor nodded.

'Wow, it's so great that you've stayed in touch for all this time,' Amy marvelled. 'I hope this little guy makes a friend for life like you two have.' She rubbed her stomach affectionately.

Eleanor smiled uncomfortably.

'I'd say staying in touch is a bit of an overstatement.' Fin laughed nervously. 'Eleanor is basically on babysitting duty while I'm over from America visiting my mum.'

'Well, I wouldn't say that,' Eleanor replied bashfully.

'I would.' He paused. 'And I'm very grateful.'

Eleanor looked up at Fin and felt a flutter of affection ripple over her.

'Fantastic babysitting skills,' Marcus said loudly, 'that's always good to know. We might have to rope you in when this one's born.' He guffawed.

Eleanor tore her eyes away from Fin's and was about to object kindly when a voice boomed across the kitchen.

'Ladies and gentlemen, if you'd like to take your seats . . . dinner is served,' Sal announced.

Eleanor didn't need a seating plan to know who she'd be sitting next to.

'Fin, you're here beside me,' Sal drawled, reaching for Fin's hand and pulling him round the opposite side of the table. 'Eleanor, you and Ben are *here*.' She gestured to the two seats directly in front of them.

'What a surprise,' Ben whispered, so only Eleanor could hear.

'Subtlety isn't her strong point,' she replied, trying to avoid any eye contact.

'Not in the slightest!' He pulled out her chair and Eleanor quickly sat down, catching Fin's eye. He seemed to be intrigued by the scene.

Eleanor shifted self-consciously in her seat. If she'd known Ben was going to be here, she might have made more of an effort. She reached for a stray curl and wrapped it round her finger, twirling it anxiously.

'I'm glad to see the curls are still with us,' Ben remarked quietly, pulling his chair in closer to hers.

'They are persistent little things,' she joked, unravelling the coiled piece of hair and letting it spring back into position. 'How have you been?'

'Fine, not much to report my end. Just been sitting patiently by my phone waiting for this girl to call me.' He sighed apathetically.

Eleanor choked a little on her wine. 'I'm sorry for not replying. It's really rude of me and I shouldn't have ignored you like that.'

'It's fine. I was teasing.' He smiled warmly. 'How long is your friend staying for?' He nodded across the table to Fin.

'Not sure actually. He hasn't said. Maybe a few weeks.' Eleanor poured herself another glass of wine hastily. 'His mum isn't well. He's here visiting her.'

'That's a shame. I'm sorry to hear that,' Ben stated solemnly. 'But please don't tell me that means we can't get date number two in for a few weeks? By the way, this' – he gestured at the surrounding guests – 'doesn't count as a date.'

Eleanor felt a rush of electricity snake up her body. 'No, no. I'll be around.'

'That's good. Although, I will need you to reply to my texts if we are ever going to meet without Sal orchestrating fake dinner parties as a ruse.' His deep blue eyes twinkled at her.

'Yeah, she really has gone to a lot of effort to bring us together, hasn't she?' Eleanor smiled wryly. 'Although I hope there is actually food, I'm so hungry.'

'Sal, when are you going to feed us, I'm ravenous,' Ben called out across the table.

'OK, Benny boy, calm down. You seemed pretty preoccupied when I last checked.' Sal smirked. Eleanor felt Fin's eyes on her and her entire body tensed.

'I can eat and flirt at the same time, you know?' Ben replied, making everyone around the table laugh.

'That's a talent if ever I saw one,' Fin chimed in.

'I can teach you if you like?' Ben joked.

'Thank you, but I'm actually taking a hiatus from women for the time being.'

'Ah, I see, newly single?' Ben asked.

'Yeah, that obvious, huh? I left LA and a relationship behind me. London is a good place to lick wounds though. There's never a dull moment.' Fin sipped his glass of water.

'Eleanor said you've come over from America. How long have you been out there for?'

'Over fifteen years now. Have you ever been?' Fin asked.

'Nope. Not really sure it's my scene. The people seem way too cool for me.' Ben laughed self-consciously.

'Trust me. If I can fit in there, anyone can.' Fin smiled and turned to look at Eleanor. 'I've never been cool, have I?'

'Oh yes, of course!' Ben rubbed his hands together. 'You can give me the intel on the younger Eleanor, can't you?' He elbowed Eleanor jokingly.

Fin held his hands up. 'Don't go down that road. You won't get a word out of me.'

Eleanor's heart surged a little. After all this time, he was still willing to keep her secrets under lock and key.

'Can't blame a guy for trying.' Ben sat back and sighed.

'To be fair, it's me who should be worried,' Fin continued, his cheeks colouring slightly at the edges. 'She has way more dirt on me than I'd care to imagine.'

'Better keep her sweet then!' Ben chuckled. 'You two must have been pretty good friends.'

'Yeah.' Fin fixed his emerald eyes on to Eleanor. 'We were the best.'

Fin

Fin had spent the last half-hour of the evening preparing for his exit. Over the years he'd managed to perfect the art of sneaking out of social events undetected. He'd learnt the hard way that actually announcing your departure and saying goodbye to a room full of people often just resulted in offers of more drinks, more conversation and an even later night. It wasn't worth it. All he needed to do was grab his coat, slink out of the door and send a thank-you message when he arrived home. Nobody would even notice he was missing. Especially tonight; after all, he'd only just met these people.

'Fin!' Sal cried, pushing her way across the room to him. 'Please don't tell me you were about to leave without saying goodbye?'

He quickly replaced the disappointment on his face at being caught with a rather over-the-top look of surprise. 'Absolutely not! I was actually just coming to find you to say goodbye.' He squirmed, praying that his lie wasn't too detectable.

Sal leant in and hugged him. 'If I wasn't the one hosting this thing, I'd be sneaking off about now too.'

Fin laughed. 'I didn't realize I was that bad at lying.'

'Nothing gets past me.' Sal released her grip and stared at him intently. 'It was really lovely to meet you, Fin. Tell me I'll see you again before you head back to America?'

'That would be really nice.'

'Good. I'll sort something out with Eleanor,' she noted.

'Sal, we need some more wine!' a slurred cry rang out from the back of the kitchen.

'Better tend to the children.' She grinned. 'Eleanor's just in the corner if you want to say bye.'

Fin hesitated for a moment before throwing his coat over his shoulder and turning back to the room full of people. He caught Eleanor's eye and gave an overly enthusiastic wave. She was standing next to that Ben guy who he'd met earlier that evening. Fin didn't want to interrupt anything; he'd felt the chemistry between them from across the table, it was palpable.

'Are you going?' she mouthed.

He nodded and before he could insist that she stay exactly where she was, Eleanor was making her way over to him, leaving Ben looking a little lost on his own. Fin had to admit, he was a good-looking man and he seemed nice.

Please turn out to be nice.

'Fin! Thanks so much for coming.' Her eyes were wide; she looked happy.

'Thanks for inviting me.'

'Not at all.' She reached out and they hugged a little awkwardly.

'Maybe we could grab a coffee next week or something?'

The words were out of his mouth before he could even register what he was saying.

Why couldn't you have just said goodbye and left?

'Erm ... sure. That would be good,' she replied, her response taking him by surprise.

'Cool. Enjoy the rest of your evening.' He nodded back towards Ben, who was patiently waiting for her return.

Eleanor's face flushed with embarrassment. 'Normally I'd be joining you as the first out of the door, but Sal will kill me if I go before the shots come out.'

'And that is definitely my cue to leave.' He did a strange bow, which he instantly regretted.

'Get back safe. You know the way, right?' she called over her shoulder as she turned to go.

'Elles, I'm all grown up now, you don't need to look after me any more,' he joked.

Her face clouded over, and for a moment he saw a hint of sadness flash across her eyes.

'Some habits die hard, I guess.' She gave a little shrug and then walked off.

*

At the request of Nurse Clara, Fin had arrived at the home earlier than usual the next day. She'd phoned him to say she had an important update on the photography project that she needed to discuss with him. From the tone of her voice, he sensed that it wasn't going to be something good.

'Fin, you actually made it in good time today.' She nodded approvingly, her shrewd eyes checking the clock on the wall.

'You sounded even more serious than usual so I came as quickly as I could.'

She shifted uncomfortably. 'Can we go to the nurses' room? It's better to talk in there.'

'Sure. Are you OK?' he asked, following her through the main door and down the corridor.

'I'm fine,' she replied, ushering him inside the little room. Fin took his usual seat by the radiator and allowed his back to rest on the metal, soaking up the warmth through his permanently chilled skin.

'What's happened?' he asked, noticing that Nurse Clara had chosen to remain standing, her body weight shifting restlessly from one foot to the other.

'It's Rudi,' she whispered, tears forming in the corners of her eyes. 'The doctor has been round today to see her.' Her voice was growing increasingly higher in pitch as she tried her best to resist the building emotion. 'He estimates she's only got a week or so left.'

'I'm sorry,' Fin offered pathetically.

'Do you think you could do something before then? With the photographs, I mean?' There was so much hope in her bloodshot eyes that to say anything other than yes would be downright criminal.

'Absolutely. I'm meeting her today; I have most of the equipment sorted, and anything I don't have I'll organize sharpish.' For the sake of Nurse Clara, Fin tried to sound in control and assertive whilst his mind buzzed with lists of things to do.

'Great. I can take you now if you'd like?'

'Let's do it.' He stood up decisively.

Nurse Clara placed her hand firmly on his arm and looked at him earnestly. 'Thank you, Fin. You're doing a very good thing, you know.'

'It's no problem,' he mumbled, embarrassed. 'Shall we?' He nodded towards the door.

'We shall.' She turned and swiftly exited the room, a composed veneer slowly re-forming over the cracks she'd exposed in her armour only moments ago.

As they walked back up the corridor, Fin began to mentally prepare himself for the sight he was going to be greeted with. If he thought his mum was frail then how would a woman just days away from death look? He couldn't imagine.

'Here we are,' Nurse Clara announced, stopping suddenly. 'Now be prepared, she's quite a character.' A wry grin flickered across her face.

Before he could ask anything further, Nurse Clara knocked firmly on the door and opened it.

'Rudi, it's me,' she called.

A deep throaty laugh emerged from within. 'I knew it wouldn't be long before you'd be back for more. Can't stay away from my husband now you know I'm about to pop my clogs, can you?'

'Stop that,' Nurse Clara quipped warmly. 'We have company. I want you to behave yourself.'

'Hey! I'm dying, surely that's the only reasonable excuse to misbehave.'

Fin couldn't help but laugh. He walked into the room and stood slightly behind Nurse Clara. The room looked nothing like his mother's. Yes, it was the same shape, with the same hospital bed, dark wooden furniture, TV unit and greying curtains, but every available surface was decorated. Pictures and photographs of smiling, laughing, happy people stood huddled in groups. Childish drawings were hung all around the room, their bright colours a stark contrast to the pale green wallpaper. Various bunches of flowers, at various stages of life, stood in vases around the bed. It was warm and, dare he say it, homely.

'See, the young man agrees with me. Don't you, lad?'

Fin's eyes focused on the woman addressing him. She was old and frail, there was no doubt about that, but there was a brightness to her, a solidity and warmth that he wasn't expecting. Her head was coated with a downy white fluff of hair, and her blue eyes were still piercing even through the milky film of cataracts that covered them.

'You make a very strong case,' he replied.

'Exactly! Now, without sounding too rude, who, may I ask, are you?'

Fin took a step forward and held out his hand. 'I'm Finley Taylor. My mum is actually a patient here.'

The old lady reached her arm out and shook his hand weakly. 'Ah, dear Eileen. How is she?'

'As OK as she can be, thanks.'

Rudi nodded knowingly. 'Now, what's this all about? Disturbing someone on death's door like this is quite uncouth, I'll have you know.'

Nurse Clara sighed exasperatedly but Fin noticed she hadn't stopped smiling since they'd entered the room.

'Well, Fin here is the photographer I was talking about.'

Realization slowly dawned upon the old woman's face and her eyes sparkled with understanding.

'How good are you, Fin?' Her sparse eyebrows knitted into a frown. 'Can you make this worn-out heap of a human being pass as visually acceptable?'

Fin smiled. 'I'm not a miracle worker. But I'll do my best.'

'Well then, you're hired! Everyone loves a trier.' Rudi let

out another deep chesty laugh, her entire body shaking with the effort. 'I like this one, Clara. I like him a lot!'

'I thought you might,' Nurse Clara replied, placing her hand briefly on Fin's back. 'I'll leave you two to it then, shall I? Fin, I'll tell your mum you've arrived and will be along shortly.'

'Thanks.' Fin took a seat in the chair next to Rudi's bed.

'Right then, Fin, what do you need from me in order to create this masterpiece?'

Fin ran a hand through his hair and thought for a moment. 'Is there anything in particular you have in mind for the photo? Anyone else you want to be in it with you? An image you want to recreate from the past maybe?' He looked at the lady in front of him and felt a wave of deep sadness. In a matter of moments this person would be no more than a memory for people. It made his heart twist in angst. 'What do you want this photograph to *say*? If that makes any sense?'

Rudi closed her eyes and took a long, slow deep breath. Underneath the paper-thin lids her eyes moved rapidly in thought. After a while she smiled and opened them again.

'Do you mind going into the top drawer of my bedside cabinet for me?'

'Sure.' Fin reached across and opened it, looking at Rudi for the next instruction.

'There should be a pile of photographs in there – take them all out and pass them here, will you?'

Fin reached in and immediately his hands found the stack of pictures. He pulled them out and passed them to Rudi, who took them from him gently.

'Where is it . . . where is it . . .' the old lady mumbled, slowly sifting through the photos, her arthritic fingers barely able to move. Fin sat back down and waited patiently in silence.

'Aha! There you are.' Rudi held a small square picture aloft.

'May I?' Fin asked, leaning over to peer at the image.

'Certainly, my boy. This is me and my husband Rupert. God, look at him, isn't he something.' She sighed, her voice heavy with emotion.

'Wow,' Fin exclaimed. 'You two made a very good-looking couple.'

'We still do, thank you very much,' she retorted. They both sat and looked at the photo for a moment. A twenty-something Rupert holding a twenty-something Rudi, dressed up to the nines at what Fin could only assume was a dance. Everything about the picture sang of happiness and carefree youth, but there was something in the way they looked at one another that spoke of a deeper connection. An undying, everlasting commitment.

'This was the first time we met,' she said dreamily. 'And the same night he got down on one knee and proposed to me.'

'What! Are you serious?'

'When you know, you know.' She sighed hopelessly. 'And boy, did we know.'

'Did he have a ring?'

'Pshht, we didn't need one. He got down on one knee and promised me that he would love me until for ever. That was all I needed.' She held the picture to her chest. 'And look at us now. He's never left my side.'

'He sounds like one hell of a man.'

'That man is the only thing I'm living for, kid.' A lonely tear escaped down her cheek. 'Do you think we could recreate this? Obviously with a few extra years added on.'

Fin looked down at the picture once more and a jolt of excitement fired through him. This was going to work. It *had* to work.

'I'll need him here on Wednesday, if that's OK? I'll sort the rest,' he stated firmly.

'So, it's on?' The old woman raised her eyebrows expectantly. 'You really think we can do it?'

'Rudi . . . I know we can.'

Eleanor

'Come on, dry already, will you?' Eleanor grumbled, twisting her curls around her fingers anxiously.

Why hadn't she followed Sal's advice and brought a change of clothes to the office? At the time, getting ready for a date in the work toilets didn't exactly scream romantic or enjoyable, and so she'd decided to go home before dinner. An idea that now she regretted intensely.

She checked the time.

Twenty minutes to go.

Suddenly she heard her phone buzz.

He's cancelling. Oh, please let him be cancelling . . .

Eleanor!

Her stomach flipped anxiously as she reached over to grab her phone. A mix of relief and frustration swept her nerves away. She didn't even wait for Sal's hello.

'Don't worry, I'm not bailing, although I am running late. Can you believe it?'

'Eleanor Levy late? That's two events on the trot. What is the world coming to!' Sal cried.

'The other night was not my fault. It was all Fin.'

'He's a fun guy,' Sal remarked.

'And that's like a five-star review coming from you.'

'I'm just *saying*, I don't know why you were being so weird about hanging out with him. He was fine. He's even kind of cute, if you go for that red-haired English rose kind of vibe.'

Eleanor felt a rush of affection. Sal was a tough crowd to win over and the fact she was complimenting Fin made her feel oddly proud.

What is wrong with you?

Why do you care?

'Yeah, he's OK,' Eleanor tried to reply casually.

'Anyway, what are you wearing for the big date?'

'Jeans and a top.'

'Wow, don't hold back on the details,' Sal replied dryly.

'I don't know what else you want to know? Black skinny jeans and it's some polo neck from Zara. And before you start,' she warned, frantically coating her eyelashes in mascara, 'yes, I'm wearing a polo neck because it's absolutely miserable outside and I don't want to get cold.'

'I wasn't going to say a thing.'

'Uh-huh.' Eleanor dusted her cheeks with some bronzer and stood back to admire her work.

That will have to do.

'Are you looking forward to it?' Sal asked, unable to mask her own excitement.

'I'm *scared*,' Eleanor admitted out loud.

'I know, but he's great and you're great and *technically* this is date three, so you're an old hand at it now! Where are you going?'

'To a little Italian place I've never heard of in Soho.' Eleanor grabbed her coat and hurried downstairs.

'Italian. Interesting,' Sal remarked.

'How so?'

'The Italians love their garlic. Not exactly setting you up for the perfect first kiss scenario, is it?'

'Sal!' Eleanor barked. 'Look, I have to go, and don't harass me for updates. I'll fill you in tomorrow at work.'

'Sure thing.'

'Wish me luck!' Eleanor begged.

'You don't need luck. See you tomorrow. Oh, and Eleanor?'

'Yes?'

'Bring some chewing gum with you. Just in case . . .'

'Oi!' Eleanor hung up immediately. She was only just managing to wrap her head around a second date, let alone the prospect of a first kiss. Her heart thrummed in her chest. Was she really ready for this? The anticipation . . . the fear . . . the worry! What if Ben was a bad kisser?

With a face like that, it would be criminal for him to be a bad kisser.

She hadn't had a proper kiss in so long – what if she had forgotten how to do it? Towards the end of their relationship, Oliver had reduced his affections to dry pecks on the lips as a perfunctory and almost robotic hello and goodbye greeting. Gone were the days when hours would pass them by, making out in her bedroom, unable to keep their hands off each other.

What had changed? Sorrow pulled deeply at her heart. *When* had it changed? In the days after Oliver had left, Eleanor spent hours reliving and recounting every memory of their time together, trying to pinpoint the exact moment that it shifted. She needed an answer. A piece of evidence to store away and direct people to whenever they asked what had happened. But the search had turned up nothing and Eleanor was still left in the dark.

'No.' She clenched her fists tightly. 'You don't get to do this today. You have a date with a gorgeous man who is probably an incredible kisser, and *you*, Eleanor, are going to be fine.' She stared at her reflection in the mirror one last time, and before she could give herself another moment to reconsider, she left the room and headed towards the front door.

*

'Hey there!' Ben stood and pulled her into a firm hug.

'Hi.' She felt herself melt a little into his arms. In fact, the moment she'd seen him sitting at the table, her nerves subsided. Everything about Ben seemed to settle her. He was solid and calming, and his face was so kind that she couldn't help but feel safe in his presence.

'You're a white wine drinker, right?' He pointed to a full glass on the table, ready and waiting for her.

'I am indeed, thank you.' She took her coat off and sat down. 'This place is so cute. I've never even heard of it.' She looked around at the tiny restaurant. It was all dark wood and chequered tablecloths, a piece of traditional Italy in the middle of central London.

'It's good, isn't it? I'm glad you approve.' He raised his glass in the air. 'To date two.'

She clinked her glass against his. 'To date two.'

'I'm sorry about Sal's the other night, by the way.' He grinned sheepishly. 'I honestly had no idea you'd be there. Although, I'm obviously glad that you were.'

Eleanor's cheeks reddened and she shyly looked away.

'You're not very good at taking compliments, are you?' He chuckled.

'Not really, no.' She felt her face grow brighter and hotter.

'What else should I know about you?' he asked curiously.

'Erm . . . what would you like to know?'

'Let's see.' He took a sip of his beer and stared intensely at her. Eleanor felt the heat travel from her cheeks all the way down to her stomach. 'What did you want to be when you were younger?'

'An artist.' The answer came without a breath of hesitation.

Ben raised his eyebrow in intrigue. 'Oh, really? So, you paint? Sculpt? Use other people's trash to make abstract artwork?'

'I used to paint.'

'Used to?'

Eleanor dropped her gaze down to the menu in front of her. 'Yeah. I don't really have the time any more.'

'Were you good?' The questions kept coming and she could sense his curiosity was not easily dampened.

'I was OK.'

Ben laughed. 'That means you were good. Do you miss it?'

Eleanor gripped the menu a little tighter, willing the thoughts of her empty spare room filled with vacant canvases and dried-out brushes out of her mind. 'Sometimes.'

'Have you ever thought about taking a class? Like joining a community group or something?'

'Erm, no I haven't, actually.'

'I did it with writing last year. Best thing I could have done. It was just for six months at the local university but it was brilliant. When I was a kid, I always dreamed of being a journalist. I'd run around writing articles on everything and anything. My neighbours found me spying on them way too many times, looking for even a whiff of scandal.'

'What happened?'

'They told my parents and I was grounded for a week.'

'No, I meant with your writing.' She giggled.

'Oh!' Ben's eyes twinkled mischievously. 'I found alcohol and girls, and then before I knew it, I'd sold my soul to the corporate world of business.'

'It gets us all in the end.' Eleanor sighed dramatically.

'That it does.' He raised his glass in agreement.

Thankfully, before Ben could pick up the painting conversation again, a young baby-faced waiter appeared at their table, holding his notepad aloft eagerly.

'Sir, madam, are you ready to order?'

'Can we have a couple more minutes, please?' Ben asked, as Eleanor nodded her head in agreement. She hadn't even managed to read the first line.

'Sure. Take your time.' The waiter gave a small bow and left.

And take their time they did. It was gone midnight by the time a rather sheepish young barman asked them politely to vacate the table as the restaurant needed to close.

'Woah, how did it get so late?' Ben looked down at his watch. 'We'd better get a move on. Do you want me to call you a cab?'

Eleanor shook her head. 'Don't worry, I'll order an Uber now.' Normally the thought of getting home at this time on a work night would have sent her into a panic, but tonight she was too full of wine and garlic-covered carbohydrates to care.

'Can I wait with you until it arrives?' He stood up and helped her with her jacket.

'Yeah, it won't be long though, so if you need to go then please don't worry.'

He took her chin in his hand and brought her gaze to his. 'Eleanor, I have nowhere to be but here, OK?'

Her entire body bloomed with warmth that she knew had nothing to do with the food or wine.

'OK,' she replied shyly, making her way out of the restaurant.

A group of twenty-something girls staggered past them, practically dragging each other along the road. 'I bet they're going to regret being out that late tomorrow.' She laughed.

'Says you!' he teased.

'Yes, *but*' – she smirked, pulling her jacket tighter around herself – 'their night looks like it's been a little different to mine.'

'Oh, really? What would you say your night has been then?' Ben grinned and took a step towards her.

'I don't know.' Eleanor tried to act as casual as possible. 'A pretty great second date?' She smiled, a little embarrassed at being so free with her speech.

'I disagree.' He edged even closer to her. 'I'd say it was the best second date I've ever had.'

Eleanor tried to drop her gaze to the pavement, but all at once his hand was on her face tilting her chin upwards.

Her body temperature soared and she felt her breath catch in her throat.

Oh God.

I can't do this.

The flutter of excitement quickly morphed into ice-cold panic. She tried to look away but Ben held her gaze firm.

'Eleanor, it's all right.' She felt his touch slacken on the side of her face. 'We can wait, I don't mind waiting.'

No!

Without thinking, she reached her arms around his neck

and pulled his face down to hers. The moment his lips touched hers, she felt her body melt. It was soft and gentle and more lovely than she could have ever hoped for.

'Waheyyy, go on, girl!' a drunken call rang out from across the street.

The magic of the moment dissolved and they both pulled away laughing.

'Who says romance is dead, hey?' Ben shrugged, his eyes sparkling intensely.

Fin

It hadn't taken much to organize the shoot. In fairness, Nurse Clara had done the bulk of the work, liaising with Rudi and her husband to sort the outfits and timings. All Fin had to do was turn up. He felt strangely excited as he arrived at the home. There was always anticipation before a photo-shoot, but over the years, Fin had found his love for the art slowly fading away. When money became the sole motiva-tion for work, passion inevitably took a back seat. But this . . . this was entirely different.

'Morning,' Fin called to the man on reception. He only ever visited in the afternoons and so wasn't used to being greeted by anyone other than Nurse Clara and her sharp eyes.

'Fin, is it?' the young man enquired.

'What gave it away?' He laughed. 'The hair or the cameras?'

'Neither.' The receptionist pointed at the bag Fin had thrown across his shoulder. 'It says your name on there.'

'Oh.' Fin smiled shyly, looking down at the branded

camera bag with his name and business plastered across it. 'Good catch.'

'Nurse Clara is waiting for you with Rudi. Do you know the way?'

'I do, thank you.' Fin nodded appreciatively as the man opened the door and let him through to the main nursing home.

As he walked down the corridor, he felt his stomach flicker with nerves. What if, after all this, they didn't like the pictures? What if there wasn't time to reshoot if it went wrong? What if Rudi . . .

No.

Don't think like that.

The sound of laughter grew louder as he neared the room. Knocking on the door, he heard the familiar voice of Nurse Clara calling him in.

'Fin, you're getting better at this whole arriving on time thing.' Her birdlike face broke into a wide grin.

'This is different.' He dropped the bags to the floor, relieving himself of their heavy weight. 'This is business.'

'Ah, of course.' She came over and stood by his side. 'Rudi, you remember Fin from the other day, don't you?'

The old lady hauled herself up a little higher in the bed. Fin noticed she was wearing the very same dress from the photograph she had shown him. 'Just because most of my organs have given out, doesn't mean my brain has stopped working too,' she joked. Fin and Nurse Clara looked awkwardly at each other, thoughts of his own mother clawing at his heart.

'And this,' the nurse continued brightly, 'is Rupert, Rudi's husband.' She gestured to an elderly man sitting by the window, dressed in a sharp, crisp suit.

'Hi Fin, so lovely to meet you.' He held out his hand for

Fin to shake. 'This isn't my usual attire, by the way.' He adjusted his bow tie. 'I'm surprised this old thing still fits me, but it must be all the weight I've lost worrying about this one.' He jerked his head in his wife's direction.

'Give over. You're losing weight because I've not been home to cook for you and all you can make is fish finger sandwiches!' Rudi chastised. 'You look bloody handsome though.' She grinned, her eyes lighting up.

'As do you, my darling,' Rupert cooed. His eyes filled with adoration at the woman before him.

'Nonsense,' Rudi scoffed. 'I look like a prune in fancy dress, but needs must, hey.' She patted her thinning hair self-consciously. 'Now, where do you want us, Mr Photographer?'

Fin glanced around the room. It was nice enough, but looking at the effort both Rudi and Rupert had made, it didn't do them justice in the slightest. His eyes scanned around for any other options. He could move some of the hospital furniture, maybe focus in on their faces rather than the backdrop. Then something caught his attention.

He moved over to the window where Rupert was sitting and peered out. His brain sparked with excitement.

'Rudi . . .' Fin turned to face the old lady. 'Would it be possible to move you?'

Nurse Clara cut in defensively. 'What do you mean, move her?'

Fin turned back to look out at the garden. How had he not seen this before? It was huge! The neatly manicured lawn sprawled out like a thick carpet. Flower beds were bursting out of their borders with flashes of purples and pinks and yellows. In one corner stood an ornate water feature, happily gurgling away. In the other, a wrought-iron swing chair, laced delicately with creeping ivy and roses.

'I mean, could we somehow get her into the garden?'

'You want me to move her to the garden?'

'Yes. Look at it. It's perfect.' He tapped on the window.

He heard Nurse Clara start to reply, but it wasn't her voice that answered him.

'Whatever you need, I'll do it.'

Everyone's eyes were on Rudi.

'Rudi, I really don't think we should be moving you in your condition,' the nurse said sternly.

'Come on, Clara, don't be like that,' she pleaded.

'Be like what?' Nurse Clara bristled in agitation. 'Worried about keeping you safe? I'm sorry, but I'm not risking it.'

'Sweetheart. I'm already dying . . . what's the worst that could happen?'

The nurse glanced anxiously over to Rupert, who was standing ready to go. 'Don't look at me. You know she's pig-headed at the best of times.' He placed his hand affectionately on his wife's.

Nurse Clara grabbed Fin's arm and pulled his head close to hers. 'You'd better make this quick. If she gets pneumonia, I'm coming straight for you,' she hissed.

'It'll be over in a flash, I promise,' he whispered back.

'Well then' – she clapped her hands together brightly – 'we'd better get this show on the road and wheel you out there sharpish!' Her fierce eyes fixed on Fin in warning.

'Ahoy there. Let's go!' Rudi cried jubilantly.

*

Fin sat back and looked at the images on the screen. Despite Nurse Clara only granting him a strict twenty-minute time slot, Fin had to admit that these were some of the best pictures he'd taken in years. There was Rudi, in her wheelchair

147

and dress, beaming from ear to ear. A woman who, for just a few precious moments, looked overflowing with life and love for the man next to her. Fin felt his throat constrict and his eyes sting with tears. Did his mum and dad ever look like that?

Don't be ridiculous.

Happy people don't have affairs.

He let his mind wander for the briefest of moments into another world where adulterous fathers chose to behave better, until he realized he could not afford to daydream. He needed to get the shots edited by tonight so they could go to print tomorrow. As Nurse Clara repeatedly pointed out, time was of the essence when it came to this project.

Fin stretched out on the sofa and grabbed his phone. 'Is it too late to get Deliveroo, I wonder . . .'

1 a.m.

Definitely too late.

'Looks like it's another packet of digestives for me then.' He sighed, reaching for the pile he'd stashed on the table. Sure, it wasn't what many people would class as a decent dinner, but needs must. Besides, what was one sleepless sugar-filled night if it made a dying woman happy?

It was almost three by the time he finished and when his phone rang and woke him up, he couldn't believe he'd been asleep for more than two seconds. His body hurt and his head was pounding. He let the phone ring off and turned over. His neck spasmed ferociously, sending shooting pains down his shoulder. Falling asleep on the sofa was never a good idea.

He closed his eyes again, only to hear his phone go off once more. He blindly reached for it and answered.

'Hello?' he grunted.

'Hi, Fin. Sorry to disturb you. Is now a good time to talk?'

The sound of Nurse Clara's voice instantly roused him. He could sense the urgency immediately.

'Yes. What's wrong? Is it my mum?'

'Your mum is fine, don't worry. It's . . .' She tried to speak but Fin could hear the falter in her voice.

'Are you OK?' he asked.

'Yes, yes, I'm fine.' She paused. 'It's Rudi.'

'*No*.' Fin hung his head. The weight of the realization was too much to bear.

'She's gone, Fin. She passed away this morning.'

Fuck.

You were too fucking late.

'Fin?'

'Yes.' His words were flat and curt but he didn't care. He had been given one job and he'd already failed at it.

'She left something for you here. We're clearing her room today but I'll keep it for you until you come tomorrow.'

'She left something for me?' Fin asked.

'Yes. A note, I think. Rupert found it by her bedside.'

Fin checked the time. 'Is Rupert still there?'

'Yes. He's here.'

He opened his laptop and began furiously pulling up the files.

'Tell him to hang on for me, OK? I'll be there in an hour.'

Fin didn't even bother with goodbye. There wasn't time for that right now. He grabbed another leftover biscuit and shoved it into his mouth.

We are not done yet, Rudi, my friend.

*

'Ah, there you are.' Nurse Clara stood up from behind the desk. Her eyes were red and slightly swollen behind her wire-rimmed glasses.

'Sorry, it took me a while to get this printed.' He held aloft a little leather-bound book.

'Don't worry, we're just finishing packing up the room. Come.' She nodded towards the door.

'How are you doing?' he asked quietly.

'OK. Relieved that she went peacefully, if I'm honest. But this place won't be the same without her.' She sighed. 'You know, it's crazy how they quickly stop becoming patients. When someone passes, it's a friend you're losing.' Her shoulders slumped slightly and Fin reached out to rest his hand on her arm. 'But it's part and parcel of the job.' She straightened up quickly, leaving his hand hovering awkwardly in mid-air.

'I'm sure it doesn't make it any easier though.'

'No.' She turned to face him and smiled a worn-out smile. 'No, it doesn't.' She took a deep breath and opened the door to her left. 'Come on.'

Fin followed Nurse Clara into Rudi's room, which was now stripped of all the personal items and splashes of joy that had previously hung from its walls. The bed was empty. The warmth had gone and Fin could feel the absence in the air.

'Ah, hello, Fin.' Rupert moved slowly towards him from his seat by the window. 'I was taking one last look. It is such a beautiful view, isn't it?'

Fin was surprised to see that his eyes were dry and his voice calm and controlled. Maybe after so much pain, seeing your loved one at peace brought comfort as well as heartache.

'It really is.' Fin held out the book he was still clutching in his hand. 'I'm sorry I was too late to get this to her.'

'You weren't late at all.' He nodded towards the bed. 'Sit, please.'

Fin was confused but didn't dare to question. He did as he was told and perched tentatively on the edge of the bed.

'This is for you.' Rupert handed him a piece of paper, his hands nothing more than lightly wrapped bones. His blue eyes crinkled as he watched Fin read.

Dear Fin,
If you are reading this, I can only assume that I am no longer of this world. I wanted to make sure to thank you before I embarked on my next great adventure. You gave me what can only be described as the most wonderful send-off. Now Rupert can look at those pictures and know that he made me just as happy at the end of our time together as he did at the beginning. He came through on his promise beautifully and for that I am eternally grateful. He was there. Loving me until the end of my forever. Thank you once again. You made this dying woman very happy to say farewell.
Yours truly, Rudi.

Fin closed his eyes and allowed the tears to fall silently down his cheeks.

'She was always one for dramatics,' Rupert said kindly, coming to sit next to him.

'She definitely had style.' Fin laughed.

'That she did.' He sighed sadly.

'These are the pictures, by the way.' Fin held the book out again and this time Rupert took it carefully from him.

'Thank you.' He opened the cover and gasped. 'Wow. Would you look at that.' He caressed the page. 'We don't look half bad, do we?'

'Rupert, if I look half as good as you do at your age then I'll count myself very lucky.'

He turned the page and burst out laughing. 'Oh my.' He placed his hand on his chest. 'There's my Rudi.'

Fin hadn't been sure whether to include the extra pictures – the ones that were slightly blurred, the ones where the couple weren't posed in position and perfectly lit – but as soon as he saw them, he knew he had to. The look on their faces, the laughter erupting out of them both. Rudi ordering Rupert around, pulling faces and pointing at Nurse Clara, who was bent over giggling. That was who they were, at their core.

'She told me about the original photo. Why it was such a special night.' Fin looked up into the lined face of the old man next to him. 'You must have pulled out some very good moves to get a marriage proposal on date one!'

Rupert let out a loud, husky laugh. 'I wish I could pretend that I was smooth enough to have moves.' He stroked the face of his wife's photograph tenderly. 'The only thing I knew was that I couldn't walk out of that room without knowing she was going to be coming with me for the rest of my life. I made her promise that she'd never leave me.' He chuckled. 'I guess she's gone and broken it now.' A tear fell on to the photo between them.

'I reckon she's still with you, in some way, shape or form. Rudi didn't seem the type to break her promises.'

'She always said if she went first, she'd haunt me until I gave up and came and joined her.' He snorted at the

152

memory. 'Thank you for these, Fin.' He closed the book and brought it up to his heart.

'I'm glad you like them.'

'I *love* them, Fin. And she would have too.'

Eleanor

'Oh, hi.' Eleanor looked up from her screen at Sal's hand, which was waving furiously in her face.

'Hey!' She smiled. 'You want to grab a coffee? I'm bored of this budget already.'

Sal looked behind her, throwing her head back and forth wildly. 'Who, me?'

'Yes, you. Why are you being weird?' Eleanor frowned.

'I just wasn't sure if you knew who I was any more. Now you're so caught up being busy in *love*,' Sal drawled sarcastically.

Eleanor picked up her pen and threw it at Sal. 'Don't be like that. It was *your* idea to set us up, remember!'

Sal laughed loudly, causing Doreen to tut disapprovingly. 'I know, I know. I'm only messing. But you can buy me a coffee for being such a negligent best friend, OK?'

Eleanor rolled her eyes and stood up. 'Fine.'

'It's going well then, I take it?' Sal asked, her eyes twinkling with glee.

Eleanor looked around anxiously as they walked towards the lifts.

'All right, paranoia, no one cares about your love life,' Sal mocked.

'I know, I'm just not used to this.' Eleanor felt her cheeks colour.

Sal squeezed her hand affectionately. 'I'm sorry. I know.' She hit the call button for the lift and pulled Eleanor into a hug. 'I think it's sweet.'

'Woah. Hugging at work, Sal?' Eleanor laughed into her shoulder. 'People will realize that you actually have a heart.'

'Behave!' Sal pushed her away and stepped into the lift. 'You give me such a bad rep. I'm really not *that* bad.'

'How many interns did you make cry last month?' Eleanor raised her eyebrow knowingly.

Sal picked at the red varnish on her nails. 'Four.'

'Exactly.'

'But that wasn't entirely my fault!' she cried. 'Anyway, this isn't about me. It's about you and Benny boy,' she simpered, her voice thick and sickly sweet.

'Ew. Don't call him that.' Eleanor stepped out of the doors and joined the queue for coffee.

'He really likes you, you know,' Sal announced casually.

'And how would you know that?' Eleanor enquired, hoping Sal couldn't hear the flip of her stomach as it somersaulted wildly.

'I asked him. Unlike you, I actually talk to people about these things.' Sal pulled her long dark hair up into a ponytail. 'Christ, I need to wash my hair. This is the problem with going to the gym before work, it just throws my routine completely off.'

'Oi.' Eleanor slapped her gently on the arm. 'Don't change the subject. What did he *say*?'

Her heart was pounding so loudly now that she was worried she wouldn't be able to catch her friend's response.

'Oh, you know.' Sal waved her hand dismissively. 'I asked him how things were going and he said they were good.' Eleanor could tell she was loving every minute of this. She willed herself to stay patient and allow Sal to continue. 'I said that I wasn't surprised because you were pretty much the best person I've ever met, and he agreed.'

'You said that?' Eleanor lowered her voice to a whisper.

'Yes! That shouldn't be a shock to you by now. You know how much I love you.' Sal shook her head in despair. 'I wish you saw what I see in you.' She turned to lock eyes with Eleanor, who quickly dropped her gaze the floor.

'And' – Sal lifted her chin with her finger – 'clearly what Ben sees in you.'

'What can I get you, ladies?' the barista interrupted. Eleanor smiled gratefully; the moment was starting to overwhelm her.

'A flat white and a double Americano, please,' Eleanor stated.

'Can you make mine a triple actually?' Sal corrected.

'Sure thing.' The barista nodded.

'A triple? Jesus, Sal, it's 3 p.m. already. You'll be bouncing off the walls all night.'

Sal shuffled uncomfortably. 'I need the energy.'

'Why?' Eleanor paid and followed Sal to the waiting area. 'What's happening tonight? Is it another big meeting or something? I can never keep up with your schedule.'

'No.' Sal's cheeks were turning pink.

'So, what is it?' Eleanor pressed suspiciously.

Sal sighed and played with the hem of her jacket. 'I . . . I may or may not have a second date tonight.'

'Sally Moreno, you dark horse!' Eleanor yelped. 'You have a go at me for not telling you things. I want to know everything. And I mean *everything*.'

'Argh. But it's way more fun to grill *you*,' she moaned.

'Not for me, it's not.' Eleanor laughed. 'It's payback time, Sal . . .'

*

For date three with Ben, Eleanor had planned much more effectively, bringing a change of clothes *and* make-up with her to work. Despite being on time, lateness always made her anxious; she still felt the queasy pull of nerves tugging at her stomach.

When did they stop? she wondered. She certainly never remembered feeling this way with Oliver.

That was different.

She shook the thoughts of her ex from her mind. It was funny – one minute he was all she could think about, all her very existence revolved around, and now . . . now there were times she couldn't even remember what he looked like. He was slowly and surely fading from her mind and her heart.

'Hello there.' Ben's voice appeared from behind her. She felt his warm hand on her shoulder.

'Hey!' She turned and went to hug him. He laughed and pulled her face up to his for a kiss. The etiquette of dating was still something she was getting used to.

'How was your day?' He opened the door to the restaurant and beckoned her inside.

'Fine. How about you?'

'Much better now.' He smiled, turning to the maître d'. 'Table reserved under Ben Ryans, please.'

'Very good, sir. If you'd like to follow Francis, he will show you the way.' He pointed to a perfectly put-together young man standing to attention behind him.

'This is very fancy,' Eleanor whispered, as they followed the waiter through the dining room.

'I know. I thought date three deserved a little class.' He winked. 'Although at this rate, by date ten I'm going to have to be organizing helicopters and weekends away.'

Eleanor smirked. 'There's going to be a date ten, is there?'

'Oh, wow.' He clutched at his chest dramatically. 'You really know how to bring a man down, don't you?'

'Your table, sir, madam,' Francis announced formally. 'I'll be over in a moment to take your order.'

'Thank you.' Eleanor sat down and took hold of the menu in front of her. She nearly choked when she saw the prices. This really *was* fancy.

Ben laughed. 'Eleanor.' He placed his hand in the centre of the table, holding it out for her to take. 'Please. Relax and enjoy. It's my treat.'

'No!' she protested. 'Don't be silly.'

'No, you stop being silly.' He leant in towards her. His comforting smell sent sparks of electricity through her body. 'If we are going to do this . . . you have to learn to let yourself be taken care of.'

She looked at him, searching his face for a sign or hint that he was anything but genuine.

What?

What are you looking for, Eleanor?

'Fine.' She exhaled, slotting her tiny hand in his.

'Good.' He lifted it to his lips and kissed the inside of her wrist. 'Now . . . what I didn't mention was that we are going to only have starters here, and then we are heading to McDonald's, where you can buy a Happy Meal, OK?'

Eleanor pulled her hand away and gasped dramatically. 'How dare you! At least make it a double cheeseburger, *please*.'

'A double cheeseburger, really?' He smirked. 'I didn't have you down as that kind of girl.'

'I think there was one month when I was about seventeen when I ate one every day after school.'

'As if.' He screwed his face up in mock disgust.

'I know. Fin told my mum in the end because he was scared that I was becoming addicted.' She smiled nostalgically at the memory. 'She took all my pocket money away in an act to curb my habit.'

'I knew Fin was a stand-up guy.'

'*Please*, you have no idea. He was the worst!'

'It's so nice that you stayed in touch. Is he still in London?' Ben asked innocently.

'Erm . . .' Eleanor felt a pang of guilt. 'I think so.'

'Maybe we could all go for dinner sometime.'

'Why?' she asked, a little too brusquely.

'Because I'd like to get to know him properly. If he's important to you then he's important to me.'

'He *was* important to me,' she said sadly. 'We aren't close any more.'

'How come?'

'You know.' She shrugged, scouring the restaurant for any sign of their waiter. 'People change, I guess.'

'Ah, I see what happened.' Ben nodded solemnly. 'He was completely in love with you and you broke his heart, didn't you!' he teased.

Eleanor forced a smile on to her face. 'You got me.'

'I knew it!' He clapped his hands together. 'And who could blame him? You're pretty lovable, aren't you, Eleanor Levy?'

'I don't know about that,' she mumbled, her body temperature rising rapidly.

'I do.' He moved closer to her, squeezing her hand gently. 'Oh, and by the way,' he whispered, his lips inches from hers, 'are you free next Tuesday night?'

'I think so, why?' she murmured, knowing that quite honestly she'd likely agree to anything he suggested right now.

'I have a surprise for you.'

Before she could say another word, he kissed her hard on the mouth, and just like that nothing else seemed to matter.

Then: Aged 16
Eleanor

'We have to be back by eleven, otherwise Mum and Dad will literally kill me.' Eleanor pulled Fin's hand so that he was facing her square on. 'I mean it, Fin. I'll leave without you if you're not ready.' She was trying to be as serious as possible, something she found incredibly hard around him.

'Eleven o'clock and not a second later.' He swayed a little on the spot, clutching his litre bottle of pre-mixed drink close to his chest.

'How much of that have you already drunk? You can't even stand up straight!' She pulled him upright, the pungent smell of whiskey and Coke pouring out of him.

'Not nearly enough, my dear,' he cooed in her ear, then knocked loudly on the door. 'You ready for your first experience of a wild house party?' His green eyes glinted mischievously.

Eleanor fiddled with the hem of her denim skirt. It had taken an hour and four different changes before she finally settled on her outfit. Apparently, dungarees and Converse were not appropriate for such an occasion, which made

Eleanor instantly decide this was not the type of event she would be likely to attend again.

'Do I look OK?' she asked nervously, adjusting the halter-neck top she'd reluctantly borrowed from Kate, who was already inside the party and waiting for them.

Fin turned to her and cupped her chin. 'You look beautiful.'

Eleanor laughed. 'You're drunk.'

'And?' He grinned widely, his freckles stretching across his cheeks. 'I'm drunk and you're beautiful. That's just the way it goes.' He shrugged his shoulders and sighed.

'You won't leave me when we get inside, will you?' she pleaded, cursing the fact she sounded like a lost little girl.

'Leave you? Don't be silly, Elles.' His face dropped momentarily, as though her question had offended him.

'I just don't know anyone here. It's all your new friends.' There was an unmistakable resentment to her tone but maybe he was too intoxicated to register it. She knew it was inevitable that things would change as they got older, but lately Fin seemed permanently attached to a new crowd. A crowd that made him stay out late, forget to call her and, most worryingly of all, a crowd that seemed to think it was funny to get drunk at every opportunity.

'You're the only person I need.' Fin took a step forward. Eleanor could feel the heat from his body. 'You always have been.' His gaze lingered on her mouth. 'You know I'm lost without you.'

Eleanor's entire body sparked with electricity. Fin's eyes darted up to meet hers, their jade green brighter than she'd ever seen them. Every cell inside her body seemed to be on high alert, prickling with anticipation.

'Really?' she whispered.

The corners of his mouth curled up at the edges and she saw his head tilt slowly towards her.

'Really.'

Eleanor's world shifted into slow motion.

This couldn't be happening. Not with Fin. Not after all this time.

She closed her eyes and allowed the moment to hold her.

'*Fin!*'

Eleanor's heart jolted. She snapped her eyes open to see the front door ajar, revealing the night's host, Jimmy Turner. The most popular boy in the year above them at school, and one of Fin's new acquaintances.

'Jimmy!' Fin cried, turning sharply away from Eleanor. 'How's it going, buddy?' He slapped him on the back and swaggered inside.

What the hell just happened?

Eleanor didn't have time to linger on the thoughts for much longer, as Fin was very quickly disappearing into the throng of dancing bodies. The music was so loud she could feel it reverberating in her ribcage. Her eyes searched wildly for Kate, but it was hard to see anyone through the heavily perfumed cigarette smoke that hung across the room.

'Come in and shut the door,' someone called out to her. Eleanor hurried inside and spotted Fin snaking his way towards the kitchen.

'Fin!' she shouted after him. 'Fin, wait up.' Everything felt out of sorts. Her brain was fizzing with confusion. All she needed to do was get to her friend and then she'd be fine, but bodies seemed to be piling in around her, blocking her view, pulling her further and further away from Fin.

Suddenly she felt someone grab her hand.

'*Eleanor!*' Kate screamed in her ear. '*You made it.*'

Her friend was wide-eyed and beaming.

'It's so busy in here,' Eleanor shouted, her voice already hoarse. 'Can we talk? Something weird just happened.'

'What?' her friend screamed back.

'*Can we go somewhere to talk?*' Eleanor mouthed, gesticulating wildly in the hope that somehow her words would register.

Kate nodded and dragged Eleanor back through the pulsating crowd of teenagers and up the stairs.

'Excuse me, excuse me, my friend needs the toilet – I think she's going to throw up,' Kate announced loudly as she pushed her through more entwined couples.

'Oi,' a gruff voice shouted after them. 'We all need a piss, love, there's a queue here.'

Kate whipped her head back sharply. 'My friend's about to vom, so unless you want to see *and* smell that, I suggest you *move*.'

The crowd instantly parted and made way for them to come through. Once they were safely inside, Eleanor sat down on the edge of the bath.

'Come on then, what's going on?' Kate asked, half listening, half adjusting her make-up in the bathroom mirror.

'I think . . .' Eleanor couldn't even believe she was about to say the words out loud. 'I think Fin and I nearly kissed.' She dropped her head with embarrassment.

'What the *hell*?' Kate squealed, running over to kneel by Eleanor. 'Are you serious? Like oh my God, at *last*, but really? What happened?' She was speaking so quickly that it was making Eleanor feel a little nauseous. 'Tell me everything!'

Eleanor looked up into the overly excited face of her friend. Doubt began to gnaw away at the edges of her mind. Maybe she was exaggerating? Maybe she'd read it wrong?

'Eleanor!' Kate shook her impatiently. 'What happened?'

'I don't know. We were waiting outside the front door. I asked him if I looked OK. Then he said I looked beautiful and . . . and he held my face. Then he started looking at me strangely . . . like really intensely. I've never seen him look at me like that before.' Eleanor closed her eyes as she recalled the moment. Her heart fluttered and her body temperature soared at the thought. 'I saw him start to lean forward and so I closed my eyes, but then Jimmy opened the door and interrupted, and then suddenly we were inside and I kind of lost him in the crowd.'

Kate's eyes grew larger and her face broke into a smile. 'What are you doing up here then, you idiot? Go find him!'

'And say what?' Eleanor shook her head in resignation. The moment had passed. What if she'd made this whole thing up?

'You don't *say* anything.' Kate winked and pulled Eleanor up to standing. 'Come here, let me put some of this on you.' She pulled out a lipstick from her clutch bag and gently started applying it to Eleanor's lips.

'Hey, how long are you going to be in there? Some of us are desperate,' an angry voice shouted through the door.

'She's being really sick . . . it's like everywhere . . . all over the walls . . . so back off a minute, will you?' Kate barked. 'Here's what you're going to do, OK?'

Eleanor nodded silently. 'You're going to go downstairs and find Fin. You're not going to say a word, just go up to him and kiss him. It's been a long time coming, nothing more needs to be said.' Kate clapped her hands in glee and let out a little shriek of excitement. 'Ready?'

Again, all Eleanor could manage was a small nod of her head. She felt sick. Maybe she actually did need to vomit. Was this really happening?

But there was no more time for thinking as Eleanor felt herself being pulled from the room and down the stairs. Everything around her was a blur. The only thing she could focus on was the feel of Kate's hand in hers and the pounding of her heart.

Suddenly Kate stopped dead. She tried to turn Eleanor away but it was too late. There in front of them, at the foot of the stairs, arms wrapped around one another, were Fin and a girl. Their faces were so tightly locked together that if she didn't know the details of him so well, he could have been anyone. But he wasn't.

The floor shifted beneath her. Tears stung her eyes as she felt her entire body run cold.

How could you have been so stupid, Eleanor?

'Let's go,' Kate hissed, pulling at her arm, but Eleanor remained rooted, unable to tear her eyes away from the scene in front of her.

'Eleanor! Move!' Kate shouted.

Fin stopped and looked up, straight into Eleanor's eyes. A wave of emotions crashed over her, so many feelings piling on top of each other that her brain didn't have time to make sense of them.

'Eleanor, there you are.' He broke into a smile and reached his hand out to her. The blonde girl who he had been attached to mere seconds ago threw her arms protectively around Fin's neck and stared menacingly at Eleanor. 'Come here and meet Danielle. I was just telling her about you. Danielle, here is my best friend in the entire world, Eleanor Levy!' He swayed a little as he stepped towards her.

Eleanor couldn't speak. There were no words. All she wanted to do was disappear and erase this moment from her life completely.

'Eleanor?' His face crumpled into confusion. 'Are you OK?' He was so close to her now she could almost taste the alcohol on him. He took her hand and squeezed it.

'Yes, sorry! Think I had one too many shots.' She snapped back into life. 'I'm going to go, but you stay and have fun.' Eleanor smiled and shook herself free of Fin's hand. 'Danielle, it was nice to meet you,' she called back over her shoulder, practically running into Kate's arms.

'Elles, are you sure you're all right?' Fin shouted after her. 'We've only just got here!'

'Get me outside *now*,' she hissed, as Kate dragged her towards the front door. 'And promise me we forget this whole night ever happened, OK?'

'OK. I promise.'

Now

Fin

His heart was already heavy by the time he walked into his mother's room the next day. Rudi's death had really left its mark on him but, thankfully, Nurse Clara had assured him that his mum was fairly lucid; he wasn't sure he had the energy to deal with the alternative.

'Hello.' She waved weakly at him from the bed.

'Hey,' he murmured glumly.

'I heard about Rudi.'

Fin dragged himself over to the chair and slumped down. 'I still can't believe it. She seemed fine the other day.'

His mum gazed away into the distance. 'She was very sick, for a very long time.'

'Yeah, Nurse Clara said.'

Fin's stomach churned with guilt. All this talk of death probably wasn't the nicest for someone heading down the same road.

'The nurses said something about you taking photographs for Rudi and her husband?' his mother enquired.

'Yeah.' He sat up taller in his seat. 'It's a long time since

I've taken pictures like that, but they looked so happy.' He paused. 'It's my job back home, you know? I'm a photographer. I have my own company.'

He hated how childlike he sounded, how even after all this time there was still the little boy inside him, desperate for approval.

'I know.' Her voice was small and somewhat sad. 'You've taken some beautiful photographs, Fin.'

Fin's look of complete and utter confusion must have spelled out the question that was racing through his mind.

'Angela,' his mother answered. 'She helped me find your website on the internet. I don't have a clue how the whole thing works, but she shows me from time to time.'

'Oh,' Fin replied meekly. 'I see.'

'You were always an artistic thing. Even as a young boy.' Her eyes glazed over a little. 'I'm glad you did something with it in the end.'

'What, and broke Dad's heart by not becoming a lawyer?' he sniped. 'I'm sure he'd be glowing with pride.'

'You know what your father was like. He just wanted the best for you.'

An uncomfortable silence planted itself between them. Fin knew he should try to fill it but he was finding it hard to in his current mood. Why, if she'd known where he was and what he was doing, had she not tried to contact him?

It works both ways, you know . . .

'Angela said little Kate Crossley got married the other day,' his mother chirped.

'She did.'

'Angela said you went?'

'Yeah . . . I was a bit of a last-minute guest,' he added sheepishly.

'That must have been lovely. I'm glad you still keep in touch. She was a nice girl. Her and Eleanor. Always such nice girls,' she remarked dreamily.

'Yeah, they are.'

'And . . .' His mother hesitated. 'I don't suppose there are any other nice girls in your life?'

Her attempt at subtlety was far from successful and Fin couldn't help but laugh. Was this what normal mothers and sons talked about? For the briefest of seconds, he wished he had something more exciting to answer with.

'No. Not at the moment. I actually broke up with someone before I came over here.'

'Oh.' Her wispy eyebrows shot up. 'I'm sorry to hear that.'

'Don't be. It was for the best,' he assured her.

'As long as you're happy. That's the main thing.' She nodded, her eyes flicking to her wedding photograph next to her. 'It's important to make sure you're with the right person.'

Fin bit back the sarcastic comments that were begging to be spoken out loud. Was she really going to talk to him about happy relationships? He anxiously glanced down at his watch. He'd barely been here twenty minutes.

'I have to go, Mum,' he stated bluntly, trying his best to ignore the guilt he felt. 'I have to meet a friend for dinner, so I should head back and get ready.' The lie was embarrassingly blatant. 'I'll see you in a couple of days, OK?'

'OK,' she whispered, but Fin was already halfway out of the room.

It wasn't that he didn't want to leave things on better terms with his mum; he just found that every time they ventured into talking about anything more serious than the weather, his long-buried anger would seep through the cracks in his defences and threaten to overwhelm him.

'Ah, Fin, there you are.' Nurse Clara was hovering by the front desk as he made his way into reception. 'Do you want a cup of tea?'

'No, I'm fine, thanks.'

'Are you sure you can't spare a couple of minutes to chat to an old nurse?'

He eyed her with suspicion. 'I've seen that look before. You want something, don't you?'

She nodded. 'Am I that transparent?'

'A little.' He smiled.

'Yes, well it seems what you did for Rudi has spread around the home. People talk in these places – there's often not much else to do, you see. Anyway, there's been another request.'

'I see,' Fin replied flatly.

'For a photographer,' Nurse Clara added for clarity.

'OK.'

'And . . . and I was wondering if you would make an allowance. I know you said you'd only do one, but you're still here and it brought so much joy to Rudi and Rupert that I thought maybe . . . maybe you wouldn't mind squeezing in another?' She took a step towards him, her eyes so full of hope.

Fin ran his hand through his hair. 'I don't know. I would love to, really I would . . . it's just . . .' He hesitated, unable to meet the pleading look Nurse Clara was giving him. 'I don't want this to become a *thing*, you know?'

'I understand.' She pushed her glasses up her nose. 'I'll let Heidi know that we'll have to find someone else.'

Have you really become the type of guy who says no to doing favours for dying people?

Fin felt the battle inside himself rage. He wanted to help,

he really did, but he didn't want to create any more ties to this place than he already had.

It's a photoshoot. Get over yourself.

'Wait!' Fin called, as Nurse Clara was halfway through the door. 'If it's just one more . . .'

She turned, her face beaming with delight. 'Just one,' she confirmed. 'Shall we visit her now? Strike while the iron's hot?'

'Can I say anything other than yes?' Fin sighed.

'Of course. It just wouldn't be wise, that's all.' Nurse Clara grinned, opening the door and beckoning him through.

Fin followed her to the door nearest the reception entrance.

'You really do like getting your own way, don't you?' He laughed.

'Naturally.' She shrugged, pausing with her hand on the doorknob. 'Now, some things you need to know about Heidi before we enter. She's quite deaf and doesn't always wear her hearing aid, so you may need to speak up.'

'Noted. Speak loudly,' Fin repeated studiously.

'She doesn't have much of a support system, so avoid mentioning husbands or partners or children.'

'OK. Anything else?' He was now very intrigued as to who this woman was behind the door.

'Yes, one last thing: sometimes she takes a bit of time to warm up to people. Don't be offended if she's rude to you.' Before Fin had a chance to even think about her comment, Nurse Clara had opened the door and stepped inside the room. 'Heidi, dear,' she half shouted, 'Fin is here to meet you.'

'Bring him in,' a cold voice summoned.

Fin took a step inside and noticed an older lady sitting

172

bolt upright in her bed, her gaze unmoving from its fixed position out of the window.

'Hello, Heidi.' He waved, hoping his exaggerated actions would make up for his lack of volume.

'No need to gesticulate at me like I'm deaf,' she sniped.

'Now, Heidi, Fin is the man who took the pictures of Rudi,' Nurse Clara continued, ignoring the glare that Fin was giving her.

'I can put two and two together, thank you, Nurse.'

'Of course you can.' Nurse Clara was already backing out of the room and into the corridor. 'Fin, I'll leave you to it.' Before he could do anything to escape, she'd closed the door and disappeared.

'Would you like to take a seat?' Heidi still hadn't bothered to look at Fin, who remained frozen and staring at the woman in front of him.

'Well? Are you going to stand there for the entirety of our meeting, or will you do as I ask and sit?' she snapped.

Fin hurriedly pulled out the chair next to the bed and sat. He thought it was best to do as she said and make as little sound as possible; he felt his presence alone was irritating her.

'I saw what you did for Rudi,' she stated bluntly, nodding to the view of the garden outside her window. 'You looked like you knew what you were doing.'

'Erm . . . thanks?' he replied quietly.

Heidi turned to look at him for the first time since he entered the room. Her eyes were large and so dark they almost looked black. She had long, delicate features and, despite her age, Fin was struck instantly by her beauty. Her thick grey hair was twisted into a long plait that fell over her shoulder. But there was no warmth to her, not a trace of kindness to be found anywhere in her expression. Nothing but wrinkled lines and severity.

'I was giving you a compliment, boy. Did you not hear me?'

Fin felt like a school kid under the watchful glare of the headteacher. He cleared his throat and spoke louder and clearer. 'I did. I said thank you.'

'You see that woman?' Heidi nodded ever so slightly to a picture standing proudly on her nightstand.

'Yes,' he said dutifully, knowing immediately who the girl with the crown and bouquet of flowers was. 'How old were you when that was taken?' he asked.

'Seventeen,' she replied mournfully. 'I'm surprised you can even recognize it's me.'

'Your features are exactly the same. It's uncanny.'

She seemed to stiffen at his response but didn't utter a word. Fin thought it best to play safe and follow her lead, distracting himself by taking in his surroundings. Like Rudi's room, all of the surfaces and most of the walls were covered with pictures and trinkets. However, unlike Rudi's, these weren't joyful family memorabilia but trophies and certificates and pageant pictures. This room felt bitter and sad, and Fin wasn't sure how much longer he could stay sitting there.

'I suppose you think me vain?' She raised an eyebrow daringly, watching him as he scanned the room.

'No. Not at all,' he lied.

'You may be a good photographer but you're a bad liar.' She flashed him the briefest hint of a smirk. 'Do you know what it feels like to have something you love so dearly and then lose it?'

'Yes . . .' Fin mumbled awkwardly, Eleanor's face appearing in his mind unexpectedly.

'Do you know what it's like to look like that,' Heidi continued, not paying any attention to Fin or his answer. She nodded at the wall of her pictures. 'To be that beautiful, with the world at your feet, and lose it all? To look at a photograph and not even recognize yourself in it?'

Fin knew his input wasn't needed. He simply sat and observed as the formidable lady began to lose herself in thought.

'Do you know how it feels to lose control of your body? A body that used to dance, and move and run and play? They say getting old is a gift. But for me it's been nothing more than a hellishly slow path to losing everything I loved.' She took a short sharp intake of breath and closed her eyes. Fin could see her long delicate hands gripping the bed covers tightly. 'I want to *feel* like me again. Just for one moment, Fin. I'd like to be beautiful again.' A single tear escaped from beneath her dark lashes.

Fin didn't dare move a muscle. He wished he had his camera with him now to capture this moment. This vulnerability. This beauty.

She opened her eyes, all traces of sensitivity and emotion wiped completely. 'Do you think you could do that for me?'

'Sure,' he stated firmly.

'Don't say it to appease me. I'm not someone who can be fobbed off and placated, you know?'

'I think you've made that very clear.' She looked a little taken aback by his honesty but stayed silent. 'I wouldn't say yes if I wasn't sure,' Fin continued. 'I just might need to rope in a little help, if that's OK?'

'Do as you wish,' she replied curtly. The cold exterior was fully back in place. 'Now if you don't mind, I'd like to sleep.'

'No problem. I'll sort everything out with Nurse Clara and get back to you on timings.'

'Fine. Just make me look beautiful in one photograph before I die, OK?' Heidi had already closed her eyes and turned her face away from him.

'Gotcha.' Fin jumped up from his seat and almost sprinted out of the room.

The minute he was outside in the corridor, he felt his body relax. He reached into his pocket and pulled out his phone . . .

Eleanor

When Ben had said he had a surprise for Eleanor on Tuesday night, this was the last thing she'd expected. A community art class? How had he even remembered their brief conversation in that little Italian restaurant?

Eleanor checked her watch anxiously. Even after her fifth walk around the block, she still had a few minutes to kill. Normally she didn't mind being early – in fact, a small part of her relished being the first one in – but not tonight. If she could find a way to slip in the back completely unseen that would be a miracle.

'You should have said no. Eleanor, when will you learn to say no?' she berated herself.

And risk looking like a boring spoilsport in front of your new boyfriend?

He's not my boyfriend.

Uh-huh . . .

'Are you here for the art group, dear?' A red-faced lady appeared out of nowhere behind her, making Eleanor jump back in shock. 'Oh, I'm sorry, I didn't mean to scare

177

you! Were you daydreaming? I'm always away with the fairies. It's a tough job getting me back down into the real world these days.' The stranger's face creased into a wide smile. 'It's a much nicer place in my head, I always find.'

'Yes,' Eleanor replied flatly.

'Yes to what, dear? The daydream or the art group?'

'Both!' She laughed nervously.

'Wonderful. Well, I'm Agatha. I run the sessions.' The lady held out her hand and Eleanor took it. 'You must be Eleanor. Our newest recruit. Shall we head in?'

Eleanor nodded mutely and began to follow Agatha towards the entrance to the community hall. 'Now, it doesn't look much from the outside,' Agatha acknowledged, her eyes flicking between the graffiti-coated walls and the peeling paint. 'But we make it feel like home.' She opened the door and gestured for Eleanor to go inside.

'I'm only here for one session,' Eleanor announced, stepping into the hallway. 'My' – *boyfriend* – 'friend signed me up as a surprise gift! I'm just going to try it out and see what it's like.'

Agatha hummed and flicked on the lights. 'That's what they all said when they started. Now I can't bloody get rid of them. Four years this has been running. *Four years*. My husband can't believe I've stuck to something for so long! Apart from him, of course. The lucky sod.' She chuckled to herself. 'Grab eight chairs and put them in a circle, will you? We're just in that room to the left. I'll get the canvases from the car.'

Eleanor didn't have time to argue; before she knew it Agatha had disappeared, leaving her alone in the corridor.

'One session. That's all,' she reminded herself, as she

opened the door on the left to reveal a large hall. It had the same musty smell that her school gym used to emit. The smell of sweating children, rubber plimsoles and dust. It was colder inside the room than outdoors and Eleanor pulled her coat tighter around her neck.

'Oh yes, did I forget to mention in my email? Bring all the layers you can. When the sun's not shining it's an icebox in here. Then the moment summer comes it's a sauna. Gives everyone something to moan about though, which strangely I always find helps their creativity.' Agatha was back and carrying eight large canvases. She placed them on the floor and looked disappointedly at the still bare hall. 'Right, where are we with those chairs then? Reggie will be here soon, and if you don't give him somewhere to sit immediately, the next hour won't be worth living.'

Within a blink of an eye, Agatha had transformed the rather sad space into an odd-looking art studio. Every chair was laden with a variety of coloured cushions; a table was placed in the centre and draped in layers of beaded fabrics. Incense was lit and portable heaters were stationed around the room, dutifully blasting their hot air into the space.

'Kettle is on and biscuits are out! Right, I think we are good to go,' Agatha announced, her hands placed on her hips. She was only a small woman – early fifties, Eleanor would guess – but there was an air about her that exuded a youthful vitality. She seemed to radiate positivity from every pore, and Eleanor had to admit she felt a little in awe of her already.

'Take a seat, dear. Not that one, that's Enid's. Or that one, that's Patrick's.' Eleanor sidestepped around the circle until she found a space that had not already been reserved. She sat and waited; it was already ten past. The class was only meant to be an hour. Did they always start this late?

'Ah, the newbie is early, I see. Keen as a bean!' a brusque voice called out from across the room. Eleanor jerked her head up to see a shrivelled old man, barely a wisp of existence, staggering unevenly towards her. 'And you've even gone and sat her next to me. You sure that's wise, Agatha? You don't want to put her with the naughty kids on day dot.' He waggled his gnarled fingers at Agatha, who had come over to accompany him to his seat.

'Come on now, Reggie. I've got to try and find someone to keep an eye on you.'

'Argh, don't fuss. I can manage by myself.' He waved her arm away and continued his slow and painful-looking journey to his seat.

'Hi.' Eleanor stood and reached out her hand. 'I'm Eleanor.'

'You're on my cushion.' He pointed accusingly.

'Pardon?' Eleanor looked behind her, confused.

'That's my cushion you've got there. Best one for my arthritic back. Nice and firm.'

Eleanor hurriedly grabbed the pillow and switched it with the one next to hers. 'Sorry, I didn't know.'

'Course you didn't. You're new.' He slowly lowered himself down into the chair. Eleanor swore she could hear his bones creaking in protestation. 'Phew. Hardest bit done. Wouldn't mind getting me a tea, would you, Eleanor? I'm parched after that marathon.' He flashed her a crooked grin and winked.

'Reginald Bates. Eleanor is not here as your servant. If you want tea, ask me and I'll get it,' Agatha scorned playfully.

'It's fine. Milk and sugar?' Eleanor asked.

'Yes, and yes. Oh, and four of the most chocolatey

biscuits you can get your hands on. Better get the good ones before Enid snaffles them all.'

Eleanor made her way over to where Agatha was standing. 'He's quite something, isn't he?'

'That's one way to put it.' Agatha chortled, pouring hot water into two cups. 'I suppose at nearly ninety he's not doing too badly.'

'Ninety? No way!' Eleanor's mouth was wide in shock. 'And he can still paint?'

Agatha cast an affectionate look towards the old man, who was adjusting himself in his seat trying to get comfortable. 'Not as well as he used to. You should see some of his early work. It's breathtaking. But yes, I'd say he can still find his way around a canvas pretty well.'

Eleanor was impressed. 'Also, I don't mean to be rude but where is everyone else? I thought the class started at seven?'

Agatha looked up at the large clock behind her and smiled. 'I probably should have mentioned that in my email too. We never start on time. And we *always* run over. But like I say, you can't really time-box creativity, can you?' She winked at Eleanor. 'Ah, here come Enid and Lance.'

*

By half past seven all of the group were seated and ready to start. Eleanor and Reggie had made their way through two cups of tea and half the packet of biscuits before Agatha finally stood up in the centre and welcomed the group.

'Hi, everybody. Before we get our brushes wet and our creative juices flowing, I'd like to introduce our newest member . . . Eleanor.'

Eleanor could feel her cheeks flush with embarrassment.

'Hi, Eleanor,' the group chorused.

'So, today we are going to be focusing on . . .' Agatha's eyes glimmered with excitement. She picked up the edges of a piece of material that was covering the contents of the table and flung it back dramatically. '*Fruit!*' She threw her hands in the air and did an odd little dance.

One of the ladies gave a half-hearted clap whilst everyone else continued to stare at the bowl of overripe fruit that had now appeared in the centre of the room.

'Pick one item, pick two, or heck . . . paint the whole bowl if you fancy! But whatever you do, make sure it reflects *you*.'

Eleanor felt the sweat bead on her forehead. All around her people were readying themselves to start. She could hear the scraping of chairs, the swirling of water and scratching of brushes, but Eleanor remained frozen, her eyes fixed on the blank page in front of her.

She closed her eyes as the ground became unsteady beneath her.

What if I can't do it any more?

You won't know unless you try.

Then all of a sudden, another voice cut through the sound of her own. Eleanor tried to shake it out of her, but her brain was forcing her back to a time and place she didn't want to revisit.

'I don't know why people continue with hobbies they aren't good at,' Oliver's voice boomed down the table. His face was blotchy and his lips were stained a menacing purple from the red wine.

'What do you mean?' one of the dinner party guests, who Eleanor hadn't yet been introduced to, asked.

'In my opinion, if you're not good at it or not going to make money from it, then why bother?' he drawled. 'It's like

Eleanor. She paints and paints and paints non-stop. Why?! She's not going to sell any of them. What's the point in having stacks of pictures that no one's going to look at taking up space in our house! She doesn't listen to me, though. Do you, Eleanor? She says until we have a baby, what else is that room being used for?' He looked up and caught her eye. '*I* haven't told her about my idea for a gym yet, though.' He threw his head back and laughed.

Eleanor felt her eyes prick hot with tears. She willed herself back to the present moment, focusing her senses on the smell of incense mixed with old plimsoles. The sing-song feedback from Agatha as she made her way around the group. The solid chair beneath her.

I can't do this.

She snapped her eyes open and was about to run when she felt the air shift slightly next to her. She turned her head and saw Reggie leaning over.

'It's only a bowl of fruit, kid.' He nodded towards the centre of the room. 'And let's be honest, how badly can you fuck up an orange?' His dark blue eyes glittered wickedly.

A lightness fell over her, settling her roaring anxiety.

'I'll show you.' She laughed, picking up her pencil and sketching the first outline on to her page.

Fin

Fin had been a little nervous when he'd messaged Eleanor, asking if she wanted to grab a coffee with him. Since the dinner party at Sal's they'd barely spoken, and although the frosty awkwardness of their initial interactions had gone, he wasn't sure they were on 'catching up over lattes' terms yet. But he knew this was more important than potential awkward silences. If he was going to pull off Heidi's request, he could not do it alone.

It will be fine. The worst she can say is no.

And then what are you going to do?

Fin slumped down further in the worn-out armchair. He'd already downed one coffee and he could feel the caffeine pumping energy waves through his veins. How many people had laid their heads here? How many difficult conversations, work meetings and salacious gossiping sessions had this chair witnessed? Were the words woven into the very threads of its brown cloth? What he wouldn't give to hear what this chair knew.

A vibration in his pocket stirred him from his thoughts.

Incoming Call: Rob.

Shit.

Fin braced himself and answered.

'Oh, hello?' Rob's voice was thick with irony. 'Is that Fin? My old best friend? The man who used to speak to me before he disappeared off to his new life in London and forgot all about his friends on the other side of the world?'

Fin winced. 'Yes, speaking?'

He knew he'd dropped off the radar, but between his visits to his mother and planning for his shoot with Heidi, the days had simply seemed to vanish. At times, his old life in America felt like it belonged to somebody else. Another version of Fin who wasn't bogged down with dying mothers and unwanted ghosts from the past. The laughter that erupted from Rob instantly melted all of Fin's unease.

'I'm sorry,' he started. 'It's just be—'

'Nah, buddy, it's fine, I was only messing. I know you have a lot going on. How is it over there? Skin dried up from lack of sun?'

Fin admired his paler skin in the watery excuse for sunlight. 'Yeah, looking pretty pasty, I'm not going to lie.'

Rob snorted. 'At least it means we'll all have a chance with the ladies for a bit when you come home.'

Fin raised his eyebrow. 'Dare I ask what happened with your blind date then?'

Rob let out a long, slow breath. 'I don't know.'

'Don't know what?' Fin checked the time. He reckoned he had five minutes before Eleanor appeared, and knowing Rob's storytelling, five minutes wouldn't even scratch the surface.

'It's hard, isn't it? Knowing what the hell goes on in their heads.'

185

Fin chuckled. 'And by "their" I assume you mean the female population?'

'Uh-huh,' Rob replied glumly.

'Too right it's hard. But apparently that's meant to be half the fun of it.' Fin pushed the memory of Camilla's face from his mind. He hadn't spoken to her since the night they broke up. Should he have at least sent a message?

She's better off without you.

They always are.

'Have you seen this woman since your ever so magical first date?' Fin shook himself back to the present moment.

'Yeah, a few times. She's actually coming over tonight and I'm cooking her dinner.'

'Wow, Rob, you must like her.'

'I know, mate. That's the problem. I'm not used to all these emotions,' he exclaimed.

Fin stood up and stretched, craning his head for any signs of Eleanor. 'You have nothing to worry about. The moment she's tasted your cooking, she'll be dumping you anyway.'

'Cheers. Thanks for that.'

'Pleasure.' Suddenly he spotted a head full of dark curls appear at the door. 'Look, mate, I'm really sorry but I have to go. My friend's just arrived.'

'Your friend?' Rob gasped. 'You've replaced me already, you cheating bastard. I thought you didn't have any friends in London.'

Fin dropped his voice, even though Eleanor was standing on the other side of the room in the queue and definitely unable to hear him. 'It's an old friend. I mean, I'm not even sure you could call us friends.'

'You've slept with her?'

'No!' Fin whispered fervently. 'She's a family friend. Anyway, I need to go. You'll be fine tonight! And I promise I'll call you tomorrow for all the details, all right?'

'Sure. Catch you in a bit, bud,' Rob grumbled. 'And remember . . . I'm your best friend, OK?'

'How could I forget?' Fin smiled. He hung up the phone and made his way across the room to where Eleanor was inching her way slowly to the front of the line.

'As *if* you got here before me?' she marvelled. 'That's got to be some sort of record, surely?'

Fin shrugged nonchalantly. 'What can I say? I'm a changed man.'

'Uh-huh. I would have been early if other people actually learnt to do their jobs properly,' Eleanor muttered. 'Do you want a drink?'

'I'll get them, I'm the one that dragged you out here after work.'

'It's fine, I don't mind.'

'Honestly, go sit. What do you want?' he insisted.

'Jesus, maybe you are changed after all,' she joked. 'I'll have a flat white, please.'

'You bet.' He did a strange salute that instantly made him cringe.

Be normal. For God's sake, just be normal.

*

'Two flat whites, a brownie *and* a slice of carrot cake,' Fin announced, delivering the stacked tray shakily on to the table.

'Wow. You really went all out, didn't you?' She took the steaming cup from the tray. 'Thank you.'

'No problem.' He sat down in the saggy armchair opposite

her. 'I hate to say it, but the coffee in London is actually pretty decent.'

'I'm surprised you even drink coffee, to be honest.'

'Why's that? Not sophisticated enough?' Fin took a big sip of his drink.

'No. It's just the Fin I remember had more than enough energy without the caffeine.'

He laughed, a tiny bit of coffee escaping from his mouth and dribbling down his chin.

'OK, maybe also the sophistication thing,' she teased, handing him a tissue.

'Thank you.' He wiped his chin quickly. 'Unfortunately, that youthful exuberance left me as soon as I hit twenty-five. I am but an old man nowadays.'

'Honestly, I swear as soon as I turned thirty, the speed of my ageing doubled.'

'Really? I think you look the same.'

'As I did at eighteen?' she cried indignantly.

'OK, maybe not. For one thing, your dress sense is a lot less cool.' He raised his eyebrow cheekily.

'*Please*. You're giving me fashion critique? Do I need to remind you of that awful poncho phase you went through?'

He let out a loud snort. 'I lived in that thing for like a month straight, didn't I?' He shook his head.

'Yes, you did,' she confirmed smugly, digging into the brownie. 'It was gross.'

'Man, I loved that poncho.' He sighed fondly.

'You were weird.'

'And you were my friend, so you must have been pretty weird yourself.'

'I like to think I was the balance. The normal to your strangeness.'

Fin's eyes widened. 'Oh, really? Do you want me to go into the time you became so obsessed with your next-door neighbour that you asked for a telescope for your birthday, just so you could try to watch him in his bedroom?'

'All right, all right. Enough about the past,' she insisted, her face reddening slightly. 'We were both weird.'

'Thank you very much.' He nodded gratefully, unable to ignore the slight sense of unease that had crept into Eleanor's demeanour.

Leave the past where it is.

What's done is done.

'Now . . .' he started.

'Now what?' She arched her eyebrow suspiciously.

'I have a favour to ask you.'

Eleanor sighed. 'Aha! So, this was why you got me the carrot cake as well as the brownie.'

'No,' he said shiftily. 'Well, maybe a little bit.'

'Go on, I'm listening.' She eyed him warily.

'Long story short.' He ran his hand through his hair. 'I've been asked to do a photoshoot for someone at my mum's care home.'

'And where do I come in?' Eleanor asked cautiously.

'It's for this lady, Heidi. She must be eighty-something now, but when she was younger, she was a pageant queen. Super glam. I mean, still is for an old lady, you know? But anyway. She asked me if I could take a picture that made her feel beautiful again. Now, I can take the shot, I can set the room up, but I have no idea about fashion or hair or make-up. As you kindly reminded me with the old poncho situation, my fashion sense is less than socially acceptable.'

Eleanor snorted into her coffee.

'So, I was wondering if you'd help me? You and Sal

maybe? Even if all you did was point me in the right direction. This woman has been through a lot, and I really want this to work.'

Eleanor looked into his pleading eyes.

'I'm telling you now, Sal won't do it.'

'How come?' Fin tried to hide his surprise. He'd been surer of Sal saying yes than Eleanor.

'She can't stand old people.'

Fin's eyes widened in shock.

'I'm serious! Ever since her grandad passed away, she has a weird thing about death and people getting old. That woman is doing everything in her power to live for ever. It would freak her out too much being in the care home.'

'OK, so Sal's a no,' he confirmed. 'What about you?'

Eleanor fiddled with a crumb of cake on the table.

'Please,' he begged.

Eleanor cocked her head and gave Fin a look that he hadn't seen in years. It was a look that seemed to be equal parts exasperation and affection, and it was one that Eleanor had used regularly growing up.

'Please, please, *please*.' Fin pushed the plate of carrot cake towards her in a final act of persuasion.

'*Fine*,' she conceded at last.

'Yes!' He punched the air. 'Thank you. Thank you!' He breathed a sigh of relief. 'Do you want to go and meet her now?'

'Oh.' She looked a little startled.

'I mean, only if you have time,' he added casually, cursing his enthusiasm. 'Seize the day and all that.'

'Sure. Why not?' She shrugged. 'But it will cost you another coffee and maybe another slice of that carrot cake.'

'Whatever you want!' He beamed.

'Come on then.' She stood. 'Let's see what on earth you've roped me into.'

*

'Well, I won't say she's the friendliest old lady I've ever met,' Eleanor whispered, as they closed the door to Heidi's room behind them.

Fin was barely able to contain his laugh. 'Yeah, I probably should have warned you about that. She can be a bit . . . *cold*.'

'Cold?' Eleanor cried. 'She ignored me the entire time. Acted like I wasn't even there.'

'Actually,' Fin corrected, 'she did comment on your shoes, remember?'

Eleanor rolled her eyes. 'Yes, to tell me they were the only decent thing about my outfit!'

'Honesty isn't necessarily a bad thing, is it?' he joked.

She glowered at him hard. 'I thought you wanted my help?'

'I do. I desperately, *desperately* do,' he pleaded. 'Please don't be put off by the rudeness. I know deep down there's more to her than meets the eye. We just have to find a way to bring it out of her. And I don't know anyone better at doing that than you. You always see the best in people, Elles.'

She shuffled uncomfortably, her gaze dropping to the floor. 'Fine.'

The words were barely audible, but Fin snatched them jubilantly from the air and pulled her into a fierce hug. 'Thank you!'

He felt Eleanor stiffen. Suddenly the closeness felt too much. He dropped his arms and took a big step back, physically creating the distance that had carved itself into their friendship long ago.

'Do you have some time or do you need to rush off?' he asked awkwardly, praying the previous ease between them returned.

'No, I can stay a bit longer. Why?'

'Would you like to say hi to my mum?' He wasn't sure why but his stomach was alight with nerves.

She smiled at him, a full, open, real smile. 'I'd love to.'

'Cool.' He nodded towards the door at the end of the corridor. 'She's just down there.'

The pair made their way towards the room in silence.

'I don't know when the last time you saw her was . . .' Fin paused before knocking, his hand suspended in mid-air. 'But she looks pretty bad now. I mean, she's sick, I guess, so it's no surprise.' He was rambling, the words falling out of him uncontrollably. 'She's also got dementia, so don't worry if she's a bit confused or doesn't remember you or . . .'

Eleanor placed her hand gently on his arm. 'It's OK, Fin. I understand.'

Of course she understands.

A knowing look passed between them. He took a deep breath and knocked. 'Mum, it's me. Fin.' He opened the door. 'I have a surprise for you . . .'

'Oh, really?' her timid voice greeted him. 'It'd better not be any more food. Angela came yesterday and brought me half the bakery. I can't look at another cupcake.'

'It's better than cake, I promise.' He heard the padding of Eleanor's footsteps following him inside. 'I brought some-one with me.'

He stepped an inch to the side.

'Look, Mum, it's El—'

'*Eleanor!*' His mother's face creased in delight. 'Eleanor, my sweet girl! How lovely to see you.'

'Hi, Eileen.' Eleanor stepped forward.

'Come, come, sit. Let me get a closer look at you.'

Eleanor obliged and perched on the seat by his mother's bedside. 'Sorry I haven't come to say hi before.' Fin watched as she took his mother's hand in hers and held it softly.

'Don't be silly. A young girl like you must have a million other things to be getting on with than hanging around with the dead and decaying.'

Fin felt the atmosphere contract. Eleanor closed her eyes briefly.

'Especially after what you've been through,' his mother continued, patting Eleanor's hand.

'True.' Eleanor sat a little taller in her seat. 'But as my mother would say . . . us Levy girls are stronger than bad memories!' she trilled, impersonating her own mother perfectly.

Fin laughed but his mother stayed solemn, her milky eyes searching Eleanor's face. 'Come now, even Angela Levy gets upset when the occasion demands it. I'll be thinking of your father this Saturday. As I always do.'

'Thank you.' Eleanor's voice cracked in response. 'That means a lot.'

Fin could see the tears spilling from her eyes.

Would it be weird if he went to hold her? To follow his instincts and wrap his arms around her as she cried?

Yes.

Most definitely yes.

Fin knew that the odd joke shared between them did not erase the years of silence. That although comforting Eleanor was all he wanted to do, it wasn't his place any more.

Instead, as the memories swirled ominously around all of them, clawing at them, taunting them, he remained frozen, rooted to the spot in silence. He was very aware of saying the entirely wrong thing and so decided an absence of words was his only option.

'I can't believe it's been that long since he passed,' his mum bleated on. 'Years have a way of running away from me at the moment.'

'I know what you mean,' Eleanor replied glumly.

'Mum. Let's talk about something else, hey?' Fin stepped forward, at last finding the courage to speak.

'Sorry, dear.' His mum squeezed Eleanor's hand. 'I didn't mean to bring the mood down. Your father was a good man, that's all.'

'Thank you, Eileen.' She exhaled sharply. 'He really was.'

Then: Aged 20

Eleanor

At 2 a.m. her mother rang. Eleanor knew before she'd even answered the phone that it was time. It was as though her whole life had been slowly building up to this one moment. All week she'd lain awake at night, staring blankly at the ceiling, her thudding heartbeat counting down the seconds until her phone would ring. That had been the deal. The only way Eleanor would agree to go back to university and not give everything up to move back home. Her mother had to call the minute there were any signs. Even a whisper of her dad's health declining and Eleanor had to be told. No matter how late or early it was. Her mother had to call.

'Mum?' Eleanor was already forcing the tears back; her voice was strained with angst.

'Darling.' Her mother was so quiet it was painful to try and catch hold of her words. 'I think . . . I think you'd better come home as soon as you can.'

Eleanor felt her body collapse. The weight she had been carrying on her shoulders ever since they got the diagnosis was finally threatening to crush her.

'OK,' was all she could muster.

'I love you. Drive safe,' her mother replied, gasping for breath between the words.

Eleanor closed her eyes for a moment, to allow the enormity of what she was about to face to hit her. This was a moment that she would never forget. A moment that she knew would change her for ever. Strangely, it was also a moment she wanted to face alone. Just for a second.

Oliver stirred beside her. 'Eleanor?' he mumbled through layers of sleep. 'Is everything OK?'

'It's time,' she cried. The hard exterior finally cracked to allow the ocean of grief to pour out of her.

He sat upright and snapped into organization mode. 'I'll get the stuff together and we'll be on the road as soon as possible.' He squeezed her arm tightly, kissing the top of her head. 'Is there anyone else we need to call?' he asked, standing up quickly and grabbing their pre-packed suitcases.

Eleanor shook the image of Fin from her mind.

'No, not yet. Let's get home first.'

*

Her dad passed away at 9 a.m. the next morning.

In the end he went peacefully. Silently. Almost gratefully. The entire family had made it to his bedside in time to hold his hands and love him right until the moment the last breath left his lungs.

She had assumed that she'd break down. That she'd scream and cry, raging at the cruelty of the world and the injustice of it all. Her father. How could they take her dad? The kindest, most joyful man she'd ever known. He didn't deserve to die. He didn't deserve to be eaten from the inside out by tumours. But now he was gone and Eleanor didn't make a sound.

Not as he passed away. Not during the excruciating silence afterwards. Not even that night, as Oliver clung to her body in her childhood bed, rocking her gently to sleep. All Eleanor felt was empty. Hollow. Tears wouldn't bring back the man she loved. Screaming wouldn't change anything. It was now a case of silent survival.

'So, the funeral is arranged for next week,' her mother stated at breakfast the next morning. 'Freya, you'll be doing a reading if you're still happy to?' She was robotic, listing the tasks as though she were planning her weekly trip to Tesco, not arranging the final farewell to the love of her life.

Freya nodded her head.

'Eleanor, have you spoken to Fin yet?' Angela reached out a hand and placed it gently on top of hers.

'No. I'm speaking to him later.'

'Do you think he'll come back?' Freya's eyes were full of hope. She loved him almost as much as Eleanor did.

'I don't know. It's a long way and tickets will be expensive.' Eleanor's heart dropped further and further down into her stomach with every word. True, they hadn't spoken that much over the past couple of months, but what with time zones and university work and her dad, organizing calls seemed somewhat impossible. It didn't matter, though. She couldn't imagine burying her father without her best friend by her side, but at the same time she knew how important this trip was for him. Every cell of her body was trying to prepare herself to be let down.

Expect nothing.

'Either way, you'll have me.' Oliver shifted his seat closer, throwing his arm protectively across her shoulders. 'I'll be by your side the entire time.' He puffed out his chest like a proud little bird.

Freya raised her eyebrows in disapproval. She knew, like Eleanor, that it wasn't the same.

'The longer you leave it, the harder and more expensive it will be for him to get back.' Freya forced another spoonful of cornflakes into her mouth and eyed Eleanor knowingly.

'I know, I'll do it tonight,' she snapped. 'Anyway . . .' She forced her voice to be as upbeat as possible, changing the subject quickly. 'Is there anything else you need me to do today, Mum, apart from sort the flowers?'

'No, I think that's all for now, darling,' her mother whispered, her salty tears making tiny ripples as they fell into her cold cup of coffee.

*

The days leading up to the funeral had passed her by in a blur. She thought on the actual day the reality might hit her, but she'd felt numb from the moment she woke up that morning, her fingers buttoning up her black dress without conscious thought or feeling. She'd let her mother brush her hair and cry tears into her tangled curls. She was a shell, going through the motions without really living a minute of it. From the second they'd stepped out of the front door, Oliver had held her hand, squeezing it so tightly she was certain he was trying to force the blood from her veins. Still, she felt nothing.

'Where's Fin?' Freya whispered anxiously, her head moving wildly around, scanning the swelling congregation for even a hint of his face.

'I don't know,' Eleanor mumbled. 'I haven't heard from

him since yesterday.' She didn't dare look behind. His absence would be too painful to register.

'We really need to make a start,' Oliver stated bluntly, checking his watch. 'Eleanor, maybe we should just accept he's not coming and get on with things?'

'Get on with things? How can you be so heartless? Fin is family,' she spat.

'I'm sorry, you know I didn't mean it like that.' He gripped her hand even tighter. 'It's just, the longer we leave it, the more painful it might be for your mum.'

Eleanor turned her head. There at the end of the row stood her mother. A faded outline of the vibrant woman she knew, cloaked in layers of black chiffon and heartbreak. She knew she was being selfish. How could she prolong this any longer?

'You're right. Let's start.' She dropped his hand and hung her head.

She kept her eyes down for as much of the ceremony as she could. Friends and family all desperately tried to catch her attention, attempting to pass their apologies across to her through a look. She didn't want it. She couldn't stand their pity. All she wanted was her best friend next to her, telling her over and over that it was going to be OK. That she'd get through this. That someday it wouldn't hurt as much. But all she had was the absence of him in her heart.

Suddenly the doors of the church opened. Eleanor's head jerked up instinctively and through the dazzling sunlight she saw someone enter. Surely it wasn't . . .? Her heart tripped over itself in anticipation. Had he come?

'Who is it?' she whispered to Oliver.

'I don't know.' He hadn't even bothered to look back.

Eleanor tried to blink the newcomer into focus. Hushed

whispers and the sounds of turning heads echoed throughout the vast church. Their intrigue sent ripples through the crowd. She craned her neck but still couldn't see. Oliver yanked on her hand.

'Your sister is about to speak. Concentrate, Eleanor,' he hissed in her ear. 'I'll go and see what's happening.'

She grabbed his hand, practically tearing it from him. 'If it's Fin, bring him here, will you?'

He jerked his head slightly in irritation and then smiled softly. 'Of course I will. Now stay here, I'll be back in a second.' He planted a dry kiss on her cheek and disappeared to the back of the church.

Eleanor turned her attention back to the front, where her little sister was braced, ready to read, her expression fixed in utter concentration. Eleanor knew it was taking every bit of strength to stop the tears from taking over her. Pride swelled in her chest. How blessed she was to share blood with such brave women.

Oliver returned just as she finished. Eleanor whipped her head around, certain her eyes would find the familiar green of Fin's, but her heart cracked in disappointment.

'It was a mistake.'

'What?' She felt the panic seize her throat.

'It was someone who came in by accident. They've gone now,' he stated coldly.

But Eleanor couldn't seem to rest. She peered behind her, willing the mourning faces to part so she could get a clear view of the door, but there it stood, firmly closed and without a Fin in sight.

'I'm sorry,' Oliver whispered in her ear. 'But I'm here. I'll always be here for you.'

Eleanor pulled her hand away from his and folded her

arms across her chest protectively. She watched the rest of the ceremony numbly. The words and songs barely registered as they washed over her. She allowed herself to be marched out of the church to the grave. She watched as they buried her sweet, beloved dad until he was no more than a mound of soil. She sat in the car and let her sister weep into her shoulder, hardly feeling the racking sobs of her tiny body against her own. Oliver's firm grip remained on her hand the entire time.

'Eleanor, you need to call the caterers and tell them there's traffic. We're going to be late.' Oliver's voice cut across her clouded consciousness.

'Huh?' She turned to look at him.

'The caterers,' he repeated. 'You need to call them; I left my phone at home. I'd ask your mother but I don't think . . . I think it's easier if you do it.'

'Oh.' She reached into her handbag and pulled out her phone. Her heart stopped.

From: Finley Taylor.

I'm sorry, Elles. All flights to London are cancelled, I'm not going to be able to make it. I tried, I really did. Please forgive me. x

Only then did she finally begin to cry.

Now

Eleanor

The week leading up to her dad's anniversary passed by, as it always did, at an alarming rate. One minute it was Monday evening and Eleanor was researching traditional 1950s pageant gowns for Heidi, the next it was Friday night and she was being handed a large glass of wine by Sal in the pub.

'How are you doing?' her friend asked. 'This weekend is a bit of a tough one, isn't it?'

'You can say that again.' She took a sip of wine and swallowed her sadness down along with it. 'I'm doing all right though. And besides, my mum's invited Fin to the lunch so at least that will be something to distract her.'

'Distractions are good . . .' Sal murmured, a note of scepticism creeping into her voice.

'Why are you looking at me like that?'

'I'm not looking at you like anything.'

'Yes, you are.'

Sal shrugged innocently. 'You just seem to be spending a lot of time with someone you were adamant on avoiding a few weeks ago.'

'Not really,' Eleanor replied defensively. 'My mum invited him to this, not me.'

'And then there's that weird old-people thing you're doing.'

'The *photoshoot* is a one-off favour.'

'All right, fine. If you say so.' Sal held her hands up. 'Also, I still don't understand why anyone would *choose* to hang out with old people. Are you sure there's not something else in it for you?' She winked.

'I'm sure.' Eleanor let out a little laugh. 'You know you will be an old person too one day?'

Sal looked at her aghast. 'Not if I can help it!'

'Hmm,' Eleanor mused. 'Whatever you say.'

'Also, speaking of getting old, I still can't believe I have my mum's seventieth coming up. I'm so pissed it's on the same day as Laura's wedding. I really wanted to go.'

Sal's words hit Eleanor like a punch in the stomach.

No.

Oh sweet Jesus, no.

'Eleanor, what's wrong?' She felt Sal's hand reach for her. 'You look like you've seen a ghost.'

'Laura's wedding,' Eleanor managed weakly.

'Yes?'

'Oliver.' The name sent nausea through her body.

'What about him?' Sal's confused face came sharply into focus.

'I haven't told Laura about Oliver. She thinks he's coming to the wedding with me. This is a disaster. I can't turn up and sit next to an empty place. It will be too late to cancel; the wedding is in like two weeks' time or something ridiculous!' Eleanor garbled, the panic pushing all of her thoughts out of her mouth uncensored.

'It's actually next weekend, but that's by the by,' Sal

corrected. 'Eleanor, don't worry. We will sort it.' The calming, steady voice of her friend soothed her slightly. 'I will sort it.'

Eleanor gulped her wine and watched as Sal pulled out her phone and began typing furiously. 'I'm emailing her now and explaining everything, just sit and keep drinking. Actually no, maybe order some food.' She eyed her warily. 'We don't want you getting drunk and disorderly.'

Eleanor's mind was racing. How could she have forgotten? How stupid could she have been?

'Done!' Sal announced. 'Honestly, Eleanor, stop *worrying*. It will be fine. It's not a big deal. If anyone can handle this, it's Laura.' Sal sat back and threw a packet of peanuts at her. 'Now, eat these while I order us some proper food.'

Sal was right: between them Eleanor wouldn't trust anyone else to help her in a crisis. Laura had been one of the senior managers in the office when she first joined the company. She was cut-throat, highly demanding and forthright, but with a heart of pure gold. Sal had introduced the pair and they had instantly clicked. Laura had left the company nearly two years ago but they had all stayed in touch.

'OK,' she mumbled. 'OK, fine.'

Eleanor allowed her breathing to return to a somewhat steady rhythm, but her eyes kept anxiously watching Sal's phone for any signs of Laura's reply.

Luckily, she only had to wait ten minutes. Sal grabbed the phone before Eleanor could reach across the table.

'Jesus, woman. Give me a second.' Her eyes flickered back and forth. 'It's fine. Laura sends her love and can't wait to give you a huge hug at the wedding. She says you're better than any man and she hopes you're doing OK. She also said that because it's so close to the day, they have already ordered and paid for Oliver's meal, et cetera, but they can delete his name from everything and you can bring a plus one instead,' Sal read aloud. 'See, I told you it would be fine.' She passed the phone to Eleanor as proof.

'Well, it's not totally fine,' she remarked. 'I need to find myself a plus one!'

'Hmmm, let me think.' Sal grinned. 'If *only* there was a deliciously handsome man who you were dating that you could bring.'

Eleanor threw a peanut at Sal, who deftly swiped it away with her hand. 'I'm not bringing Ben! It's way too soon. I'll ask Freya.'

'Fine. Have it your way.' She shrugged.

'Speaking of men . . . how is it going with that guy?' Eleanor scolded herself for not asking sooner.

Sal fiddled with the label on the wine bottle coyly. 'I don't know. I think it's going well . . .'

'That's a good thing, isn't it?'

'I guess.'

'You guess?' Eleanor pressed.

'Yeah, but . . .' Sal stopped picking the label and looked at her square in the eye. 'I think I really like him.'

Eleanor couldn't help but burst out laughing. 'And that's a bad thing?'

'No,' Sal huffed, tearing off strips of label and pulling them anxiously apart. 'I'm not used to it, that's all.'

'I hear you.' Eleanor took the paper from her hand and tossed it aside. 'Honestly, I get it. But what is it that you've told me about a million times these past few months?'

Sal shrugged, feigning ignorance.

Eleanor drew her eyebrows together and sat up stiffly, doing her very best Sal impression. 'Get out of your comfort zone, Eleanor.'

'Oi. I do not sound like that.' Sal smirked. 'And besides, you *do* need to get out of your comfort zone. I'm always uncomfortable, I don't think I can handle any more.'

Eleanor refused to let Sal divert the conversation back to her. 'You can. If anyone can, it's you.' She flicked a rogue scrap of paper across the table at her friend. 'Now . . . are you going to tell me about this man or not?'

Sal smiled shyly, refilling her glass of wine. 'What do you want to know?'

'Erm, how about *everything*!' Eleanor cried.

'His name is Paul, he's forty-two, has his own consultancy business, lives in Wimbledon.' Sal reeled off his credentials formally.

'Come *on*, Sal. I need more than this. I want a photo; I want all the details of the dates. You can't hold out on me.'

Sal sat back and folded her arms. 'Fine, I'll tell you anything you want to know, if you go and order us another bottle?'

'Deal!' Eleanor stood up immediately, allowing the thoughts of her dad to momentarily take a back seat.

*

The drive to their mum's on Sunday had been conducted in near silence. Neither Freya nor Eleanor felt like talking. What was there to say? Besides, they knew they would need to save as much of their energy as possible for handling their mother.

'Are you ready?' Eleanor turned anxiously to face Freya as they slowly dragged their feet up to the front door.

Freya took a deep breath. 'As I'll ever be.' She reached out and squeezed Eleanor's hand briefly. 'We'll be OK, we have each other. And Fin.'

'True.' Eleanor's anxiety settled momentarily at the thought of Fin's presence. Slowly, she knocked on the door. 'She won't be too wild with guests around.'

'Fin's hardly a guest,' Freya shot back.

All of a sudden, the pink front door swung open to reveal their mother, standing and smiling with her arms wide open. 'My babies. It feels like a lifetime since I last saw you both.' She pulled them into one of her fierce embraces and held on tightly.

'OK, Mum, you're hurting me now,' Freya groaned.

'Sorry, sweetie, I forget my own strength sometimes.' Their mother released her grip and smiled adoringly at them.

'How are you?' Eleanor asked tentatively.

'Fine. Fine.' She waved her hands as though her grief were nothing more than an irksome fly. 'Come in. Lunch is nearly ready and Fin's already here,' Angela stated, before turning around and disappearing into the kitchen.

Slowly Eleanor hung up her coat and walked into the kitchen. A photograph of her dad had been placed proudly in the centre of the table. God, she missed him.

'Right, come on now, sit yourselves down. We have a lot of food to get through.' Her mum laughed, unloading dish after dish on to the table.

'Hey.' Fin waved at her from across the table. The look of relief on his face at their arrival was undeniable. She knew how it felt to be on the receiving end of her mother's mania. Support was a necessity.

'Woah, how long did this all take?' Freya marvelled at the piles of food on the table.

'Oh, it was nothing. You know I like to make your dad's favourites and, my word, did he have a lot of favourites!' She chortled.

Eleanor's heart shook once again at the memory of her father.

'Fin, are you OK there?' Angela fussed.

'Fine, thank you. It all looks wonderful, Angela,' he replied.

'Sit, girls, please!' their mother insisted. 'And help yourselves,' she said, piling Eleanor's plate with potato salad and shepherd's pie.

'Thanks, Mum, I can do it.' Eleanor moved her plate away ever so slightly.

'Don't be silly. Just because you're not skeletal these days, doesn't mean I'm not going to feed you up.' Angela heaped spoonfuls of mashed potato on to her plate. 'You should have *seen* her at her worst, Fin. She was disappearing before my eyes. Terrible to see, absolutely shocking,' her mother continued, as though Eleanor had in fact already disappeared. 'I kept telling her, men don't like bones! If she's going to get herself back out there and dating, she needs to plump herself up again. Am I right?'

Fin forced a giant forkful of steak and kidney pie into his mouth. Eleanor knew he was trying to avoid any wrong moves. All he could do was nod in agreement.

'See, Eleanor! I know you don't like to believe me, but Fin agrees. Now have another helping, will you?'

Eleanor was about to protest when Fin opened his mouth and mumbled something inaudible.

'What was that, dear?' Angela asked. 'I couldn't hear you over the pie in your mouth.'

'Sorry.' Fin swallowed hard and cleared his throat. 'I said . . . I think she looks great. As she is.'

Eleanor blushed with embarrassment.

'Aren't you a total sweetheart.' Angela pinched Fin's

cheeks. 'But there's no need to lie to make her feel better. Honesty is the best policy in these situations, I find.'

Eleanor stole a glance at Fin, whose cheeks were the colour of his hair.

'I wasn't lying,' he mumbled under his breath, and Eleanor flashed him a grateful smile.

He's sticking up for you.

Say something!

But Eleanor remained resolute in her silence, slowly making indents into the mountain of food on her plate. Everyone seemed to follow suit, speaking only to pass more dishes or refill glasses.

Angela cleared her throat ten minutes later. 'Now, are we all done eating? You know I always like to say a few words on this day to remember your father.' She lightly touched her fingertips to the photograph, wiping a smear of gravy from the frame.

Eleanor inhaled sharply and closed her eyes. She felt her sister's body tighten next to her. She could hear Fin shuffling uncomfortably in his chair.

'He was the love of my life,' their mother declared, as though she were addressing the funeral party once again. 'There was never a moment that I didn't want to be near him, and he gave me the greatest gifts I could have hoped for . . . my two girls. Although he's gone, I think of him every day. I miss him more than words could ever express, but Richard, we love you. We always have and we always will.'

The tears were silently snaking down Eleanor's cheeks. Her throat felt so tight, it hurt to breathe. She didn't dare look up. She didn't want Fin to see her cry. In fact, she didn't want anyone to see her cry.

'Thanks, Mum,' Freya mumbled, once again proving herself to be the stronger sister. 'To Dad?' She raised her glass in the air.

'To Dad,' they all chimed, Eleanor still fixing her gaze anywhere but on the people around her.

Angela stood up suddenly. 'Right, who fancies dessert?'

'I'll sort it,' Eleanor replied flatly, wiping her cheeks with her sleeves. 'You've done enough, Mum.'

'I'll help,' Fin volunteered, jumping up from his seat.

'No, Fin, you're our guest, sit down. Freya can help her sister,' Angela insisted.

'Honestly, please let me. It's the least I can do.' He was already over by the oven before Angela could say anything more. Eleanor had turned her back to him and was scraping the dirty plates into the bin. He shuffled over quietly. 'Are you OK?' he whispered.

She turned to face him, catching her puffy-eyed reflection in the oven door.

'I'm fine.' She replied, willing the tremor in her voice to steady itself.

'Are you really?' he asked again, his voice so soft and warm that for a moment Eleanor nearly forgot herself and burst into tears on his shoulder.

'Thank you but honestly, I'm OK.' She composed herself slightly. 'Anyway, how are *you*? I admire your courage for being here,' she tried to joke.

'I'm good.' He grabbed the empty plates and began loading them into the dishwasher.

'You won't be saying that after the six desserts you've got coming your way.'

'Six!' he cried, dropping one of the forks on the floor. 'Surely there aren't six?'

'There are indeed. It's the same every year. Treacle tart, apple crumble, chocolate cake, pavlova, trifle and profiteroles.' She opened the oven door and pulled out two of the aforementioned puddings. 'All of my dad's favourites.'

'Wow. I mean, good job your dad had amazing taste in desserts, but seriously? How are we supposed to get through all of them?' he asked, the look of fear growing heavier on his face.

'It's a marathon, not a sprint. Here, take these. I'll get the rest.'

Eleanor couldn't help but laugh as she pulled a gigantic pavlova, trifle and mountain of profiteroles out of the fridge and placed them on the table; Fin looked as though he were close to tears at the sight of them.

'Thank you, darling.' Angela placed her cool hand on Eleanor's cheek affectionately. 'Now, Fin, how is that photography project of yours going?'

'It's good actually. Eleanor and I are going to be shooting a lady called Heidi this week. I was thinking Saturday if that works for you, Elles?'

'Sure,' she replied casually. 'Shit, wait, no!' she swore, dropping the apple crumble on to the table with a loud thud.

'Eleanor! Language. What kind of a lady uses such profanity?' her mother chided. 'And mind my crumble, please.'

'Sorry. Eurgh, I totally forgot.' She rubbed her face in frustration.

'What?' Freya asked.

'I've got to go to Laura's wedding on Saturday and I need to find a plus one. I forgot to tell her that Oliver and I split up.' She added the last bit quietly.

'Forgot?' Angela queried. 'Or conveniently held off telling her in the hope you would be reunited?'

'No,' she snapped back in offence. 'I genuinely forgot.'

'Good.' Her mother nodded in satisfaction. 'Because as much as I am desperate to see you wed and content, he wasn't right for you.'

'Thank you for that,' Eleanor mumbled through gritted teeth.

'And anyway, how on earth did you forget such a crucial piece of information?' her mum continued.

'I had a lot of things going on, OK?' Her voice was rising. 'Don't you think I haven't beaten myself up over it already? I don't need you joining in too.'

Angela bristled slightly and grabbed Fin's plate. 'No wonder you can't find a plus one with an attitude like that,' she remarked, loading his plate with spoonfuls of trifle.

'Are you free, Frey?' Eleanor begged, ignoring her mother's slight. 'Please tell me you're free?'

'This Saturday?' Freya winced. 'I'm sorry. You know I would, but Sam . . .' She wrung her hands anxiously. 'Sam has something planned for our anniversary. I think he's taking me away for the weekend.'

'Isn't that *sweet* of him, darling! Goodness, what a gentleman.' Angela beamed. 'Doesn't Sam have any single friends he could loan out to Eleanor for the night?'

'Absolutely not!' both sisters said in unison.

'Is Sal not around?' Fin suggested.

'Nope. She can't come.'

'What about Be—' But before Fin could finish, Eleanor had kicked him hard under the table.

'Well, what a shame, dear. It looks like you'll have to go by yourself. Luckily you had Kate's wedding as a practice run!' Angela patted Eleanor's arm patronizingly. 'Now, Frey, tell me . . . where do you think Sam is whisking you off to?'

'I'll come.'

Eleanor raised her head sharply.

'What did you say, Fin darling?' Angela asked.

'I said, I'll come. To the wedding. If you want.'

The words seemed to linger in the air between them all, everyone's eyes fixed on Fin's face, which seemed to be turning a very radiant shade of beetroot.

'Only if you need someone, of course. It's just . . . I'm free on Saturday, that's all,' he mumbled.

'Oh.' Angela placed her hand on her chest. 'How *lovely* of you, Fin! Isn't that sweet? Are you sure you'd want to give up a precious weekend like that?'

Fin shrugged, fiddling with a soggy piece of sponge cake on his plate.

'It's fine. Like I said, I really don't mind.' He glanced up at Eleanor, who hadn't yet been able to form a sentence in her mind.

'Well . . .' Angela shot Eleanor a pointed look. 'Are you going to thank Fin and accept his kind offer?'

Time seemed to slow to a painful crawl. What the hell was she supposed to do? Surely he didn't *actually* want to come to a wedding with her? Eleanor felt the eyes that had been locked on to Fin's face slowly turn their attention to her.

Say something.

Anything!

'Erm, thanks, Fin.' Her cheeks were starting to match the colour of his own flaming-red face. 'Only if you're sure?'

'One hundred per cent.' He nodded. 'You know me and weddings,' he joked awkwardly.

God help me . . .

'Ah. I remember my wedding day like it was yesterday,' Angela said dreamily.

Freya rolled her eyes and shoved a profiterole into her mouth. 'We've heard this a million times,' she moaned.

'So once more won't kill you then, will it?' Angela smirked. 'It was 1979 . . .'

Fin

The rest of the afternoon at Angela's had gone fairly seamlessly, although Fin couldn't remember ever eating so much in his life. The next morning he'd woken with a stomach still full of cooking and a head still full of regret about his outburst. By the time he'd got to the home that afternoon, he was all but tempted to text Eleanor and retract his offer.

She said yes.

Get over it.

'Hi, Fin.' Nurse Clara's customary greeting welcomed him into reception.

'Hey, how's it going?' He could sense things were a little hectic, from her ruffled hair and manic smile.

'Busy,' she confirmed. 'I'll pop by in a bit, but the last time I checked in your mum was fast asleep. Hopefully she'll come around soon.'

Fin nodded and made his way down the corridor, leaving Nurse Clara to the mountain of paperwork that sat piled up on the desk. Unsurprisingly, his mum was still out for the count and didn't even stir as he settled himself down in the chair by her bed. Fin looked around the room listlessly. He wasn't very good at sitting still without distraction, especially not when confronted with so many unwanted thoughts and memories.

Leave, she'll never know you were here.

Fin rose from his seat and then planted himself firmly back down. He couldn't go, not without saying hello. His past few visits had already been shamefully short, and after seeing Rudi's quick demise Fin was very conscious of how cruel time could be.

Put the TV on then.

I can't, it will wake her up!

Well, think of something . . .

Fin leant into the chair, balancing his weight on two legs. He rocked back and forth for a while, contemplating all the other things he could be doing with his time.

Eating biscuits and watching Netflix?

Hardly important business.

This was why he liked to be busy. Distraction drowned out the noise inside his head; without it, the voices could become overwhelmingly loud. Fin scanned the room in search of some form of entertainment. His eyes quickly passed over his parents' wedding photograph, allowing the flicker of resentment to burn freely. He craned his neck and saw another photograph tucked behind it. A small bundle of flesh with a mass of ginger hair was peeking out from the glass. Fin's heart leapt with recognition and he was about to reach over and grab it when he noticed, next to the pictures, a weathered and worn-out puzzle book. He carefully plucked it from the bedside table.

'Aha! You should keep me busy for a while,' he muttered under his breath, flicking the pages open to a blank crossword.

'Four down . . .' he murmured, lost in thought. 'Where gardening could be child's play.' Fin flicked his pen against the front of his teeth. 'Oh!' he exclaimed. 'I got you. Nursery.'

A croaking noise pulled his attention away from the puzzle. His mum was stirring, stretching her withered limbs and opening her eyes. The second she saw him, she gasped.

'Are you all right?' He edged closer. She looked too fragile to even touch.

'You came,' she breathed.

'Of course I did. Are you OK?' He tried to assess her for any potential damage.

'You came back, Brian.' She sighed with relief. 'I knew you would.'

Fin jerked his head back.

What?

'Brian.' She shot out her bony hand and grasped his wrist tightly. 'I've missed you. Please don't go again.'

Fin looked around for any source of help. What the hell was he supposed to do in this situation?

'I'm not Br—' he stammered, her grip on his arm tightening.

'I know you say you love her. I know you say this time is different, but please. You have to stay with us,' she pleaded. 'Fin needs us. Don't you see that?'

'You're confused,' he whispered, fighting the urge to pull her hands off him. 'I need to get help.'

'*No!*' she screeched, her eyes blazing with panic. 'Don't leave. You can stay with her. I don't care, just don't leave us, *please*. Not until Fin is at least old enough to move out.' Tears were falling down her cheeks. 'He needs us more than ever. A united front, Brian. That's what he needs. We can be a family again, I know we can. We've done it before, right?

I've turned a blind eye for the sake of our son before. Can't you let me do it again?'

Fin felt as though his heart were breaking for the both of them. He was rooted to the spot, floored by the wave of questions that assaulted him.

'Brian.' She shook his arm. 'Say something. Say you'll stay?'

Suddenly he snapped back into life. 'Mum, it's me, Fin.' His voice was shaking despite his best efforts. 'I'm going to get some help, OK? I need you to wait right here.' He slowly unpeeled her fingers from his wrist.

'*No*,' she screamed again. 'Brian, come back.'

Fin turned and practically sprinted from the room, unable to stand the look on her face any longer.

'Don't leave me, Brian,' she wailed. 'I'll be better. I'll do better.'

He slammed the door behind him and hurtled down the corridor, the cries of his mother echoing loudly through the home.

'Nurse Clara,' he shouted as he burst into reception. 'It's my mum. She . . .' He shook his head. 'She needs help.'

'It's OK, Fin.' She sprang into action immediately, coming round the other side of the desk and placing a firm, calming hand on his back. 'Wait right here. I'll go to her now.'

Fin shook his head even harder, wishing he could shed the last few moments completely. 'I can't stay here.' His heart was racing and his head was whirring. He needed to go. To think. To scream. To be anywhere but here. 'I have to go.' He stood up and headed towards the exit.

'Fin, please wait,' Nurse Clara called after him.

'I'm sorry.' He didn't even bother to look back. 'I can't. I can't do this again.'

Then: Aged 14

Fin

'So, is Dad going to be gracing us with his presence tonight, or will this be night three of him working late?' Fin asked sarcastically as he sat down for dinner.

'Don't be like that, Finley. You know his job is high-pressure, especially at the moment,' his mother replied, anxiously chewing her lip.

'Nice to see you're both still sticking to the same pathetic cover story.' He sighed, reaching over and helping himself to a slice of pizza. His mum said nothing, but simply sat and stared at the clock whilst pushing her salad around her plate.

'Yeah, my day was great, thanks for asking,' Fin continued through a mouthful of cheese. 'School was fine. Got top marks for my art assignment, not that you give a shit.'

'Don't swear, please.'

'Why? Dad does. He practically swears every other word,' he remarked bitterly. Fin knew he was being especially difficult tonight, but he found he couldn't help himself.

'Yes, but your father is an adult. And like I said, he's under a lot of pressure at the moment.'

'Oh yes, poor him. I forgot how difficult life must be for *him*,' Fin snarled. Just as his mother was about to speak, the front door opened.

'Brian!' his mother called, practically leaping from her seat in excitement. 'Brian, have you eaten? I've just served up dinner!'

'Jesus, Eileen, it's nearly nine o'clock. I told you not to wait for me,' the gruff voice of his father barked out from the hallway.

'I know, but Fin wasn't hungry earlier so we waited a little later to eat tonight,' she stuttered pathetically.

The sound of his mother's lies made the blood boil furiously under Fin's skin. He didn't like how she was when his dad was away, but he absolutely *hated* what she became when he was around.

'Bloody kids. If you let him think he can do what he wants, Eileen, he'll take the piss.'

'It's fine. Come on, come and eat.' His mother re-entered the kitchen, a feverish smile on her face.

Fin shoved the last piece of pizza into his mouth and stood up. There was no way he was going to be able to spend even a minute sitting at the same table as his father. Not tonight. The anger was already threatening to overwhelm him.

'Where do you think you're going, kid?' his dad boomed, his large frame swaggering through the doorway.

'To my room,' Fin stated flatly, making his way over to the dishwasher.

'And who gave you permission to leave the table?'

'I did.' Fin turned and stared at his dad. All six foot four of him, with his large muscular frame and thatch of bright ginger hair. There was a ruddiness to his cheeks, which Fin knew meant he'd been drinking. There was also a wry smile on his face, which Fin also knew meant trouble.

'And I suppose you think you're the big man of the house these days, do you?'

Don't rise to it.

Don't let him get to you.

'Do you?' his dad pressed.

'Well, if there's a vacancy then I suppose someone has to fill it.' Fin shrugged, shoving his dirty plate into the dishwasher and slamming it shut.

'What do you mean by that?'

Fin made to leave but his dad side-stepped to block his way.

'I'm talking to you, Finley. Answer me.'

'Brian, come on, let the boy leave. He's probably got homework to do,' his mum bleated meekly from behind. 'Just sit down and have some food with m—'

'I don't want any of this crap food,' his dad thundered, his small watery eyes still fixed on Fin's face. 'I want to know what our good-for-nothing son meant by what he said.'

Fin took a deep breath and began to count to ten in his head. It was something Eleanor had taught him to do whenever he felt stressed or overwhelmed. He closed his eyes and brought the image of her face to his mind. His best friend. The only person in the whole world who seemed to care that he existed these days.

One . . . two . . . three . . . four.

'Are you stupid, boy?'

Five . . . six . . . sev—

'Oi!' Suddenly his dad's face was so close to Fin's that he could smell the toxic mix of alcohol, cigarettes and a strange floral perfume on his skin.

'*What?*' Fin's eyes flashed open. 'What do you want me to

221

say?' he hollered, all semblance of control disappearing at once.

'How dare you shout at me! Show some goddam *respect*, will you?' his dad spat, showering Fin in tiny flecks of sour saliva.

'*Respect?*' Fin cried. 'You don't even know the meaning of the word. You'll get my respect when you stop treating Mum like a doormat. Staying out late "working".' Fin laughed sarcastically. 'What kind of work are you doing that requires you to come home reeking of booze and cigarettes and other women's perfume?' He could feel the heat rising from his skin as the pain poured out of him uncontrollably. 'I am not a fucking child any more. I see through your pathetic lies, and even though Mum is too in love with you to do anything about it, I'm not. I'm sick of it. I'm sick of *you*.'

Fin could see his dad's jaw clenching as the veins on his forehead rose threateningly to the surface.

'Get. Out.' His dad's voice dropped to almost a whisper.

Fin cocked his head and took one long look at his dad. The man he had adored and looked up to for so much of his life, now nothing but an embarrassing, lying fraud.

'Happily,' Fin snarled, pushing past and running out of the front door.

Now

Eleanor

It was a long time since Eleanor had taken a day off mid-week. When they'd first started working in London, she and Oliver had often called in sick and spent an impromptu day in bed together. Sometimes, if they were really feeling wild, they'd get on a train and take a random trip somewhere for a couple of days. But then things changed, their jobs became more serious . . . he became more serious. After the fifteenth lecture on responsibility and the importance of clean attendance records, Eleanor had stopped the attempts at spontaneity and reserved her holidays for Christmas and summer only. Now look at her. Setting an 'out of office' on a Tuesday evening with absolutely no care in the world.

So you can go and visit an old people's home.

Totally rock and roll!

'You coming?' Sal called impatiently.

'Yeah, give me two seconds,' Eleanor replied, shutting down her laptop and shoving it into her bag. It was rare for the pair of them to be leaving the office at the same time and

Eleanor knew Sal was desperate to get out. Pre-8 p.m. exits were once in a blue moon for her.

'Come *on*.' Sal looped her arm through Eleanor's and practically dragged her to the lifts. 'I don't want anyone from accounting to see me, otherwise I'll be here until gone midnight.' She looked around shiftily.

'I don't know how you do it. I know I say it all the time, but it still baffles me. Does Paul mind that you work late?' Eleanor asked as they stepped quickly into the lift.

'He doesn't have a choice.' Sal shrugged. 'Besides, he works similar hours so it doesn't matter that much.'

'The perfect match,' she remarked.

'Yeah, something like that.' Sal laughed. 'Although he doesn't have an Eleanor to keep him sane every day like I do.' She flashed her a grin.

'Not every day.' Eleanor grimaced. 'Remember, I'm not in tomorrow,' she reminded Sal, as they stepped out of the lift and into the foyer.

Sal's face crumpled in disappointment. 'I still think it's weird you're voluntarily using your annual leave for something like that.'

'I might as well. I've got about three weeks' holiday to take.' Eleanor paused. 'And now my romantic trip to France is off the cards, I might as well use it.'

Eleanor's feelings towards Oliver had mellowed significantly in the past few months, but the thought of their two-week trip to France immediately sent a sharp pang of sadness through her chest.

Sal's eyes narrowed in disdain. 'Fucking Oliver,' she spat.

'Exactly.' Eleanor walked briskly, trying to keep up with Sal's long strides. 'Anyway, you know the company policy.

"Use it or lose it." So I might as well get rid of a day where I can.'

'Fair enough. I dread to think how much I've got left over.'

'Well, maybe *Paul* will decide to whisk you away on a romantic weekend sometime soon,' Eleanor teased.

Sal pushed her away gently, her cheeks already reddening. 'I could say the same for you and Benny boy, couldn't I?'

'Ew, I told you before, don't call him that.' Eleanor cringed.

'All right, stop being dramatic. Are you going to his tonight?'

'Yeah.' Eleanor stopped outside the tube station. 'But I'm going to get the bus, so this is where I leave you.' She pulled her friend into a tight hug.

'OK, well *enjoy* tonight.' Sal winked. 'And try to have fun tomorrow with the oldies.'

'Don't call them that!' Eleanor chastised. 'I'll be sure to give you a full debrief on Thursday.'

'Can't bloody wait.' Sal rolled her eyes, disappearing into the throng of commuters descending into the station.

*

It took her a lot longer to get to Ben's than she'd anticipated; the rush-hour traffic was particularly abysmal and she may or may not have got off at the wrong bus stop. It didn't help that her bag was so heavy, containing not only her laptop and overnight clothes, but also all of the stuff she needed for the shoot tomorrow. She hoped Heidi liked the dress she'd found. To see a smile, even just a hint of one, on her face would be like a gold medal for Eleanor.

'I wish you'd told me you have the day off tomorrow,' Ben called over his shoulder. 'I would have joined you and we could have done something fun.'

Eleanor stood and sipped her tea, watching as he moved expertly around the kitchen. 'Sorry, it was a bit of a last-minute thing. I'm helping Fin with this photoshoot and we were meant to do it this Saturday, but then I had this wedding drama so couldn't. He wants to get it done soon in case . . .' The image of Fin's frail mum drifted across her mind. 'Well, before he goes back to America.'

Ben clattered and clanged various pots and pans, but Eleanor knew she had his full attention. That was the wonderful thing about Ben, she noticed; he could multi-task better than anyone she knew.

'His mum not doing great?' he asked, plating up a huge bowl of spaghetti carbonara. 'Please, sit.' He nodded towards the dining table. 'I'm pretty much done here.'

Eleanor stayed standing; she liked watching him cook. 'They don't think she's got long.'

'I'm sorry.' He turned to face her properly. 'How are you feeling about it?'

'I'm fine.' She picked at the chipped edge of her mug. 'If I'm honest, I'm more worried about how Fin will take it.' An old familiar worry curled itself around her heart.

He's not the same person any more.

Let it go.

'It's going to be hard, but at least he'll have a good support network. I don't know about his friends in America, but having you around will be a comfort, I'm sure.' Ben smiled and Eleanor couldn't help but feel a sense of calm radiate through her.

'Maybe.' She shrugged. 'Anyway, do you want me to take anything through?' she asked, quickly changing the conversation.

Ben shot her a knowing look and handed her a plate of

garlic bread. 'Expert change of subject, Ms Levy. Take this and I'll be with you in a second.'

Eleanor sat herself down and looked around. It was a nice flat, spacious and warm. She'd felt at home from the very first moment she'd stepped inside. There was something secure and safe about the place that made her easily relax. In a strange way, kind of how she had felt when she first met Ben.

'Voila!' Ben placed the rest of the food between them and raised his glass of wine. 'Cheers. I hope you're hungry. I *may* have over-catered.'

'When you've been brought up by my mother, you know how to eat for a hundred.' She touched her cup of tea against his glass.

'Oh, really?' He raised his eyebrow curiously. 'Is she a bit of a feeder?'

'A bit!' Eleanor exclaimed. 'Honestly, on Sunday she made seven different main courses and six desserts. There were only four of us eating.'

'No way.' Ben's jaw dropped. 'Is that a normal Sunday lunch for your family? If so, I'd better start stretching my stomach in preparation.'

Eleanor paused, her forkful of pasta halfway to her lips. Was she going to tell him? Was it too soon to explain? Her stomach jolted as though someone were tugging at her just behind her belly button.

'Eleanor?' Ben was leaning forward, his hand outstretched. 'Are you all right?'

She put her fork down and took his hand. 'Yeah, I'm fine.' She took a deep breath in and forced out the words that were lurking at the back of her throat. 'It was actually the anniversary of my dad's death on Sunday. My mum has this ridiculous tradition of cooking all his favourite meals, hence all the food.' She dropped her gaze to the space between them.

Immediately he was by her side. 'Eleanor, I'm so sorry.'

She rested her head on his firm shoulder. 'That's OK. It's been nearly fifteen years and I always think it will hurt a little less this time, but it never does.'

He lifted her chin so that her face met his. 'He was your dad. Of course that's going to hurt.'

She wanted to turn her head away – the intensity of the moment was threatening to break her defences completely – but Ben held her gaze firmly. He leant in and kissed her forehead.

'Thank you,' she whispered, a single tear escaping down her cheek.

'Not at all.' He stood up and sat back down on the other side of the table. 'Thank you for telling me. It means a lot.'

A quiet settled over the pair of them, as light and fine as dust. Eleanor had spent the past few years fearing silence. It was painful and awkward, and if it ever reared its ugly head she would desperately fill it with any topic she could find, simply as a way to prove to Oliver that she was interesting. But this was different. For the first time in a long time, she actually found she was enjoying it, the sounds of each other breathing and eating and hearts beating.

'Wait, did you say you had a wedding drama this weekend?' Ben sat back and pushed his empty plate away from him.

Eleanor wiped a fleck of sauce from her mouth and smiled. 'Yeah. I had a mad dash to find a last-minute plus one. But luckily Fin stepped up and saved the day.'

'Really?' Ben's face dropped. 'That's good.' He fiddled

with his empty wine glass and stood up suddenly. 'Do you want any wine or are you OK with tea?'

Eleanor eyed him suspiciously. 'I'm good for the moment. Are you OK?'

'Yeah.'

'Ben?' she asked, sensing the change in atmosphere immediately. 'What's wrong?'

'I don't know.' He drained the dregs of his wine and shrugged. 'I guess I'm wondering why you didn't ask me?'

Eleanor stood up and walked over to him. She removed the glass from his hand and put it on the table, taking his hands in hers. '*Because* I didn't know if it was too soon to ask! You forget, I don't know how this whole dating thing works.'

'I don't know if anyone really knows how it works, to be honest,' he replied glumly. Eleanor could tell he was still feeling put out.

'I'm sorry.' She gave him a little squeeze. 'Fin volunteered and my mum had already pretty much accepted on my behalf anyway. It's all been a bit last-minute.'

'OK,' he mumbled.

'Would you have even wanted to come? To a wedding where you don't know anyone?' she asked.

'Well, I quite like weddings.' He raised one of her hands to his mouth and kissed it softly. 'And I definitely like *you*.'

A ripple of electricity shot through her centre. She felt the sparks tingle right to the ends of her fingers.

'Look at you getting all red and embarrassed.' He laughed, stroking her blazing cheeks. 'But for future reference, if you ever need a plus one to a wedding, I'm your man.'

Eleanor took Ben's arms and wrapped them around her, placing her face against his chest. 'Sure thing, Mr Ryans.'

'Good. Now let's eat dessert.' He kissed the top of her head. 'I've only bought one, though. I hope that's OK.'

'That's perfect!' She smiled, watching as he disappeared back into the kitchen.

Fin

Even though Nurse Clara had called Fin later that afternoon to reassure him that his mother was fine and much calmer, he still couldn't quite shake the unease he felt every time he thought about going back to see her. The sound of her voice would haunt him, and the skin on his wrist still bore the half-moon indents from where her nails had dug in so deep. Seeing her so distraught brought back too many unwanted memories that were getting harder and harder to ignore.

'Now, why in the world do you look so nervous?' Nurse Clara remarked, as Fin walked through into reception on the Wednesday morning.

'I don't, do I?' He tried to rearrange his face hastily into some sort of smile.

'Heidi won't bite, you know. The woman is eighty-five years old!' The nurse laughed.

'I know that.' Fin hoisted his camera bag over his shoulder. 'I just want her to be happy with the pictures. That's all.'

'And I'm sure she will be. You are a beautiful photographer, Fin.' Nurse Clara tilted her head and smiled at him sweetly, her sharp eagle eyes softening for a moment. 'Eleanor is already here, by the way.'

Fin scoffed. 'Of course she is.' He followed Nurse Clara through towards Heidi's room.

'Are you planning to use the garden again?'

'I think so. It looks like it might rain, but I reckon it will hold off until we finish. Bloody English weather.' He rolled his eyes.

'Enjoy it while you can. I reckon you'll be surprised at how much you miss it when you go back.'

'Not likely.' He adjusted his bag over his shoulder once again and hovered outside Heidi's door.

'You know where I am if you need anything, all right?' Nurse Clara placed a hand on his shoulder before continuing down the corridor.

'Right.' He gripped the door handle and turned it slowly. 'Heidi? Eleanor? It's Fin. Am I OK to come in?' he asked tentatively.

'Considering you are the photographer, Fin, and therefore pretty essential to this whole set-up, I'd imagine coming in would be a rather good idea,' Heidi replied bluntly.

Fin took a sharp inhale and pushed the door open. If he hadn't heard the sarcastic snipe of her voice, he'd be hard pushed to believe it was the same woman sitting in front of him that he'd met previously. She was sitting proud and tall in the chair. Her grey hair was smooth and sleek, curled ever so slightly under at the edges and dotted with pearls. Her eyes were closed as Eleanor reached across and continued to lightly dust her skin with a pink shimmering powder. The dress she wore was spilling into pools of dark red silk around her feet. Fin stood there silently, trying to take it all in.

'You look beautiful, Heidi.'

She simply opened one eye, stared at him, then closed it again. Fin placed his bag down and waited whilst Eleanor completed her finishing touches.

'There!' Eleanor announced proudly. 'All good to go, I think.' She turned to look at Fin with a huge grin on her face. 'Happy, Mr Photographer?'

'Very. Thank you.' He nodded in approval.

'Who cares what he thinks,' Heidi said dismissively. 'I'm the one having their photo taken. Maybe it would be a good idea if I could see what you've done with me?'

Fin saw Eleanor visibly tense as she passed over a large hand-held mirror to Heidi. Nobody breathed as it was lifted to her face. The silence was excruciating.

Eleanor went to speak but Heidi held up her hand to stop her. Fin was just about to launch into a rant about manners and how Heidi needed to find some very quickly, when he heard a tiny little gasp. Eleanor and Fin locked eyes in panic.

'If you don't like it, I can take it off and we can start again,' Eleanor gushed, fumbling around in her bag.

'No.' Heidi's voice wavered.

Fin made to step forward when she spoke again, this time her voice firm and steady. 'It's fine. Thank you.'

Fin was still looking at Eleanor in confusion. He didn't have a clue what was going on. Then Heidi dropped the mirror to her lap; her eyes were misty and brimming with tears.

Fin smiled at Eleanor, who seemed to deflate a little with relief. 'It's all right to be happy, you know, Heidi?' He edged closer, hoping to reach inside the small gap in her armour she'd exposed.

The old lady stood so quickly that Fin nearly tripped over himself in surprise. 'Thank you for the inspirational talk, Mr Taylor, very moving indeed.' She bristled, smoothing down the creases in the front of her dress. 'But your advice is not needed, nor is it wanted. Shall we get on with it?'

He nodded mutely, stepping aside to let her walk past. Eleanor hovered by her side gingerly, uncertain whether to offer her support or not. 'I am fine, dear,' Heidi quipped. 'No need to fuss.'

Eleanor still lingered close behind as the old lady made her way down the corridor and out into the garden. Fin took up the rear with the equipment, his resentment growing with each step taken.

Be professional.

Take the pictures and be done with it.

'Where would you like me?' Heidi stood, hands on hips, surveying the grounds. 'It's rather chilly, so as quickly as possible if you wouldn't mind.'

'Yes, madam,' he grumbled, reaching for his camera bag. 'If you go and sit on the bench over there, that would be great. Eleanor, can you come and grab this for me, please?'

'Sure,' she replied, walking quickly over to join him. 'Look,' she whispered, 'I know she's being a complete arse, but you saw her face earlier. It was like you said to me, this *means* something to her. Come on, Fin, don't let her rattle you.'

'Who says I'm rattled?' He forced his voice to become bright and nonchalant.

'You've run your hands through your hair about twenty times, plus you keep clenching your fists.' She flashed him a smug smile.

'Eurgh.' He sighed. '*Fine*. I'll try to be nice. And if not nice, then civil.' He handed her his tripod. 'You did an amazing job on the hair and make-up, by the way. The artist still lives!'

Eleanor's face instantly dropped. 'Oh no.'

'What's wrong?' he asked, indicating the spot opposite the bench where they needed to set up.

'I forgot to cancel art club yesterday.' She dragged the tripod along the ground, which made Fin's insides cry out. Did she know how much money she was hauling haphazardly through the mud?

'You're going to art class? That's great!'

'Yeah.' She blushed. 'Not so great when you don't turn up for them though.'

'Maybe not,' he agreed.

'I'm not used to having so many social plans – I forget that I need to actually organize my life a bit more now there's things in it.' She laughed sadly to herself.

'Organization is overrated.' He lifted one leg of the tripod up off the grass. 'I think spontaneity will be good for you.'

'Just because that's the way you choose to live your life doesn't mean it's the right way, Fin.' She smirked.

'Excuse me?' Heidi's cry cut through their warm back-and-forth. 'Am I going to be left to wither away over here while you two chit-chat?'

Fin gripped the metal leg of the tripod a little tighter. He opened his mouth to speak, but Eleanor gave him a familiar look of warning and then painted a giant smile on her face.

'Sorry, Heidi, we were sorting the equipment out. You know how these technical things can be a little complicated.'

'Funnily enough, I don't,' she stated flatly. 'I've only ever been in *front* of the camera.'

Fin took a deep breath in and allowed his frustration to subside. 'Make sure you're in a position you're comfortable with, Heidi.' He quickly assembled the equipment and peered through the camera lens. 'I'm going to take a few test shots to make sure the lighting is all OK.'

'Whatever,' Heidi mumbled, fixing herself into a serene pose. She had clearly done this before, her body finding the light as naturally as if she were a flower tracking the sun across the sky.

'Perfect,' Fin marvelled. 'Right, are we ready?'

'I've been ready for what seems like hours.' She rolled her eyes at Eleanor, who he could see out of the corner of his eye was relishing the whole interaction.

Fin chose silence as his best option and happily began to lose himself behind the lens. As cold and cruel as her exterior was, Heidi seemed to bring a softness and elegance through her eyes. He was loath to admit it but she was truly striking.

'How long do you think you'll be staying for then, Mr Taylor?' Heidi asked.

'Not sure. Depends on how my mum does,' he murmured, focusing his attention on angling the camera.

'Ah, yes. Eileen.' Heidi nodded almost imperceptibly. 'She mentioned she had a son, but I wasn't totally convinced you existed until your recent visit.'

Fin felt his heart begin to pound violently in his chest, the abated anger rearing its head once more. He gritted his teeth and continued to stare down the camera lens.

'I live in America, so it's quite a long way to come over.'

'Why?'

'Why what?' He peered over at her.

'Why do you live in America?' she asked, her face betraying no hint of emotion. He quickly looked across at Eleanor, who shrugged her shoulders, also seemingly clueless as to the intention behind Heidi's questioning.

'I kind of ended up there after travelling. I got a job working at a photography studio from someone I met in Bali.'

Heidi continued, her tone becoming more interrogative with every word. 'And why were you travelling?'

'Why does it matter?' he sniped, unable to keep the bitterness from his retort.

'It's just that, in my opinion, people only travel as an excuse to run away from something they'd rather not confront.'

He stiffened, his hand gripping the camera so tightly his knuckles were turning white.

'I was young and wanted to see the world.'

'Hmmmm.' She adjusted her position perfectly to catch the shower of sunlight that had peeked through the clouds. 'And why didn't you return?'

He was about to boil over when Eleanor cut in. 'You must have travelled all over the world in your pageant days, Heidi? Where was your favourite place?'

Heidi simply waved her hand dismissively in Eleanor's direction. 'Mr Taylor?' She arched her eyebrow, willing him to take her bait. 'Were you not close to your family?'

'Not really.' He grimaced.

'And what about Eleanor here? I thought you said you were best friends?'

'We were.' He felt the sweat beading across his forehead. He didn't want to go into this. Not now. Not with her. And especially not in front of Eleanor.

'Well then, why on earth didn't you return? Was there nothing to come back for?'

'I'm not sure why it's any of your business,' he spat. Memories were creeping out between the cracks of their hiding places, visions of his former self crowding his sight, making it impossible to see anything other than what he'd been trying to forget for so long.

'Forgive me.' She softened a fraction. 'I didn't mean to dig up old wounds, but I am an observer of people. A lifetime on your own will do that to you.'

He didn't know why he even felt inclined to give this rude, nosy woman an answer, but something inside him was bursting to justify his behaviour. He needed her to know that he wasn't a coward. That his choice to leave was bigger than she could imagine.

'Of course there were things to come back for.' He fixed his eyes firmly on to Heidi's. 'There was a lot to come back for. I just couldn't see it at the time.'

He felt his face flush, his eyes finding Eleanor's. 'I don't need you to berate me or judge me for it. I'm doing enough of that myself as it is.' He felt his entire being focusing on Eleanor, every atom in his body pulling towards her. 'But all I can do is be here now.'

The pair stared at each other in silence. It took all of his will not to open his mouth and let the mountain of unsaid thoughts and regret pour out of him. He widened his eyes and prayed she could see directly into his mind, like she could all those years ago.

'Very well,' Heidi interrupted brusquely. 'Are we done here? I'm freezing.'

Eleanor smiled at him. It was a kind, knowing smile. He felt his body ease and the tension melt out of him.

'Mr Taylor?' Heidi pressed. 'Are we done here?'

'Please say yes,' Eleanor mouthed desperately.

Fin laughed. 'Yes. We're done.'

'Good. Now, Eleanor dear, will you help me up? I've been sitting here so long I fear my joints have forgotten how to work.'

Eleanor

As the date of Laura's wedding grew closer, Eleanor couldn't stop the onslaught of anxious questions from invading her thoughts.

Should she have asked Ben if he minded her taking some-one else?

No. He's not your boyfriend.

Should she have just gone by herself?

And sat next to an empty place like a loser? No.

Would it be weird spending so much time with Fin? They were most definitely over their awkward silent phase; in fact, the last couple of times they'd been together she'd actually had a lot of fun . . . but this was different. What if they ran out of conversation?

It's a wedding. There are loads of people to talk to.

Even as she stood waiting in the hotel reception for his arrival, Eleanor's mind was ablaze with nervous energy.

'It will be fine,' she reassured herself. 'You'll be fine.'

She glanced anxiously at the clock hanging over the

reception desk. 'What won't be fine is if you turn up late, Fin,' she hissed.

With Fin being such a last-minute addition, he'd been forced to stay in a bed and breakfast slightly further out of town. There was no way Eleanor was offering to share her room; they may have become more friends than strangers over the past few weeks but that was definitely a step too far! Besides, what on earth would Ben have said about that?

Oh God. Ben.

She reached for her phone and typed out a quick message, trying to avoid the ticking clock at the top of her screen, teasing her with every passing minute.

Hey, sorry, was caught up in getting ready! I'm here safe and sound, waiting for Fin who is unsurprisingly late! I'll call you tomorrow when I'm back in London? Maybe we could grab dinner? xx

Eleanor was still getting used to the idea that someone else cared about her whereabouts. It was a nice feeling knowing that there was another human being thinking about her, worrying about her, missing her. She stowed her phone back in her bag and sighed. Any minute now and the coach would arrive.

I'll get on it with or without you, Fin.

She turned to take one last look in the large gilded mirror behind her. Eleanor felt a bloom of pride. At last, she could look at her reflection and recognize herself. Her cheeks were no longer hollowed, her eyes no longer dull and sad. Her previous withering frame had more or less been restored to its strong former self and so this time, when it came to wedding outfits, she'd had the pick of her old dresses to recycle.

This was a particular favourite of hers, a green flowing slip dress. It hugged her in all the right places and was soft as butter to wear.

'Eleanor!' A cry from outside made her jump. She turned to see a beacon of red hair running towards the hotel reception. 'Please don't kill me, it wasn't my fault, there was a problem in my room and they had to move me which took ages, and then I needed to change and . . . wow.' The wild, chaotic figure of her friend stopped in front of her. His eyes were wide, taking her in slowly.

'All right. You don't need to look so surprised. It's not like you've never seen me in a dress before,' she joked awkwardly, feeling the areas where his gaze lingered flush with heat.

'Sorry,' he apologized, looking rather flustered. She hadn't meant to embarrass him, but she could see his cheeks blushing.

Good start, Eleanor.

'It's fine. At least we match, hey?' She smiled, nodding towards his green tie and pocket square. 'I was worried we were going to have a repeat of prom.'

Fin's face instantly turned a deeper shade of red. 'Look, how was I to know that when someone says to match the colour of their dress, they only mean your tie?'

'Who would assume it was the entire suit?' Eleanor exclaimed, remembering the moment Fin arrived at her doorstep in a hideous lilac suit he'd somehow managed to find.

'Yeah, well, we had a good night in the end, didn't we? No harm done!' he murmured bashfully. 'Have we missed the coach?' He craned his neck to check the time behind her.

'No, it should be here any minute.'

'Phew.' He looked at her seriously. 'I am sorry I'm late. And you really do look beautiful.' He offered his arm, adopting an exceptionally posh accent. 'Shall we wait outside for the carriage, madam?'

She looped her arm through his and sighed. 'Fine.'

'My undeniable charm still works, then.' He laughed loudly. 'All of my dates seem to exude a similar level of extreme enthusiasm.'

'Firstly. This is not a date,' she stated firmly, feeling another surge of warmth radiate through her.

What is going on with you, Eleanor?

'And secondly, I don't believe you for a second. Women always used to fall at your feet.' She eyed him shrewdly. 'It's the freckles, I reckon.'

'That was in my youth, dear Eleanor,' he moaned dramatically. 'These days it's a very different story. I mean, look at our friend Heidi, for instance!'

'I'm sure underneath those multiple layers of ice-cold steel her shrivelled heart beats a little louder for you,' she remarked sarcastically, as they joined the group of guests waiting for the coach.

'Unlikely,' Fin replied. 'The pictures turned out pretty great, though. I did some editing last night.'

'I had no doubt they would,' she replied truthfully. 'I mean, she looked better than me and I'm about fifty years younger than her.'

'Don't be stupid. Look at you. You'd give Heidi a run for her money any day.' He smiled.

Eleanor's stomach did a strange little flip and her neck suddenly felt very hot.

'Aha, here it is!' Fin pointed at the large white coach turning into the car park. 'It's hardly rushing, is it? I could have had time for a quick power nap at this rate. Come on, let's try and get the good seats at the back.' He grabbed her arm and pulled her towards the vehicle.

'You're such a child.' Eleanor laughed, trying to shake off the odd tingling feeling in her chest.

'I never got to sit at the back at school. So now every time I get on a coach, I make it my mission to get the back seats.' He shrugged as though this were the most normal thing in the world to admit.

Eleanor felt a pang of guilt. 'You told me you didn't mind sitting at the front.'

'What?' he asked, clambering on to the coach.

'At school. When we used to sit at the front, you said you didn't mind it. That you didn't like the back seats.'

'Oh.' He paused mid-step, his foot suspended in the air. 'Well . . . your travel sickness was so bad you couldn't sit anywhere *but* the front. I told you that so you didn't feel bad.'

'Fin!' A childish annoyance quickly replaced the guilt. 'You shouldn't have done that.'

'It was no big deal.' He leapt up on board and was halfway down the aisle when he stopped suddenly. 'Wait, do you still get sick? Do we need to go back?' The panic on his face was comical.

'No. I'm fine. Just find a seat and sit down, there's a queue behind me,' she scolded, sounding scarily like her mother.

'OK, let's go here,' he announced proudly. 'Do you want the window?'

'Sure.' She shuffled into the seat. 'Now, some rules for today . . .'

'Here we go,' he scoffed, falling in beside her.

'What do you mean by that?' She scowled.

'Nothing.'

'Yes, you did, or you wouldn't have said it.'

'I'm just saying, it wouldn't be right if we went somewhere or did something without you trying to organize and plan everything. You like to be in control, that's all.'

'No, I don't,' she protested.

'Yes, you do.' He grinned. 'It's not a bad thing, don't worry.'

'I'm not worried,' she huffed, adjusting her dress unnecessarily. 'Anyway, all I was going to say was don't, whatever you do, let me do shots tonight. Tequila and weddings are never my friend.'

He relaxed back in his seat and stretched his long legs out. 'Gotcha. Absolutely no tequila.' He raised an eyebrow at her cheekily. 'Anything else before we set off?'

She shot him a deadly look. 'No. That's all.'

'OK, as you wish.' He closed his eyes and leant back against the headrest.

What I wish is that you would stop being so infuriating . . .

Fin opened one eye and smiled at her. 'You OK over there, grumpy?'

Eleanor unfolded her arms, which had found themselves unconsciously crossed over her chest.

'I'll be fine when you stop talking,' she sniped back, unable to stop her lips curling up at the corners.

'As you wish . . .' He laughed.

'Stop saying that!' she cried, slapping him gently on the arm.

'As you wish . . .'

*

Eleanor was hot and sweaty and out of breath, but she didn't care. She was having the best time, throwing her arms in the air and moving her body instinctively to the music. She hadn't danced like this in years. Free, wild, and not caring about what anyone thought. Maybe it was the palpable excitement that was sparking in the air. Maybe it was the copious amounts of alcohol she'd consumed . . .

Or maybe it's being around Fin . . .

Eleanor eyed the flailing limbs belonging to Fin and pushed the ridiculous thought from her mind.

'You want a drink?' she called into Fin's ear.

'What?' he tried to shout over the music.

'A drink?' Eleanor mimed taking a sip from an imaginary glass.

Fin held up his half-full tonic water and shook his head. How the man had managed to survive without a drop of alcohol and still be able to keep up with the intoxicated she had no idea. It was rather impressive, and deep down Eleanor felt a spark of pride for the man her friend had become. The Fin she remembered before the darkness. The Fin who made everything fun.

'*You want to get some air?*' she shouted.

'*What?*' Fin screamed back, sweat beading across his freckled forehead.

'*I need some air.*' She pointed towards the far corner of the room. Everything was swimming in and out of focus, but she could just about make out the double doors that opened out on to the perfectly manicured grounds.

'*OK,*' he hollered back, taking her damp palm and pulling her towards the exit. She felt giddy on a heady mix of adrenaline and alcohol. Her body was glowing from the inside with the fuzzy warmth of tequila shots.

'You want to sit or walk?' Fin asked, opening the doors, allowing the cool night air to greet them.

'Sit. Definitely sit.' Eleanor rubbed her throbbing feet and gestured towards a low wall by the edge of a crowd of smokers. As she walked, she felt her balance wobble. Everything was starting to sway and she grabbed hold of Fin's arm to support her.

'Wait, wait just a moment.' Fin stopped her just as she was about to lower herself down on to the wall. 'You can't get a dress like that dirty.' He took off his jacket and laid it down on top of the bricks.

'Finley James Taylor, a gentleman? Who would have thought it!' she jested, reaching her hand out to touch his cheek but retracting it at the very last minute.

'I'm full of surprises,' he teased.

Eleanor slung her shoes off and placed the pads of her worn-out feet on to the chilled earth. At once she felt grounded, the energy that had been raging through her body slowly retracting into stillness.

'Look at the stars. Aren't they're magical?' she marvelled, letting her head fall backwards as she tried to absorb the enormity of the sky above her.

'You don't get skies like this in LA,' Fin mumbled, flinging his feet out in front of him like a little boy. 'Too many goddam cars.'

'I'll never forget what my dad used to say. If ever there's a problem you feel is too big or too scary, look up and remember you're part of something way bigger.' She sighed.

'Your dad was a wise man,' Fin said softly.

'He was. He really, *really* was.' It was hard enough not to get upset over her dad when she was sober, but now there was no chance at restraint. Tears stung her eyes and her heart contracted in angst. 'Oh Fin, how on earth did we end up here?' Eleanor rested her head on his shoulder.

'At the wedding? Wow, I didn't realize you were *that* drunk.' He laughed.

'No, you idiot. How did we end up *here*?' She gesticulated wildly. 'Drunk and single at a wedding at thirty-four years old?' She sighed.

'I'm not drunk. And you're not single,' he stated.

'Yes, I am,' she slurred slightly.

'What about Ben?'

'Technically' – she raised a pointed finger at Fin – 'I'm not his girlfriend.'

'Not yet.' He grinned.

Eleanor shrugged, her head rolling forwards. 'Won't be long until he gets bored of me and goes.'

'Hey. Don't say that.'

'Why? It's true. Sometimes I look in the mirror and don't even recognize myself any more. Like . . . who *is* this woman? This boring, stuck-in-her-routine, grown-up *woman*,' she garbled.

'Stop with the "old" thing, because if you're old, I'm old and I refuse to believe that.' He nudged her affectionately.

'*Fine*,' she lamented. 'I'm old*er* than I was.'

'Better.'

'And more boring.'

'No! Not boring.'

'I spent my New Year's Eve getting drunk on wine and crying over the fact I couldn't even think of *one* resolution, not one thing I wanted to do for the year ahead. I had to use this stupid journal thing Freya got me to help. You want to know what I wrote?' She swayed a little.

'Go on . . .'

'Talk to my mum more. Big fucking whoop!' She began to

howl with laughter. 'Oh, wait, and drink less. Which I'm clearly failing at.'

'I should probably have done both of those a long time ago.' He dropped his head.

'I'm sorry. I didn't even think.' A flash of guilt cut through her thick tequila fog.

'Don't be silly. It's fine.'

The pair exchanged a loaded look.

'Your New Year's sounds a total blast compared to mine.' He smirked. 'Mine was spent breaking up with my girlfriend, who decided to throw a large number of very solid items at my face. Then I stayed home while all my friends went out and got completely shit-faced. I woke up and had to fly for nearly eleven hours next to a guy who felt the need to not only take up every possible speck of room available to him, but also tell me in detail about his messy divorce from his third wife.'

'Jesus Christ, that sounds bad.' Eleanor burst out laughing, the force of it nearly sending her toppling backwards off the wall.

'Woah there. Steady on!' Fin caught her, his hand warm against the small of her back. He pulled her upright and held her steady. 'I don't think either of us want this night to end with you in an ambulance, thank you very much.'

Through the cloud of the alcohol Fin's face was only a blur. A haze of freckles and red hair, but a haze that she'd know anywhere, even after all those years apart. His hand lingered at the base of her spine and she could feel the warmth from his skin through the thin fabric of her dress. There was a pull deep inside her navel. A tugging, a longing, a memory. The way he was looking at her. The force of her

heart beating in her chest. This moment. They'd been here
before. The years melted away and before she knew what
was happening, her lips were on his. The smell of his skin
sent comforting waves through her body. The weight of her
nearly knocked him backwards, but he steadied himself and
she felt him pull her closer. His hands were holding her
tightly, his mouth on hers.

She was kissing him.

Eleanor Levy was kissing Finley Taylor.

And in that moment she never wanted it to stop.

Fin

It took a moment for him to realize what was happening. One minute they had been fine. Then she was crying and now . . . now they were kissing.

You can't kiss her, she's drunk!

But she kissed me.

He pulled away, stopping it as quickly and abruptly as it had started, not allowing himself a moment to think about how strangely wonderful the kiss had felt. He held her out in front of him; her eyes were still closed and her lips slightly parted.

'Eleanor, I'm sorry, I jus—' But before he had a chance to finish, she pushed him aside and threw up violently on the ground next to him.

'Christ, Elles.' He pulled her hair back, trying to capture every one of her loose curls.

'Eurgh,' she moaned between retches. 'I'm so sorry.'

Fin held her up, supporting her weight as she emptied her stomach on to the grass, much to the disgust and horror of passing guests. It took a good few minutes before she had finished.

'How are we doing down there? I mean, who knows if there's anything left to throw up at this point.' He bent over and placed a cool hand on her forehead.

Eleanor stood up slowly. 'I'm good. I think I'm good.' She groaned. 'Please can we go?'

'Sure.' Fin wrapped his arm around her shoulders and began to walk them both towards the car park. He was trying as hard as he could to focus on keeping her upright, his body taking the full weight of hers, but his mind was still reeling from their tight embrace.

Did that really just happen?

Fin shook the thoughts from his mind, forcing himself to concentrate on the task at hand. He gently lowered Eleanor on to a little wall outside the front of the venue.

'I'm going to get a cab sorted – just wait here for a second?' he asked, praying that she would manage to stay upright for at least a few moments.

'Mhm.' She nodded, her face shockingly pale against the smears of make-up streaked across her skin.

Fin looked around helplessly. It was getting cold and he wanted to get Eleanor back to her room and cleaned up as soon as possible. Did they even have Uber out here?

Of course they don't – you're in the middle of bloody nowhere.

'Coach,' Eleanor croaked from behind. Fin waved her away dismissively as he began to google local taxi numbers.

'The *coach*,' Eleanor shouted.

'What about the coach? I'm trying to find us a taxi here.'

She looked up at him, her eyes rolling in different directions before settling on his face. 'The coach runs every half-hour back to the hotel. Check the time, there might be one soon.'

Fin looked at his phone. Ten minutes. They only had to wait ten more minutes! He rushed over to where Eleanor was perched precariously and threw his suit jacket over her frozen shoulders. 'How is it that even when you're absolutely wasted you still manage to be better at organizing things than me?'

She smiled and snuggled in close to him, a waft of vomit hitting his nostrils. 'Because I'm Eleanor Levy. And you are Finley Taylor. The two best friends that ever there were,' she sang sleepily.

'You're not wrong there, Elles.' He kissed the top of her head and squeezed her tightly.

'I'm sorry,' she mumbled.

'It's fine, everyone gets sick. God knows you've cleaned me up enough times.'

'No.' She raised her head. Her dark eyes were large and pleading. 'I mean . . . I'm sorry for kissing you.'

'Oh, that.' His stomach jolted. 'Don't worry about that. We all do stupid things when we're drunk.'

'Yeah.' She let her head fall heavily on to his shoulder once again. 'Yeah, we do.'

*

It hadn't been the easiest task getting her up to her hotel room. By the time the coach had dropped them off, Eleanor was pretty much fast asleep. In the end he'd picked her up and carried her in; not the most dignified way for her perhaps, but definitely the simplest and most efficient way for him.

'Come on, Elles, I need you to help me for a second.' He lowered her on to the bed and lifted her head up. 'You need to drink all of this, OK?' He handed her a bottle of water

253

from the minibar. 'I'm going to get a flannel to wash your face.'

'Fine,' she mumbled, opening the bottle and sipping it slowly.

Fin kept an eye on her in the bathroom mirror as he dampened a flannel and found some make-up wipes on the side. 'How we doing in there?' he called. 'I hope you're still drinking?'

'I'm tired. Can you hurry up, please?' she whined.

'Oi, I'm not the one who appears to have consumed half the bar and couldn't handle their liquor,' he teased, grabbing a dressing gown from the back of the door and returning to join Eleanor on the edge of the bed.

'Sorry we can't all be sober as a judge like you,' she replied haughtily. 'And *someone*,' she shouted, pointing her finger at him, 'was supposed to not let me drink said alcohol.' She grabbed a face wipe from his hand and rubbed her cheek aggressively.

'Excuse me? Since when was I your babysitter?'

She laughed loudly in his face. 'Wasn't I yours for about sixteen years?'

Fin didn't say anything but took the wipe gently from her hand and stroked it lightly over her eyes.

They sat in silence while he cleaned her face.

'Hey,' she whispered, as he removed the last traces of make-up. 'I was only joking, you know? I didn't mind looking after you.' She sighed, the alcohol still strong on her breath.

'It's fine.'

'Can I go to sleep now, *please*?' Eleanor whimpered.

'Soon, but I do think we need to clean your teeth or you'll never forgive me.' He wrapped the dressing gown around her shoulders and hurried back to the bathroom, returning with toothpaste in hand. 'Now, squeeze a bit of this into your mouth with some water and swill it around.'

'You're so gross.' She grinned.

'Trust me.' Fin handed her the tube. 'If anyone is gross right now, it's you, my friend.'

She shot him a deadly look.

'Hurry up, and when you're done, shuffle back and lie down.'

Despite the deep scowl on her face, Eleanor did as she was told and crawled towards the top of the bed. 'But where will you sleep?' she muttered, curling up on her side.

'I'll sit with you for a bit and then grab a cab to my hotel.' He threw the dirty wipes in the bin, and took another bottle of water and placed it on the bedside table next to her head.

'Don't be silly,' she grumbled. 'Stay here.' Her voice was thick with sleep.

'I can't do that.'

'It's fine. I don't snore.' She chuckled to herself.

'Yes, you do.' He pulled the blanket up over her and smoothed the hair from her face.

'No, I absolutely do not.' She opened one eye lazily. '*You* snore.'

Fin couldn't help but laugh. She sounded so like the young Eleanor of his past, stubborn and righteous. 'I know I do. That's why you always left me to sleep by myself when we went camping. I'd wake up freezing and on my own! Terrible friend, you were.'

A small hand darted out from the covers and smacked him on the arm. 'I was the best.'

He tried to manoeuvre her hand back under the duvet.

'Say it!' she insisted. 'We were the best, weren't we?'

'Yes.' He sighed, tucking her back inside the warm covers. 'We really were.' His heart strained with affection.

'Will you stay with me until I fall asleep? Like old times?' Her breathing was already growing deeper and her eyes were fully closed.

'Of course.' He lay down next to her and watched the slow rise and fall of her chest. 'Just like old times.'

Then: Aged 18

Eleanor

Her heart was in her mouth. She could barely breathe. Every time she tried to inhale, her throat would close up and she'd choke on the tears that she was fighting back.

He's fine.

He'll be fine.

The words played over and over in her mind as she willed her feet to move just a little faster.

Why was it taking so long to get to him? The seconds were crawling past; time was like a long corridor that she couldn't see the end of.

Eleanor had been at work when she'd got the text. Luckily, she'd been on her break, otherwise it didn't bear thinking about when she would have seen it. The three indiscernible words on the screen took the air out of her lungs and made the world shift beneath her feet.

From: Finley Taylor.

Hel3lp. Nt goofd.

The phone almost dropped from her hands.

'Roy? Roy!' She ran into the cafe, wildly searching for her boss.

'Eleanor, what's wrong?' Roy wiped his hands on his grubby apron and placed them on her shoulders. 'You look like you've seen a ghost!'

'I need to go. I'm sorry. I'll work a double shift next weekend. I'll do whatever you want, I just really need to leave. Like right now.'

She started pacing back and forth, her mind already planning the fastest route to his house.

Will there be traffic?

What if the bus is late?

Can I run?

Every second she wasn't moving was a second she couldn't afford to waste.

'Of course! Is everything OK? Are you all right to go alone?' Her boss looked around at the half-full cafe. 'I'd offer to drive you home but I can't leave the customers.'

Eleanor stopped and looked at him. Affection washed over her. His big, kind eyes seemed to know without words the significance of the crisis.

'I'll be fine. Thank you, Roy. I promise I'll make it up to you.'

She managed to force her face into a tiny smile before throwing off her apron and running out of the back door.

'Be safe, Eleanor,' he called after her, but she was already sprinting down the street.

Hold on, Fin, I'm nearly there.

Her top was drenched with a mix of sweat and tears. But she wouldn't stop. She couldn't stop. The moment she saw his front door her heart skipped a beat. Then all at once she froze. Her body jarred into complete stillness.

What would she find in there?

The thought flashed across her mind and she felt her stomach drop through the floor.

No. Don't think.

Just get to him, Eleanor.

She shook her head and forced her legs back into action. Her entire being became laser-focused on getting into the house.

The door opened at her touch.

'Hello?' She cursed herself for the fear that had crept into her voice.

Silence.

Her heartbeat rang out loudly in her ears.

'Fin?' She peered into the lounge, scanning for any sign of life. '*Fin.*' Her voice echoed through the empty room.

'Up here.' A faint cry, barely audible, carried down from upstairs.

Her body was moving before her mind could even register. She was in complete survival mode, running on nothing but fear and instinct.

'I'm here. Don't worry, I'm here.'

The smell hit her as she reached the top step. It took everything not to gag as the heady mix of vomit and alcohol assaulted her senses.

She paused at his bedroom door, her pale shaking hand lingering for just a moment in mid-air.

He needs you, Eleanor.

She closed her eyes and stepped into the room.

It was pitch black. The curtains were drawn and it took a moment for her eyes to adjust. The air was thick, cloying almost. Instantly she felt the walls closing in on her, and the urge to run back into the fresh safety of outside was overwhelming.

'I'm going to turn the light on, OK? I need to be able to see you.'

A muffled groan of acknowledgement came from somewhere in the depths of the darkness.

The moment she flicked the switch, the true mess of the situation confronted her. Clothes covered every inch of the floor. Mixed in amongst them were piles of sick and splashes of blood.

Blood? Why is there blood?

And then Eleanor saw him. Lying in the corner of the room sprawled out like a rag doll, limbs splayed at all angles.

She ran to him immediately. His head was cut and bruised and there was a pool of sick gathering by his side. She didn't want to cry. She didn't want to show any sign that she wasn't in control.

Her friend.

Her beautiful best friend.

'Fin. Can you sit up for me?' She gently cradled his head in her lap, stroking his matted damp hair.

'Mhm.' His eyes flickered open. The piercing green met hers. A flash of consciousness. 'Elles,' he mumbled. 'Please help.'

A sob escaped from her. 'It's OK. You're OK.' She tried to soothe him. 'But I'm going to have to call for help. I can't do this by myself.'

His hand grasped her arm so tightly she could feel his nails digging deep into her skin. 'No!' he cried, panic pouring out of him. 'Eleanor, please. Just me and you. Just us . . . like old times.'

She paused. It was the tiniest hesitation in which, for a second, she imagined giving in to her logical brain; betraying Fin's wishes for once in her life and doing the sensible thing. The thing she should have done a long time ago.

Call someone.

This has gone too far.

You can't do this again.

'We need to get you cleaned up before anyone else sees you,' she whispered, pushing the voice of reason aside swiftly.

'Thank you,' he groaned, closing his eyes again.

'Can you sit up for me?' she begged. He was too heavy for her to lift alone. 'I can't do this if you don't help me.'

Slowly, very slowly, he moved himself up to sitting. Dark purple bruises flushed angrily against the pale white skin of his arms. Her heart surged with angst. There were so many questions she wanted to ask but she knew now was not the time.

'Thank you,' she whispered softly in his ear. 'Now, can you stand for me?'

'Mhm.' Another slight nod of the head. Thankfully Eleanor was strong; trying to take his weight was not easy. Eventually they were upright, and only then was the full extent of the chaos revealed.

His clothes were ripped; cuts and bruises flashed aggressively through the material. She didn't know where to hold him for fear she would hurt him even more.

'I think . . . I think I've had an accident, Elles.'

His voice was so small and childlike it pained her to hear it.

'You can tell me what happened after we get you cleaned up, OK? We need you sober before we do anything.' All she could focus on was keeping him moving, one foot in front of the other towards the bathroom.

'No,' he moaned. 'I've had an *accident*.' His head dropped down and Eleanor followed his gaze.

His trousers were soaked through.

'I'm sorry, Elles. I'm so, so sorry.'

'I know you are. I know.' Her voice remained surprisingly calm despite her heart breaking in her chest.

*

It took over an hour to get him cleaned up and safely back into bed. Eleanor had almost had to get in the shower with him for fear he'd fall over and crack his head on the tiles. The entire time she had to block out his desperate cries of apology in order to maintain some semblance of emotional control. Her tears wouldn't help anyone.

As soon as his head hit the pillow, he fell asleep. If she hadn't witnessed all the destruction, she could easily be forgiven for thinking he looked at peace. But Eleanor knew there was trouble brewing behind his calm serenity.

Only when she was certain he was lost to the world of dreams did she allow herself to cry. Curling herself around his slight frame, she held on and breathed in the smell of his freshly washed T-shirt, and sobbed.

When did it all get so complicated?

Eleanor closed her eyes and prayed for the simple days of childhood, when all that mattered to them was playing outside, getting pizza for dinner and being able to have sleepovers. Now everything seemed out of control. The only person in the world she thought she knew inside out was becoming a mystery to her. Was this what growing up was?

I don't want it.

Take it back.

She woke from an anxious sleep still wrapped around Fin, who was now awake and staring at the ceiling.

'How long have I been out for?' she groaned.

'Not long.' He was quiet, not even daring to look at her.

'How do you feel?' She sat up and brought his face down to meet hers.

'Like shit.' He managed a slight smile. 'Elles, I'm so so—'

'Look.' She held her finger up. 'You've apologized enough. Trust me, if I hear another sorry come out of your mouth, I'll do more damage to you than you've managed to do to yourself.'

The tears started to run down his cheeks, silent rivers of salt falling on to the sheets between them.

'All I need you to do is promise me you'll stop this madness. Have you seen the state you're in?' She gently held up his arm, now tinged a deep blue. 'You're hurt, Fin. Really hurt. What happened?'

He closed his eyes.

'You can't remember, can you?' She didn't want to get angry but the frustration was starting to break through her defences.

He shook his head.

They both sat in silence, allowing the gravity of the situation to fill every inch of space between them. It was heavy but it needed to be felt.

'Thanks for not calling my mum. Or my dad.'

'I can't keep doing this.' She let the weight of her head fall into her hands. '*You* can't keep doing this.'

'I know. I'm going to stop, I really am.'

'I wish I could believe you, but I can't. It's happened too many times, Fin. This is getting serious. You need help.'

'But I have you.' He smiled weakly.

'You won't have anyone if you carry on like this. You'll be dead.' The words punctured the air with more force than she'd intended. She didn't care; she needed him to know she wasn't playing around any more.

'Come on, Elles. Don't be so drama—'

'*Don't you dare,*' she hissed. 'Don't you dare do that. This isn't a joke. This isn't a one-off drunken night. This is a problem, Fin, and you need professional help.'

He was staring at her now, his eyes filled with terror.

'If you don't tell your mum about this, or get yourself some help . . .' She stood up and took a deep breath in. 'I will.'

'Elles, please,' he begged.

'No.' She shook her head. 'I love you too much, Fin, to lose you. You tell them or I will.'

Now

Eleanor

Eleanor began to stir. Her entire body hurt as she tried to turn over on to her side. Her stomach ached deeply and her head felt as though someone was raking their nails along the inside of her skull. It took a while for her to come around fully. Her eyes were gummed shut with sleep and her mind was hazy.

'What the hell happened?' she moaned, tasting the remnants of tequila, mint and . . .

'Oh God,' she cried, looking down at her sick-stained dress. The realization forced her upright. 'No. No. No.' She grabbed the cover and pulled it over her face. When had she been sick? Not at the wedding. Please, not at the wedding. Why had she gone to sleep in her dirty clothes? And what the hell was this dressing gown doing wrapped around her?

Eleanor closed her eyes and willed herself to focus. She remembered the ceremony, she remembered the dinner, she remembered dancing. Everything was fine until that point. Where had it gone wrong? She sifted through the fragments of her memory and felt her stomach lurch in protest. There she was, at the bar, with Laura and her new husband and an entire tray of shots.

Why?

Why, Eleanor, why?

A part of her wanted to lie here for the rest of the day, dissolve into the bed sheets and languish in pity. But the smell of her was too wretched to sit with, and she knew she somehow had to get up and get ready to drive home. Slowly she sat up, her head swirling with lights and colours. She set her hands down and carefully lifted her fragile body up to standing. Then she saw him, curled on the floor.

'Fin?' she whispered.

What was he doing here? Why was he—

Then it hit her. A memory dragged through the scrapyard of her consciousness, assaulting her senses.

Launching herself at Fin.

Kissing Fin.

'Oh no.' Her hand flew to her mouth. Her stomach heaved, guilt and confusion threatening to drown her.

She ran into the bathroom, her body springing to life with the sparks of adrenaline. Throwing herself under the shower, she turned the water up to the hottest setting and scrubbed at her skin. She wanted to erase the entire memory, remove its traces from her and emerge anew, but the thoughts were whirling around faster than she could keep up with.

Did he kiss you back?

Does it matter?

Yes!

When was I sick?

Oh God, no . . .

Straight after?

Oh God, yes . . .

'Argh!' she screamed into the burning stream of water.

A loud knocking on the door stopped her immediately.

'Eleanor?' Fin's voice drifted through the steam. 'Are you OK in there?' he called.

'Yes. I'm fine,' she shouted back, overly bright and way too breezy. 'I'll be out in a second.'

'That's OK, as long as you're all right,' he replied.

All right? This whole thing is anything but all right.

She allowed herself five more minutes under the shower before stepping out to face him.

'Hey! How are you feeling?' He was sitting on the edge of the bed, folding up the blankets he'd used for his makeshift bed.

'I can't say I'm feeling my best.' She grimaced. 'How are you? Sleeping on the floor can't have been too comfortable.' She hovered awkwardly, unsure whether to sit or stand or crawl back into bed. Her body throbbed with the hangover.

'I've slept on worse, trust me.' He smiled.

Eleanor pulled her towel tighter around her, the damp curls trailing down her back sending a chill along her spine.

'Sorry, you probably want to get changed and stuff,' Fin mumbled, his face turning a shade of red that matched his ruffled hair. 'I'll head back to my hotel and get cleaned up.' He stood and made his way to the door. 'Are you going to be all right to drive?'

You kissed him.

You kissed that face and then vomited all over him.

'Elles?' His voice cut through her whirring thoughts.

'Oh – yes.' She pulled her mouth into a forced smile. 'I'll be fine. I'll down a coffee or twelve and then come by and pick you up. Say in an hour?'

267

He nodded, a strange expression clouding his face. If only Eleanor had a fully functioning brain cell left to decipher it. 'See you in an hour.'

The moment the door closed, Eleanor threw herself on to the bed and screamed into the pillow.

Eleanor Ruth Levy, what the hell have you done?

*

Thankfully, by the grace of God, there was a Starbucks en route to Fin's bed and breakfast. One large triple-shot latte later and Eleanor was feeling semi-human again. The shower and the change of clothes were also doing wonders for her well-being. She pulled up in the car park and waited; unsurprisingly she was early.

Eleanor turned the radio on in an attempt to prevent any swell of thoughts creeping up on her, but the music was way too loud and jarring. Instead, she reached into her bag and pulled out her phone.

Hey. I'm waiting in the car park when you're ready x

Short, sharp but civil. Perfect.
Maybe he doesn't remember the kiss?
Was he drinking?
Of course he wasn't drinking.
Well then, he remembers . . .
She leant back against the headrest, praying the force of impact would knock the voices from her crowded head. Suddenly a blast of cold air shot in from the left-hand side. She slowly turned her head to see the freckled face of Fin, peering in through the open door.

'Well, don't you look like a brand-new human!' he joked,

eyeing her in mock surprise, clambering inside the car. His face was fresh and full of life. His green eyes sparkled at her, making her lips tingle rather unconsciously.

'Trust me, I don't feel it on the inside,' she mumbled, praying for her heart to stop racing in her chest as she turned the engine on. 'Ready to go?'

'Sure am,' he replied, settling down into the seat beside her.

They drove in silence for the first hour, Eleanor focusing all of her energy on the road ahead, leaving no room for thought or conversation. Every few minutes she would steal a glance at Fin as he slept soundly, face pressed up against the window, steaming it with his breath. Clearly, he'd had just as bad a night as she had.

Probably worse.

He was looking after you, remember.

Her foot pressed down on the accelerator harder than she'd intended. The car lurched forward and jolted Fin from his sleep.

'Sorry. I'm so sorry.' Eleanor winced as Fin wiped the trail of dribble from his chin.

'No, it's fine,' he replied groggily, stretching himself out as far as he could manage within the confines of the tiny Yaris. 'How long have I been out for?'

Eleanor checked the time quickly. 'Maybe an hour or so.'

'Ah, must have been more tired than I thought.'

'Not even Whitney Houston at top volume could wake you up,' she joked.

'Really?' he replied, aghast.

'No! My head hurts too much for the radio.' Eleanor sighed, the ache behind her eyes still lingering like unwanted storm clouds. Dark, heavy, and too close for comfort.

'I see.' Fin reached his hand slowly towards the radio and raised an eyebrow playfully. 'So me putting some music on now at full blast would *not* be a good thing?'

Eleanor narrowed her eyes. 'Don't you dare,' she warned.

'Oops.' Fin chuckled, hitting the on button and turning the sound up high.

'Fin!' Eleanor cried over the music that was blaring out of the speakers.

'Come on, it's Oasis. How can you not want to sing along to Oasis?' He began to sway back and forth, waving his hands in the air like an inebriated fan at a festival.

Eleanor wanted to be mad. She wanted to reach over and shut the music off completely. But before she knew what was happening, she was opening her mouth and singing along as loudly as she could. Joy erupted from the depths of her as Fin joined in with a poor attempt at a harmony. Together they sounded atrocious and normally Eleanor would have been mortified at her pitchy notes, but for some reason she didn't care one bit.

Three awfully performed songs later and Eleanor's hangover seemed a distant memory.

'Eurgh, I hate this song,' she moaned as the music changed.

Fin graciously turned the radio down and leant back in his seat. 'I'd forgotten how fun it is to sing like that.'

'When do you *ever* sing like that?' Eleanor scoffed.

'I have been known to do the odd karaoke session once in a while.'

'Really?' Eleanor replied.

'Yes, and I resent how shocked you look at that.'

'Not shocked.'

'No?' Fin teased.

'More like disturbed.'

'Oh, come *on*,' Fin huffed, folding his arms childishly across his chest. 'That's just mean.'

'I'm kidding.'

'You'd better be.' He uncrossed his arms and stretched them above his head. Eleanor couldn't help but notice his T-shirt lift up to reveal a taut strip of stomach.

Stop staring, you creep!

This is Fin.

'That singing really took it out of me.' Fin yawned. 'I'm exhausted.'

'I think that's probably more to do with how little sleep you got last night. And that is most definitely my fault.' Eleanor felt her grip tighten on the steering wheel. She was reluctant to bring the mood down but knew she'd have to bring up last night at some point; better to say something before he did. Get it over and done with. Sooner rather than later.

'Was I completely awful?' She turned to look at Fin briefly.

He shook his head and smiled. 'No, you were fine. Apart from being a bit sick – well, quite a lot sick – you were harmless.'

A familiar flash of self-loathing punched her hard in the chest.

'Did anyone see me?'

'No. We were outside. All very discreet,' he assured her.

'Phew.' Eleanor felt her body relax. 'The thing is . . . I don't really remember anything about that bit of the night.' She spoke the words slowly and deliberately. 'I mean, the only reason I know I was sick was because . . .'

'You saw it all over your dress?' he quipped playfully.

Eleanor blushed with embarrassment. 'Yeah, exactly! Everything else is blank,' she lied. 'I don't remember anything. Like nothing at all.'

'Oh.' Fin's face fell for the briefest of moments. 'Of course you don't.' He tore his eyes away from hers and began fiddling with his seatbelt. 'You were pretty drunk, so that's not surprising.'

'Yeah.' She forced a laugh. 'Me and tequila really need to break up.' The joke landed awkwardly between them. 'So, anything I said or . . .' She paused; did she really need to say this? He clearly wasn't that bothered or concerned. He hadn't even mentioned the kiss! 'Or anything I *did*,' she continued. 'Could we erase it permanently from our minds, please?'

'No problem.' Fin turned his head to stare out of the window. 'Consider it done.'

*

The rest of her Sunday was spent in a restless haze of naps and carbohydrates. Ben had called her twice, but Eleanor couldn't face speaking to him. Even seeing his name flash up on the screen sent waves of sickening guilt through her. There was no way she could see him today. Her nerves and heart couldn't take it. Luckily, she'd managed to palm him off with a very apologetic and very hungover text. He'd been so sweet and so Ben-like about it, even offering to drop food and supplies over to her flat. The guilt cut her even deeper.

By Monday morning the hangover had all but gone, leaving only the emotional scars behind. The best way to get through the day was going to be by immersing herself completely and silently in PowerPoint decks and Excel spreadsheets. Meetings were an absolute no. Her team would have to find a way to fend for themselves for once. Her brain needed tasks and logic and focus. What she didn't need was conversation and thinking time.

It was a drunken kiss.

One stupid kiss.

And with Fin . . . of all people! It meant nothing.

'She lives! Another wedding survived.' Sal's voice rang out behind her. Eleanor jumped, throwing her notebook off the desk.

'Jesus, twitchy much?' Sal handed her the book and perched on the edge of her desk.

'You're the one who crept up behind me, what did you expect!' Eleanor snapped.

'Woah.' Sal held her hands up defensively. 'What's up with you?'

Eleanor sighed. 'Nothing, I'm sorry. I don't feel so great.'

'Tequila?' Sal smirked.

'Don't.' Eleanor squirmed. 'Why do I do it to myself?'

'Because you're a sucker for pain, like most of the human race. Was it good, though?'

'Yeah, it was fine. How was your mum's party?'

'It was boring. Standard family stuff.' Sal shrugged. 'Come on, tell me more about Laura's! I saw some of the pictures, she looked stunning as per.'

Eleanor hesitated. Normally Sal would have been the first person she told about her drunken antics, but Sal knew Ben, and Eleanor knew what she'd done was stupid. Surely there was no point making more drama than was necessary?

'You know, it was your classic, expensive, elegant and tear-jerkingly beautiful wedding. What did we expect from Laura?'

Keep it high-level. No detail. Don't give her anything to go on.

'And Fin?'

Eleanor's stomach tensed.

'What about him?'

Sal's eyes narrowed. 'As in . . . did he have fun?'

'Oh yeah. Loads of fun. I think he disappeared off at some point with one of Laura's new work colleagues.' Eleanor's voice had become extremely loud and a little too high-pitched. 'Didn't see him for most of it.'

'I see.' Sal folded her arms across her chest and continued to eye Eleanor suspiciously. 'Are you sure everything's all right? You're being weird and I don't know why.'

Eleanor felt beads of sweat blossom on her forehead. She pulled the corners of her mouth into an unwilling smile and forced herself to calm down.

'Just a lot of deadlines for this week, and I think I over-compensated my hangover with too much coffee this morning. I'm not built for triple shots like you.'

'Hmmm. Well, if you're sure.' Sal raised an eyebrow. 'Make sure you lay off the caffeine for the rest of the day, though, OK? You know how wired you get.'

Eleanor nodded obediently. 'Sure thing.'

'Good. I have to run; I've got a new intern starting and apparently I have to be around to show face.' She sighed.

'Enjoy!' Eleanor called, silently sending luck to the poor, innocent intern that was about to experience the full force of her friend.

'Thanks, I'll try.' Just as Sal was about to walk away, she paused. 'What are you doing this week, by the way? Fancy drinks one night?'

'Definitely. Although I can't do tomorrow, I have art club.'

'Art club?' Sal couldn't hide the surprise from her face.

'Yeah.'

'So you're painting again?' She nodded approvingly. 'If you ever need a nude subject, you know where I am.' Sal winked.

'Unfortunately we're still on fruit at the moment, but I'll be sure to bear your offer in mind for the future.'

Sal flashed her a wicked smile. 'Please do.'

As Eleanor watched her friend walk away, she couldn't help but feel relieved. She'd survived, albeit rather clumsily, her first encounter with Sal. Eleanor had been sure that five minutes into the conversation she would be confessing the whole sorry tale, but she'd managed to keep her mouth shut and her secret safe. Fin wasn't going to say anything, she was sure of that. The Fin she knew couldn't stand confrontation, and she prayed that his feelings on that hadn't changed.

The Fin you knew wouldn't have kissed you back.

'No.' She clenched her fists determinedly. 'No more Fin.'

Fin

He had been staring at the computer screen for so long his eyes physically ached. Sunday had been a write-off; the events of the night before had taken more out of him than he'd thought and he'd spent the whole afternoon asleep on the sofa. He needed to get Heidi's pictures finished as soon as possible. He didn't want anything hanging over him when he left for America. His ties to the UK would be clean cut after his mother passed, no more baggage or loose threads.

So, just like that, you're going to go and disappear from Eleanor's life again?

He kneaded his eyes with the palms of his hands, pushing the thoughts out with brute force. Fin had hoped focusing on the pictures would be the perfect distraction, but clearly thoughts of Eleanor weren't going away any time soon. He was confused. He knew the kiss didn't mean anything – she was drunk – but it was so nice to be back on talking terms he didn't want anything to ruin it. Did he need to bring it up? Make sure they were OK?

No. Leave it alone.

He needed to talk to someone about it all, but who? His mother? Absolutely not. Nurse Clara? He laughed at the very thought.

Fin glanced at the time. It was 8 a.m. on a Monday morning in London; would Rob really be up so late on a Sunday night?

'Only one way to find out.' He reached for his phone and searched his call list. His friend answered immediately.

'Hey, buddy.' The sound of Rob's voice brought a smile to Fin's face. It was like an instant dose of Californian sunshine. 'How are you?'

'All right, mate. Surprised you're awake!'

'Pshhht, you know me. I'm a night owl by nature.' Rob sighed. 'What's new with you? How's your mum doing?'

Fin closed his laptop and sank back into the sofa. 'Not good, although I swear I say that every time someone asks, yet she still lives to fight another day.'

'Probably where you get your stubbornness from,' Rob quipped.

'Probably. What's going on with you? Still in the throes of love?'

'Behave!' he sneered. 'But yeah, I'm still with Rachel. It's going surprisingly well.'

'Have you told her about your meat-eating tendencies yet?' Fin joked.

'I had to, mate. It was killing me. Going out to eat and seeing all those big steaks coming past me while I picked at my mushroom and tofu burger. She doesn't seem to mind. Maybe that's what love is, hey?'

How the hell would I know?

'Must be. I'm happy for you. When I'm back we'll have to

go for drinks or something? I want to meet this woman, check that she's real and all.'

'Yeah, for sure. The Finley Taylor stamp of approval is mandatory for any woman in my life.' Rob's voice was bursting with glee. 'Now tell me, have you met up with any other old friends you're planning to replace me with lately?' he teased.

Fin's lips tingled at the memory of Eleanor's kiss. 'Erm . . . well, about that.'

'*I knew it*,' Rob exclaimed. 'Who are they? How fun are they? Who do I need to push off the top spot?'

'It's not like that. It's just . . .' Fin ran his hand through his hair.

'What happened?' Rob replied knowingly.

'It's nothing really.'

'Doesn't sound like nothing,' Rob insisted.

'Well, long story short, I ended up going to a wedding with that old friend on Saturday. She needed a plus one, I volunteered my services; all very casual and low-key, you know?'

'Ever the gentleman,' Rob remarked.

'Yeah, quite.' How the hell was he going to explain this? There was so much to his and Eleanor's friendship that words alone wouldn't do the story justice.

'OK, so you're at the wedding with this friend of yours,' Rob prompted.

'And we kissed,' Fin blurted out.

'Cool. And?'

'And . . . she was drunk.'

'How drunk?'

Fin paused, already cringing at the memory. 'So drunk that she threw up afterwards.'

Rob's laugh was so loud Fin had to hold the phone away from his ear.

'Hey, come on!' he cried shamefully.

'Sorry, mate, but that is brilliant. How bad are you at kissing?' The raucous laughing continued for a good minute longer. 'Sorry, sorry. Carry on. You've smooched her, she's thrown up. Then what?'

'Nothing.'

'Nothing?'

'I took her back to her hotel room and put her to bed,' Fin relayed.

Rob paused. 'And you really are just old friends?'

'Yes.' Fin hesitated. 'Just friends.'

'So then what's the issue? No offence, but we all do stupid stuff when we're drunk. If you don't have feelings for the girl and you're mates then it's fine, right?'

Fin breathed in deeply. 'It's just, she says she doesn't remember anything from the night. I feel strange not saying anything. Should I tell her? I don't want things to be awkward between us.'

'No. Oh, hell no,' Rob said firmly.

'Why?'

'If she hasn't said anything then steer well clear. If girls want to talk about something they will. Otherwise leave it well alone. It will only make things weirder if you bring it up now.'

Fin let the advice settle in his mind.

'Just because you never stray from the tonic water these days doesn't mean the rest of us are angels.'

'True. I am a gift from God,' Fin teased, trying his best to ignore the million thoughts racing through his head.

'One that makes girls vomit with his kissing technique.'

'Hey! It wasn't me, it was the tequila.'

'Sure,' Rob scoffed. 'Right, buddy, I'd better get some sleep. Keep me posted on everything.'

'Thanks, mate. Will do.'

Fin hung up the phone and tried to muster some of the calm that Rob exuded.

It's fine.

Everything is going to be fine.

*

The pictures didn't take long to edit. Heidi was such a perfect sitter that the touches he needed to make were minimal. He only hoped she'd be as pleased with the results as he was. As soon as he was finished, he decided to go over to the care home. What else did he have to do with his day?

'Heidi?' He knocked lightly on the door to her room. 'It's me, Fin. I've got something to show you,' he called softly.

'Come in,' she replied curtly.

Fin opened the door and entered to find Heidi in her usual position, sitting upright in bed, staring blankly out of the window.

'I've finished the pictures. I thought you'd like to see them and maybe choose a couple for me to print?' he suggested hesitantly. Once again, she hadn't even bothered to turn and face him.

'Sure.' She sighed as though his very presence was an effort for her.

Fin sat down in the seat by her bed and pulled the laptop from his backpack. 'I edited them slightly, mainly to adjust the lighting. If I'm honest, they were pretty perfect as they were.'

Heidi turned her head and looked down at the screen he

held aloft. 'You'll have to bring it closer.' She tutted. 'My eyes aren't what they used to be.' She chewed on her thin lips anxiously. 'Nothing is.'

'Why don't I put this here?' He stood, placing the computer on her lap. 'All you need to do is click this button' – he pointed at the right arrow – 'to move through the pictures.'

The old lady nodded in understanding, her eyes focusing on the image in front of her. Fin watched silently, trying his best to glean any inclination of her feelings towards his work. She was as readable as concrete.

It took all of his control not to speak but finally, after what felt like hours, she raised her head and cocked it ever so slightly to one side. A tiny flicker of movement appeared at the edges of her mouth.

'Thank you,' she said resolutely. 'These really are . . .' Her eyes were glassy and her voice cracked. 'These are perfect.'

'I'm glad you like them.' He nodded appreciatively. 'Which ones shall I print?'

Heidi turned to look back at the screen and clicked through the reel of photos. 'These three.' She paused, her expression softening a little. 'Please.'

'Sure thing.' He took the laptop back, marking the pictures she'd chosen before stowing the computer back in his bag. 'I'll drop them off this week.' He swung his backpack over his shoulder and made to leave.

'Fin?' Her voice caught him as he was halfway out of the door. He turned back to face her, the fierce facade nearly all put back into place. 'Pass my thanks on to Eleanor, please.'

Fin smiled. 'I will, don't worry.' He made to go but once again her words kept him rooted.

'Oh, and Fin?' She raised a wiry eyebrow. 'If it were

me . . . I wouldn't let go of that one, now you've got her back.'

'Pardon?'

'You heard me,' she replied bluntly.

'I think you might have read that situation a little wrong, Heidi. Eleanor and I are just friends.' He laughed awkwardly, unable to push the memory of her kiss from his mind.

'That much is obvious.'

'Oh.' A flicker of disappointment sparked in the pit of his stomach. 'Well, what did you mean then?'

'I *meant* . . .' Heidi let out a sigh of indignation, looking once again out of the window. 'As someone who has spent the majority of her life by herself, friends like that are hard to come by. When you find them, personally I would think it criminal to walk away from them.'

'Right.' He smiled weakly. 'I'll bear that in mind.'

'Goodbye, Mr Taylor.'

'Goodbye, Heidi.' Fin retreated quickly, closing the door quietly behind him.

He stood for a moment in the hallway, bemused by Heidi and her parting words. There was obviously more to her than met the eye; underneath those thick layers of steel seemed to live a human being, but he was dammed if he knew how to get her out for more than a few seconds at a time.

'Hi, Fin.' A young nurse emerged from the room next door, pulling him out of his thoughts. 'Survived your meeting with Heidi, I see?' She grinned brightly, her eyes betraying her tiredness with their dark circles.

'Only just,' he joked. 'How's my mum doing?' he asked, knowing his mother would always hide the truth from him when he asked her directly.

The nurse gave him an encouraging smile. 'The doctor

came by earlier and gave her some more pain relief. When she's awake she seems very upbeat, but she is sleeping a lot.' Notes of sorrow pierced through her enthusiasm. 'Are you going to pop in and see her?'

'Yeah. I was on my way now,' he replied.

'She'll love that,' the nurse chirped. 'Anyway, I'd better carry on with my rounds. See you later.' She waved and scurried away in the opposite direction.

'See you,' he replied to the blank space left in front of him.

Eleanor

By Tuesday evening, Eleanor's fingers were itching for the brush. It was funny how quickly the urge to paint had returned after only one session. A sleeping beast awoken from its slumber, the cravings crying out to be sated.

'Hello, Eleanor dear,' Agatha half sang, half shrieked as she walked into the hall. 'We feared you'd never return, but here you stand and your seat awaits.' She pointed across the room to the empty chair next to Reggie, who was already in place and not looking happy about it.

'Thanks, Agatha.' Eleanor moved quickly across the room, reeling from the spotlight that had been unceremoniously shone on to her.

'Thank the Lord you came back,' Reggie grunted. 'She was on at me non-stop. Blamed me for your no-show.' He nodded towards Agatha, who was busying herself at the refreshment table. 'Said I must have offended you. Can you imagine? Me? Offensive?' He waved his wrinkled hand dismissively. 'Never!'

Eleanor placed her jacket on the back of her chair and

smiled. 'No, in fact you are the epitome of warm and welcoming, aren't you, Reggie?'

He clucked indignantly. 'I wouldn't go that far, but I may be a little warmer and a *little* bit more welcoming with a cup of tea and a biscuit in my hand.'

'Would you now?' She eyed him shrewdly. 'Good job I was heading over there myself. I'll bring back the supplies.'

'Get the jam-filled ones,' he shouted at her, as she walked over to join Agatha. 'Before everyone else gets their greedy paws on them!'

'His daughters thought that coming here might soften him up. Bring him a little joy.' Agatha giggled as she unashamedly stirred five sugar lumps into her tea. 'I think we're working our magic, don't you?' She winked and handed Eleanor the selection box of biscuits.

'Definitely.' She grinned.

'We're very pleased you're back.' Agatha leant in close, dropping her voice to a whisper. 'And I think this next little project will be much more up your street than a mouldy old pear.'

'Oh, really?' Eleanor was intrigued.

'Indeed. Come now, as soon as everyone is gathered, I can reveal all.' She tapped a finger slyly against the side of her nose and returned to the centre of the circle, leaving Eleanor with the task of carrying two teas and a plate of biscuits back across the room.

'Hurry up, will you?' Reggie grumbled. 'Enid's going to be up there soon for seconds by the time we've even tasted a crumb.'

'You won't even get that if you carry on shouting at me,' she snapped back.

Agatha clapped her hands together in delight. 'Oh-ho, Reggie, you'd better be careful. Looks like our Eleanor here takes no prisoners. Come, everyone, sit, sit! It's time to announce our new and exciting project.'

Eleanor half walked, half ran back to her seat, trying not to cry out as the hot tea splashed over the sides of the cup and on to her hand.

'I've known most of you for a very long time now. And it's clear that your talents deserve more to play with than some pieces of old fruit and store cupboard items. It's time we levelled up.' She spoke with such energy that Eleanor could almost see the sparkles of light beaming from her. 'So, I thought we could experiment with a bit of *imagination*.' She whispered the word dramatically, eyeing the group desperately for a reaction. All that was returned was the shuffling of chairs and the loud chewing of biscuits.

'Right!' Agatha steeled herself. 'What does that mean, I hear you cry. Well, let me tell you.' Her audience remained silent and blank-faced. 'I will provide a word which will be your theme for the next month of classes. You will paint or create a piece of art that, to you, encapsulates this word fully. You have complete creative freedom as long as it relates back to the theme.'

Nods passed between the group.

'We will present our works at the end of the month and have a little group celebration. Sound good?'

More nods and a few murmurs of 'yes' rippled around the circle.

Eleanor felt the air bristle next to her as Reggie moved in close. 'I bet you that last jammy dodger that the word is love.' He dropped his voice for her ears only.

Eleanor took a sip of her tea. 'This last jammy dodger?' She held the biscuit in question aloft.

'The very one.'

'I don't think Agatha is that transparent. I have more faith in her than that.' Eleanor put the biscuit down and held her hand out to Reggie. 'You're on.'

He took it and shook it firmly. 'Big mistake, kid.' He chuckled, seating himself upright once again.

'Would you like to know the theme?' Agatha rubbed her hands together, her eyes so big that they occupied half of her glowing face.

'Tell us already, will you?' Reggie cried.

'All right, calm down, you keen bean.' Agatha chortled. 'The theme of the month is . . . "forget me not",' she trilled, throwing her arms wide in joy.

'That's not one word!' Reggie barked. 'Forget me not?' he huffed. 'What does that even *mean*?'

Eleanor looked around the circle at the others' equally confused faces. Agatha's arms dropped limply to her sides, her excitement brutally extinguished.

'I thought it was a clever play on words, you know?' She looked around for some support.

'Yes. It's really clever,' Eleanor found herself announcing loudly.

What are you doing, Eleanor? Shut up!

But the defeated look on Agatha's face was too painful to ignore.

'You could have forget-me-not, the flowers . . .' Eleanor continued. 'Forget-me-not, the colour blue, or not wanting to be forgotten by someone. Someone or something that we've lost. There's so much to play with.'

'Or paint with.' Agatha winked, cheered on by Eleanor's support. 'Is everyone OK with that?'

Another round of hushed agreements signalled the group's acceptance of their task.

'Brilliant. Well then . . . ready . . . set . . . paint!' Agatha whooped.

Eleanor picked up her winnings, turning the biscuit proudly in her hand. 'Looks like this is mine then, doesn't it?'

'She said *word*. One bleeding word,' Reggie sniped. 'How is it my fault if she can't stick to her own rules?'

'Don't be a sore loser. It doesn't suit you.' Eleanor smiled, shoving the entire biscuit into her mouth.

'I tell you what, I'd rather forget this whole stupid class if I'm honest,' Reggie grumbled.

'Why don't you draw a bunch of flowers, colour them blue and be done with it then?' Eleanor turned her attention to her rather large vacant canvas.

'Because that would not reflect my immense skill and talent.' He cracked his fingers painfully and began pulling out various drawing utensils from his bag.

'Forget me not,' Eleanor whispered to herself, closing her eyes and allowing her mind to wander freely.

Then all at once, his face appeared before her, as clear and real as if he were standing right in front of her.

'OK, Dad.' She reached for a pencil. 'Let's do it.'

*

By Friday night her avoidance plans had been thwarted. Ben had surprised her by turning up on her doorstep with take-out and dark chocolate.

'If the lady won't come to me, then I guess I will just have to come to her.' He shrugged, handing her the plastic bags full of food.

'Ben!' She was thrown completely, her mind a blur of thoughts and her heart a whirr of feelings. 'You really shouldn't have.'

'I wanted to see you.' His smiling face dropped. 'Wait, are you busy? Sorry, I didn't even think. Do you have people over?'

Eleanor couldn't help but laugh. 'No, it's fine, come in.' She turned and walked back into the kitchen, her stomach growling in response to the spicy aromas wafting from the bags in his hands.

'Pretty full-on week for you then, hey?' he asked, leaning his sturdy frame against the worktop. He couldn't look any more different from Fin if he tried.

Why are you even thinking about Fin right now?

I'm not thinking about him.

I was just observing.

Well, don't.

'Yeah, it's been busier than I expected.' She unpacked the boxes, trying not to meet his gaze. 'How was yours?'

'Fine. Same old, same old for me.' He came and stood behind her, placing his hands around her waist. The touch of him made her skin prickle with goosebumps. 'Definitely much better now.' He nuzzled his face into the back of her neck.

'Hey!' She melted a little. 'We'd better eat or this will get cold.'

'Argh,' he groaned as Eleanor pulled away. 'You're killing me over here. I haven't seen you in so long.' Ben ran a hand across his shaven head.

Just like Fin.

She shook the thought from her mind and busied herself with grabbing fistfuls of cutlery.

Pull yourself together.

She turned to face him, her lips curling into a wry smile. 'Well, Mr Ryans, the quicker we eat the quicker we can . . .' She paused, surprised by her own boldness. 'Do *other* things.'

His blue eyes flashed with excitement. He grabbed the food and ran to the table. 'Hurry up then, what are you waiting for?'

'You're ridiculous.' She laughed. 'Only here for one thing. Typical.'

'Yeah.' He looked up at her, fixing his eyes on hers with an intense gaze. 'I'm here for you.'

Eleanor's body burned with a confusing mix of longing and guilt. She forced her eyes away from his and laughed self-consciously. 'And look at that, here I am.'

'I love it when you get all shy.'

Eleanor shot him a glaring look.

'All right, all right, I'll be quiet and eat.' He reached over and took one of the trays of food, unloading it hastily on to his plate. 'How's Fin doing?'

Eleanor's hand faltered, slopping curry sauce all over the table.

'What do you mean?' she asked warily.

Ben continued plating up, seemingly unaware of her reaction. 'As in . . . how's he doing? How's his mum?'

Eleanor willed her pounding heart to quieten; it was practically beating out the confession against her ribs.

'I haven't actually spoken to him since the weekend. I'll message him later.'

No, you won't.

Another pang of guilt stung her. Guilt about kissing Fin. Guilt about not speaking to Fin. Guilt sitting here with the lovely Ben, thinking about the kiss with Fin. How many more feelings could she realistically carry in her tiny heart?

'Remember, us men don't tend to find talking about our emotions easy.' He twirled his Singapore noodles around on his fork. 'He might need a little encouragement.'

She flashed what she hoped was a sincere-looking smile. 'Gotcha. Do some poking.'

Do some poking?

What the hell are you saying, woman!

Ben choked with laughter. 'I mean, if you want to say it like that, then sure!' His eyes twinkled cheekily. 'But don't do *too* much poking. Save some for me, please.'

Eleanor's cheeks flushed pink again. 'Stop that.' She slapped him gently on the wrist.

'You said it, not me.' He winked.

Silence settled over them, comfortable and calming as it always was between them. Unfortunately, the same could not be said for Eleanor's inner world. Her anxious mind was never easy to deal with, but tonight it was reaching new heights.

'By the way, what are you doing next Friday?' Ben asked, pushing his cleared plate away proudly.

Eleanor narrowed her eyes suspiciously. 'Nothing . . . why?'

'Do I need a reason for wanting to take my girlfriend out for dinner?' He grinned.

Eleanor's mind tripped over itself.

Girlfriend?

Did he say girlfriend?

'Look at your face!' He laughed loudly. 'You look terrified.'

'No, I don't.' She rearranged her expression hurriedly. 'I wasn't expecting you to say that.'

'The dinner part?' He leant in and smirked. 'Or the girlfriend part?'

'You know what part,' she cried childishly.

'Well?' he asked.

'Well what?'

'Will you come to dinner with me on Friday?' Ben reached his hand out and placed it over hers. 'As my girlfriend?'

Her storming mind quietened at his touch. 'I'd love to,' she replied, sparks of anticipation dancing across her skin.

'Good.' He grinned. 'Now, my next question is . . . what's for dessert? Because I'm really hoping it's you.'

'You are *so predictable*.' She shrieked as he pulled her on to his lap and began kissing her neck.

Fin

There had been no word from Eleanor since she'd dropped him back at his flat after the wedding. He supposed this wasn't unusual – it wasn't as though they talked much normally – but somehow her silence felt pointed and deliberate. He thought about messaging her a number of times, but what was there really to say? How are you? Want to go for a coffee? No. Rob was right. If she wanted to talk, she would talk. It just sucked that his only real social life in London had been through Eleanor, and now he was back to Netflix and care home visits. And he found neither particularly enjoyable.

'Hey, Mum.' He closed the door behind him as quietly as he could, dropping his voice the moment he saw her sleeping. He tiptoed as lightly as possible across the room and into the seat next to her bed. As he was about to pull his trusty crossword book from his bag, he noticed a large cardboard box towards the end of her bed. Scribbled across it in big black marker pen was his name. He cast a quick glance at his mother, who was still out for the count, and carefully slid the chair towards it. He tried to lift it up but it was heavier than he expected, so instead he left it on the floor and came to sit beside it on the carpet.

Intrigue was bubbling to the surface, but right alongside it was a pang of caution.

Should you really be opening this without her knowing?

It's got my name on it!

The voices argued back and forth until eventually the strength of his curiosity won out. He checked to see if the box was sealed, but thankfully it wasn't. Carefully, without making a sound, he opened the large cardboard flaps and peered inside.

His heart sank a little in disappointment.

'Photographs and paperwork,' he grumbled, pulling a stack of old pictures and ring binders out and on to the floor. 'Basically admin.'

'Fin?' his mum called out groggily. He shoved the paperwork back in the box and closed the lid quickly.

'Hey!' he replied, a little too brightly.

'What are you doing down there?' she asked suspiciously.

'I dropped my pen and was trying to find it without waking you.'

'Oh. Have you got it?'

'Yeah, all good.' He waved his pen enthusiastically in the air. 'How are you feeling?'

'So, so.' She inched her way up a little, the effort of such a minuscule movement plain as day on her face. 'Did you find anything good?'

He came to sit next to her bed and frowned. 'What do you mean?'

'In the box you were rifling through over there.' She chuckled hoarsely.

'Ah.' He smirked guiltily. 'You caught me.'

'You never were a very good liar,' she mused. 'It's probably just a bunch of old junk to you, but it's all the memories I kept from the house before I came here. I thought you could see if there was anything you wanted to keep when . . . you know.' She looked down sadly at her ghostly hands. 'When I die.'

Fin recoiled at the bluntness and the almost casual way she spoke the words. Even though it was obviously fast approaching, it was still a topic they hadn't touched upon since his arrival. Maybe avoiding the hard conversations ran in the family.

'Thanks. I'll take a look later.'

'It's not going to be long,' his mum continued. 'The doctor came to see me yesterday and things seem to be progressing fairly quickly now.'

'I'm sorry. Is there . . .' He went to reach for her hand but halfway through decided against it. 'Is there anything I can do? To help?'

'Yes, actually there is.'

'Sure, what is it?'

'I want you to call your father.' She closed her eyes as though to steady herself.

'What?' he objected fiercely. 'No!'

'Fin.' She sighed, opening her eyes. 'This has gone on far too long. You said you'd help me.'

'Yes, and I meant things like get you your favourite food or buy your favourite flowers.' He knew he sounded childish and petulant, but he couldn't help but feel blindsided by her request. 'Not this. Anything but this.'

'Please. This is for me. It's important to *me*.' She spoke softly, almost wearily.

Fin sat in silence, chewing the request over and over in his mind. Was he really going to be able to say no to a dying woman? Did his hatred for his father really run that deep?

'Does he know you're here?' Fin asked quietly.

'No. I'd like you to tell him.'

'Why?'

'Because he was my husband for twenty years, and before I die I want him to know I forgive him.'

This was too much. Any ounce of patience Fin had left immediately vanished.

'*How?*' he cried. 'After everything he did to you. To us?' Rage was surging through him, uncontrollably taking over every one of his senses. 'Tell me how, Mum? How can you forgive that? He left us. He left *you* all alone.'

'I wasn't alone,' she whispered.

'Yes, you were. You used to say it all the time. You'd cry constantly about how lonely you were without him. How unfair it was that he could do this and be happy and remarry and you were stuck by yourself.' Memories cut through him like razor blades. 'Do you know how many times I had to listen to you cry yourself to sleep over this? I was fifteen, Mum. *Fifteen.* All I needed was my mum. All I wanted after he left was for you and I to be together. To create a decent home. Yet all you ever did was pine after him. I wasn't good enough. Nothing I could offer was good enough.'

'That's not true.' She scrunched her eyes up tightly.

'Really? Even after I left to go travelling, the only times I'd hear from you were when you wanted to talk about Dad. It was always about him.'

'I know.' She shook her head in despair. 'Don't you think I look back and wish I could have done it differently, Fin? Don't you think I look back and hate myself for being that way?' Her breathing was growing heavier, her chest rising and falling rapidly.

'But it hasn't changed, has it?' he shouted, forcing himself to stay seated as the frustration threatened to lift him from his chair. 'Even now, on your deathbed, you want me to call him. Yet it took a complete stranger to call me behind your back to let me know you were sick. How do you think that makes me *feel*, Mum?' His voice cracked as he spoke the last word. All of the years of pain he'd so artfully buried were now free from their hiding place.

'I didn't think you wanted me in your life any more. You stopped writing to me when you moved to America. I tried to call a couple of times but you didn't answer. I just assumed you had started a new life, without me. And you know what? How could I blame you? I was hardly mother of the year.' She threw her head back as the tears ran down her papery cheeks. 'And I didn't call you when I got sick because I didn't want to burden you. You'd spent enough time picking me up off the floor and caring for me. I didn't want to put you through any more of it.'

Fin couldn't speak. The anguish on his mum's face was almost unbearable, but the flames of anger were still burning brightly.

'I failed you, Fin. On so many levels I failed you, and it took me too long to see it. I'm sorry, and I don't expect you to forgive me, but I don't want to die with any resentment or any regret. I want to go with a clean slate. So please, will you help me?'

Fin closed his eyes and let his head hang for a moment.

'Will you call your father for me? *Please.*'

'Fine. I'll do it.' He kept his voice devoid of emotion; he needed to try and distance himself as much as possible from his own feelings. 'When? When do you want me to call him?'

The look on her face said enough. 'You want me to call him now, don't you?' He stood reluctantly. 'Do you have his number?'

His mother nodded. 'In my address book on the side.'

'I'll be back in a second.' He turned to leave, grabbing the little book and shoving it hard in his pocket. Just as he was about to close the door, he stopped. 'You were wrong . . .' He looked back over his shoulder at the tiny figure, with her hopeful tired eyes. 'It was never a burden. You were my mum.'

He didn't even wait for her response before closing the door gently behind him.

*

Just do it already.

Call, tell him the news and hang up.

Fin knew he didn't have the luxury of time to waste, but it didn't stop him from standing outside procrastinating. He'd left his mum more than ten minutes ago, and still he hadn't called.

'Simple,' he muttered, pacing back and forth along the main road outside the care home. 'It's simple.' Fin looked down at his phone and hit call.

'Hello?' It took two rings for his father to pick up.

'Hi . . . is that Brian?'

Why the formality?

Because I can't call him Dad, can I?

'Yes . . . speaking.' The booming voice of his father vibrated into his ear. 'Can I ask who's calling?'

'It's Fin.'

There was an audible intake of breath and then a deathly silence.

'Finley Taylor,' he repeated, as though it wasn't clear the first time.

'I knew who you meant.' His father sounded a little flustered. 'Are you OK?'

'I'm fine.'

Keep it short.

'It's Mum,' he continued. 'I don't know how much you know, but she's asked me to call and tell you that she's sick. Really sick. As in . . .' – he clenched his fists tightly and forced the words out as quickly as possible – 'she's-not-got-long-to-live sick.'

The only sound from the other end of the phone was deep laboured breathing.

'So, yeah . . . She wanted me to let you know.' Fin paused. 'Are you still there?'

His father cleared his throat. 'Yes. I'm here.'

'Good.' Fin wasn't quite sure where to go next. He had been expecting the call to be awkward and painful but not silent. His father hadn't ever had a problem with words. In fact, he had always spoken too much and too loudly, in Fin's opinion. This was new territory and he didn't like it one bit.

'Is there anything else?' his dad stated mechanically.

'Erm.' Fin kicked the ground hopelessly. 'She wants you to know that she forgives you.'

Everything went quiet again; even his dad's breathing became barely audible.

'That was it really,' Fin finished.

'Right.' His father cleared his throat. 'Well, I'm sorry to hear that.'

Fin waited. Surely there was something more? There had to be something more. But the silence continued.

'And that . . . I hope she's not in any pain.'

'You hope she's not in any *pain*?' Fin laughed. 'For Christ's sake, her body is being eaten from the inside out by cancer. She's got dementia and she's stuck in a care home, bedbound and drugged up to her eyeballs on pain medication.' The words were flowing out of him, the pain, the frustration, the pent-up emotion emptying itself at last.

'That's not my fault,' his dad replied bluntly. 'I'm sorry it's happened to her, but she's not my responsibility any more.'

Fin wanted to scream, to throw the phone across the road and break it into tiny pieces.

'Nobody is asking you to take responsibility for her. I'm just asking you to stop being a complete and utter prick of a human being for once in your life and show some humanity to the woman you were married to for twenty years before she dies. It's not hard.' He could feel his vein throbbing in his temple, the anger surging through his entire body.

'Like I said. Please tell her I'm sorry.' It was like listening to an automated machine, blindly spouting the same infuriating response over and over.

Fin gripped the phone as hard as he could. 'Don't worry, I'll make sure to pass on your heartfelt condolences.' He paused, the words impatiently pressing their way to the front of his mind.

Don't do it.

It's not worth it.

He's not worth it.

But it was too late. His mouth was open and the toxicity pouring out of him before he could think twice about stopping. 'And believe me, one day, you will be sorry. You'll be so sorry that you won't know what to do with your pathetic self, and I hope, goddammit, I hope that there's no one around to make you feel better or tell you it's going to be OK. I hope you wake up one day very sorry and very alone.' His hands were shaking and his voice was trembling. 'Because that is the least you deserve.'

Fin hung up before he dared speak another word. There was nothing more to be said. He was done and it was finally time to move on.

Then: Aged 18

Fin

Fin checked the time. He still had a good two hours before his taxi was set to arrive and his mum wouldn't be home for at least another four.

You can do this.

Everything is going to work out fine.

Fin took a deep breath and focused his attention on what was left to do. He had finished most of his packing, he had his visa application ready, his tickets, his passport and his letter to Eleanor written and sealed. The only things outstanding were making some sandwiches for the plane and trying to sneak as many snacks and cereal bars as possible from the kitchen.

'*Fin,*' a loud voice called from outside his window.

He dropped to his knees and prayed that he hadn't been seen.

'It's too late, I saw you in the window,' Eleanor continued to shout. 'If you don't come down and let me in, I'll stand here screaming until you do.'

She wouldn't do that . . .

'*Finley Taylor.*' Her voice reached an even louder volume. '*Don't try me.*'

She really would.

Reluctantly, he got up from the floor and peered out of the window. There she was, his best friend in the entire world glaring up at him, hands on hips and a deep scowl on her face.

'Any time soon would be good.' She pouted angrily.

Fin ran his hands through his hair. He knew there was no escaping now, so very slowly he made his way out of his bedroom and down the stairs. Every step he took, excuses and lies swam temptingly around his mind.

She doesn't have to know.

One more lie won't hurt her.

But the moment he opened the door, he knew any attempt at deceit would be useless. Eleanor only had to look at him a certain way and the truth would always come spilling out. She was the only person in the world he had been able to be honest with, except for the past couple of weeks. Guilt swirled sickeningly inside him.

I had to lie.

It was for her own good.

'Aren't you going to invite me in?' She frowned.

'Sure.' Fin stepped back and made way for Eleanor to pass. The moment the front door was shut, she turned on him.

'So, what's all this about then?' she asked, the anger leaving just enough room for the hurt to appear. 'You've practically disappeared off the face of the earth the last two weeks. I've called. I've texted.' Fin went to open his mouth but Eleanor cut him off. 'And don't give me the "I've been sick" bullshit any more. You're fine. I know you're fine. So why are you avoiding me?'

Fin put his hands in his pockets and felt his shoulders slump forward. 'I had some stuff to sort out,' he offered weakly.

'Stuff?' she pressed, her voice sounding scarily like her mother's. Fin was about to comment on their likeness when he realized that maybe now was not the time.

'Yeah. Stuff.'

'Cool, well don't blow my mind with details or anything,' she snarked.

'I don't know what you want me to say.' He shrugged.

'I want you to tell me why you're avoiding me! Why my best friend in the entire world has stopped talking to me?' Her face flashed with concern. 'Is this because I told your mum about the other night?'

Fin's shame crawled up his throat and began to wrap its cold fingers around his heart. Although he didn't remember much about the night she'd found him passed out, fragmented flashbacks told him everything he needed to know. 'No.' He shook his head.

'It is, isn't it?' She took a step towards him and narrowed her eyes. Fin tried to avoid her gaze but it was pointless. She was so close to his face that he could smell her skin and feel her breath mingling with his.

'Fin, I'm sorry. I was worried about you. I've never seen you like that and I had to tell someone,' she pleaded, her coat of angry armour falling by the wayside. 'You said everything was fine after you talked to her.'

'It *was* fine, until she went and told my dad.' Fin could feel the resentment burning hot in his stomach, melting the shame away with its intense heat.

'Oh.' Eleanor took a step back. 'What did he say?' she asked tentatively.

'Just the usual.' Fin gritted his teeth. 'That I was a pathetic waste of space and how ashamed he was to even call me a son. How he was booking me into a rehab facility whether I liked it or not. That the only way I would ever make something of myself was if I grew up and stopped acting like a child.' Tears were building behind his eyes but he forced them to stay put. He didn't want to cry. Not over his dad.

'I'm so sorry. I had no idea.' Eleanor softened. 'Are you going to go?'

'To rehab?' Fin laughed. 'No. Not a chance in hell. I'm leaving.'

Eleanor's face crumpled in confusion. 'What do you mean, leaving?'

'The country. I'm getting out of this shithole. Away from my arsehole of a dad and pathetic pushover of a mum. I fly tonight.' He winced as Eleanor's mouth fell open.

'No.' She took a step towards him and reached for his arm. 'Don't go. You can't go.'

'I have to.' He moved away from her. 'I can't stay here, Elles. Surely you can understand that?'

'But what about me? I'm still here.' There was so much angst in her voice that Fin was finding it hard not to change his mind right there and then. To promise to stay with her for ever and to never leave. But he couldn't. He wouldn't be a burden on her any longer. He knew if he stayed she'd do everything to make sure he was OK. It wasn't right. It wasn't fair.

'You'll be fine. You'll go off to uni and make loads of new friends, and then you can come and visit me in all the cool places I end up.' He attempted a smile, but Eleanor's face remained stony.

'I don't want other friends. I want you. What about the plans we had? You promised me.'

Fin could feel the urge to stay growing with every word she spoke. This was exactly why he hadn't wanted to see her before he left. He'd known it would be too hard to say good-bye like this.

'We're not kids any more, Elles,' he snapped. 'I'm going whether you like it or not.'

'Well, screw you for being so goddam selfish,' she spat, turning on her heel and storming out of the door.

*

Just under two hours later and everything was ready to go. Fin had scribbled a quick note to his mum, letting her know his plans. She may not have been the best parent in the world, but she didn't deserve her son to leave without at least some explanation. The interaction with Eleanor was still sitting uncomfortably in his heart, but he couldn't think about that right now. If he gave her even one second's thought, he knew he'd never leave.

There was a loud knock on the door.

'Hello?' he called tentatively.

'Taxi for Mr Taylor?' a chirpy voice replied.

'Coming!' He hauled his rucksack on to his back and took one last look at the house. The house that had once been a source of security and solidarity was now full of bitter words and unspoken resentment.

'Do you need any help with bags?' the taxi driver asked through the door.

Fin opened it and stepped out. 'No, all good. I'm travelling light.'

'Nice. Quick trip somewhere, is it?' the man asked.

'Not quite.' Fin grinned, following the driver down the front path and to the black car waiting on the side of the road. 'I'm going to India actually.'

'Jesus, how long for?'

'No idea.' He threw his bag into the boot of the car and felt the enormity of his decision slowly dawn on him.

'Brave lad. I like that.' The man nodded approvingly. 'Right, shall we get to it then?'

Fin walked over to the passenger side and was about to open the door when he saw a figure running towards him. He narrowed his eyes and saw the familiar mass of curly brown hair flying out in all directions.

'*Fin*,' Eleanor's voice rang out. '*Hold on.*'

'I'll wait inside.' The taxi driver winked, before disappearing into the front seat.

'Don't go yet!' Eleanor shouted again. Fin watched as her tiny figure came closer and closer until she was standing in front of him, panting, sweating and red in the face.

'Eleanor, what on earth are you doing?'

'I had to say goodbye,' she puffed.

Fin couldn't help but laugh as the sweat poured from her face. 'Christ, how far did you run?'

Eleanor put a hand on her waist and winced. 'From mine. Fastest I've ever done it, to be honest. If I wasn't in so much pain, I'd be pretty pleased with myself.'

'I'm sorry about earlier,' he mumbled.

'Me too.' She stood and looked at him hard. 'Can I come with you to the airport? You know, to see you off properly.' Her eyes were sparkling, the light brown shimmering almost gold in the dying sunlight.

'Elles.' Fin wiped a damp curl from her face and felt his

heart fill with a bittersweet mix of love and loss. 'I wouldn't have it any other way.'

'You're my best, Fin.' She sighed.

'You're my bestest, Elles,' he replied, opening the car door and jumping inside.

Eleanor

Eleanor knew she was being immature, but somehow not talking to Fin made forgetting about her impulsive kissing episode a lot easier. Out of sight, out of mind. That was the key. It also helped that between work, art classes, Ben and lunches with her mother, Eleanor was able to stay fairly distracted and busy.

'I'm actually *starving*,' Freya remarked as she clambered out of the car. 'I think I might be disappointed if we don't have five puddings.'

Eleanor laughed feebly, her mind still consumed by thoughts.

'Honestly, the look on Fin's face the other day when the trifle came out was a picture,' she scoffed. 'I felt like he was about to cry! It's so nice that he's back. I've missed him.'

'Mmm, yeah.'

'Do you think he'll stay around long after his mum passes? I don't want him to disappear again.'

'Yeah,' Eleanor replied distractedly.

'Excuse me. Are you even listening?' Freya barked, shaking her shoulder gently as they walked up the path towards their mother's front door.

'Yeah, sorry.' Eleanor tried to focus. 'I'm attempting to zone out before we get inside. It's a new tactic I'm trying,' she joked.

'Not a bad idea.' Freya looked at her, impressed. 'Shall I do the honours?' She nodded to the pink front door, her hand ready to knock.

'Please. Be my guest.'

Freya rapped hard on the door. Normally their mother was ready to greet them from the moment their feet touched the gravel drive, but today there was silence.

'Mum?' Eleanor called, as Freya knocked a little harder. Silence.

'Where the hell could she be? You don't think she's got a man in there, do you?' Freya's eyes widened in horror.

'Ew, absolutely not! Angela Levy mates for life. There's no way she's with another man,' Eleanor replied, trying desperately to convince herself at the same time.

'*Mum*,' Freya shouted, banging loudly on the door.

'All right, give me one *second*, will you?' the raised voice of their mother called from within. There was a distinct wobble to it that they hadn't heard before.

Eleanor and Freya looked at each other in confusion.

'Does she sound OK to you?' Freya whispered.

But before Eleanor could respond, the door opened.

'Mum?' Freya gasped, staring at the figure in front of them. The brazen woman draped in swathes of beaded chiffon and layers of embroidered silk had been replaced with an old woman in a dressing gown. The usual made-up face and blow-dried hair instead looked pale and bare and limp.

'Mum, are you OK?' Eleanor asked, perplexed.

'Come. Come in,' she whimpered, pulling the soft cotton robe around her more tightly and ushering the pair inside.

Nobody spoke; the situation was too surreal for either sister to comprehend. Eleanor tried to make sense of what was happening, looking around the house in search of any clues. Their mother led them into the kitchen and sat down in the chair.

'Frey, make some tea, will you?' Eleanor found her voice at last. 'Mum, what's going on? Are you sick?'

Angela gave a little hiccup of a laugh. 'No, no, I'm not sick. Although I can see why you'd think that.' She smoothed her fluffy hair self-consciously. 'I didn't want you to see me like this.'

'You look fine.' Freya placed her hand tentatively on her shoulder.

'*Please.*' Their mother snorted with derision. 'I didn't even look this bad when I gave birth to you, darling, and that was an ordeal to say the least.'

Freya gave Eleanor her 'over to you' look, and turned back to busy herself with the tea.

'OK . . . you look awful,' Eleanor stated bluntly, trying to emulate her best version of Angela Levy's tough love. 'Why do you think we're so worried? Forgive us for thinking the worst.'

The edges of her mother's lips gave a little pull upwards; the briefest hint of a smile appeared on her face.

'So . . .' Eleanor continued. 'What's happened?'

'Well,' Angela sighed. 'Everything was fine. I got up, did my yoga stretches, had a little chat with your father.' Freya gave Eleanor a very concerned look but she ignored it. There would be plenty of time to discuss their mother talking to their dead father later. 'And I was about to make my breakfast when the phone rang. It was one of the nurses from Eileen's care home.' Her voice began to tremble. 'Eileen,' she whispered, shaking her head in despair. 'Oh, poor Eileen.'

Eleanor's mind was racing. She wanted her mum to hurry up and tell her what had happened, but she knew she had to be patient.

Angela managed to steady herself and continue. 'The doctor says it's only a matter of days now. I knew it was coming. We all knew it was coming. I mean, she barely keeps her eyes open when I visit, and I have been assured by the nurses on multiple occasions it's not just when I come to see her!' A glimmer of the Angela Levy humour sparkled through the clouds of sadness. 'But hearing it like that, it . . . I suppose it took me back to when your father passed. Those final days. The heaviness of it all. Then before I knew it, the doorbell was ringing and here you both were. I must have been sitting here for hours.'

Eleanor's thoughts were immediately filled with Fin.

'I'm sorry, Mum.' Freya came and sat down at the table, passing her a big cup of tea. 'That really sucks.'

'Yeah.' Eleanor reached her hand out to her mum. 'It does.'

'Hmmmm.' Her mother sighed, taking tiny tentative sips of her drink.

'Did they find out today?' Eleanor asked, trying to subtly establish how bad a friend she'd been to Fin.

'No. The doctor came to see her a couple of days ago, I believe.'

'Oh,' she replied glumly.

'I'm surprised you didn't know already,' her mother went on curiously. 'Have you not spoken to Fin?'

Guilt clawed at her throat. 'No, not really. I assumed he'd let me know if anything really bad happened.'

A look of disbelief broke out on Angela's face. 'Eleanor!' she gasped, all traces of the meek and mild woman that had been sitting in front of them disappearing instantly. 'His mother is *dying*. Did you really expect him to reach out to you? He's a man. They don't talk.'

'And you think I can make him? I don't even really know him any more.'

You know him well enough to kiss him.

'Yes, you do, my dear! He's the same boy you grew up with underneath it all. Anyway . . .' – she bristled, planting her mug down hard on the table – 'do you think I got a word out of your father voluntarily? I don't think so.'

'Sorry. I've been preoccupied.'

'Psht,' her mother scorned. 'A poor excuse if ever I heard one.'

'It's true!' Eleanor insisted. 'Besides, this isn't about me right now. It's about you. Are you OK?'

All at once, her mother looked down, as though only really seeing herself for the first time. 'Good Lord, this won't do,' she announced with disgust. 'I'm going to shower.'

'Are you sure you don't want to sit for a bit longer?' Freya asked cautiously, eyeing Eleanor warily.

'Darling, I think I've been sitting around moping for quite long enough,' she replied. 'Sitting doesn't do anything for anybody.' She stood up decisively. 'Eleanor, make sure you

313

call Fin, and Freya, make us some sandwiches. There's plenty in the fridge. I won't be long.'

And with that, she left.

'Wow.' Freya stared at Eleanor, still looking bewildered. 'We need a serious debrief in the car home.'

'Big time.' Eleanor stood and began clearing away the half-drunk cups of tea. 'Now come on, if we don't have a full spread laid out ready for when she's done, we'll be in a world of trouble.'

'What about Fin? Aren't you going to call him?'

'I'll do it later; it will be much easier to talk away from the prying ears of mum,' she replied.

'Good plan.' Freya smiled, opening the fridge door and peering inside. 'Ooh, there's a quiche in here, do you reckon we can eat that?'

Eleanor tried to smile through the guilt. 'Freya, this is still our mother we're talking about. I reckon she's expecting us to eat everything!'

*

It seemed that a shower, four rounds of sandwiches and three slices of quiche was enough to bring Angela Levy back to life. Both Freya and Eleanor had insisted on staying on into the evening, fearful that once left alone, the dressing gown and blank staring may be at risk of a swift return. But they had been sent packing with reassurances and Tupperwares of food.

'That was really weird, wasn't it?' Freya said as they set off in the car.

'So strange,' Eleanor agreed, still quite unable to believe the state they'd found their mother in.

'I don't even remember her being like that after Dad died,'

Freya commented. 'Except at the funeral of course,' she added sadly. 'After that day, I swear she turned back to normal.'

A sharp pang of realization struck Eleanor. 'I don't think she did.' She stole a quick glance at her sister. 'She just pretended to, for our sakes.'

Freya rested her forehead against the window. 'Shit.'

Neither spoke for a long time, Eleanor fiercely trying to bat away thoughts of her sad broken mother wrapped in a dressing gown, crying silently over their dad in secret.

'I wonder how Fin is taking it.' Freya broke the silence, her words so pointed that Eleanor couldn't even pretend to feign ignorance.

'I'm sure he'll be fine,' she replied positively. 'It's different now. He's different.'

'If you say so.'

'I do say so,' she said confidently, prickles of anxiety coursing across her skin. 'I'll call him as soon as I get in.'

'It must suck; he'll have no family now,' Freya said quietly.

'Yes, he will,' Eleanor protested. 'He's got his dad. And I think some cousins and an aunt somewhere up north. He has family, Freya.'

'Right.' Freya scowled. 'Because his dad was such a gent, wasn't he?'

Eleanor gave an exasperated sigh. 'I get what you're saying, but he'll be OK.' She reached her hand out and gave her sister's arm a gentle squeeze. 'He's got us, remember? We'll always be his family.'

'I suppose so.' Freya leant her head back and closed her eyes. 'Just make sure you call him, OK?'

Eleanor looked at her sister, her face etched with worry.

315

Sometimes she forgot that it wasn't only her life that Fin had disappeared from. Her sister had loved Fin nearly as fiercely and deeply as Eleanor had. His absence had left marks on her heart too.

'I promise. The moment I get in, I'll call.'

*

Eleanor had called three times and texted twice. At what point did concern blur the line with harassment? Freya's troubled little face loomed in the back of her mind.

Fine.

I'll call him one more time.

She picked up her phone and tried again. No answer.

'Can't say I didn't try, little sis.' She was about to throw her phone on to the sofa when she felt it buzz in her hand.

Incoming Call: Finley Taylor.

'Hey,' she answered immediately.

'Eleanor, what's going on, is everything OK?' He sounded panicked. 'I've got four missed calls from you.'

'Sorry. I was trying to get hold of you to see how you were doing and you weren't picking up.'

'Because I was in the shower!' he replied, still sounding a little flustered. 'Jesus, I thought there was an emergency or something.'

'No. Just me being impatient.' She tried to laugh it off. Maybe four missed calls was a *bit* much.

'Anyway,' she carried on casually. 'How are you?'

'I'm fine,' he replied suspiciously.

'That's good.'

God, this is painful.

'Nurse Clara been on at you for any more photoshoots?'

She asked, a false brightness in her voice, 'I still need to see Heidi's finished pictures.'

'Eleanor,' he replied sternly, 'can you please stop the awkward small talk and tell me why you're ringing me . . .'

She cringed at her poor attempt at navigating the conversation and dropped the facade. 'I was at my mum's today for lunch. The care home called her this morning to tell her about your mum. She was in a pretty bad way and I wanted to check to see how you were doing.'

He laughed, a faint sad laugh. 'I see.'

'So . . .' She began to pace up and down her living room. 'How are you?'

'I mean, it's not the best news I've ever had.' He sighed. 'But it was to be expected.'

She closed her eyes and imagined his face as he spoke, deflated and weary with the weight of the grief. His hands anxiously running through his wet hair.

'Yeah, but that doesn't make it any less painful,' she replied softly. 'I remember when Dad passed, it felt like I'd been thrown under a bus. Everything hurt to an unbearable degree but at the same time I was completely numb. It was the weirdest thing. I just wanted to disappear.'

Eleanor felt a tear fall from her eye. She had never spoken about this before, not even with Freya. What was it about Fin that made her feel so at ease?

'I'm so sorry,' Fin replied softly.

'It's fine. I'm fine.' Eleanor gathered herself together. 'My point was, even though we had months and months to come to terms with Dad's sickness, it was still a shock. Remember, you've barely had any time to process this whole thing.'

'True.' He let out another long sigh. 'I guess I just didn't expect to feel so sad about it all. And there's going to be so much to organize, I have no idea where to start. You know planning is *not* my forte. I feel so useless, Elles.'

The way he said her name made Eleanor want to reach down the phone and hold him close to her. 'You're not useless.' She tried to keep her voice firm and composed, pushing her emotions aside. 'And you won't have to organize anything by yourself. I promise. You've got me. You've got Freya and you have Angela goddam Levy on your team. The most organized woman in the world!'

Fin let out a snort of laughter. 'This is true.'

'I'm serious. Anything you need, just ask.'

'Thank you. That means a lot.'

'If you want to go for a drink or something tomorrow, I'm free after work if you're about?' She was hoping her offer sounded much more 'casual friends hangout' rather than 'concerned parent check-in'. Unfortunately, she reckoned it was very much the latter.

'No, that's OK. I'm going to head over to the home tomorrow and stay there as late as possible.'

'Sure. That makes sense. Send your mum my love, and Freya's. We're all thinking of her.'

Tears filled her eyes as the memories of her own dad sprung up to greet her.

'I will.' Fin took a deep breath. 'Anyway, I should probably go and get changed. It's not warm enough here to stand around in your towel all day!' he joked clumsily. 'I called you straight out of the shower.'

'Oh, of course. Go get dried!' she replied, grateful that nobody could see the flush on her face at the thought of Fin in a towel.

What is wrong with you, Eleanor?

'And sorry for scaring you earlier with my stalker calling behaviour.' She laughed loudly, trying to bat away the image of a half-naked Fin from her mind.

'That's OK,' he replied kindly. 'See you later, Elles.'

'Right . . . yeah . . . see you later, Fin.'

Fin

His mother's health deteriorated rapidly over the next couple of days. It was even quicker than he expected, and the nurses' smiles were becoming harder and harder to force whenever they passed him in the corridor. Even Nurse Clara's resolve was beginning to show signs of weakening. Fin was now visiting daily, arriving as early as his stubbornly weary body would allow and staying until dinner. Not that his mother noticed; she spent the majority of it asleep or confused, opening her eyes for brief moments when a nurse encouraged her to eat and then swiftly shutting them in refusal. It was painful to watch, and as ashamed as he was to say it, most of the time Fin kept his attention firmly fixed on the crossword puzzle in front of him.

'How's she doing today?' Fin asked as he passed Nurse Clara on the way to his mum's room, more out of habit than anything else.

'She's awake,' Nurse Clara replied. 'In fact, she's been awake all morning.'

'Really?' Fin paused. 'That's good!'

'It is, yes.' The nurse stuffed her hands in her pockets and gave Fin a strange, uncomfortable sort of look.

'But . . .?' Fin narrowed his eyes, sensing Nurse Clara's hesitation.

'But . . .' She sighed. 'It's quite common for people to get this way, before . . . well, right before the end. It's called a surge. They seem energetic, lucid even. It's a kind of final burst of energy. We don't know exactly why it happens, but it does.'

'Right.' He nodded in acknowledgement, the foolish bubble of hope that had formed in his chest bursting instantly at her words. 'Thanks for letting me know.'

'I'm sorry it's not better news. I really am.' She smiled wistfully, reaching her hand out and placing it gently on his shoulder. 'You know where I am if you need me, OK?'

'Yeah, I do.' Fin turned and continued his walk along the corridor. Each step he took brought with it even more anxiety and dread. Was this the final time? Was this the moment he'd been preparing for? Now it was here, he wasn't quite sure if he was ready to face it.

It's not about you right now.

She's dying.

She needs you.

Fin took a deep breath in and closed his eyes, drawing upon every single morsel of energy he had. He raised his hand and knocked loudly on the door.

'Mum, it's me, Fin.' He paused, preparing himself for whatever he was about to be faced with. 'Can I come in?'

*

Nurse Clara wasn't wrong when she said his mother was awake, but he had to admit, it wasn't quite the 'surge' of energy he had imagined.

What did you think she was going to be doing? Dancing and singing round the room?

His mother groaned and twisted her lips into a thin smile of welcome.

'How are we doing today?' he asked tentatively.

'Mmm, I've felt better,' she whispered hoarsely.

'I can imagine.' He took up his usual seat by her bed and drew her tiny hand into his. 'Can I get you any more pain relief?'

'If I have any more, I think my blood would be 100 per cent morphine,' she wheezed, her breathing laboured and heavy.

Fin gave a small chuckle and swallowed down the lump that had formed in his throat. He couldn't cry, not when she was being so strong.

'I don't think I have long now.' She closed her eyes and gave the faintest squeeze of his hand.

'Come on . . .' he tried to jest. 'What would Angela say if she heard you talking like that?'

His mother opened her eyes and let a single tear fall down her cheek. 'Pass me the box, Fin.'

'Huh?' He leant in closer, her voice barely scratching the surface of his hearing.

'The box.' She lifted her free arm up and pointed at the end of her bed. 'Bring it to me.'

At once Fin remembered the large cardboard box his mother had caught him rifling through the other day. He slowly let go of her hand and went to retrieve it. For a box full of paperwork and pictures, it was deceptively heavy.

'Look inside. There's a wooden box – find it and open it.'

Fin did as he was told and retrieved a small, beautifully carved box from the bottom. He turned the little key and opened the lid. Inside sat piles of letters; there must have been nearly thirty at first glance.

'They're yours,' his mother whispered. 'They're all yours.'

Fin pulled out the envelopes and saw, as his mother had said, that every one was addressed to him.

'What are they?' he asked, turning them over in his hands.

'I wrote to you. For so many years I wrote to you.' The tears were falling thicker and faster now, tiny sobs punctuating her already strained breathing. She held out her hand and Fin placed the pile on to her palm. Slowly, she sifted through them, each one causing a flicker of recognition in her eyes. At last, she stopped and handed him one. 'I was planning to send this to you in my final days. Read it.'

Fin took the letter and turned it over in his hands. He carefully opened it and pulled out a small A5 piece of paper.

Dear Fin,

I'm sorry for any inconvenience this letter causes, and I pray you understand why I have chosen to do this in this way. I am very sick. In fact, by the time you read this, I will most likely be dead. A few years ago, I was diagnosed with dementia and then a couple of years after that terminal cancer. I hope you'll forgive me for dumping this on you now, and understand that after all I put you through, I didn't want you to have the burden of looking after me. I don't expect that or want that from you. I let you down as a mother in so many ways when you were growing up, I don't deserve a moment of your time or care.

Although it's been years since we have spoken properly, I need you to know that not a day goes by when I don't think of you, my darling beautiful boy. The son I

*was so lucky to have. I am sorry for all the time we
missed out on, the birthdays and Christmases that we
spent estranged. It is my biggest regret that I didn't keep
calling you. That I didn't try harder to be in your life, no
matter if you wanted me or not. I should have been there
regardless. But in my own way I was . . . here are letters
that I wrote for you. On days when I wanted to talk to you
so badly I thought my heart would burst from my chest, I
wrote to you. I know I never said it enough when you
were younger, but before I go, I need you to know how
deeply proud I am of you. And that I will love you in this
lifetime and the next. Everything I have is yours and you
are free to do with it as you wish. I trust your judgement.
I only hope you can find it in your heart to one day forgive
me for the lack of mine.*

   Yours,

   Mum x

The words on the page were practically swimming in his tears by the time he finished it.

'Mum,' he breathed, unable to pull his gaze away from her words.

'I'm sorry,' she sobbed. 'I am so, *so* sorry.'

Fin lifted her hand to his lips and kissed it. He could feel her pulse throbbing beneath her skin. Her heart doing its best to keep going, fighting the battle it was soon to lose. 'I love you,' he cried.

'I love you too.' She patted his sodden cheek. 'Even though you're always late.'

Fin choked out a laugh. 'Yeah . . . sorry about that.'

She smiled, her milky eyes glistening at him. 'My darling boy. I have to go now.'

'No!' he cried, gripping her hand so tightly that he could feel the bones shift under his grasp. 'Please, Mum. Don't leave me.'

'I've never left you.' She closed her eyes and took one last deep breath. 'I never will.'

Eleanor

Do I text again?

How many times is too many times?

Eleanor forced her concentration back to the freezing community hall and the drawing in front of her. It hadn't changed much from last week; maybe a few extra pencil sketches here and there, but the primary feature of her artwork so far was blank space. Ever since she'd hung up the phone to Fin on Sunday night, she hadn't been able to shake him from her mind. It was making concentrating extremely difficult.

'Having trouble, kid?' Reggie asked, pausing his own painting to look over at her.

'Hmmmm,' Eleanor murmured, analysing the rough outline of her father's face. 'I was never good at portraits,' she confessed.

'Why paint one then?'

'Because I wanted to paint my dad,' she replied, deep in thought.

'Wanted?'

'What?'

'You said *wanted* to paint your dad,' Reggie repeated. 'Do you still want to?'

Eleanor thought for a moment. 'You know what, I don't think so.' The tiny seed of an idea planted itself into her consciousness. 'I think . . .' She took one last look at the pencil strokes in front of her. 'I think I need to start again.' She grabbed her eraser and began furiously rubbing her canvas clean.

Reggie laughed. 'Inspiration has struck! Oh, to be young and able to wipe the slate clean,' he mused wistfully.

Eleanor dusted the shavings of rubber from her top and looked at her neighbour suspiciously. 'Since when were you so whimsical?'

'Since I became a ninety-year-old man and therefore could do whatever I liked.' He grinned at her.

'Fair enough.' She adjusted herself in her seat, admiring her blank canvas. 'But I disagree.'

'There's a surprise,' he remarked sarcastically.

'I do!' she insisted. 'I think you can start over at any point in your life. I saw my mum do it after my dad died. She's doing all sorts of things she never dreamed of doing.'

'That may be so.' He picked up his brush and dipped it lightly in water. 'But I haven't got the time for it.'

'If you say so.' She smirked, knowing there were some fights not worth having. 'What are you painting?' she asked, swiftly changing the subject.

'Don't run away from a good argument.' He paused, rotating his wrists one way and then the other.

'I'm not! I'm interested.' She peered over, trying not to flinch at the sounds of his clicking joints. 'Maybe I can learn something from you.'

'Sarcasm will get you nowhere,' he quipped, brandishing his pencil at her. Eleanor caught the end in her palm and held it tightly.

'Now, now, no need to be aggressive,' she warned.

'I wasn't being aggressive. It's old age, sometimes I lose control over my limbs.' He winked, pulling the pencil back out of her grip.

'Good job I have my youthful reflexes then, otherwise who knows what damage you'd cause.'

He eyed her warily and then turned his canvas towards her ever so slightly. Eleanor tried to hide her surprise at the sketch of a young man staring back at her.

'Something wrong?' he asked.

'No.' Eleanor tried to wipe the look off her face quickly. 'I guess . . . I guess I assumed you'd be painting your wife.'

'Who says that's not my wife?' He frowned.

'Oh.' Eleanor's hand flew instinctively to her mouth. 'Sorry, maybe it's the angle . . . or the lighting . . . or,' she stuttered, tripping clumsily over her words.

'Jeez, woman! You should see your face.' Reggie let out a loud snort. 'Course that's not my wife.'

'Who is it then?'

Reggie turned the picture away from Eleanor and she felt him stiffen slightly at her question. 'He was a close friend.'

'Was?'

'Yes, was,' he replied bluntly.

'Did you fall out?'

'*We'll* fall out if you keep hounding me with questions.' He shot her a warning look.

'I lost contact with my best friend, although he came back recently. It was really weird at first but now . . .' Eleanor mused.

Now what?

328

A feeling of warmth bloomed in her stomach.

'He's dead,' Reggie interjected bluntly.

'What?'

'My friend. He's dead.'

'Oh.' Eleanor cursed her stupidity. 'I'm so sorry.'

'It's fine.' Reggie hesitated. 'Actually, I only found out becau—'

'Everything OK over here?' Agatha's face appeared from behind Reggie's canvas, stopping his words dead in their tracks. She tried to peep over at Eleanor's but she pulled it closer, out of Agatha's way.

'Fine, all fine over here.' Eleanor smiled, trying to hide the frustration. She was sure Reggie had been about to tell her something important before Agatha's abrupt interruption.

'Good, good,' she chirped. 'As long as this fellow over here isn't distracting you too much.' She turned to Reggie. 'How are you getting on?'

'Aggie.' Reggie smirked. 'Everything is wonderful.'

'Now, hold on a second.' Agatha frowned exaggeratedly. 'What have I told you about calling me that. Nobody calls me that apart from my mother! You're terrible at times, you know that, Reggie?' She beamed affectionately. 'Isn't he terrible, Eleanor?'

Eleanor nodded in agreement. 'The *worst*.'

'All right, enough with the insults, thank you,' Reggie puffed. 'Now, is this an art class or what? Some of us want to do some proper painting.' He shot Eleanor a look out of the corner of his eye. 'So, leave me alone and let me get on with it, will you?'

'There we go. That's the dedication we like to see!' Agatha punched the air proudly, moving around the circle to inspect another work of art.

Eleanor picked up her pencil and closed her eyes, bringing Eileen's face into view. She wanted to paint her as the woman she knew growing up. The lady who was full of life and joy, and who would sneak her and Fin sweets when his dad wasn't looking. She wanted Fin to have a piece of that Eileen to remember, because she knew how easy it was to forget when you had to be the one to bury them.

'I'm so sorry about your friend,' she whispered, opening her eyes and beginning to sketch.

'Thank you,' Reggie replied. 'Me too.'

*

Eleanor had left the class feeling energized and excited. As lovely as it would have been to have a portrait of her dad, her new idea felt much more important to paint. At least it could be something for Fin to take back with him when he left. A little piece of London life all the way across the ocean in LA.

Her heart sank at the thought of him leaving. His arrival back into her life had been unexpected and at first, she thought, unwanted. Now, though, she quite liked the idea of having him around for longer. It definitely wasn't the same as before but it was certainly a friendship.

What part would you call a friendship exactly?

The part when you were ignoring him or when you were drunkenly kissing him?

The memory of the kiss suddenly hit her. Fin's lips on hers. His arms around her waist, holding her closer to his body.

No.

You were drunk. It didn't mean anything.

330

She pulled her jacket round her and turned the corner into her street. As she got closer to her flat, Eleanor could see someone standing outside her front door. She narrowed her eyes to try and bring the person into focus, but it was no use. It was too dark and she was too far away.

It's fine.

They'll leave in a minute.

But they didn't. They stayed. The shadowy figure was pacing up and down her porch.

Stay calm.

If in doubt, walk straight past.

She quickly pulled her hood up over her head and began to pick up her pace. Tucking her hands into her pockets she tried to slow her breathing, but it seemed to keep catching in her chest. As she approached, she noticed the person had crouched down on to the step, their back facing away from her.

What the hell are they doing?

She opened the front gate and almost jumped out of her skin when the person stood up and turned to face her.

'Eleanor!' he cried.

'Oliver?' Eleanor blinked, unable to process the fact that her ex-boyfriend was standing outside her front door.

It's technically his front door too.

Shut up.

'What the hell are you doing here?' she demanded, her fear quickly morphing into anger.

'Sorry.' He held his hands up in surrender. 'I didn't mean to scare you.' He took a step closer to her, the streetlamp throwing his features into an orange glow. It was funny; looking at him now, the face she thought she'd spend the rest of her life with looked old and a little tired.

'Well, you did.' She folded her arms defensively, the post-art class bubble officially burst.

'Can I come in?' he asked meekly.

'Why?' she asked, her brain still trying to work out the reason for his visit.

He wants the flat back.

Violent waves of panic crashed over her.

This is it. He's kicking you out.

'You don't need to look so scared.' He laughed, reaching his hand out to touch her arm. Eleanor found herself recoiling; the thought of him holding her was unbearable now.

'Ouch. OK, I deserved that,' he acknowledged.

'Oliver.' She was pleading now, aching to know why, after all these months of complete and utter silence, he was now standing in front of her on her doorstep. 'What are you doing here?'

He dropped his head and wrung his hands nervously. 'I came . . .' He lifted his chin to look at her. 'I came to say I'm sorry. I came to see if we could talk things through.'

Eleanor felt the ground shift beneath her. A thousand questions assaulted her at once, making her sick with confusion. Emotions collided into one another, crashing and screaming for her attention.

'I know.' Oliver took another tentative step towards her. He was looking at her as though she was a wild animal ready to bolt at any second. 'I know I left, and I know I have no right to show up on your doorstep like this and ask for another chance, but . . . Eleanor, I'm going crazy without you. I made a mistake. Surely you can see that. Look at me! I'm a mess.'

She didn't move, she didn't dare move an inch.

This isn't real.

This is a dream or some kind of hallucination.

'I was an idiot and I want to come back. Come back to you, to our home, to our life together.' He made his eyes so big and hopeful that it sent a spike of resentment through the core of her.

'What life?' she replied coldly.

Oliver's face fell. 'Our life, the one we built together.'

'No.' She shook her head. 'It wasn't our life. It was *your* life. I just happened to be a part of it.'

'You don't mean that.' He laughed, as though her words were nothing more than nonsense.

'Yes, I do.' She found the rage rising up from the very bones of her. For months after he left, she'd dreamt of seeing Oliver again. Of this very moment. Him, coming back to her. Pleading for a second chance. A chance to resume her life as it was before he broke her heart and walked away without a glance. But that wasn't her any more. That Eleanor no longer existed.

Oliver went to speak but she cut him off. 'Do you know what I would have given to hear from you after you left? I was *dying* to speak to you, Oliver. I didn't leave this flat for weeks. I couldn't get up. I couldn't get up because it hurt too much to exist in a world without you. All I wanted was an explanation for why you broke up with me. But there was nothing. You couldn't even be bothered to call me. After sixteen years the only thing you could do was send me an email about the fucking finances for the fucking flat. And now you want me to take you back?'

He shifted uncomfortably, squirming with every true word she spoke. 'Because that was how it worked, wasn't it?' She narrowed her eyes and took a decisive step towards him, pulling herself up tall and proud. This was her home now. This was her life now. 'You dictated everything. You decided every little bit of our life together, and the worst part is that I let you do it!'

'Eleanor, we can do things however you want,' he simpered pathetically. 'I can change. I *have* changed.'

She took a moment to look at him. To stare into the face of the man she would have given her life for, to try and find any scrap of longing or desire. But the only thing left inside her was pity.

'And so have I. I don't want you back. I don't want you anywhere near me. Do you hear?' She was so close to him that she could see his pupils retract in shock. 'Do. You. Hear. Me?'

'You can't do this.' His sweet exterior swiftly switched into furious outrage.

Eleanor felt her phone buzz in her pocket.

'Eleanor? Do you hear me?' he demanded childishly. 'I want my half of the flat. I want what's owed to me.'

She wouldn't have been surprised if he'd started stamping his foot and wailing. How had she ever found him attractive? How had she ever thought of *marrying* him?

'Fine.' She reached into her coat and pulled out her phone. She needed as many excuses to get Oliver to leave as possible. Maybe she could threaten to call the police? Maybe . . . she could threaten to call Ben!

'Fine what?' he stammered.

'Fine, we can sell the flat. I don't care. I just want you to go—' Eleanor looked down at her screen and felt her heart collapse on itself. 'Oh God.' Her hand flew to her mouth.

No.

Not tonight.

'I know what you're doing, Eleanor, and it won't work,'

Oliver spat viciously. 'Pretending there's an emergency so I have to leave, and you get to go inside and enjoy the home that I practically paid for.' The venom was putrid on his breath and his face twisted in bitterness.

'Fin's mum just died.' She closed her eyes and let the words sink in.

'Excuse me?'

She clenched her fists tightly. 'You heard me. Don't make me say it again.'

'Fin? Since when was he back on the scene?' He laughed. 'Don't pretend you care about that waste of space again.'

Eleanor remained completely still, the tears falling hot and fast down her cheeks. 'I need you to leave, Oliver.' She kept her voice calm and composed. 'I need you to leave right now or I will call the police.'

He gave a short, sharp snort of disgust. 'You say you've changed, Eleanor, but look at you. The minute that good-for-nothing lowlife calls, you drop everything and go running. It's pathetic.'

'*No*,' she roared, the anger practically exploding out of her. '*You* are the pathetic one, Oliver,' she hissed, pushing him away from her hard. 'Now *go*.'

Oliver stared at her dumbfounded before turning on his heel and leaving with an indignant grunt. Eleanor didn't even bother to check where he'd gone; the only thing she needed to do right now was to call Fin. To call her friend. To be there for her friend.

Fin

The week following his mother's death passed in a blur of lawyers, funeral directors and countless phone calls. The only way he managed to know up from down and what to do next was because of Angela's strict instructions. By the morning of the funeral, Fin was bone tired but relieved. Everything was sorted and ready for the final goodbye.

'The car is going to be here in about ten minutes to take us to Mum's.' Eleanor was sitting next to him on the sofa. She'd been by his side nearly as much as Angela. How easy it was to fall back into old habits, he thought. How hard it would be to leave her, when all of this was over.

'Sure.' Fin began to wring his hands nervously. 'Do we need to go over the list one last time?' he asked, clutching at any form of distraction.

'No, we're good.' She adjusted herself to face him. 'It's going to be fine, I promise.'

He lifted his eyes to hers.

'I'm scared,' he whispered, the words falling out of his mouth quite unconsciously.

She placed her hand against his cheek and rested her forehead against his. 'I know. Trust me, I know, but you will get through this.' Her words soothed him, so soft and hopeful that with each one he found his breathing ease and his mind quieten. 'And I'll be here, every step of the way, OK?'

He didn't speak. He didn't dare do anything to break the moment. The feeling of her skin on his, her breath on his face and her voice in his ears. So close. So close he could feel the memory of her lips kissing him.

'Do you hear me, Fin? I'm here,' she repeated.

There wasn't time for words any more. He leant forward and pulled her mouth on to his. All the pain, all the grief, all of the emotion spilt out of him and into her. He needed her. He needed to feel her.

'Fin!' She pulled away sharply. 'What are you doing?'

He opened his eyes. The shock on her face hit him deep in the stomach.

You complete and utter idiot.

What the hell were you thinking?

'I'm sorry,' he mumbled shamefully, the mocking jeering voices in his head growing louder in their laughter. He couldn't look at her. He couldn't stand to be in the same room as her. He needed to leave. He needed to get out of here.

'Fin, look at me,' Eleanor pleaded, as he stood and began to pace up and down the room. 'It's OK, I know you're upset and emotional and you di—'

'The car will be here soon.' He turned away from her, grinding his teeth so hard that his entire jaw seared with pain. 'I'll wait outside.'

'Fin!'

337

He heard her call after him, but it was too late. He slammed the door and walked away without a second glance.

*

It wasn't a big funeral. In fact, barely a handful of people showed up to pay their respects to his mother. Her life, remembered by a group of humans whose number he could count on two hands. How small had her world been? How much had she truly lived? The questions taunted him throughout the entire service, drowning out the impersonal words recited by the priest, screaming over the tuneless hymns that were sung without any trace of enthusiasm, silencing the tears that were streaming down his face. The only other thing he was aware of was Eleanor's presence next to him the entire time. He'd replayed the memory of their kiss over and over, his shame growing with each rerun. Her surprise had now mutated into disgust, her face contorting into an almost offended repulsion.

'Fin?' Angela's voice stirred him from his thoughts as they stood outside the church. 'Are you coming back with us? I've got food laid out at mine. I'm sure you could do with a cup of tea. We all could.' Her eyes were red raw and her face older somehow. Could grief leave its mark so quickly?

'I don't think I can,' he muttered. 'I need some space. I'm going to head back to the flat.'

He felt her hand gripping his tightly. 'You don't have to do this alone. You know that, don't you?' The words were said with such force that Fin felt them land directly on his heart with tiny little thuds.

'Thank you. I really do appreciate it. But I'll be fine.' He turned to leave before she could make any further attempt at persuading him to stay.

As he made his way out of the churchyard, he kept his eyes fixed firmly on the path ahead. He couldn't stand to look at the graves any longer. Why his mum had wanted to be buried he'd never know. The thought of her lying in the cold earth, dissolving slowly into the ground, made his skin crawl. No. Much better to be cremated, he thought. Burnt and scattered somewhere. Easier. Simple. Plus, why have a grave if there was no one there to visit it?

'Fin, hold on a second!'

He glanced quickly over his shoulder to see Eleanor running towards him.

Leave me alone.

Please just leave me alone.

'Wait!' she shouted, her footsteps getting louder as she closed the gap between them. Fin tried to pick up his pace but she was by his side in seconds. 'At least let me drive you home?'

'Thanks.' He carried on walking. 'But you don't have to do that.'

'*Fin,*' she begged. 'Don't do this, please.'

'I'm not doing anything. I just want to be by myself.' He quickened his strides, hoping that she would give up and go.

'Hold on!' She pulled at his arm. 'I'm scared if you go home alone you'll do something stupid.'

He stopped abruptly, still unable to meet her gaze.

'Promise me you won't do anything stupid,' she pleaded, reaching for his hand. Memories of their younger selves swam shamefully in his mind. After all this time, she still didn't trust him. How stupid he was for thinking anything could have been different between them.

'I promise.' He snatched his fingers away from hers. 'I'll be fine.'

He could feel her eyes burning into the back of him as he continued to walk away.

*

By the time he got back to the flat, the numbness had begun to wear off. Sharp stabs of guilt pricked his skin whilst undulating currents of loss rippled through his chest. He couldn't bear the enormity of his feelings. He needed more numbness and he needed it now.

Fin headed to the little cupboard in the corner of the kitchen and opened the door. He'd discovered Rob's alcohol stash a few days after arriving at the flat. At the beginning of his recovery, he would have probably poured them down the drain and replaced them when he left. How foolish to think he was past that.

'Hello, old friends.' He reached in, grabbed the first bottle his fingers touched, and made his way over to the sofa. Whiskey. His favourite poison.

Straight from the bottle?

Come on, at least be classy.

He placed the bottle on the coffee table and ventured back to the kitchen for a glass. It was true, his mother deserved a proper send-off, and drinking from the bottle was anything but proper. He threw himself down, coat and shoes still on, and laid his head in his hands.

'What are you doing, Fin?' He sighed, the emotions of the day, of the past few months, sitting heavy on his shoulders.

You don't have to do this.

It's not worth it.

The memory of Eleanor's face loomed darkly in his mind.

The look on her face after he kissed her: so repulsed, so embarrassed.

Don't think about it.

Just do it.

He reached for the bottle. As he poured the amber liquid into the glass, the smell alone made his head spin. He closed his eyes and held the rim to his lips. If he was going to do this, he at least had to try and savour every moment. Besides, it was one drink. Things were different now. He had *control* now.

Fin held the glass in mid-air and brought the image of his mother to his mind. The old frail shadow of the woman he'd spent so much time with the past few months. The young, carefree version of his mum who had laughed and played with him as a boy. The broken, crumpled heap of his mother, who had cried herself to sleep on the bathroom floor when he needed her most.

'To you, Mum. May you rest in peace.' He raised his drink and downed it in one.

His throat seared and his stomach convulsed at the touch of the liquid. He closed his eyes tight and allowed the burning sensation to engulf him. Then slowly, very slowly, he felt it.

Nothing.

At last. He felt nothing.

Fin reached for the bottle and poured himself another. He needed one more.

One more glass of nothing.

*

There was a knocking. Somewhere just outside his reach was a loud, hard knocking. He tried to swat it away with his hand but his limbs were too heavy to move.

'Leave me alone,' he mumbled, the words catching on the dryness in his throat.

'Fin!' a familiar voice shouted. 'Fin. Let me in!'

His eyes sprung open.

'Finley Taylor, I know you're in there,' Eleanor barked. 'Open this door or I'll call the police,' she demanded, the knocking getting louder and louder with each passing second.

Fuck.

'OK,' he called back hoarsely. 'I'm coming.'

Carefully, cautiously, he sat upright. The room gave a horrifying lurch and he closed his eyes quickly. When he opened them again, thankfully everything had returned to its rightful place and he forced himself to stand. He edged his way over to the door and slowly opened it.

'Jesus Christ.' Eleanor stood, hand outstretched, ready to hammer at the door once again. She stepped across the threshold without asking and placed her hand on his arm. 'You look like shit.'

'Thanks.' He laughed sarcastically. 'I buried my mum today, so forgive me for not looking my best.' As hard as he tried, he couldn't stop his words from slurring, blending into one another in a haze of whiskey fumes.

'How much have you had?' she asked, steering him back into the flat towards the sofa. Her eyes clocked the empty bottle and he could see the shock in her eyes.

'Don't, Eleanor. I don't need more of your disappointment today,' he spat angrily, shaking her hand off him.

'Disappointment?' She looked confused.

'Nothing. Don't worry.' He dismissed his words with a flick of his wrist, praying the image of her face this morning would erase itself from his mind. Her features had transformed into a grotesque caricature; the revulsion in her expression was sickening.

'Of course I'm worried.' She sat beside him and placed her hand softly on his cheek.

No. He wasn't going to go here again. She couldn't barge into *his* flat, sit on *his* sofa, and act all tender and loving after rejecting him that very morning.

'Don't do that,' he snarled, pulling her hand from his face.

'I know you're angry and upset, but you don't need to take it out on me.'

He could feel his heart pull inside his chest; he didn't want her to see him like this.

'You need to go.' He stood, trying to put as much space between them as possible.

'I'm not going anywhere when you're in this state.' She got up from the sofa and marched into the kitchen. 'You need to drink some water and eat some food.'

'No.' He shook his head. 'You don't get to *do* this.'

Eleanor handed him a glass of water. 'Do what, Fin?' She looked at him curiously.

'*This*,' he shouted, unable to control himself any longer. 'Looking after me. Pretending you care.'

'I do care.'

'Do you? Really?'

'Of course I care,' she insisted. The sadness in her voice was only making him want to drink more.

I need to drink more.

'You don't care, Eleanor. You feel sorry for me. There's a difference.'

'This is nonsense. You're talking nonsense,' she stated flatly, as though he were nothing more than a dramatic child throwing a tantrum.

'Stop treating me like a kid, Eleanor. You don't need to tell me off.' He pushed past her back to the alcohol cupboard. He crouched down and reached in to retrieve another bottle of numbness. This time it was gin.

'Well, stop acting like one then,' she shouted.

Fin unscrewed the top of the bottle and took a deep mouthful, relishing the look of panic on Eleanor's face.

'Stop!' She was in front of him, pulling his arm down. 'You're only going to make things worse.'

'But it's OK for you to get drunk and do whatever the hell you want?' he spat viciously. The anger inside him seemed endless.

'I don't have a problem with alcohol, though, do I?'

Fin snorted and took another sip. 'Could have fooled me, when you launched yourself at me and then practically passed out in your own vomit.' He staggered forwards an inch, finding a perverse pleasure in the horror on Eleanor's face.

'That was different,' she muttered.

'Oh, so you *do* remember that night?' He laughed cruelly, taking another swig from the bottle. 'Whatever – it doesn't even matter. You don't need to be here and you don't need to look after me any more,' he snapped. 'You relinquished your role as carer a long time ago.'

'I'm not trying to look after you. I'm trying to be your friend.'

'Really? Is that what we are? Friends? Come on, Eleanor, I'm an inconvenience to you. I always have been. You know what?' He gave another cruel, sharp laugh. 'I bet you were relieved when I went away. Did you a favour. No more caring for poor pathetic Fin.'

'Stop, you don't know what you're saying.' She was pacing back and forth, her face etched with fear.

'Yes, I do.' He wanted to hurt her. He wanted her to feel as much of the pain that was coursing through his veins as possible. 'Do you know why I left?' He stood, his face so close to hers he could see every streak of gold and orange in her eyes. 'I left because it was too fucking humiliating to be around you any more. Do you think I didn't see the way you looked at me? I hated it, Elles. The pity. The worry. The constant *fear*.' He ran his hand through his hair. 'I didn't want to be that to you. I was embarrassed. I went so I could sort myself out and come back as the Fin you knew before.'

'I wasn't embarrassed. I just wanted to help,' she whimpered.

'And then lo and behold, I came back and found out that as soon as I left, you disappeared off to uni and found Oliver. Safe, dependable Oliver. At last, someone who didn't need picking up off the floor and caring for.' The toxicity was spewing out of him and he knew he wouldn't be able to stop even if he tried. 'He made it *very* clear that you were better off without me.'

Eleanor stopped and stood still in front of him. The fear on her face had been replaced by confusion. 'What do you mean, he made it clear?'

Keep it together.

He took another swig of gin and let the cool liquid steady him. 'Nothing. I didn't mean anything. I'm drunk, Eleanor . . . remember? I always say stupid shit when I'm drunk.'

'No.' She inched closer. 'You said when you came back . . . tell me what you meant. When did you speak to Oliver? When did you come back?'

'It doesn't matter.' Fin tried to step away, but his balance was off and he could feel his legs shaking unsteadily beneath him.

Don't do this. You promised yourself you wouldn't do this.

'It doesn't matter because he was right, wasn't he? I was a fucking waste of space and you were better off without me.'

'*When did you speak to Oliver?*' She was nothing but pure, wild fury, and Fin practically felt her words slap him across the face. '*When did you come back?*'

'I didn't,' he mumbled, edging away from her.

'Tell me,' she demanded.

'No.' He shook his head, praying for this to be over. Why had he opened his stupid mouth? Why had he done this to himself?

'*Tell me,*' Eleanor screamed, her hands on his shoulders, shaking him hard.

'I came back!' he cried. 'I came back for your dad's funeral.'

'No.' She dropped her hands as though his confession had burnt her. 'No, you didn't.'

'I did.' He sighed. 'I came back but I was told to leave.'

'*You're lying,*' she roared.

'I'm not. I wish I was, Eleanor. But I'm not. I came back for you. Of course I came back for you.'

Then: Aged 20

Fin

Mumbai airport was noisy and crowded. Fin tried not to push too hard as he made his way through the hordes of people queuing in complete chaos. That was what he loved about India. The seemingly unorganized mayhem that always ended up taking you exactly where you needed to go. It was manic and magical and everyone seemed to understand the system. There was a logic buried underneath it all that Fin was yet to master. Right now, however, he would have killed for some of that quiet, English matter-of-fact order. His brain was overheating and his thoughts were as hard to catch hold of as the air in his lungs. He checked the time.

'Shit,' he cursed. 'Come on, come *on*. Where are you?' He scanned the boards, looking for his flight number. 'Yes! London Heathrow . . . delayed.'

His heart sank.

'No. No. For fuck's sake, *no*,' he cried, his hands pulling at his overgrown hair. He looked around and saw his airline check-in desk; the queue was so long it was merging with five others. 'Please, don't do this to me,' he groaned. 'Not today.'

Fin hauled his bag over his shoulder and ran to join the end of the line. Every minute that passed he felt his skin get hotter, his chest grow tighter and his heart pound louder. It took every ounce of restraint he had not to scream and throw the people in front of him out of the way, clear the path to the front desk and demand they get him on the next flight out of here. As long as he was moving, he would feel better. Being standstill and stuck across the other side of the world was unbearable, especially when he knew what his friend was going through.

Don't think about her. It won't help anything.

Fin clenched his fists and willed Eleanor's face out of his mind. He needed to focus on what was happening right now. He had to find some semblance of control amidst the madness. Just as he felt like he had steadied himself, an announcement reverberated through the check-in hall. It was tinny and muffled and hard to hear over the swell of the restless crowds, but he found the words he needed.

'London Heathrow. Cancelled.'

But before he knew it, tears were filling his eyes and spilling down his cheeks. Fin dropped to his knees and began to shake with frustration. 'No. No. *No!*' he sobbed, crudely wiping his face with his hands.

'Come now,' a kind voice cooed above him. 'Take this.'

Fin looked up and through his blurred vision could see an older lady smiling at him, a tissue in her outstretched hand. On her hip sat a disgruntled baby, its dark curls even wilder than Fin's sun-bleached mop of hair.

'Take it.' She waggled the paper at him. 'It's dirty in these places.'

Fin accepted the tissue gratefully and wiped his face. 'Thank you,' he mumbled, suddenly embarrassed by his outburst. 'I'm sorry about that.' He stood slowly and dusted himself down. She was right; the floor was filthy.

'Psht.' She shooed his apology away and began bouncing the round baby up and down. 'Are you OK?'

The question sent a ripple of sadness through him once more. 'I just really need to get home.'

'You have an emergency?' She arched her eyebrows and stopped jiggling her babbling child. Her dark brown eyes fixed him with a serious look, and Fin could feel the knot of tension intensifying its grasp on his throat.

'Kind of.'

'Family emergency?'

Fin closed his eyes and thought of Eleanor's dad. The man who had been more present in his childhood than his own father, always ready and willing to offer words of wisdom or a place to be when he had nowhere else to go. A man that was adamantly in his corner, no matter how troublesome Fin had been.

'Yeah.' The tears started again. 'Someone's died and I need to be home for the funeral.'

The lady nodded brusquely and then turned to an older boy behind her. He was sitting, headphones on, plugged into his Walkman and eyes glued to his comic book. She unceremoniously pulled out one of the earpieces and handed over the baby, muttering firm instructions that Fin couldn't quite make out. Before he had a chance to ask any questions, the lady had grabbed his hand and was pulling him out of the queue.

'No!' he protested, grabbing his bag just in time. 'Please, what are you doing?'

349

'Trust me,' she stated, dragging him through the mass of confused-looking people towards the front of the line. Fin kept his head down, his cheeks blushing brightly at the scene the pair were making, but every time someone stopped to question them, his fierce protector would passionately put them in their place with words Fin had no way of understanding. Before he knew it, he was thrust in front of a young, meticulously made-up woman behind the check-in desk.

'Can I help?' she asked, eyeing the odd-looking pair with equal parts confusion and suspicion.

'I need to get to London. I have to . . .' Fin shook his head, hot tears pricking his eyes. 'I have to get home.'

'OK, sir. Well, the flight from Mumbai direct to London has just been cancelled . . .' She tapped her long painted nails on the keyboard in front of her.

Fin let out a groan. His impassioned friend began another one of her emboldened rants, whilst all Fin could do was stand there meekly and uselessly.

'OK, OK.' The young lady nodded, continuing her tapping. 'Right. It's going to be tight, but if you run, I'm pretty sure I can get you on an internal flight to Delhi and then from there you'll go to London.'

Fin's heart rose from the pit of his stomach.

'There's a bit of a wait time at Delhi, but I think it's your best option right now. Shall I go ahead and book?'

Fin didn't have to think – not about the already severely overdrawn number in his bank account, not about the wasted ticket he was throwing away, and not even about how late he was going to be arriving home. All he needed was to keep moving.

'Yes, please. Do whatever you need to do,' he urged.

'You'll be fine now.' His friend turned to him, a wide smile on her face.

'Thank you.' Fin could feel the tears returning, but this time they were not so heavy, they were almost joyful.

She placed a warm hand on his cheek and fixed him once more with her dark coffee eyes. 'Get home to your family safe.'

'I will. I promise.'

*

Two flights and seventeen hours later, Fin was exhausted. He had barely slept on the plane, his anxiety keeping his body running on high alert. He'd had to wash and change in the Heathrow airport toilets, not even minding the curious looks he was getting from his fellow passengers. There was no time for showers or haircuts; in fact, the funeral was already in full flow by the time his taxi pulled up outside the church. But it didn't matter. He was here. After everything, he'd made it.

'Just here is fine, mate,' he instructed the cab driver, who had barely stopped as Fin opened the door and jumped out. He threw his bag over his shoulder and sprinted up to the church entrance.

Take a breath.

He stood, dusted down the cheap suit he'd bought back in India, and slowly opened the heavy wooden door. It creaked loudly on its rusted hinges, and Fin winced as the noise cut through the heavy grieving silence within. He was about to peer through the crack when suddenly the door lurched away from him.

'Get outside,' a stranger's voice hissed.

Fin did as he was told and stepped back a little. A young

man had sneaked out silently through the door and was standing in front of him, looking less than impressed.

'I'm so sorry I'm late. You wouldn't believe the nightmare I had getting here.' Fin could feel the stranger's disapproval raking over his entire body. 'I'm Fin.' He held out a hand but the man simply looked at it with growing disdain.

'I know who you are,' he jeered. 'And I'm not willing to hear your lame excuses as to why you're turning up halfway through a funeral.'

'They aren't excuses. My flight got cancelled and I had to go thr—'

'Like I said. I don't care.' The man took a step closer to Fin. 'You need to leave.'

'Excuse me?' Fin couldn't help but notice how well put together this stranger was. His crisp black suit fitted him beautifully; his dark brown hair was coiffed and gelled to perfection. Even the white flower in his buttonhole looked like it was holding its breath, standing to attention. 'No offence, but who even are you? I've never seen you before. I'm sure if you go and get Elles, she'll clear this whole thing up.'

'I'm *with* Eleanor,' he smirked, elongating her name ever so slightly. 'I'm Oliver. Her boyfriend.'

Really, Elles? You picked someone like him?

Fin pushed the judgement to the back of his mind for now; he needed to focus on getting in that church and by his friend's side.

'Well then, you'll know how much she would want to see me.' Fin grimaced.

'Hmmm, I'm not so sure about that.' Oliver looked him up and down with repulsion. 'You see, I'm not quite sure why anyone would want their delinquent, no-good *drunk* of a schoolfriend showing up at their dad's funeral months

352

after disappearing off to the other side of the world and' – he laughed cruelly – 'sleeping in God knows what conditions. You're a state. You're probably drunk and I don't want you near Eleanor.'

Fin's fist clenched reflexively; it was aching to swing out and punch the tiny smug face in front of him, but he held off. 'I'm. Not. Drunk,' he stated.

'Sure. Like all the other times you weren't drunk?' He raised an eyebrow mockingly. 'Eleanor's told me everything about you, Fin. You may have pulled the wool over her eyes for years, but it won't work with me. You're no good for her, and there is no way I'm letting you come back and ruin her life again. She's better off without you. They all are.'

Fin went to speak but the words vanished from his mouth the moment they formed on his tongue. He wanted to push past Oliver and run to Eleanor's side, but he couldn't. His feet were rooted to the spot and his entire body had turned to lead.

He's right.

That's why you left, remember?

'No.' Fin shook the doubt from his head and forced his body forward. But Oliver was there quicker than he imagined, grabbing his arms and throwing Fin to the floor.

'Now, get the hell out of here or I swear I'll call the police.' He tutted patronizingly, turning away from Fin, who was still sprawled out on the earth. 'This is a day of mourning . . . have some fucking respect, for once in your life.'

Now

Eleanor

'But . . . then . . . why?' She sunk down on to the sofa, the weight of Fin's revelation dragging her down by her ankles. 'Why didn't you call? Why did nobody see you? What happened?'

This isn't real.

He didn't come back.

He told you himself he didn't come back.

'You texted me saying you had missed your flights. *You* told me yourself you weren't coming.' She balled her fists and ground them deeply into her forehead.

'I lied. I was embarrassed.' Fin's voice had lost all of its drunken bravado and was now so small it was barely audible.

'Of what? It was my dad's funeral. I *needed* you. For fuck's sake, Fin, why didn't you just come and see me?'

'Because I got drunk. After everything that Oliver said, I went and fucking drowned my sorrows in a pub somewhere. I don't remember where. I don't even remember how I got back to my mum's, but I did. I was a state,

Eleanor. I was everything he said I was. I couldn't look at you after that. I wanted to go away and come back better. Not worse.'

'You think I cared about that? How selfish can you *get*?' Suddenly she stood. She had to get out, get away from him; from the memories, from the lies. 'I have to go. I can't do this.'

'Elles, please,' he whined pathetically. 'I'm sorry. I just wanted to be better.'

'And all I wanted was my best friend by my side as I buried my own fucking father.'

'But I wanted to be more for you.'

'Well, we don't always get what we want, do we?' She pushed past him and stormed out of the flat, slamming the door as hard as she could on her way out.

*

The moment she got outside, the rage burst from her. It rose up her throat and tore from her lungs in a deafening scream. People in the street whipped their heads around wildly, trying to identify the source of the pain.

'It's rude to stare,' she shouted, cursing the onlookers' judgemental glances and hushed whispers.

Her body was trembling, the emotions crawling over her skin, making her want to tear herself apart. She needed to walk. She needed to cry. She needed to go back inside and give Fin a piece of her mind.

No.

He doesn't deserve any more of your time.

But still she stayed, pacing up and down outside his building. Something was holding her there, rooted, clinging to the source of her pain. His face, his words, kept flashing through her mind, assaulting her with their cruelty.

Do you know why I left? I left because it was too fucking humiliating to be around you any more.

'No. He was drunk, he didn't mean it,' she announced to no one.

I came back for you.

'Argh.' She clawed at her head, willing the sound of Fin's voice to stop repeating over and over.

'Excuse me. Are you OK?' a timid voice called out.

Eleanor snapped open her eyes and saw a twenty-something girl staring at her with a mix of concern and caution.

'I didn't mean to interrupt but you sounded quite upset,' the woman continued. 'I thought I'd check if you needed any help?'

Eleanor stared at her blankly. Part of her wanted to direct the remaining shreds of anger at this nosy stranger, to tell her exactly where she could shove her curiosity and her help, but Eleanor was too tired. She was done fighting.

'I'm fine.' She sighed, trying to stop the tears from streaming down her face whilst simultaneously mustering her very best sane and calm expression. 'It's been a long day, that's all.'

The young lady nodded. 'I see.'

Eleanor knew she wasn't fooled.

'Do you want to call anyone? I can wait with you while you do.' The woman smiled kindly.

'No.' Eleanor reached inside her pocket and pulled out her phone. 'My boyfriend's ordered me an Uber, it will be here soon,' she lied. 'Thank you, though.'

'Sure.' The stranger gave her one last look of concern and hurried off down the street.

You could call Ben?

And what? Cry down the phone to him?

No, thank you.

If there was one thing she'd learnt over the past few months, it was how to calm herself down. To soothe her own pain. To be her own support system. Maybe that was what happened when you had your heart broken, she thought, as she made her way down the street in the opposite direction to the kind stranger . . . it grew back harder and more protected than before.

*

When Eleanor woke the next morning, she was expecting her phone to be full of apology texts and missed calls from Fin. As she reached over to check, she couldn't help but feel a little disappointed that the only notification she had was a text from Ben.

He's stubborn. You know he's stubborn.

'He's an idiot,' she muttered, tossing her phone aside and hauling herself out of bed. 'That's what he is.'

He was drunk. He didn't mean what he said.

Eleanor closed her eyes and replayed the argument in her head; the vicious exchange of words, the shouting, the cruel laughter. It was too much to bear. Drunk or not, Fin did not deserve one more minute of her time.

By Monday afternoon the silence felt excruciating. She'd almost given herself whiplash the number of times she kept glancing over at her phone screen, in the vague hope of seeing Fin's name pop up.

What if something has happened to him?

What if he's hurt?

'It's not your job to look after him any more,' she told herself through gritted teeth, trying her best to concentrate on the screen in front of her, whilst images from the past flashed through her mind. That time she found him in his room . . . so beaten and bruised.

'No.' She shook her head. 'He's an adult now. He's fine.'

'Everything OK over there, Eleanor?' Doreen's concerned voice called out. 'You look a little . . .' She paused and cocked her head to the side, the bouffant of scarlet hair remaining perfectly in place. 'Out of sorts.'

Eleanor plastered a smile on to her face. 'Yes, yes, I'm fine. Just can't get the wording right for this presentation, that's all,' she bumbled awkwardly.

'I see,' Doreen replied, not looking the least bit convinced by Eleanor's assurances.

Get it together. If he wants to speak to you, he'll call. Otherwise let it go.

A sudden twinge of sadness pulled at Eleanor's heart. Could she really imagine a life without Fin now? After everything that had happened, would it really be so easy to let him leave again?

You might not have a choice . . .

But on Tuesday morning, Eleanor had got her wish. She woke to six missed calls and three voicemails from Fin. It was a relief to know he was alive and there was a part of her that wanted to pick up the phone and call him back immediately, but something stopped her.

Let him stew, the perverse voice in her head jeered.

Make him wait just a little bit longer . . .

Eleanor's anxiety was at an all-time high the entire day. She could barely keep it together to go to work let alone socialize, and she had been very tempted to cancel her art class. But as much as she tried to convince herself otherwise, she knew she couldn't cancel. Her soul needed to paint, to create, to dump all of her angst on to something outside her own heart. But she wasn't in the mood to talk, and she most certainly wasn't in the mood for Reggie and his sarcasm. She'd made sure to get there early and chose a seat on the opposite side of the room.

'Playing hard to get, are we?' a gruff voice whispered in her ear.

Eleanor cursed herself for jumping, but she'd been staring so hard at her still very blank canvas that Reggie's appearance had taken her by surprise.

'No,' she mumbled, feeling her face flush. 'This was the first empty seat I saw when I came in.'

'Huh,' Reggie commented. 'I guess it is pretty rammed today.'

Eleanor reddened even more as she looked around at all the vacant chairs.

'Mind if I join you over on this side?' he asked, already seating himself next to her. 'Might be good to get a different perspective on things.'

'Be my guest.' She smiled.

'Agatha!' Reggie barked. 'You wouldn't mind getting me my cushion and bringing my canvas over here, would you? Eleanor and I are getting new perspectives.'

Eleanor gritted her teeth and tried to remain calm. She knew he was trying to provoke her. If she could block him out and focus on painting then everything would be fine.

'Ohhhh, shaking things up, are we? I like that!' Agatha beamed. 'You sit right there, Reginald, and I'll be over with your things in just a tick.'

'Perfect.' He sat back and folded his arms. 'And I suppose

you're too grumpy to get the tea and biscuits today then?' he remarked.

'I'm not grumpy,' Eleanor replied.

'OK. If you say so.' He let out a long, slow sigh. 'At least I'll get some painting done, I suppose. What with you being all quiet and sulky.'

'I'm not sulking.' She grimaced.

'OK,' he mused. 'I could really murder a chocolate digestive right about now.'

Eleanor whipped her head round to look at him. 'If I get you a biscuit, will you be quiet?'

'Get me five and I'll think about it.' He grinned cheekily.

'Eurgh,' Eleanor grunted, standing up and storming over to the refreshment table. When she returned, she found Reggie leaning forwards and inspecting her canvas.

'Here you go.' She thrust the plate of biscuits in front of him. 'Now, do you mind?'

'You've got a good eye, for someone who says they can't do portraits,' he commented.

'I didn't say I *can't* do them. I just said I wasn't very good,' she corrected pedantically.

'I see. My apologies, I must have misheard.' He popped a digestive into his mouth gleefully.

She didn't bother to reply. She knew it wasn't fair that she was taking her frustration out on Reggie, but who could blame her when he was being so incredibly annoying? Eleanor forced the rest of the room to dissolve around her, and picked up her paintbrush. For a good twenty minutes she worked uninterrupted, her hands finding their way instinctively across the picture, her mind settling at last.

'Cookie?' A hand appeared next to her face, brandishing a crumbling biscuit.

'No, thank you.' She continued to paint.

'Sure? It's the last one,' Reggie pressed.

Eleanor inhaled deeply. 'What do you want, Reggie? Normally you're begging me to be quiet, and now that I am you can't seem to leave me alone.'

The old man popped the cookie into his mouth and chewed thoughtfully. 'The thing is,' he mumbled, mouth half full, 'it doesn't work this way around.'

She looked at him, confused. 'What doesn't work?'

He swallowed and gesticulated back and forth between them. 'This. Us. We don't work this way around. I am the grumpy, silent old man and you are the bright, sunshiny young woman. That's the way it goes, you see.' He shrugged his shoulders. 'So, are you going to tell me what's wrong so I can get back to being miserable or what?'

Eleanor couldn't help but smile. 'It's nothing.' She leant back in her chair.

'Doesn't feel like nothing.'

Eleanor paused for a moment. 'You know that best friend I told you about? The one who recently came back into my life again?' Reggie nodded. 'Well, his mum died and it was her funeral on Saturday. He got pretty drunk and we had this big fight.'

'And?' The old man raised his eyebrows expectantly.

'And what? I'm annoyed about it,' she snapped.

'People argue all the time. Heck, I don't think there was a week that went by without me and the wife arguing.'

'This is different.'

'How?'

Eleanor shrugged. 'He was so angry. He was so . . . *mean*.' The echo of his words still made her wince in pain. 'He's never spoken to me like that before. Ever.'

'Hmmm.' Reggie picked up his pencil and began to fiddle with it. 'Have you talked to him since?'

'No. He's called me a bunch of times but I don't want to speak to him.'

'Why not?'

'Because I don't.' She swiped her brush across her canvas a little too viciously, leaving a big splodge of paint in its wake. 'Argh, look at this mess.'

'Stop.' Reggie took the brush from her hand. 'Take a minute before you make a complete cock-up of what was looking like a very nice piece of work.' He flashed her a little smile. 'Look, I'm going to be honest with you. Men are idiots. Trust me, I am one.' He patted her hand gently. 'And . . . men are even bigger idiots when they've been drinking. He probably didn't mean half the things he said. Give him a chance to explain himself without half a bottle of poison in his veins.'

'More like three litres of the stuff,' she grumbled.

'Wow, no wonder he was a complete arse then.' Reggie chuckled, sensing Eleanor's anger abating slowly. She gently wiped away the garish blob of paint from her picture, and sat back to assess the damage.

'Did you two ever fight?' she asked.

'Who?'

Eleanor nodded at Reggie's half-finished portrait. 'You and your friend.'

'Only once.' A sad smile bloomed on to the old man's face. 'It was a big one, though.'

'Really?' Eleanor's curiosity was rearing its head.

'Hmmm.' He sighed, a long deep sigh.

'How did you make up?'

He sat back in his chair, staring forlornly at the picture in front of him. 'We didn't.'

'Oh.' Eleanor was desperate to know more but she knew Reggie was not a man to be pushed into talking, so she busied herself with cleaning her brushes and mixing new paints.

'We didn't speak for over fifty years,' he continued quietly. 'By the time I got back in touch . . . he was dead.'

Eleanor stopped her ruse of activity and stared into the crinkled eyes of her friend. 'I'm sorry,' she replied softly.

'It's OK.' He waved his hand, dismissing her apology. 'It was my own fault. I don't know if you know this about me, but I can be very stubborn at times.' Reggie gave a strained excuse of a smile.

'You can't blame yourself entirely. Two people make up a friendship, it wasn't just you.' Eleanor couldn't stand the sadness in his eyes; it was too much for her already bruised heart to take.

'No, but I was the one who walked away.'

Eleanor's stomach lurched, the unanswered voicemails and missed calls from Fin sending prickles of guilt across her skin.

She forced her attention back to Reggie.

'Why didn't you go back? What happened?'

The old man closed his eyes and shook his head.

'I'm sorry, I didn't mean to pry,' she apologized, praying that the disgruntled, vibrant Reggie that she knew and loved would return and replace this broken, deflated version.

'I was too scared,' he whispered. 'Back then, things weren't like they are now. It was a different world.'

Eleanor didn't dare breathe; she simply sat and stared at her old friend.

'I told myself the moment had passed,' he continued sadly. 'We were young and stupid and we didn't know a thing about the world. We'd both moved on and it would be wrong to find him again. I was married. I had a *wife.*' The words were flowing freely, as though every one spoken relieved him of some heavy burden. 'I thought about him every day. Every single day, and yet I did nothing until it was too late.' He shook his head and gave a small, weary laugh.

Questions exploded in her mind, all firing at once so that she couldn't hold on to one long enough before another erupted and distracted her.

'Reggie,' she managed feebly. 'I'm so sorry.'

Her friend looked at her and smiled, his eyes so tiny buried under the folds of papery skin. 'Eleanor, the only thing you need to be sorry about is making the same mistake as this old fool.'

'But . . . did you . . . did your wife ever find ou—'

'I need to finish painting.' Reggie turned his attention back to the canvas, shutting down the conversation immediately.

'OK. Yes, of course,' Eleanor replied, blushing at her insensitive and inappropriate questioning. 'I'm sorry if I overstepped the mark.'

'I've told you the only thing you need to be sorry about, Eleanor.' The old man smiled but his voice was firm and serious. 'Speak to your friend. Please, before it's too late.'

*

The moment Eleanor got home she dialled his number.

Voicemail.

'Come on, Fin . . .' she urged, trying again. 'We can't keep doing this for ever.'

Maybe he's gone back to America.

Maybe he was calling to say goodbye.

'Argh, pick up!' she groaned as the sound of his answering machine greeted her yet again.

Eleanor hung up and began scrolling through her phone to her own unanswered messages. She dialled the number and waited.

'You have three new messages. First message received Tuesday, 3 April at 2.45 a.m. from Finley Taylor.'

Eleanor began to pace up and down, nervous energy forcing her to move. The moment the message played, her body froze in fear.

'Hello?' A lady's voice was shouting over the deafening sound of sirens. 'Hello, I hope you can hear me.' She sounded scared. Who even was she? Why did she have Fin's phone? Questions fired through Eleanor's mind but she tried to focus her attention on the stranger's voice.

'My name is Emma and . . . and I'm with your friend. You're the first person I could find on his call list. Please, as soon as you get this, go to St Joseph's Hospital. He's been in an accident. There's been an accident.'

Eleanor felt the entire world shift beneath her.

'Second message received Tuesday, 3 April at 3 a.m.'

'Hello.' This time a deep, gruff male voice spoke. 'Is this Eleanor Levy? My name is Mike Cardoza and I'm a paramedic. Your friend Fin has been hurt in an accident and we need you to head to St Joseph's Hospital as soon as you get this.'

She couldn't breathe.

It's too late.

Oh my God . . . I've left it too late.

Eleanor didn't even wait to listen to the third message. There was simply no time.

Fin

It was funny, he thought, as he lay in the middle of the road, watching the blood collect in deep red pools around him. Funny that this should be the way he went. After all these years and everything he'd been through, he'd die sober, after being hit by a Ford Fiesta, smashed to pieces in the middle of the road. Fin closed his eyes, the flashing lights and screech of sirens like shards of glass crunching through his brain. He was aware of panicked voices and concerned whisperings. People poking and prodding him tentatively, as though he may crack at their touch. Didn't they know he was already too broken for that?

'Fin, I need you to keep your eyes open for me, OK?' Someone was by his head, talking loudly in his ear. 'My name is Mike and I'm going to be getting you to a hospital as quickly as I can.'

It's too loud and too bright.

I just need to sleep.

'Fin, can you hear me?' the voice asked. 'I need you to

open your eyes. We've called your friend Eleanor and we've asked her to meet us at the hospital.'

No. She can't see me like this.

He tried to speak, to tell this man that no matter what, Eleanor must not see him like this, but his mouth was too full of blood and his tongue too heavy and swollen to form words.

'Don't try to talk, we need you to keep as still as possible.' Fin felt himself being lifted into the air. 'It's going to be OK. You're going to be OK,' the man repeated.

Eleanor

'Next, please,' the receptionist called.

'Hi!' Eleanor practically hurled herself at the young man. 'My friend was brought here yesterday morning. I don't know where he is but I was told to come to this hospital,' she blurted. 'A man named Mike . . . a paramedic called Mike left me a message and I only listened to it last night because I'm a complete stubborn idiot. I came here as quickly as I could but you turned me away because visiting hours were over, but now I'm here and I'd really like to see him, please.' She had barely paused for breath, and the young man was looking as though he'd been hit by a hurricane.

'Name?' he said slowly, his face still a little startled.

'I'm Eleanor Levy.'

'No. I meant the patient's name.'

Eleanor blushed at her mistake. 'Oh . . . it's Finley Taylor.'

'One moment, please.' He began typing into his computer, all the while his eyes flicking back to Eleanor as though she herself could do with being admitted. So what if she hadn't managed to wash her hair this morning, or even put a brush through it? And did it matter that she was wearing the same clothes as yesterday because she'd barely been able to sleep all night and her brain couldn't function properly?

'OK, he was moved out of intensive care to orthopaedics so you'll be needing the third floor. Follow the signs and check in at the reception there,' he announced.

Intensive care.

The words sent shock waves through her.

God, Fin, what have you done to yourself?

'Thank you,' Eleanor mumbled, darting her head back and forth, trying to find the stairs.

'The stairs are over there.' The receptionist pointed to the left, clearly sensing her flustered disorientation.

'Right, yes, over there.' She dashed across the foyer, weaving between the milling crowds. Everyone was going too slowly – didn't they have somewhere to be? Someone to see? Eleanor raced up the stairs, through the door and along the third-floor corridor. She didn't care that she was breathless and sweating by the time she arrived at the reception. She had to know he was all right. That was all she needed.

'Hello, are you OK there, sweetie?' A jolly red-haired lady looked up from her computer.

'Hi,' Eleanor panted. 'I'm here to see my friend. His name is Finley Taylor.'

'Oh ho! You must be Eleanor?' The lady's face shone even brighter than before.

'Err, yes, that's me.' The confusion gave way to guilt. Clearly they had been waiting for her to arrive.

'Wonderful. Let me see if he's out of surgery yet.' She peered over the desk. 'Helen?' she called. 'Helen, my love.'

A thin, tired but cheery-looking nurse poked her head around the corner. 'Yes?'

'I've got Eleanor here for Fin. Is he out of surgery yet?'

'No, he only went in a couple of hours ago.' She turned to look at Eleanor. 'I can take you through to wait for him, if you'd like? He shouldn't be too long.'

'Yes, please,' Eleanor replied, willing the swarm of questions to stop buzzing around her head for just a moment.

'Of course, come with me,' Helen beckoned, disappearing behind the corner she had been peering round.

Eleanor hurried after her, nodding her thanks to the kind receptionist. The pair walked in silence along the corridor, the only sound coming from the faint beeping of machines and clattering of equipment. Everything seemed to shine and squeak and smell of disinfectant.

'Here we are. He's in the bed in the far corner.' The nurse pointed into one of the wards; a large room with four beds along each side, all filled with a variety of broken and bruised-looking humans. All except Fin's.

'Is he . . .' she began, unable to hold the questions back any longer. 'Will he be OK? The man downstairs told me he was in intensive care.'

The nurse smiled and placed her arm reassuringly on to Eleanor's. 'He had a nasty accident but he's through the worst of it. He's broken a lot of bones and recovery won't be quick or easy, but he'll be all right.'

'OK.' Eleanor breathed a sigh of relief. 'OK, good. Thank you.'

'Pleasure.' The nurse nodded and then checked her watch. 'I have to go, but I'll come and give you an update when I know more about when he'll be coming out. In the meantime, take a seat, or grab a coffee. There's a Starbucks on the fourth floor.'

'Sure.' Eleanor smiled appreciatively and made her way across the ward to Fin's corner of the room. She'd had enough coffees this morning to last her a lifetime, her anxiety so bad that she'd been unable to stomach anything solid. She settled herself down in the visitor's chair by the empty bed and took out her phone.

From: Ben Ryans
Hey. How's it going? Was wondering if you wanted to grab some food tomorrow night or go and see a movie? I miss you. X

I miss you.
Seeing those words written down made the knot in her stomach twist even tighter. She hadn't told Ben about Fin's accident yet. She wanted to assess the damage for herself first before worrying anybody unnecessarily. Eleanor was perfectly capable of handling the situation by herself; she'd done it many times before.

Sounds wonderful. I'll call you tonight to sort out the details? xxx

She paused, her fingers hovering tentatively over the send button. Quickly she added a 'miss you too' and fired off the message. It wasn't that she didn't mean it, it was that, in all honesty, she wasn't used to someone being so affectionate and open with their feelings. Oliver was to the point. He was logical and practical, and words of affirmation were saved for special occasions and holidays. Ben, however, was a different story, and it was taking Eleanor a little time to adjust.

'Eleanor?' a voice called gently from behind. She jerked up her head and stuffed her phone back into her pocket, turning around to see a different nurse standing there. She was smaller and a little older but had the same tired eyes as Helen.

'Yes, that's me.' Eleanor stood, eager for any news of Fin's arrival.

'Helen told me to come and update you. Fin's out of surgery and in recovery. He's taking a while to wake up from the anaesthetic but it's nothing to worry about. I'll come and let you know when we're bringing him up.' She was holding a bag that she handed over to Eleanor. 'These are his personal effects that we recovered – I didn't know if you wanted to hold on to them for him. ICU brought them up just now.'

Eleanor took the plastic bag and held it close to her chest. 'Thank you.'

'Pleasure.' The nurse turned and scurried away.

Eleanor sat back down and steadied herself. She could already see the pile of bloodied clothes folded up at the bottom. She reached inside and pulled out his watch, the screen smashed and the hands frozen in position. A cruel reminder of the time of impact forever more. Eleanor placed it on her lap and continued to rummage around, pulling out his wallet, his cracked and lifeless phone, his jeans and finally his coat. She held it close to her, breathing in the smell of his skin, his sweat, his blood.

How could this have happened?

Eleanor held the battered jacket out in front of her and began to refold it neatly. As she did so, she felt something in the inside pocket. Reaching in, she pulled out an envelope. It was crinkled and crumpled but still in one piece. She turned it over.

Eleanor Levy
129 Ursuline Road
London
E18 1HP

Her stomach dropped sickeningly; her hands began to shake so violently that the envelope nearly fell from her hands.

You can't open it . . .

But it's for me.

Eleanor looked around nervously, checking for any prying eyes or disapproving witnesses. But it was only her and the letter and her conscience. Slowly she opened the envelope and pulled out an A4 piece of paper, littered with the familiar untidy scrawl of her friend's handwriting. She tried to bring the words into focus as her mind began to spin.

Dear Eleanor,

By the time you read this letter, I'll probably be back in LA. I wish I had the courage to say all of this to your face, but we both know my ability to have difficult conversations is lacking and so I'm hoping this letter will make do instead.

Firstly, I want to say how sorry I am. Not only for the stupid, stupid things I said in our argument the other night, but for the lifetime of promises I made to you and broke. The times when I wasn't there for you as a friend. For running away from my problems but leaving you to deal with yours by yourself. I let you down as a friend in more ways than I care to imagine, and I wouldn't be surprised if you decide never to speak to me again. But

374

there's something I need to tell you before you make that choice . . .

These past few months have been some of the hardest I can remember. I was so afraid to come back and visit the past, but despite all the heartache and pain, there has been one thing that has made everything feel better. And that's you, Eleanor. Having you back in my life has been more than I could have dreamed of. I have never met anyone like you and I don't think I ever will. Seeing you again, being around you again, has made me realize just how much I lost when I left all those years ago. You were the other half of me back then and that piece has been missing ever since.

Before my mother died, she gave me a bunch of letters she'd written to me but had never sent. Letters for my birthday, letters she wrote at Christmas, letters when she was bored or missing me or lonely. All the things she wanted to say but never could, because she didn't know how, or maybe she was too afraid to.

I'm sorry it's taken me so long and I'm sorry I'm too much of a coward to say this to your face, but Eleanor, I love you. Not just as a sister or a best friend. I love you like I want to be the one holding your hand, waking up next to you, kissing you and then cleaning the sick off you when you vomit on me after. I love you, Elles, and even though I am only saying it now, I think deep down I always have done. I know we've made a lot of promises over the years and none of them we've ever kept, but I can promise you this. Until the day I die, I'll be thinking of you and wishing you only the best, because you deserve it. You deserve it all.

Yours always,

Fin

Eleanor held the letter in her hand. She couldn't think. She could barely breathe. She shoved the paper into her pocket and ran. She ran out of the ward. She ran down the corridor and past reception. She ran straight into the thin nurse called Helen, practically knocking her off her feet.

'Woah there, Eleanor, what's going on?'

'I'm sorry.' She shook her head, tears soaking her cheeks. 'I have to go. I have to leave right now.'

'But Fin will be back soon. He's on his way now. He's fine, everything with the surgery went well.' The nurse tried to soothe her, but it was no use. She didn't understand. She'd never understand. Eleanor felt the walls of the reception closing in on her, her lungs shrinking, her breath so small it was barely a sip of air.

'I can't,' she sobbed. 'Tell him I'm sorry. Please . . .' She pushed past the nurse and hurtled down the corridor. 'Please tell him I'm sorry,' she called back.

Fin

Fin began to stir. His brain cautiously woke to a confusing blend of sounds and smells. For one glorious moment he forgot entirely where he was. It wasn't until he opened his eyes fully that the reality came crashing down around him.

'Ah, Fin, there you are.' A red-haired nurse, whose face he vaguely remembered, was by his side. 'How are you feeling?'

He gave himself a minute to assess, his mind still operating at half-speed.

'Tired,' he mumbled.

'That will be the anaesthetic.' She smiled. 'Are you in any pain?'

Fin closed his eyes. His entire body seemed to be in some level of pain, not searing or sharp or coming from anywhere in particular but a low, deep thrum of hurt radiating throughout.

'Kind of,' he replied quietly.

'OK.' She patted his arm lightly. 'I'll give you another dose of morphine in a bit and see how you feel after that.

The surgery was a success, and . . .' Her small almond eyes sparkled. 'You had a visitor.'

Fin's brain jolted into action.

'What?' He tried to sit up but his body was a dead weight.

'Yes, your friend Eleanor came.'

His heart was pounding. Where was she? If she had come to see him why wasn't she here?

'Where is she?' he croaked, his eyes looking around his tiny curtained bay for any traces of her.

'Erm, she left in a bit of a rush actually.' The nurse's face creased in confusion. 'I think there was some sort of emergency. But not to worry.' Her expression smoothed itself back into a warm smile. 'I'm sure she'll be back soon.'

An emergency?

His mind began to race with the possibilities.

'Oh, before I forget.' The nurse pointed at the pile of belongings on the chair by his bed. 'ICU brought those up whilst you were in surgery. Your friend must have been sorting through them before she had to go. Would you like me to put them away for you?'

Fin's stomach contracted violently. Something was trying to fight its way to the front of his awareness, but the cotton-wool lining of the anaesthesia was keeping it at bay.

'No.' He shook his head slightly. 'Can you pass them here, please?' There was a quake in his voice that he prayed only he'd noticed.

'Sure.' She hurried around his bed and handed him the pile of items. 'I'll be back in a bit with that morphine. Meanwhile, stay put and don't wander off anywhere, will you?' She laughed loudly at her own joke, tapping the plaster cast around his leg gently.

Impatient to look through the heap of damaged goods in

his hands, Fin could only offer half a smile in response. He waited until he was alone before he began his inspection. There was his watch, frozen in time and cracked. His phone, dead to the world, covered in scuffs and scratches. Fin turned them over in his hands, mourning their wounds just as keenly as his own. But there was something more important he needed to find; everything else would have to wait. He sifted through the remnants of his torn and bloodied clothes until he found his jacket. The sleeves were ripped and hanging limply by their stitches, but the main body was still intact. Fin reached inside and felt for the letter. The letter he had placed carefully in the inside pocket so that it would be safe, hidden from the world and kept close to his heart.

Where the hell is it?

He turned the material inside out and shook it. It had to be here. Someone must have found it and put it with his stuff. Panic joined the pain throbbing in his head. He rifled frantically through the rest of his stuff but it wasn't there.

She'd found her letter.

And she'd left.

She'd read his words.

And she'd gone.

She couldn't even bear to say goodbye.

*

The rest of the night was spent in a series of disturbed dreams and fitful waking. Fin's mind couldn't settle. Images of Eleanor reading his words and fleeing continued to haunt him and the pain in his body was making it hard to relax. By the time the morning came, he was desperate for something to take the edge off and lull him into a deep and mindless sleep.

'Good morning.' A different but still oddly familiar nurse poked her head around the curtain. Fin was lying wide awake, his body so tired it was frozen still, but his mind continued to whirr relentlessly. 'How did you sleep?' she asked, unable to hide the flicker of concern on her face as she registered him properly.

'Not great,' he replied flatly, the effort of speaking already proving an exhausting task.

'I can see that. You look spent! Was it the pain?' She picked up his notes from the end of his bed and began to study them intently. 'It says here you had the maximum dose of morphine so it should have taken the edge off somewhat.'

'Hmmm,' Fin replied pathetically. 'Bad dreams.'

'Ah.' The nurse nodded. 'That would make sense.' She came back round to stand by his head, placing a warm gentle hand on his shoulder. 'Let's get you some breakfast and see how you feel after that. I'll check with the doctor if there's anything more we can do. Sound like a plan?'

'Thank you.' He sighed, closing his eyes and letting his head sink back fully into the scratchy pillow beneath him.

'Try and rest, I'll be back with your food shortly.' He heard her soft voice disappear behind the swish of the curtain.

And try he did. The entire morning was spent with his eyes half closed and his mind focused determinedly on sleeping, but it was no use. At best he drifted off into a strange half-dream state where flashing lights and screeching car tyres woke him abruptly. He had no true memory of the accident, only fragments of sensations. The smell of the tarmac as he lay face down in his own blood. The sound of panic and screaming. The crushing impact as the force of the car hit him. Maybe it was better that way. Not knowing fully what his own stupid actions had led to.

Ignorance is bliss.

He sighed and tried to find another comfortable position, a task made extremely difficult when his range of motion extended to turning his head and moving his arms. How the hell was he supposed to get back to LA in this state? Surely he wouldn't be cleared to fly for at least a few weeks. Cold dread snaked through his veins, but he didn't have too long to dwell on it as he heard voices approaching his bay.

'He might be asleep so let me pop my head in and check. He had a rough night last night and so if he's dozing, I don't want to wake him. Fin?' a tentative voice called out.

The red-haired nurse's face appeared between the blue cloth curtains. 'Oh. Hello there, wide awake I see.' She beamed cheerfully. 'There's someone here to see you if you're up for it?'

'Yeah, sure.' Fin tried to sound calm but his heart was beating furiously. Had she come back? What on earth was he going to say to her? Maybe he could pretend it was all a joke? The questions were suddenly silenced as the curtain was drawn back.

'Freya?' He couldn't help the tone of surprise.

'Fin!' she cried, almost flinging herself on to the bed. 'What the *hell* happened? You look awful.'

The pang of disappointment was swiftly replaced by warm affection. 'Thanks.'

'Can I sit?' she asked, nodding towards the empty chair by the window.

'Of course.' He tried to sit up a little higher. 'What are you doing here?'

'Eleanor called and told me what happened. She asked if I could come and see you.' Freya settled herself down and pulled out a plastic bag. 'Here . . . I picked up some supplies on the way over.'

Fin peered inside and saw about ten packets of chocolate digestives. But his mind was still stuck on Freya's words.

She couldn't stand to see you herself so she called Freya.

'Now, can you please explain what happened? The nurse said something about surgery and Eleanor told me it was a car accident.'

'Yeah.' He shrugged. 'I don't remember much, to be honest, but . . . apparently I walked out in front of one and got pretty smashed up.'

Freya winced at his blunt account. 'You walked in front of it?' Her eyes were wide and the young girl he'd grown up with appeared before him.

'Not on purpose!' he insisted. 'It was an accident.'

'Right.' She eyed him suspiciously.

'It was. I promise.'

'Were you drunk?' Freya's face dropped. 'Eleanor said something about you drinking.'

Fin tried to sit up but the pain held him down. 'No.' He shook his head furiously. 'I had some drinks the night of my mum's funeral, but after that nothing.' His voice was straining as the desperation clawed through to the surface. 'You have to believe me. You both have to believe me. I was sober.'

'OK.' She reached her hand out and placed it on his arm to calm him. 'I believe you.'

He took a couple of seconds for the anxiety to subside and then reached into the bag and pulled out a packet of biscuits. 'You want one?'

'Go on then.' She smiled, sitting back in the chair.

'How did Eleanor sound?' he tried to ask casually.

'Fine.' Freya took the packet from his clumsy hands and ripped it open. 'A little stressed maybe.'

'Stressed? Did she say why?' He cringed at his lack of tact, but Freya seemed oblivious.

'Nope. I'm guessing work.' She sighed, taking a bite out of her digestive biscuit. 'She's always stressed with work.'

'Are you seeing her soon?'

Freya curled her legs up underneath her on the chair. 'Wasn't planning to until Sunday. The lunches with Mother dear still continue.'

'OK,' he mumbled dejectedly.

'I'm sure she'll be back to visit you, though,' Freya chirped brightly. 'How long do they say you'll be here for?'

'I don't know. The doctor is coming round later for an assessment. I guess I'll find out more then.'

'Will you let me know as soon as you do, please? We're worried about you.'

'We?' he asked curiously.

'Yes! Me and Eleanor.' She smirked. 'I haven't told Mum yet because God knows the last thing you need is her flapping around your bedside when you're trying to recover.'

Visions of Angela Levy bursting on to the ward swathed in silk, crying his name dramatically, gave Fin a little burst of levity.

'It would probably be quite entertaining, though,' he mused, going in for another biscuit. 'Mainly for the other patients.'

'Exactly. Oh, by the way, do you want me to pick up anything from your flat and bring it here? Toothbrush, deodorant, books?' Freya asked.

'Only if you don't mind.' As much as Fin was counting on a quick exit, looking down at the various stitches, plaster casts and bandages, it was probably safer to prepare for a long recovery.

'Of course I don't mind.' She reached into her bag and pulled out a pen and paper. 'Tell me what you need and I'll swing by later and pick it up.'

'Thanks, Frey. It won't be much, I promise.' A sickening thought struck him. 'You'll also have to excuse the state of the flat . . .' He glanced down at his hands, remembering the pile of empty bottles he'd left in the recycling bin. 'It's going to be a bit of a mess.'

'That's fine,' she replied, ignorant to his unease. 'I know you worship the ground Eleanor walks on, but she can be messy as hell when you live with her,' she teased.

Fin's heart dropped into his stomach.

'Frey?' He glanced up at her.

'Yes?'

'Will you check in on Eleanor for me?'

Her eyes narrowed and she looked at him shrewdly. 'What's going on?' She leant forward in her chair. 'Did something happen?'

'No,' Fin lied, shaking his head adamantly. 'I worry about her, that's all.'

'I think the only thing you should be worried about is yourself right now. How many bones did you break? You're more plaster cast than skin!' She flicked his leg gently. 'But fine – as it's you, I'll check.'

'Thank you.'

'Now, back to this list . . . I've got here deodorant, tooth-brush, toothpaste . . . underpants?'

Eleanor

Eleanor had been lying on the floor for what felt like hours. She knew she should get up but it was comfortable down here on the carpet, sprawled out on the ground. What other options did she have? She'd tried everything. Drinking hadn't helped. Eating hadn't helped. Crying hadn't helped. Running hadn't helped. Now, she was learning that doing nothing didn't help either.

Ben or Fin.

Fin or Ben . . .

She balled her hands into tight fists and slammed them down hard on the floor.

'There isn't even a choice!' she hissed through gritted teeth. 'There. Is. No. Choice.' She beat every word out angrily on the carpet, scrunching her eyes closed and begging her brain to stop thinking for one moment. There was nothing to think about. Her life could and would and *should* keep on going as it was. She was happy. She was starting over. She was with Ben.

'I'm with Ben,' she repeated out loud, bringing the details of his kind, broad face to her mind.

Is that why you've been ignoring his calls?

All at once, Ben's blond, shaved hair became blazing red, his chiselled cheekbones dotted with freckles. His face merged and morphed into Fin's.

No.

Stop thinking about him.

He was drunk. The words mean nothing.

A loud knock on the door startled her but Eleanor stayed where she was. If she ignored it for long enough, the person would leave and she could get back to drowning in the incessant bleating of her own inner thoughts. But the knocking continued, growing louder and more urgent.

'*Eleanor*,' her sister's voice boomed through the letter box. 'I know you're in there – open up.'

Eleanor stayed resolutely still, slowing her breathing down so that the tiny inhales were almost inaudible. She needed to disappear, to find a way to become completely invisible.

'I've just been to Fin's to pick up his stuff and there are empty bottles everywhere. What the hell is going on, Eleanor?' Freya's voice was becoming increasingly fretful.

'*Eleanor.*'

Suddenly her phone screen lit up and began to vibrate violently.

'I can see your phone ringing through the window,' her sister continued to holler. 'I'm not stupid . . . let me in.'

'I'm sick,' Eleanor groaned pathetically. 'I don't want you to catch it.'

'Eleanor Ruth Levy . . . don't make me call Mum,' Freya threatened.

She wouldn't dare!

'You've got ten seconds to get your arse up and open this door, or I swear to God I'll be on the phone to her.'

Eleanor sat bolt upright. Resentment simmered under the surface of her skin but she forced herself to standing and made her way over to the front door.

'Ten . . . nine . . . eight . . . seven . . .' Freya counted down.

Eleanor placed her cheek against the cool wood of the door and closed her eyes.

Make it quick.

Show her you're alive and get her out as fast as possible.

She opened the door, assembling her face into the best 'I'm totally fine, now leave me alone, there's nothing to worry about' expression she could muster.

'Christ, what happened to you?' Freya remarked, her eyes scanning the length of her.

'I told you, I'm not feeling well.' Eleanor folded her arms defensively across her chest, very aware she hadn't showered and was still wearing her pyjamas.

'That's what Sal said. She said you hadn't been in work since yesterday.' Freya stepped closer, inching her way into the flat with every word. 'And do my eyes deceive me? Are those six empty ice-cream tubs lined up on the countertop over there?'

Eleanor whipped her head round and saw the evidence immediately.

Idiot.

You absolute idiot.

'I had Sal over last week and forgot to take them out to the recycling,' she lied.

'Bullshit.' Freya pushed past her and stormed into the living room. Eleanor could do nothing but follow and wait for her sister's reaction as she took in the scene. Pieces of paper were scattered on the floor; half-drunk mugs of tea huddled in groups; biscuit wrappers and crisp packets sprawled their contents out on to the carpet.

Freya stood, completely speechless, in the middle of the room.

'I wasn't expecting visitors,' Eleanor murmured.

'I can see that.' Her sister sounded dumbfounded. 'What's going on?' Freya turned. 'And don't lie to me. This' – she gestured around the room – 'is not nothing. And what I saw at Fin's flat is *definitely* not nothing.'

Eleanor perched on the edge of the sofa and closed her eyes. She'd been hiding away in an attempt to avoid the very moment she was now faced with.

You don't have to tell her.

It will only make things worse.

Lie, Eleanor. For Christ's sake, find a way to lie.

She felt her sister's stare burning into the top of her head.

'The day of Eileen's funeral, after I left Mum's, I went over to Fin's. He was drunk when I got there.'

'Well, I'm not surprised judging by the number of bottles in his bin,' Freya commented. 'Go on . . .'

'We argued.' Eleanor's voice trembled but she managed to regain composure. 'It was bad. Really bad.' She shuddered at the memory.

'Have you spoken to him since?'

Eleanor shook her head; the burden of Fin's words was becoming too heavy to carry by herself.

'Why not? Surely whatever was said can be forgiven, especially now he's holed up in the hospital?' Freya implored.

'Over there' – she pointed by Freya's foot – 'is a letter from Fin. I found it in the belongings the hospital gave me when I went to visit. Read it.'

Eleanor watched as her sister reached down and fished the letter from the floor. She tried to analyse any hint of emotion as Freya read the piece of paper. Eventually, her sister came to sit next to her on the sofa.

'Wow,' Freya whispered.

'Yeah.' Eleanor sighed.

'So . . . what are you going to do?'

'I don't know,' she replied feebly. 'After I read it, I completely freaked out and ran away before getting a chance to see him.'

'Well, you have to do something.' Freya shook the letter in front of her face. 'You can't just ignore this and hide away in here for ever.'

'I know that,' Eleanor snapped. 'Don't you think I know that?'

'And you haven't spoken to Fin since?'

'No.'

'Have you told Ben?'

'No!' Eleanor cried.

'Are you going to?' Freya asked, her questioning starting to grate abrasively on Eleanor's brain. This was why she wanted to figure things out on her own before involving anyone else. It was already complicated enough without adding other people's commentary to the mix.

'I don't *know*.' She stood and began to pace back and forth. 'It's such a mess.'

'Let's simplify it then,' Freya said breezily, as though this was nothing more than a difficult homework question. 'What if we ignore Ben for a second.'

'How can we ignore Ben? He's my boyfriend.' Eleanor flung her arms up in the air. 'I have a boyfriend, Freya.'

'And do you like him?'

Eleanor was staring at her sister in amazement. How stupid was she? 'Yes, I like him! What's not to like? He's nice and kind and treats me better than I've ever been treated before in my life.'

Freya shrugged nonchalantly. 'Just because someone is nice to you, doesn't mean you want to be with them. There are plenty of nice people in the world, Eleanor.'

'This isn't helping,' she grumbled, her mind feeling even more full than it had before her sister barged in and began grilling her with idiotic questions.

'I'm trying to get to the bottom of how you really feel, that's all. If you liked Ben so much then Fin's letter wouldn't be a problem, would it? If you had no feelings for Fin whatsoever then there would be no room for confusion.'

By this point Eleanor felt fit to burst. 'Obviously I have feelings for Fin. He's my friend. He *was* my best friend. He was who I spent my whole childhood loving. But he left, Freya. He left and when he did come back . . . he couldn't even show up for me.'

'He came back?' Freya interjected.

'For Dad's funeral. He made it back but Oliver told him to go. Said he wasn't wanted. And instead of standing up for himself, he went and got drunk and felt too ashamed to tell me. He left without saying a word.' Eleanor could see Freya's jaw fall open. 'Then, guess what? Fourteen years later, he decides to return and confess his love to me in a drunken letter. I mean, who knows if he even *meant* what he said?' Her voice was so loud now, the frustration of it all erupting out of her.

'He wasn't drunk,' Freya stated firmly.

Eleanor jerked her head in confusion.

'What do you mean, he wasn't drunk?'

'I asked him.' She shrugged. 'He promised me he wasn't drunk the night he had the accident.'

'And you believe him?'

'Completely.'

Eleanor's world shifted once again.

'OK, so you have feelings for them both,' Freya stated bluntly. 'What do you want to do?'

'I don't know.'

'Yes, you do. What do you want?' Freya replied.

'Aren't you listening to me? I. Don't. Know.' She clawed at her hair, scratching her fingernails deep into her skull. 'I've tried to write down the pros and cons. Endless lists to help me try and work out what to do, and I still don't know.'

'You can't *think* your way out of this one, Eleanor.' Freya stood up and placed her hands firmly on her shoulders. 'What do you want?'

Eleanor needed to move. She needed to walk the frustration out of her, but Freya was still holding her tightly, keeping her still. 'I don't know.'

'What do you want? *Who* do you want, Eleanor?'

Images of Ben and Fin flashed across her mind. 'I don't know,' she moaned.

'Ask yourself, what do you want?' Freya pushed, her voice firm and stern.

'*I don't know*,' Eleanor screamed.

'*Yes, you do*,' her sister shouted back.

'You don't need to shout at me.' Eleanor tried to pull free from her grasp, but Freya clamped down harder.

'Yes, I do, because for Christ's sake you're not listening. You haven't been listening for years. This is *your* life, Eleanor. Yours. Do you hear that? It's. Your. Life.' Freya shook her hard with each word she spoke. 'You let Oliver take over completely. You straightened your hair because he wanted you to. You stopped painting because he wanted you to.

Goddammit, you work in that godforsaken job that you *hate* because that's what you think you should do. You went on that date with Ben because Sal wanted you to. You turn up to Mum's for lunch every other Sunday because she wants you to.'

Freya relaxed her grip slightly and Eleanor wrenched herself free. Her sister's words filled her brain until it became so crowded it was all a jarring blur of white noise. She tried to speak but nothing came out.

'You do everything that everyone else wants you to do. You always do everything for everyone else.' Freya softened. 'So, I'm asking you. What do *you* want? What does your heart *want*, Eleanor?'

Eleanor closed her eyes and willed her brain to quieten.

What do you want?

She breathed in deep, guiding her attention away from her thoughts and down deeper into herself.

What do you want, Eleanor?

Everything went quiet. The external world around her melted away until all she could hear, all she could feel, was the thudding of her heart in her chest and the sound of a name repeating over and over between the beats. The sound of *his* name. After everything . . . it was his name . . .

Fin

Fin woke gradually, the pull of sleep refusing to relinquish its grasp on him completely. He could sense the familiar movements around him, the nurses coming and going, the chatter of the ward beyond his bay, easing him from his dream state and welcoming him back to the monotony of life in the hospital. Since Freya left, time had slowed itself down to barely a crawl. The only way Fin could pass the day was either to stare out of the window or sleep.

'Jesus Christ!' he gasped, his body shocked fully into waking. There was someone staring at him from the chair by the window. A pair of large and piercing eyes. He sat upright and saw, to his confusion, that it was an oversized painting of his mother.

'Sorry, I didn't mean to scare you.'

Fin turned his head at the sound of her.

'Eleanor?' he whispered, blinking furiously to make sure he wasn't still dreaming. But there was no doubt about it: she was there, standing at the end of his bed, her voice flat and emotionless.

'I did it for my art class project.' She pointed at the picture. 'We were given the theme "forget me not". I thought I would paint my dad, but then . . . everything happened with your mum and I thought it would be a nice thing to do for you,' she continued, her expression still completely unreadable. 'Something for you to remember Eileen by.' She wasn't even looking at him now, her gaze fixed on the painting.

'Thank you.' He reached for the canvas but it was too far away. His hand fell limply by his side. 'It's amazing.'

She gave a tiny, silent nod in response.

'I bet you didn't think I'd go to these lengths to get you to talk to me again, did you?' he tried to joke. 'Always one for extremes, me.'

'You don't get to do that.'

'Do what?' He winced in pain as he tried to pull himself upright. Eleanor remained standing, her expression fixed and unimpressed.

'You don't get to joke about this, Fin.' She lifted her eyes to meet his at last. 'You don't get to laugh this away or pretend it never happened. This happened, Fin, and you have to deal with the consequences.'

'I'm sorry. I didn't mean to s—' But once again she cut him off.

'Didn't mean to what? Come back into my life after disappearing for years? Didn't mean to reel me back in and be my friend again? Didn't mean to get steaming drunk and get hit by a car and nearly die?'

'I wasn't drunk when I had the accident.' He locked his eyes on to hers and prayed she could feel the importance of his words.

'So what were you doing wandering the streets at half two in the morning then?' Eleanor asked accusingly.

'I couldn't sleep so I went for a walk,' he replied earnestly.

Eleanor folded her arms across her chest but stayed silent.

'After our argument I pretty much passed out. I woke up the next day feeling worse than death. I realized . . .' The words stung as they formed. 'I realized what a total mess I'd been. The next day I found a local AA meeting. I went along the night of the accident. Those things are pretty intense, you know? They bring up a lot of stuff, even after all this time.' Fin could feel the familiar discomfort making its home in his chest. 'I had so many things on my mind and I'd written you that letter and I was supposed to be flying back the next day, so I just thought . . . Fuck it, I'll go and post it now. Walk around for a bit, get some fresh air.' He knew the story sounded like a pathetic stream of lies, but he hoped Eleanor would believe him. 'I wasn't looking where I was going and then . . .' He shrugged, knowing she could fill in the gaps. 'I didn't mean for things to end up this way,' he continued, not caring that his voice was loud enough for the other patients to hear.

'Right. Well, they did.'

'I know, and all I can say is I'm sorry. If I could take it all back, I would.'

Eleanor shifted awkwardly. 'Even the letter?'

Fin dropped his gaze to the floor, his face burning with the memory of those words he'd written.

'No. Of course not.'

'Are you sure?' Her voice had softened a little but he didn't dare look at her.

'Yes. That part I did mean. I *do* mean.'

'And what . . . You were going to casually post me the letter containing your confession in it whilst you hopped on a plane back to America? Disappear off again without a backward glance to your life in LA? You don't get to do that, Fin. Not any more. You don't get to run away.' Her voice cracked and Fin lifted his eyes to hers. They were watering and her cheeks were flaming.

'I know that. And I know that I've been a complete and utter idiot, and I've said I'm sorry.' He wished he could do more than lie pathetically and helplessly in his bed. 'I made peace with my mum before she died. I know I'm never going to make peace with my dad, and for the first time in my life I feel OK about that. But I can't leave here not having made things right with you, Eleanor. Not again. So can we please forget about it and go back to how it was before the funeral? Before I screwed everything up yet again?'

She stared at him hard, her eyes blazing. 'No. I'm sorry, but we can't do that.'

Fin's heart groaned under the weight of her words. 'Why?' he whispered, tears falling thick and fast down his cheeks.

'Because.' She took a couple of steps closer to him. 'The way we used to be didn't work. The way we used to be was a lie. We made all these stupid promises that we never kept. We pretended to be something we weren't. Can't you see, that doesn't work.' The anger had almost faded completely, but he found the sadness that had replaced it even more difficult to listen to.

'So that's it then?' He wished she'd never come back. Seeing her, saying goodbye like this, was too hurtful and too heavy. His broken body couldn't take it.

'No.' She reached out her hand and placed it on his arm. 'Not if you don't want it to be.'

'What do you mean?' He looked up at her.

'I mean, the old way wasn't working so we need to start

again.' She handed him a piece of paper. Fin's hand was shaking as he reached out for it, his eyes so full of tears that it took him a minute to focus on the words.

'What is this?' he asked.

'Read it.' The corner of her lip curled ever so slightly.

I, Finley James Taylor, and I, Eleanor Ruth Levy, agree to abide by the following rules:

A spark of anticipation ignited somewhere deep in his stomach. 'Is this . . .?'

'Go on . . .' She was smiling fully now. 'Read it and see.'

1. Stop making promises we can't keep.
2. Stop running away when things get hard or difficult or awkward or painful.
3. Talk. Whatever happens, never stop talking.
By signing this agreement all previous promises, pacts and agreements are hereby deemed invalid.

Fin's heart both rose and fell at once. The fact that she still wanted to be in his life was a relief. She wanted to be his friend. After everything that had happened, she still wanted him as her friend. But that didn't stop his heart from aching from her unrequited feelings.

'Do you have a pen?' he asked.

'Have you read it all carefully?' There was a hint of mischief behind her smile.

'Think so, looks pretty self-explanatory to me.' He scanned over her words once again to make sure.

'OK.' She shrugged and handed him a biro.

Fin took hold of the pen and signed hastily at the bottom

of the page. 'Do you want this back or do you already have a copy?'

'No, that one's for you. Keep it.'

Fin still couldn't understand why she was looking at him like that. As though there was a joke he was missing, or a secret he hadn't been told yet.

'Right, I'd better go. I'll make sure Freya or I pop in tomorrow.' Eleanor picked up her bag and slung it over her shoulder. 'Do you need anything?'

'No, I'm all good, thanks.' Fin folded the pact in half and went to put it on his bedside table. 'I'll see you to—' He stopped suddenly, his eyes catching something written on the back of the paper.

'What's this?' he asked, turning the page over and reading the line of handwriting he'd missed. His heart almost stopped completely at her words.

4. If both parties find themselves single at the age of thirty-five then they must not get married but instead . . . start by going on a date.

It took him a moment to fully comprehend what he was reading.

'But . . . but I don't . . .' he stammered.

'Don't what?'

'I don't understand. Are you?'

'Am I what?'

'Single?'

'Oh, that.' She shrugged casually.

'Eleanor?' he pressed, his heart aching with suspense.

'It shouldn't matter really . . .' She laughed. 'Because *technically* I'm not thirty-five for another couple of months.' She jabbed her finger at the piece of paper in his hand. 'Those are the rules.'

'Since when have we ever stuck to the rules?' He didn't know what was racing faster, his brain or his heart. Adrenaline was flooding his system and his entire body was on high alert.

'I really have to go; I'm going to be late.' She smirked.

'Eleanor!' he shouted. 'Come back.'

'I will.' She turned to look over her shoulder, her legs still carrying her further and further away from him.

'Do you promise?'

'I promise.' Eleanor stopped and placed one hand on her heart. 'I'll always come back for you, Fin.'

After: Aged 37

Eleanor

'Is everyone ready to go?' the harried-looking photographer whispered loudly.

Eleanor looked around at the group of people huddling together under the entrance to the church. It was just their luck that today, of all days, it had decided to rain.

It's fine. Everything will still be fine.

She smoothed down the front of her dress and took a deep breath. 'Ready,' she confirmed, as right on cue the music switched and the entrance song began to play.

'Ladies, remember: walk slowly, smile, and try not to look directly into the camera,' the photographer instructed as the large wooden doors creaked open. 'You all look beautiful,' he added.

Eleanor took a step forward and felt her stomach knot at the sight of the congregation, their excited faces peering anxiously for the first hint of the bride. She relaxed her face and began to walk, trying to keep her eyes focused on the floor in front of her. Everyone had told her that she needed to walk at half her normal speed – it was an important moment, the crowd needed time to absorb it – but it was hard not to feel like a complete idiot as she edged her way down the aisle. She could hear the trademark sniffs and rustle of tissues rippling through the crowd and had to focus all her energy on trying to keep her own tears at bay. Her eyes locked with the sea of glistening faces. There was Laura, her not-so-new husband and their two children. There was Ben with his fiancée Millie, smiling as kindly as ever as she passed. And then there was Fin, smiling at her with his green eyes and red hair shining even brighter under the lights of the church.

No.

Don't do it.

You will ruin your make-up if you cry.

She tore her eyes away from him and swallowed down her tears, forcing her attention on the other beaming faces looking at her. At last, after what felt like an age of walking, Eleanor reached the altar where a very nervous-looking Paul stood waiting for his bride. Eleanor gave him the most reassuring smile she could muster before turning to watch her friend make her grand entrance. The crowd gasped in unison as Sal stepped through the doors, a sight so beautiful that for a moment Eleanor forgot to stick to the rules and let the tears fall from her eyes.

She was on strict instructions not to cry. Sal had been very clear on that. It wasn't going to be a day of crying. It was going to be a day of drinking and celebrating and laughing. Sal did not do emotions, even on her own wedding day.

*

'There you are!' Fin grabbed Eleanor's hand and pulled her towards him. 'Did I mention how incredibly beautiful you

look, even after bawling your eyes out for most of the ceremony?' He kissed her delicately on the cheek.

'Don't.' She shot him a warning look. 'Sal's already had
the make-up lady touch me up twice.' Eleanor took a large
sip of champagne, looking anxiously around to make sure
everything was running smoothly. Being maid of honour
was a big task, but being maid of honour to Sal was a whole
different ball game.

'Relax, everyone is having a great time.' Fin squeezed her
hand, soothing her instantly. 'I've also been eyeing up the
photographer. He looks pretty great. Do you think he'd be
interested in coming to help us?'

Eleanor finished her drink and reached out for another
from a passing tray. 'He's busy! Don't you dare bother him.
If Sal catches you being a distraction you'll be in big
trouble.'

'Me? A distraction?' He grinned cheekily at her. 'How
very dare you.'

She narrowed her eyes in disapproval.

'I'll catch him on his break,' Fin continued. 'It will take
less than five minutes, I promise. You know we need volun-
teers. Come on, Elles. We have to take every opportunity we
can.'

Fin's eyes were wide and pleading. The charity was still in
its infancy but growing fast, and every bit of help they could
get was critical at this stage. Fin had decided to go back to
the care home and finish off the work he'd started when his
mother was sick. Word had got out and all of a sudden he
was offering the service to three local care homes and hos-
pices. It had been Eleanor's idea to make it an official charity,
and now their side-project was becoming so big that they'd
had to start pulling in reinforcements.

'Fine,' Eleanor conceded. 'Do it, but do it quick.' Her eyes caught Sal's from across the room. 'I have to go . . . I think we are readying ourselves for the big bouquet throw.'

'I'll get warmed up, shall I?' he teased.

'Yes, I want you out there ready and raring to go.' She winked and began to wend her way through the crowd towards the bride.

'There you are!' Sal cried, practically launching herself at Eleanor. She turned to address the couple in front of her. 'I'm sorry, I have to attend to some more bride duties. You know how it is.' Sal didn't even wait for their response before waving goodbye and dragging Eleanor across the room.

'Sorry about that.' She released her grip on Eleanor's arm. 'They're my mum's cousins, who are so incredibly boring that if you even entertain them in conversation you'll be stuck for hours. I needed you to save me.'

'That's my job.' Eleanor saluted.

'And you're doing amazingly.' Sal smiled. 'I can't believe that I'm actually *married*.' She waved her left hand wildly in front of Eleanor's face.

'I know. It's crazy! But good crazy. Like . . . the best kind of crazy.'

Sal pulled her in close and hugged her tightly. 'It won't be long before it's your turn.'

'Please,' Eleanor scoffed. 'I'm back at school training to be a bloody art teacher. We definitely don't have the money for a wedding right now. Plus, Fin is running the charity and doing his freelance work, so we also don't have the *time* for a wedding either.'

'Whatever you say.' Sal let go and eyed Eleanor seriously. 'But don't leave it too long – I want to look drop-dead gorgeous and young in all your wedding photos, OK?'

'Fine. Now, enough talk about my pretend wedding day . . . let's get back to your very *real* wedding day. According to your carefully and ruthlessly planned schedule, you should be throwing your bouquet right about now.'

Sal looked at her watch anxiously. 'Fine. You go and rally the crowds. I need to find a way to haul myself and this big old meringue dress up those stairs.'

'Be careful!' Eleanor called after her friend. 'We don't want any accidents, please.'

It didn't take long to get everyone together. A group of young, fairly intoxicated and extremely giggly girls were pushing their way to the front of the crowd, their hands and arms outstretched, ready to snatch the flowers from the air. Eleanor found Fin lingering somewhere near the back.

'You've got no chance of catching it from back here,' she whispered in his ear.

'Now, that's where you're wrong, Eleanor. Do you really think Sal is the type of woman to do a half-arsed throw?' He pointed at the bride, who was already limbering up at the top of the stairs. 'That bouquet is going to come flying all the way back here, where I will be ready to catch it.'

'Don't call me Eleanor, it's weird.' She scowled.

'Don't scowl or I'll tell Sal's make-up artist you need another touch-up.'

'Touché.' She leant her head gently on his shoulder. It had been nearly three years since Eleanor and Fin had gone on their first date. She still had to pinch herself sometimes that after everything, after all they'd been through, Eleanor Levy and Finley Taylor were together.

'Right, are we ready?' Sal bellowed. 'Three . . . two . . . one . . .'

There was an audible gasp as the bunch of flowers arced

through the air. Eleanor saw it coming closer and closer, watching it as though it were on a film . . . not heading to her . . . not about to land directly on top of her head.

'Catch it!' a wild voice called out from the crowd.

Eleanor snapped into action and seized the bouquet from the air. A roaring cheer erupted and she felt her cheeks blush.

'Congratulations.' Fin nudged her. 'Looks like you're the next one down the aisle.'

'Oh, really?' She turned to face him, holding the slightly bruised flowers between them.

'Well . . .' He placed a warm hand behind her head, his fingers caressing her soft, tamed curls. 'How about this? If we're both still together by the time we turn thirty-eight . . . I'll marry you.' He grinned.

Eleanor's body tingled with a delicious warmth, her heart dancing in her chest. 'Is that a promise?' She raised an eyebrow inquisitively.

Fin lowered his face to hers. The face she'd known her entire life. The face she'd loved and would continue to love for her entire life. 'I promise.'

Acknowledgements

Everyone told me that the second book is the hardest to write and my God . . . isn't it just! I wouldn't have been able to make it through without the following people:

My family – for always supporting me and being my biggest cheerleaders. A special thanks goes to my sister who witnessed many moments of writer's block and endured many 'ending option' discussions when we lived together. Thank you for being the best person I know; I will for ever look up to you.

My friends – to all of you, from all chapters of my life. Without you my world would be a much less wonderful place, but I have to give a specific shout-out to the incredibly fierce, incredibly funny and unbelievably talented women I have in my life. I am blessed to know you and be in such amazing company.

To the real Eleanor Ruth – thank you for letting me use your name and for being the edgiest girl I know.

My 'day ones': Amy, Rosie and Naomi – always and for ever.

My actual real-life work wife, Karis – thank you for the countless hours of Starbucks debriefs, endless WhatsApps of support and for being the main reason I got up every morning and came to the office. I'm glad our love has continued outside the confines of the office – till death do us part.

My incredible team who have once again made this book something I am extremely proud of:

Sarah – to whom I owe so much. Thank you for everything you do. You're nothing short of remarkable – a real-life wonder woman.

Sally – who was instrumental in getting this book to where it is today. Your kindness, patience and brilliance are something I feel very lucky to have experienced. I am eternally grateful.

Hayley, Hana, Ruth, Holly, Lara, Becki, Viv, Claire – thank you for all of your support and love for this book. Without you, the story of Eleanor and Fin would be going nowhere. It is an honour to work with you all.

And finally, to my readers. It still blows my mind that people are picking up the words I've written and reading them. It means more than I can say, and every comment, review and message brings so much joy to my heart. I feel so very blessed and grateful to you all. Thank you, thank you, thank you.

x

If you enjoyed *Last Time We Met*, you'll love
Emily's debut novel, *Before I Saw You* –
a heart-warming and funny romance

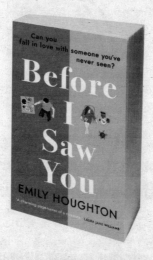

CAN YOU FALL IN LOVE WITH SOMEONE YOU'VE NEVER SEEN?

**Alice and Alfie are strangers. But they sleep
next to each other every night.**

Alfie Mack has been in hospital for months recovering
from an accident. A new face on the ward is about as
exciting as life gets for him right now, so when someone
moves into the bed next to him he's eager to make friends.
But it quickly becomes clear that seeing his neighbour's
face won't happen any time soon.

Alice Gunnersley has been badly burned and can't
even look at herself yet, let alone allow anyone else to
see her. She keeps the curtain around her bed firmly closed,
but it doesn't stop Alfie trying to get to know her.
And gradually, as he slowly brings Alice out of her shell,
might there even be potential for more?

Available in paperback, eBook and audio

Page TURNERS

Great stories.
Unforgettable characters.
Unbeatable deals.

WELCOME TO PAGE TURNERS.
A PLACE FOR PEOPLE WHO LOVE TO READ.

In bed, in the bath, on your lunch break.
Wherever you are, you love to lose yourself in a brilliant story.

And because we know how that feels, every month we choose
books you'll love, and send you an ebook at an amazingly low price.

From tear-jerkers to love stories, family dramas and gripping
crime, we're here to help you find your next must-read.

Don't miss our book-inspired prizes and sneak peeks into
the most exciting releases.

**Sign up to our FREE newsletter at
penguin.co.uk/newsletters/page-turners**

SPREAD THE BOOK LOVE AT